Some Trouble Investing in Wine

Nicholas Jones

Published and available from
TheEndlessBookcase.com

This book is available in both paper and electronic format.
Available in multiple e-book formats.

The Endless Bookcase Ltd
Suite 14 Stanta Business Centre, 3 Soothouse Spring
St Albans, Hertfordshire, AL3 6PF, England

ISBN: 978-1-914151-26-2

GW00569761

About the Author

Nicholas Jones writes fictitious books about things that could be happening right now. The first book tells the sobering story of what may have happened in late 2019, to the business of investing in French fine wines.

After more than 35 years in business, Nicholas attended a six-month writing course to convert from a fact-based business person to a storyteller. His clients would probably say it was inevitable given the number of stories he told them over the years. He now intends to spend a lot more time writing about business and imagining what is really going on inside them.

Disclaimer

All characters, organisations (except the brands mentioned) and events in this publication are fictitious and any resemblance to real persons living or dead is purely coincidental.

Acknowledgements

I have been bothering **my wife Gillian** for most of the last forty years about my desperate need to write books based on things that could be true. She encouraged me to get on with it, then helped with the story and the editing of this first effort, over a great deal of wine. So many thanks and much love for her tenacity.

There are of course several people and organisations that helped to make this possible and below I salute them:

Robert Basier (unfortunately no longer with us) where I spent many summers starting in the 1980s teaching me to taste the best of Bordeaux. An exacting teacher who successfully helped me to develop a lifelong love of the best wines.

Charlie Martin, an entrepreneur and Bordeaux wine connoisseur who helped me with wine investments and over long languid lunches explained the workings of the Bordeaux market.

The Faber Academy and Caroline Green for helping with the transition from civilian to a writer.

The New Bloomsbury Set or should I say my fellow Faber trainees. Thanks for the encouragement and for you, I included some of my readings in this book. I bet you can't wait for me to try out book 2 on you!

Marcus de Maria, a Wealth Educator who I worked with for a while. Such an interesting speaker and a great man in his industry.

Ju Ju Missy for her help in making sure the French is really French and not from that website!

Carl French, who I have worked with several times over the years, thanks for trusting me with this!

To my girls, Gill and Harrie

with love and thanks

Contents

Some Trouble Investing in Wine

· · · · · · · · · · · ··

Part One - Should we Invest in Wine?

Prologue: Cote d'Azur, France, Summer 2019

It was hot, really hot, the sun blazing down on Le Vieux Port de Marseille through the bright blue sky. Leisure boats were dancing in the gentle harbour swell while locals strolled and visitors jogged. People were sitting in the cafés enjoying cooling drinks, talking about what they would be doing later and the rest of the week. If they stayed long enough, it was the "yellow vesters", the President, British tourists, terrorists and maybe even the upcoming rugby season. But it was all good-natured, it was too hot for vexation.

Unfortunately, this was not true for everyone. In a steaming warehouse hidden by sprawling buildings overlooking the harbour, a gang of men were hard at work like 18th century slaves driven on by a modern day gangmaster sporting a stolen police matraque.

"Ouch! Pardon monsieur, it won't happen again, pardon monsieur, sorry sir." Good, he's gone now. Our French men like to be treated well and called sir. They shout at us most days when we are late or don't do things right or want to have a pee. But they are not too bad they don't hit us very much unless they are already angry, or something has gone wrong. Our French chief Yves, who has a giant friend, is quite nice he talks to us and thanks us for what we are doing. His bosses M. Pascal and M. Martin have been here but they just walk around, don't say much and take away boxes from the cellar.

The work is not too difficult, but it can be harder when the big truck arrives with a belly full of liquid. Sometimes they say the place looks a mess, but we have a way of working that gets it done easy. At one end of our building, some brothers are cleaning what they told us were claret bottles. This is a very strange name I don't know why they don't just call it red wine. Down at the other end, we put the bottles into wooden cases and nail them closed. Then my brothers put them onto platforms ready for transportation.

I work on filling the wine bottles from the big silver tanks the truck leaves for us every week. I think the truck goes back to the port but I don't know for sure. I say this because I think some of the wine comes from my home, but I can't be sure of this either, but my brothers think so. When the bottles are full, we have to make sure the level is right, then we squeeze a cork into the top to stop it from running out, sometimes it is hard to do and the corker breaks and we are yelled at. Our French man looks at all the bottle tops and then wraps some stuff around the top to hide it. Mahamid is very skilled, he polishes the bottle then puts on the label so they know who owns it. The wooden cases are all different and many have pictures of big houses, they call them chateaux. I don't know where these places are but the labels are very pretty. We must be putting their wine in the bottles for them so they can drink it or maybe sell it because there is a lot. It's good to know that we are making them happy. My brothers sometimes call us slaves but I just laugh at their jokes. I don't have to wear chains as they used to in America. I believe I am a guest in this country and helping the French who let me come here from my very poor country.

We are not allowed to go near the French men that work with the white powder. They are kept in a cellar down some stairs. I went there when I helped my friend carry a box. It was full of paper money and when I looked around me I could see lots more money being put in a machine and shuffled like when we play cards. Then they wrap it in plastic like the fruit we buy in the market, I don't why they do that it must be to keep it clean. Down there smelt very strange and there was a lot of white powder being mixed as you do for bread and then they put that in plastic too. They told me that people put the powder on their face, mainly on the nose, it makes them feel good. I don't know what they do with so much money but I wish I could have some more and then I could leave here and enjoy France.

I am called Hakim and I have been here for one year soon, I came with my blood brother, but I have not seen him for some time. I hope he has found somewhere good and is not lost or dead. The French men told us it would be easy work and we would be able to leave after one year but I think that cannot be true as many of my brothers are still here. My close brother is now Sami and we always try to work together. We both wanted to leave our home and come to France, we have heard many stories about how good the houses are. There are I think ten of us staying in my house it's better than home although there are too many people in it. We have running water, even though it is not always hot, electricity for lights and heaters usually work. We have our own beds, but not much space to move around or store our belongings. But it is what we need to live. They give us food in the morning and give us rest time in the middle of the day when they eat. We can cook something in the evening but it is difficult with so many of us. But they give us bread and cheese. We are not allowed to drink anything but water or some orange juice. Most of us do not drink alcohol as we are strict, but it would be good to have some tea. If we want to pray they sometimes let us in the day if they are in a good mood and not being shouted at by M. Pascal. But we have a little time when the sun appears and when the sun goes down. Although it is difficult to know what time it is especially when the cold months come.

I would like to go to England but that is a long way from here. We are worried about England leaving Europe, they say it will be much harder for us to get there when it is no longer England, but a place called large Britain or maybe it is big Britain. That seems a strange name, I prefer it to be called England because we know who that is and we prefer their football teams to the French. I like Manchester City because my cousin has sent me a picture wearing a blue shirt of Riyad Mahrez before I came here. I don't know when I will be able to go and see him.

Our French men tell us they are keeping our money to pay for everything, but there must be some leftover, they only give us 50 euros each week. We wonder if we should tell someone that we are working here for so little money, but we don't know who. I can't buy much, but we have a secret phone which we share. I make a call home when it is my turn, I think it will be tomorrow this week.

Yesterday some police came to our house, one of them was a woman which is strange I think. They said nothing to us and were very friendly with our Frenchmen, maybe they are cousins. We were worried that they might think there was too many of us in one place and tell us there was not enough room, so some had to go home. We tried to hide but they saw us but said nothing so it must be alright for us to be working here.

Chapter 1: St Albans, a Tuesday morning in September 2019

"I think you're just being mean," the lady presenter shouted accusingly. The audience stopped whispering to stare at her, then glanced at him waiting for a reply. "Did you hear me? I said you're being plain mean to these lovely people," she repeated. He still said nothing, they wondered what was going to happen, they knew the man was in charge he told them earlier. But they liked what she was saying about them. "Roger, I think you can do much more than that," she continued in a loud voice. They were transfixed, having spent the day enjoying the seminar, the two presenters who entertained them had fallen out and they weren't sure why. The man looked at them accusingly as though they were in league with her. There was absolute silence, the audience stared at the male presenter. Surely, he must say something to her or to them, they waited.

"Okay," he replied and they all let out a deep breath then started to breathe normally. "I understand why you think that," he turned to the audience with tears in his eyes. "Lydia is right, I was only thinking about what would be easier for the company. I am so sorry for what I was going to do. We have spent the whole day together and I have grown to love you people. I sometimes forget that you are most important, we must always help you first. Can you forgive me?" They nodded, they were embarrassed at the way they had ganged up against him and supported the lady. Now they hated her and loved him, "I don't care what the rest of the company thinks I am going to do the right thing. So, I will give a third off our "**Jubatus for Currency"** training and support package – "**The world's fastest-moving investment strategy"** not just for the first five," he put one hand up. "Or the first eight people," holding up both hands, one with thumb and one finger down. "But the FIRST TEN people," holding up two hands, "who run up to the front and stand alongside me." There was a clamour amongst the audience, they stood and started to run to the front of the room some nudging others out of the way to make sure they didn't miss out. There were twelve slowly counted out by Lydia. "Twelve," he echoed. "Who were the last two up?" he asked the line. No one confessed but some looked guilty. "Well, in that case, shall I just pick two orrrrr LET'S ALL HAVE THE DEAL" he shouted as he raised his arms. The room erupted with cheering. It was another good day for Investment Mentor 4U, thought the staff listening in the office next door.

The company had been running since 2009. It had a slow start but in the last five years, revenues had increased by at least 20% a year. Success had come by expanding in the richer Northern European countries where people had an appetite for taking a risk to make money. The owner and Chief Executive is Andre Devries, aged 38, a former banker who left because he wanted to do something more exciting.

He made an appearance at the beginning of the Foreign Exchange Workshop to whet the appetite of the attendees. He told them the well-practised story of how his parents fled South Africa for the UK when he was only five. Then onto how his father died unexpectedly leaving him and his brother to be looked after by their sick mother. But they never gave up hope and he made it to become an Investment Banker, before setting up his own successful business. Most of this was true although he left out the bits about private school, rich uncle and lots of failures. They listened intently as he told them it was all about getting the mind right, focusing on what is important and not letting anything get in the way. He claimed his only motivation was to help others to get where he was now. He walked over to the window and pointed to his brand new Porsche Cayenne Coupe.

"I got that a few weeks ago," he continued, most of them got up to look. "It cost me a fortune, I just love it, I paid for it through my investments and not with our company's money. I follow my methods without question, if you do the same, believe in what we do, you can have one too. All I ask is that today you look at HOW you can make money then learn the way TO DO IT on our future courses."

They clapped, he bowed and left. If things had been slow, he would have gone back in, but he also heard the cheers for the Lydia and Roger show. Going back now might distract the audience from signing up for the premier courses, which cost more than £15,000 – available through a finance agreement at modest rates. *They are so good at the finale,* he thought. *I must make sure they never leave,* he chuckled.

Andre's company is engaged in selling investment training to people who want to develop a second income which could become their first if they do well. The training is intense at the beginning and involves either foreign exchange or one of the main stock markets. It is not based on teaching an investment strategy to create a portfolio but rather teaching how to trade by following the movements of the big players in a chosen market. It entails increasing the individual's capital by placing multiple small buys or sell bets, to win more than you lose. For the right kind of person, it is a good way to minimise risk whilst building up a sizable return over many years.

To help sell its training services Investment Mentor 4U had a small equity and FX investment group following its strict methodology so they could then claim:

- Low Risk but High Reward is the name of the game
- Watch us do it!
- Follow our methods and you can pile up the cash too

Today he was more interested in confirming the marketing copy for the next seminar. He was struggling to find the right words;

- Make £250.00 each day for twenty minutes of work

- You just can't fail, it's impossible to fail, no you would be stupid to fail if you follow the rules! In fact totally mad if you fail, completely insane even

I give up I'm not in the mood for invention, he decided.

He switched to thinking about his research into new investment products. There were several studies on the go; property, gold and most interesting, wine. Paintings, watches and gold coins had been discounted, given how much information would be needed to develop a method he could package. But, and it was a big but, in this highly competitive business, only his superior methodologies and money already spent kept his customers loyal. Now he needed new opportunities for the more adventurous to gamble on or invest in. He was receiving daily reports about all kinds of prospects, including cryptocurrencies which were on offer from a couple of his competitors. His customers were politely asking about these new options, soon they would demanding, perhaps going elsewhere, but not yet. He still had some time.

Andre began to read a circular from a Wine Investment House promising at least a 15% return on investment. Onto Google he went, to peruse the Bordeaux wines they were suggesting. His saunter through the chateaux led him to the grand cru and eventually the premier crus. *Wow look at the price of the Rothschild wines, he thought. Unbelievable, every time I look at the prices I wonder who would drink a bottle worth £1,000 just for lunch, or dinner for that matter? Just a few cases of that would buy me another Porsche,* he chuckled looking at the details. But what about all that scamming stuff I read about, *I need to know so much more before I can come up with,*

"**Strategies to make you money, methods to make you loads of dosh,**" he said out loud. Then he lost interest in the wine and turned back to his marketing work.

"I just love this job," he said and then began thinking, making money with like-minded people who also want to make money, be rich and are willing to work and follow our methods. Unfortunately, most of them will just get their brains scrambled looking at a screen full of numbers all day. "BUT," he said and started thinking, what they need is a new unbelievable system that does everything for them, and laughed. In the meantime I need a killer strapline, what is it? Something powerful to get both prospects and existing customers to buy into our latest investment methods. No doubt it will come to me, hopefully soon!

In his previous job at the bank, things had gone badly for Andre, he had lost heavily after backing a hunch that a US pharma company would bring a bowel cancer drug to market. Unfortunately, the company's chief executive was arrested on racketeering charges, leading to a fifty-year sentence. The company collapsed and the drug was lost along with confidence in his ability. The failure affected him for many years, he even thought about ditching finance and opening a wine store, or a French restaurant. "Doing something useful, providing great food and great wine to people who appreciate the finer things and have money to spend," he told his mother.

Maybe he would have done that if his US-based uncle had bought into such a plan. His father's brother had been willing to help him even when he left his highly paid job, at Fertigungsbank in the City, to set up in St Albans. He often wished they could spend more time together.

He returned to his laptop to continue his sloganizing, but he was getting hungry and it was time to go and spend time with his team. But first, he texted "The King" to ask her what they were doing that evening. The response was fast, telling him she was working late and he was being visited by a wine salesman or had he forgotten. *Yes, I did,* he thought, a *good thing she reminded me. Perhaps I should ask the Wineman to tell me how he got into the wine business. Maybe he will also tell me why he wants to give me free coffee cups rather than wine glasses.*

Sharing the first floor, of the recently built St Albans offices, was its owner, BloedStone Investment Ltd a UK company with financial connections to the Isle of Man. The regional head was sitting at his desk in a modern white and grey office thinking about his appointments for the week. The business was now eight years old and took its name from its chairman's US company. It specialised in finding loan and equity finance for medium and large companies as well as acquiring investments for itself. The directors and shareholders were mostly ex-military, of one kind or another, who teamed up shortly after the 2008 banking crisis. The UK's breakthrough came when they managed to secure investment for a Saudi Arabian tanker fleet, netting them 5% of 2 billion US dollars. Stones as it is often called invests mainly in businesses and property in the UK, France, and Germany.

Jackson Ritchie, one of the founders of the company, tall fit and in his mid-fifties was formerly a partner in a major consulting company but gave it up to join his old military friends in building the investment business. Although his wife had initially taken the news badly, success and seemingly unlimited wealth had helped change her mind. Cassandra gave up teaching to become a successful author of crime novels. She never asked about their wealth, just accepted much of it was invested in high performing assets, or property, such as the large house in St Albans and overseas apartments where sadly, they never seemed to go.

Jack continued to work because he was good at what he did and so far, had not found anything better to do. Success was now being a hero amongst his fellow investors by finding a Unicorn company to generate vast amounts of money. Cass showed little interest in bragging rights, being a successful writer and having two daughters was fine with her.

The second in command Avery King was much younger than Jack at 38. The King was tall and in great shape from her boxing workouts, pilates and running. To her, the Yorkshire three peaks walk was a good warm-up for a cross country run, although she would admit to slowing up. Avery, a Harvard graduate, with thanks to a wealthy mother and surgeon father, became a Chartered Accountant working on Mergers and Acquisitions before joining Stones as Finance Director.

It seemed that she had been destined for great things at one of the big four auditors but had fallen under the spell of one of the senior partners, it all ended badly. Jack understood how the senior partner must have been drawn to Avery who was more than just a great accountant. She had a terrific body with the most magnificent breasts, which he never tired of looking at. A guilty secret he kept to himself.

On leaving the auditors Avery was given a substantial payoff and chose to set up her own company providing FSA regulated advice. She was acquired by Stones after taking a small ground floor office in the St Albans building. Soon after that, she obtained her current lover Andre from along the corridor. They met when he almost ran into her beautiful E400 Mercedes cabriolet while trying out his new Porsche.

The diary called for Jack to meet a prospective client who believed they could sell a low alcohol gin to over 75s rivalling the consumption of normal gin to under 35s. He had already decided it would be a waste of time, believing older drinkers would want the flavoured fully leaded version. *Maybe people in the forties to fifties needing to keep a clear head might be interested but even so, can't see it,* he thought. The project was put forward by someone Jack had already invested with so he had to show willing. Before that meeting, Jack was supposed to follow up with a man who had come to the office to speak to Avery about raising cash for his fishing business. He said he was one of Jack's old troopers, so she thought they should see him. Any chance of that happening quickly vanished with the placing of a hand on Avery's bottom. Such a #MeToo offence caused Avery to deliver an angry rebuke along with a strong suggestion he should do something unpleasant to himself. *I think I will ignore that task for a while and perhaps he will go down with his boat,* thought Jack.

Next came a start-up investment prospect, who wanted to introduce a business for clients to "try a fine wine before investing'. Jack recognised the difficulties with such an operation, especially the cost of sale and time-wasters just wanting to drink. However, he knew of a profitable company that used a similar model for good wine, but they had a dedicated following who were willing to pay twice the price of supermarket wines for unusual vintages. For investable wine, he reckoned the prospects would have to pay up to £100.00 a night for the privilege of tasting. Jack did not believe that would happen, like most people he could not understand how anyone could seriously say they truly appreciated the difference between a £50.00, a £100.00 and a £1,000 bottle or could even pick out which was which. But the company ran a separate wine investment business that might also want cash, so it made sense to view the start-up.

Jack knew gin and wine investments were becoming popular so people naturally wanted to borrow to exploit the interest. He was happy to help with the right opportunity but it had to be more than just an idea. The last wine investment request he put forward was from a company called www.BordeauxInvestments Group.com. It was rejected after they failed to properly demonstrate, to Robbie, the Stones UK Chief Executive and Nicky, the UK Chairman a comprehensive grasp of the world wine market. The two men, self-proclaimed connoisseurs of wine, were the inspiration behind the Stones acquisition of the very beautiful Chateau du Carys – a third growth from St Emilion.

Jack began thinking, *some people just want me to find investors stupid enough to give them money to turn an idea into a saleable product and then see if anyone wants to buy it.* Jack spoke out, "are this lot going to be a waste of time like that Bordeaux mob." Then he thought, *unless they have solid research, preferably with checkable names and addresses they won't even get in front of any real investors. They will just get people like me to charge them for advice and strip them of what little cash they have. Perhaps I should just call them and tell them they should get a proper job and stop wasting time. Good ideas are everywhere, I have good ideas. But who wants to pay to try them out?*

Jack would be very professional, weigh up the case for funding to see whether he could help by assembling a sufficiently compelling business plan for investment. If he could, then Stones would help with the initial documents, send them out to the usual suspects and maybe punt some cash themselves. Prospective investors would no doubt charge for them to come and pitch. The whole exercise could cost £10-£20,000 with no guarantees that they would get any more than smiles and warm words. "Unless of course, they have something seriously coolllllllll, said Jack hoping it would happen soon.

Ok, that takes care of Thursday so what shall I do the rest of today and tomorrow, he was thinking. *Perhaps I should do some prep for the meeting or do my expenses. No, all too dull, I think I will go and annoy the staff, especially the King,* he decided and laughed.

"Hi Miss King, is anything exciting happening?" he asked. She glanced up from her white desk, covered in customs and excise books, sheets of papers, calculators, PC and laptop, to give him one of her looks. Jack could never understand how accountants could work in all that clutter.

"You bored again?" she asked. "What about all your clients don't any of them need you to get money for them? Or did you make them all rich?" she chuckled.

"Yes, of course, I am very busy talking to that nice man who appreciates a good rear?"

"Don't you wind me up with that horrible man," she got serious.

Jack was laughing but standing back in case she threw something at him. "No, I am just socialising like a good boss should like it says it in the management books." She turned away to get back to her papers. "I was going to ask you if you wanted to come with me," a new look clearly said NO. Her eyes widened her neck reddened as she thought of what she would like to do to the man. "Only joking you don't need to come" Jack noticing the speed at which her temperature was rising and withdrew. "But I might need you to crunch some numbers if I decide to meet with him. Who knows perhaps it would make sense to get involved with the old lecher. By the way, what do you know about wine investment?" he continued. "I will have to get right up-to-date on the market if I am going to judge whether to recommend we invest in the fine wine project. I don't want the guys rejecting them like they did the last one. I was debating whether to ask Robbie what he thinks before I waste any time. I know that he put more than £300,000 into some Rothschild wines and was threatening to drink them at his restaurant. I can't believe he would do that."

"Actually," she replied. "You should probably speak with Andre he is thinking about teaching wine investment as part of his portfolio. He keeps nattering on about wines and how much they cost then goes out and buys any old South African wine he can get his hands on. He even has some man going round to do a wine tasting tonight. But as you know I will be here working on the numbers for the property deal in Yorkshire you and Tinny seem to like so much," she made another face.

"I thought he was in stocks and FX rather than stuff like wine," said Jack ignoring the jibe about the property introduced by Tinny's sister.

"He is but he has been studying the wine investment market and was trying to tell me something about the scams that have been going on over the last few years, apparently, some are still hidden or about to happen, I didn't pay too much attention as I was more interested in watching the rugby."

"Are you two still in love as one loves wine and the other rugby?" This time she ignored him and went back at her papers. She wanted to get back to her numbers so she could confirm her previous conclusion that the property project did not stack up.

Jack slouched in the chair opposite Avery but resisted the temptations of putting his feet on her desk and gazing at her breasts. Avery could see he wasn't going away so she said, "in answer to your question I know quite a lot about drinking wine but not much about investing in it. I prefer red at any time, although pink in the sunshine is pretty good too. Yes we are still in love or maybe lust because it's only six months, and yes he is quite sweet, no his new car is not better than mine and not really that fast. Is there anything else I can help you with today or can I get back to my books?"

Jack straightened up and replied. "I can see you are no fun today, so I will go and upset someone else."

"No please don't, can't you find something else to do?" she asked.

"Ok, I am going to pop along and see your boyfriend about getting together to talk about and probably drink some wine," she nodded at this suggestion. "Okay I will go then," she nodded again and he left.

At the other end of the corridor, Jack introduced himself and asked whether he could have a quick word with Andre. The receptionist hesitated and went away to check. "He is just saying goodbye to some visitors, but he will be out in a few minutes," said the young man and asked if Jack would like some tea or coffee or water while he waited. Jack declined and slumped into a comfy leather settee to wait.

"Hi Jack," said Andre as he suddenly appeared, "we have not really met." Jack stood up to shake hands and introduced himself. Once they were both sitting, Jack explained he needed to research the fine wine market for an upcoming meeting with an investment prospect. Andre smiled then told the Stones Director that he was considering adding wine to his investment training portfolio. Then followed up by talking enthusiastically about his research so far.

"You know it is really funny you should be asking me about this today as I have a meeting arranged with a wine guy tonight. He is bringing over some wines for me to taste. I am not sure how good they are going to be, but his company also do wine investment and I want to pick his brains about what goes on in the business as well as drinking his samples," Andre laughed.

"How about we get together next week, on say Tuesday, for me to buy the drinks and pick your brains to see what you have found out and try to work out how wine investment can be made profitable," suggested Jack. "I think it is for us at Stones, as we bought into the best vineyards and own a chateau."

"Deal. Let's go straight from here and exchange stories, it could be fun," agreed Andre smiling broadly and offering his hand.

"Okay good, see you later," Jack went off back to his office impressed by Andre. He could see why he was a great salesperson and a suitable companion for Avery.

Chapter 2: St Albans town centre, Tuesday evening

Avery returned to her financial analysis of the property company Jack had met a few days earlier. She studied the monthly revenue streams, expenses, assets and liabilities before deciding that the company had cash missing covered up by inflating property valuations. The Stones investment was needed to avoid running out of cash. Avery wondered whether it was just a mistake that could be explained, she was not a property expert. It was time to finish for the day but before speaking with Jack and Tinny she would play dumb and ask their accountant to explain what she had found. This might be a big disappointment, Robbie liked the property as well. She studied the results of the company search, it revealed nothing. "Enough," she said to herself. "Time to go."

The Stones Finance Director packed up her papers and stuffed them into her big leather bag with her laptop. A ritual performed just in case she got the urge to do more work later while slowly drinking her favourite Provence Rosé wine loaded with ice. She called it her working drink because it held its taste, lasted longer, besides helping her to relax and stay under four units a night. In her rush to get to the stairs, she crashed into someone. She was partly to blame, reading phone messages on the go she looked up ready to do battle.

"Oh gosh, I am so sorry; did I hurt you?" a playful Andre asked pretending innocence. He had been reading his phone too but saw her first. Avery stepped back and the anger disappeared.

"YOU, now I wonder why you're rushing to get home," she said with a knowing smile.

He stepped forward, she pursed her lips waiting for impact, "why Miss King I was rushing to see you," he gave her his naughty boy look.

Avery gave him an umm, a different look and a brief kiss. "Off you go and don't call me when you get drunk as I will NOT coming over to see you. I will be drinking some of my own wine," but reserved the right to change her mind depending on how much she had to drink. He kissed her again and ran down the stairs to his car to disappear in a cloud of dust and noise. She strolled over to her Mercedes, decided to put the top down and drive with the breeze blowing through her hair. Stopped in traffic, she thought about Andre's physical attributes and her appetite for lean and muscular, not to say sophisticated men. When unattached she had flirted with the idea of having a toyboy, *perhaps I will when Andre is too old* and chuckled to herself. Traffic clear, she drove to her home on the northern edge of St Albans.

Andre lived near the town centre a mere fifteen minutes going the direct route or double when he went roaring down to London Colney for some provisions. He liked living there because it was a short walk to the many restaurants, he was not a great cook. The penalty for this deficiency and his penchant for drinking big reds was time spent exercising – mainly running and weights. Now in his late thirties, he had managed to build the body of a cruiserweight boxer, which received a pass mark from Avery. The process had started more than twenty years before as captain of the school rugby team and carried on through his days at Cambridge. An injury to his left knee while playing part-time in the Rugby Championship had ended his career. Multiple operations never properly fixed the problem. Now he maintained what he had built through hard work.

On the short trip, he began to wonder if it was such a good idea to have the Wineman come round to his house. *What if he brings crap wine or won't leave or worse, talks for hours. I wonder what this guy is going to bring tonight, but I do fancy a few glasses of big 14.5% cabernets,* he laughed out loud. Andre is a salesman and optimist, how could it go wrong?

After he completed his usual parking drama avoiding scrapes, he climbed out worrying about what he was going to eat and wandered inside to be greeted by Mills. His visitor was due at 6.30 pm therefore gone by 8 pm, he decided. But before he could do anything else, he had to feed the cat or he would get no peace.

Andre just managed to change his clothes before the doorbell rang and Mills looked up from the sofa to see who had disturbed her snoozing. "Cool," he said to Mills as he got up to answer the door. "That must be the Wineman come to get me drunk." In fact, there was a Wineman and a Winewoman standing on the doorstep. The man with a big case and the woman with a big smile. The man gave his name and Andre responded, "please come in," leading them to the sitting room and pointing to the unoccupied sofa behind the coffee table.

"Thank you, we are from Redbridge Global Wines following your request to taste some of our special wines before you buy. My name is Michel Canning and this my associate Rosalba Babineaux." Another big smile from the dark-haired, dark-eyed, petite and beautiful French women. "I bring mostly red wine as you say you prefer it."

"I'm Andre and ready to try your wines, so what do you need from me?"

"I have some glasses but if you would prefer, we can use yours," he replied.

Michel opened his oversize pilot case and revealed his first offering, a French Rhone. He removed the cork and put half a shot or roughly a mouthful into the first of Andre's oversize glasses. Michel told Andre about his company, how they did business and why it is so important to "taste before you buy'. The man continued with the tasting process; look, sniff, taste and judge, in some detail. Andre ignored the first two steps in the evaluation process went to the third by downing the wine after a quick swirl, then to the fourth by deciding it was okay. *Now I wonder if I can have a proper glassful?* he thought. It was soon clear, the Wineman wanted to talk through all four stages for the rest of the six wines including, a two-year-old red wine from Australia with a picture of a cowboy on a bucking bronco on the label, an Italian Barolo and a couple of wines from Bulgaria and Romania. Andre was worried that this was going to take all evening. Michel kept talking about special vineyards, exceptional wine and exclusivity.

Andre was downcast, struggling to hide his disappointment. This is not what he had expected, wine tasting to him was silky Bordeaux, beautiful Rhone and bold Riojas. He did his "thumb up the bottle bottom" tester and these were as flat as the wines. Even after the six mouthfuls, the French couple kept talking about the company at a dreary half speed. *How can I get rid of the man?* he thought looking over at Mills who had turned her back to them. He had planned to ask the Wineman about the business, but it would be a waste of time and he was getting hungry. Perhaps the most interesting thing was that the two sat a little too close together and were too smiley and touchy. "Do you have a price list?" was his solution. Out came a couple of pieces of paper and Michel started to talk about the specials. Andre briefly studied the price list to discover the wines were all over twenty pounds per bottle. He judged that the local supermarket wines were of better value especially when they had 25% off events. His stomach rumbling from missing lunch but he ignored the discomfort and asked questions about the wine industry while pretending to study the price list. "I understand you also do wine investment stuff at your company. That sounds interesting to me as I do some investment work on FX and Stocks."

"Yes, we do and have been very successful at it," Michel replied. "We give good deals to new investors, you can start with a small investment and work up." The Wineman continued to sell the virtues of investing in wine and the women continued to smile.

21

"So how did you get into the wine business?" Andre asked now he had created an opening. "Do you like it?" he continued.

The man was very open and replied, "I saw an ad in the Advertiser searching for salespeople for a wine company to work in the UK and just applied. I had been selling all sorts of stuff over the years and thought if I worked for a wine company I would get free samples of French wines."

"Do you?"

"No, not really, they are a bit strict about giving us discounts in case we start to offer discounts to our friends."

You need to give discounts for this crappy stuff especially at these prices, thought Andre. "Where are you based? Is it close by?"

"We have a small office in Dartford down by the bridge near the docks where the freight ferry operates. Our main location is in the South of France. We operate the wine investment from the UK and also keep small quantities of wine so we can do these visits."

Andre knew very little about that part of London except it was the bridge he had to cross to get down to the Euro tunnel. "Do you have any interesting stories about investing in wine given it's so expensive? I bet a few scams are going on with the good stuff," finally getting round to what he wanted to know about, although hunger was still calling.

Michel hesitated but did not seem to be in any hurry, then he said, "well yes, I have heard some stuff about vineyards changing the year of the wines they release from a moderate to good year."

"How does that work?" asked Andre.

"Well, I heard that when they bottle say 2010, which is a good year, they also put some into bottles labelled 2009, which was a great year. That way they make much more money when they export it to China. No one would ever know except the vineyard owner and possibly the workers."

"Oh that sounds plausible I suppose as some of the vineyards have huge cellars," responded Andre wondering why unscrupulous vineyards didn't do that all the time. He decided it would certainly be worth Jack talking to this man and would arrange it. But for now, he asked, "do they sell any wine down at your warehouse? I could go down and pick it up," returning to an exit strategy.

"Probably not, we are only "try before you buy" but I will find out for you," replied the Wineman.

"In that case, I will have six bottles of the Rhone please, it's good," *or rather least bad,* he thought. Andre produced his credit card which the Wineman took and wrote down the details on a sheet of paper. "What no card machine? Shall I just call up the website and pay direct?" he pulled out his smartphone.

"No, we are still a little old fashioned, we put the payment on paper then process it back at base along with the order details. Hope that is alright for you," he continued. The couple kept talking about the wines, the company and all sorts of stuff that Andre thought was drivel, except he had to wait a week for delivery. Finally, Michel and Rosalba finished and Andre saw them out. Mills stood up stretched and left through the cat flap. Andre was alone, hungry and thirsty, it was time to go eat.

That was almost a waste of time, he thought. "Anyway it's Chinese for me," he shouted and left his house. On the road outside he saw Michel in a car gesticulating wildly at someone who appeared to be shouting at him and Rosalba. He paid no real attention, he was hungry and not surprised someone was slagging him off for selling the "shit" stuff and spending so long at it!

Chapter 3: St Albans North, Tuesday evening

Avery arrived home about seven after stopping to pick up some dinner. She was now well into her bottle of Provence Rosé and thinking about how much she enjoyed her current job, liked the company but wanted to do a lot more on investment projects. Just preparing the time consuming financial reviews was no longer challenging enough. Although being the Chief Financial Officer certainly was and the salary and bonus payments were more than adequate. She decided to discuss things with Jack and Robbie. "The other problem," she announced, "you are getting lazy. You must get out and go back to running first thing in the morning." Then she began to wonder how Andre got on with the wine tasting, she decided not to call him instead started up Netflix to watch another episode of the series she was following. It was too slow, she drifted back to her former lover "R" and the trip where their relationship came to an end.

It had been the third time they had met in the Cote d'Azur but the first in Bandol. She pictured the beauty of the small town with the improbable casino and thought, *surely it must be one of the most beautiful places I have ever been to. A place that is nearly always warm in the winter and hot in the summer.* In the past, she talked about living there but there were still too many things going on in the UK for that to happen.

She sipped her rose and thought about that day, *the distressed message from her lover, "call me when you get this." Not how's my King, hi Avery or hi babe. She remembered rushing through Arrivals before calling him, thinking he must have missed his flight. Calling him again and again, no answer, leaving messages. "Are you alright? I got your message to call, where are you?" What's wrong?" He finally answered.*

"She knows about us and is…" he said sounding upset again. "I went to my sister's flat I couldn't get on the flight. I'm too upset."

"What are you saying?" she replied with a sinking feeling in the stomach. *"We need to talk about this, are you coming down here or shall I come back?"*

"I don't know, what am I going to do now. She's really angry and talking about all kinds of stuff." He was crying, *"I can't think what to do next, she might…,"* all he did was talk about himself.

I loved him deeply, he was so kind and generous, but it was all an act? He chose to go back to his rich wife and all their possessions. He did not love me, he loved having a young mistress and nothing more. What a shit, tears filled her eyes, *what a waste of my life and love on that bloody traitor.*

She returned to the present, *"I must stop thinking about him and move on,"* she thought having drunk most of the bottle. *He's gone and now I have Andre, who has made a pretty good start. He's strong and has been through some bad times, poor thing. But now I am older and wiser, he has much to do before I will allow myself to love him.*

"No more wine for me, an early night is called for and I'll clear up in the morning," she announced to the room and went to bed.

Jack was back home with his wife, in a large three-story multi-million-pound property north of the city centre, where they had lived for the last five years. It was not far from Avery. They had acquired it with the Stones shareholder dividends. Despite having plenty of money Jack still couldn't do everything he wanted, especially eating. To keep his weight down he had to eat low-fat meals during the week. Tonight it was some chicken concoction followed by skinny cheese and crackers washed down with some red wine. What he really wanted was fish and chips with mushy peas and tons of stilton washed down by a flood of red wine and a 10-year-old port. He was still working on finding a diet that would keep him at his best weight of under 90 kilos. He was always hungry which occasionally made him bad-tempered. It was so irritating that his wife was one of those people who could eat anything and never put on any weight.

Cass his wife of twenty-five years, was in the study working on her latest book about an underage runaway. It was a crime novel that she hoped would be another bestseller. They had two daughters both away at university.

Jack switched on his piped classical music. He liked technology and in particular wifi-enabled systems fed by his private network. He mostly used them for working with other Stones associates or checking how long the gardener spent working or whether the newspaper had been delivered. He checked his watch and decided he had about thirty minutes before Cass would reappear. Jack had learnt that writers disappear to another place where it was impossible to talk with them. She would never notice that she was being serenaded by Bach's Piano Concerto Number One or any other number. They were happy to leave each other to get on with their own projects. It had worked well for them over the years.

He began to think about his upcoming meetings with Andre and then the start-up project. *I know of two ways people invest in wine, first by putting money into a fund that someone operates and secondly, a specialist company that recommends wine for a commission then the person buys it for their own account. In the last case, the wine usually stays in customs until it is offloaded to someone else at a profit. Andre is thinking about teaching people how to acquire their own wine and manage their own account like it were stock or foreign exchange. The wine company the guys rejected, wanted to do the fund thing and raise money to make it bigger. Robbie rejected that because he does not believe that the lower growths they were going to buy, would make enough of a return after the fees are taken out. I think the start-up is in the commissions camp but has only suggested a sales approach so far. Robbie used words like insane when I explained what I knew about them, although he was still happy for me to check it out, just in case there is a brilliant idea for us to invest in or a brilliant guy to hire.*

'Hi babe,' Cass said rousing him on her return from her cave. Have you eaten yet? I'm starving."

"Yes I had some rubbish, but I'll have another glass with you."

The couple spent some time talking about the day, but it was soon time to get to bed and be fresh for the morning. The city seemed content with the cool autumn evening, some of the braver people sat outside eating, drinking and enjoying the conversation.

Away in North London later that night, Michel Canning had received a request and was wondering how to deal with it.

Chapter 4: St Albans, Saturday morning

Finally, it was Saturday and Andre thought he was dreaming as a bell rang over and over again. He tried to turn off the alarm but it continued. He awoke in a daze after spending the previous evening with Avery and a bunch of friends having an impromptu wine tasting. His stories about the Wineman and his smiley companion had caused much laughter and his downfall. He looked around the bedroom for Avery. *What happened to her?* he thought *where did I lose her or is she somewhere in the house?*. He glanced into the other bedrooms and stumbled down the stairs to find the only female was Mills, stretching and getting ready for her breakfast. The bell kept ringing. He finally managed to get the door open to find himself looking at two police officers wearing big vests and big belts. A sinking feeling in the stomach as he ran through all the things that could have gone wrong with his car the night before. Then remembered he wasn't driving so began worrying that something must have happened to Avery. He asked.

"Hello, officers, what's happened?" and waited for the bad news.

"Are you Andre Devries?"

"Yes, has something happened to my girlfriend? Or has someone complained about my car? Or Mills?" trying to get all the possibilities out.

"Sir, this is nothing to do with your car, girlfriend or your partner," to which Andre blew a breath. "We need your help. Can we come inside please? We would like to ask you some questions."

"Of course, but Mills is my cat" he said stepping back to let them in before closing the door and leading them to the sitting room. Mills was doing her guard dog imitation sitting up watching the police intently as they intruded onto her territory.

"Sorry Mills, you will have to wait for breakfast we have visitors," he told her. She looked unhappy and continued to stare at the invaders in case they made a wrong move.

"What can I do for you officers?" he said slightly nervously.

"Mr Devries do you know Thierry Martin?" said the older of the two.

"No, that name does not sound familiar, I assume it's a man."

"Yes it's a man, are you absolutely sure you have never met him?" the officer pressed. "We believe he visited you."

"No, I am sure, I would remember him with a name like that. In my job, you have to remember clients" names. So, no, I have never met him, who is he?"

"Are you sure?" the younger officer asked again and produced her phone having called up a passport photo which she thrust at him.

"Oh, that looks very much like a younger Michel Canning, the wine guy that came round on Tuesday evening with his smiley, no sorry, his colleague. He was a nice guy, but he was selling pretty crappy wine. Anyway is there a problem he seemed okay to me? he repeated. "He did have a bit to drink but he had a friend or a colleague and she was driving I think. Did he have a crash or something?" Andre was starting to prattle.

"Mr Devries, that is not Michel Canning but Thierry Martin a French national. It appears he has been working under an assumed name in the UK for some months as a wine salesman. At this time we are not sure why or how he obtained the necessary papers. His employers reported him missing after visiting his flat yesterday, that's Friday and finding only his partner who is also an employee of the company. She confessed she had not seen him since he left the flat on Wednesday morning. He did not go to work on Wednesday or return home that evening and has been missing ever since. No one has been able to reach him by phone or e-mail. It seems that neither his employers nor girlfriend knew him as anything other than Michel Canning. We are concerned that he may have been here to carry out some sort of criminal activity and we are actively searching for him. That means, apart from his girlfriend, you were one of the last people to see Mr Martin when he visited you here on Tuesday evening. Please tell us what happened and try to include everything, as it might give us some ideas about where he is."

"Ok, but let me feed Mills and then make some tea. Would you like some?" Andre asked and both officers relaxed a bit and were eventually served with their desired version of the drink.

Andre began telling the officers what happened and kept repeating there was nothing unusual about the man. Indeed, if anything he was a caricature of a dull salesperson who had just left a training course. He suggested Michel came across as someone who genuinely wanted to sell wine even though it was not what Andre would buy. Occasionally they cut in and asked questions or sought clarification. Then the officers asked him if there was anything odd about his female colleague.

"I think her name was Rosa something, but they were not a sales team, they were closer than that," declared Andre. "She spent most of the evening with a big smile showing off beautiful white teeth. I assume she was his girlfriend or partner. She must have come to give him support or something. I have his business card somewhere." To his relief, he remembered putting it on his desk in the study and quickly retrieved it. "Here it is."

Michel Canning – Wine Advisor the card announced followed by the company details.

"Not sure what else I can tell you," he continued as he handed it over. The police stood up to leave then stopped as he remembered. "There was one odd thing though," he blurted out.

"It probably means nothing, but when I went out to get some Chinese food I saw Michel in his car with two other people. They had the interior lights on. I think the one in the back was the girlfriend but I don't know about the other. I assumed it was his boss as the person was waving their hands around as they were talking. The police conferred between themselves which gave Andre the opportunity to ask questions about the missing man.

"Is he a scammer? Wouldn't be surprised that wine was pretty rough and expensive. He wrote down my credit card details, do you think he will sell them? I probably won't get my wine, will I?" he said glancing at the officers for comfort. "What are you going to do?" he continued now a little concerned.

"Sir at the moment we don't know what he has to do with your wine or credit cards. At this stage, we are following his movements and talking with everyone who met or spoke with him over the last few days. But you probably should contact your credit card company to make sure it is not being used.

"Shit, ok, I will, I wonder what happened?" But the police were not engaging and made a second and successful attempt to leave. Andre closed the door behind them feeling more intrigued than worried about the unexpected development. *This sort of thing happens on NCIS or NYPD he thought. I bet the guy has done his deed, whatever that was and run off back to France. He was certainly no terrorist. I am surprised he would leave that girl behind though or maybe she was in on whatever it was.* "Or more likely drank his own wine and is lying dead in the gutter somewhere," he said to Mills and laughed. "What do you say Mills?" the cat looked at him, produced a huge yawn in answer and flopped over onto her side.

His phone beeped with a text,

Are you still alive and do you remember me, my little drunky pooh!!? If so, don't be late for the game, we are meeting at noon in the usual place. Axx

He replied:

I am, but why did you go and leave me? I have been with the police all morning. I thought they came to take me away haha! Tell you more when I see you. Andre x

"Mills, when you get hungry just pop round to see your Auntie Tess she will have your tea ready for you," he said. Then he texted Tess to check she would be in. The next-door neighbour, a former glamour model now in her late fifties but still doing the odd modelling session, always had food for Mills. She agreed one night while flirting with Andre that she would look after his cat when he was out late or away. For Tess, Mills was the next best thing to being able to look after Andre. She had often thought how nice it would be if she was Avery spending every night riding his muscular body like her former co-stars.

Chapter 5: St Albans town centre, Tuesday

After a few more days working on his latest best deal, Andre left to meet up with Jack at the Garibaldi pub hidden away in the back streets of St Albans. Although Andre was a huge wine drinker he knew about good beer and some of the best was available at this victorian pub. Tonight, they would be drinking only pints and talking about wine. Jack arrived first and picked out a table in the bar which looked like it would allow for a bit of privacy. As he hung his coat on the back of a chair Andre breezed in. Seeing Jack he headed straight for the bar and called out.

"What you havin?"

"Pint of the Fullers to start me off please."

Andre carried the pints over to the table where they spent time talking about the pub, the city, the office block, their companies and how good things would be when we finally left the EU. Andre continued by giving his now enlarged account of the Wineman's visit. It majored on the terrible wine he was selling, that he was really a criminal and finally how the scoundrel disappeared having carried out a crime, leaving his forlorn but attractive girlfriend behind to live in poverty. Jack was able to laugh at the funny story the incident had become.

Towards the end of the second pint, they moved onto the subject of wine and the fact-finding mission that Jack had embarked on to better understand certain elements of the wine industry. "I am being asked to raise cash for a couple of companies in the wine sector. One of them runs an investment fund and acquires investable wines for individual customers for fees. So far we have turned them down because we are struggling to see how they can make enough revenue to pay the 3x multiple we require in order to invest. I am looking to see if we can reverse that decision because we may be missing something. The second company wanted to get people to invest in fine wines after tasting them. We can't see how this can be made into a business with the "cost of sale" being too high. Prospects would simply drink the wine, then tell them to take a walk when they were asked to invest up to £1,000 per bottle." He continued, "as far I can see a wine fund is like a property fund without the rental income. The investors bet that increasing wine values will swell the fund so they can get a return by selling their shares. For the wine they acquire on behalf of individuals, the company gets a return by hiding their fees in the price the customer pays. In both cases, this only works if the wine continually increases in value. Once that stops, like musical chairs, you get left standing and lose. On the other hand, with wine classified as a "wasting asset", it's free of capital gains tax, so if you get it right, you can make a lot of cash and keep it," he chuckled.

"Yeah, it's a strange market, I have been looking at it for a few years now," replied Andre. "I would like to add it to my training courses, but I just can't shake off the feeling it's become a market for the growers and advisors rather than investors. Remember I work on behalf of the individuals who put money into schemes while you work on behalf of companies that provide them. I believe that a lot of the potential returns are taken out of the deals before it gets to ordinary investors. For example, if you buy wine from a trader he takes profit out through the fees which may never be recovered if the wine fails to increase in value. I have not found any "paid on results" companies they all want money upfront. Then there is the risk that if you buy in the barrel and the wine is not great it will never produce a return and you lose again. All this is good for you, provided you can get enough punters to place bets."

Andre pressed on, "I believe in the early days, individuals could make a good return on investing in wine still in the barrel, but as chateaux and vineyards were taken over by the money men, like your lot, this changed. The chateaux pushed up their prices to take a much larger margin before release. The good news is the market is not as volatile as say, gold or manic like Bitcoin because it operates by year. If you have the right year you can make money if it's a bad year you lose it or make very little.

At that point, Jack suggested they take a break, order some food, relieve themselves and get more drinks so they could continue. With two pints of ESB for a change and some cutlery, they started again with Jack seeking more information.

"If as you say the market is rigged in favour of the suppliers, then it sounds like it might be a potential investment for my wine fund guys if not for you. But is that true?" Jack was still wrestling with whether a rigged market would always give advantages to his side and even then would that be enough.

The delivery of food stopped the conversation and they reverted to talking about Andre's business and how he financed it. Jack spoke about his investors and their appetite for the opportunities they could exploit by having cash to use as a weapon. After a while, the conversation returned to the wine business and Andre began again.

"Look there is a rumour of a secret fine wine lake in Bordeaux that is being managed like the gold mines in South Africa or OPEC for oil. The chateaux particularly the first and second growth, Premiership and Championship in football terms, are keeping the supply side under strict control to maintain the high prices. There are good years like 2005, 2009, 2010, 15 and 16 and bad ones like 2002, 3 and 4 or 2011 and probably 17. They must have felt they needed to do something to keep their businesses in constant growth rather than have peaks and troughs, especially if they are owned by listed companies."

"Back in the mid-noughties when they had a great harvest and great wines they made a lot of money from the Chinese and Russians using them as currency and gifts. Crucially they continued to control supply, rather than reducing prices, by building underground storage facilities to hold more stock. When they had a bad harvest or the wine was not that great they just stored it hoping they could get rid of it later without wrecking the market. Initially, they sold it to dealers as something other than real chateau wine to be "mixed down" and sold to supermarkets. But they still had too much so they stored it. Then unfortunately for them, demand for top wines declined as both the Chinese and Russian presidents cut down on the corruption and stopped the "wine for friends" culture. That left the vineyards with stacks of wine in storage they can't get rid of without ruining the market. Sometimes they invent petite chateau to sell the wine at a much-reduced price. Alternatively, they will have to find a way to destroy it as the supermarket channels are now clogged with cheap wine from outside Europe. That's partly why the supermarkets can afford to those twenty-five per cent off events."

"Does this happen at all of the French chateaux?" asked Jack beginning to think that he may be heading for a call with Robbie about Chateau de Carys.

"No I don't think so and there are still great wines to be had at good prices but not for investment. There are also several scams affecting the fine wine world. I guess the best-known scam was a few years ago when a bunch of Nicaraguan cartel guys put Bordeaux labels on Rhone bottles. Apparently, it took US customs a few minutes to compute what was wrong, they had never seen such a faux pas before and wondered whether it was a new type of wine," laughed Andre.

"I bet someone took a hit for such a screw-up," Jack laughed. "What else have you heard of?"

"Perhaps the most worrying scam is the one where the label on the bottle is changed from one vintage to another" continued Andre. "There are great differences in wine quality, for example, a 2010 vintage Latour is worth around £9000 for six, while 2011 is worth about £4000. With this sort of difference, some of the lesser Bordeaux chateaux might be tempted to label 2011 wines with 2010 labels and make a lot more money. This sort of scam could be executed by the chateau or by an independent bottler. The fact is, most people can't tell the difference between the two years even if they had the chance to sample them next to each other. In any case, who can do that when the wine is so expensive? In reality, it is not about who drinks the wine it's about who believes in it and so invests in it." But at least there is something to drink, unlike Bitcoin where there's nothing.

"Or, just bottle any old wine and stick a fancy label on it and make a fortune," added Jack. "It makes you wonder what you're drinking. How do the fine wines get sold in the first place?" he continued. "Do the investment companies go to the chateaux and order up wine when they're boxed? sorry cased or whatever it is called."

Andre began to explain, "from what I understand Bordeaux chateaux use people called "Négociants" to sell their wine before bottling. Many believe that this is the reason why Bordeaux has become so successful and of course expensive. This whole process caused a bit of difficulty with the Chinese as they wanted to buy direct to get big discounts. Unfortunately for them, demand far outweighs supply for the most investable wines so they had to play the game or get no wine at the release prices. Indeed, most of the wine for China made its way to Beijing via Hong Kong. The other issue for the Chinese was they thought that if a wine fell in value before they got it they could walk away from the deal. Of course, that is not allowed so they don't get the best deals and then buy later for more money. Then in 2011, a number of the First Growth chateaux abandoned the sale of their wines En Primeur. This has killed off the early investment profit leaving trading and shortage to drive up prices."

"If you speak to a wine broker or fund owner, they will show lots of examples of first growth wines producing average returns on 10-20% over a ten year period. Once you get a few bad years in the mix then it can take the return down to around 5% and you can get that if you are prepared to lock your money away for 5-10 years." He concluded with, "hence my quandary, how can I teach people to invest in wine unless I know the wines and vineyards like I know the companies on the exchanges?"

"Ok well let's just take another break and get another drink," suggested Jack whose head was spinning with the volume of information being heaped upon him.

With fresh drinks, Jack decided to summarise what he had heard, "so what you are telling me is that you believe the wine market is a difficult place to operate in as an individual. It may be ok if you invest with the right fund manager but there are better ways to guarantee a good return, if not as interesting. Plus, you think the vineyards could be scamming the investors, who won't know because they never drink the wine and those that drink the wine won't know, because they can't tell the difference. Have I got that about right?"

"Yea not a bad summary I suppose," replied Andre. "Where does that leave you?" he asked laughing. He finished his beer and began to feel very drunk.

"I am not sure, but I think I've had plenty of beer. But thanks very much for all this information. I can see why our CEO is not keen on the investment fund and thinks the start-up guy is crazy. I need to think some more, plus have Avery work through the numbers. By the way, how are you two getting on?" he asked with a cheeky smile and raised eyebrows.

"Good thanks," looking a bit sheepish. "Time to go," they shook hands and departed on shaky legs.

Chapter 6: St Albans, Friday evening and Saturday morning

Andre was getting ready to leave and the doorbell rang. *What's happening? I'm trying to get out,* he thought. *It must be my Amazon delivery, but I only just ordered it.* He opened the door without looking, then stepped back to get his coat off the stand shouting, "hang on." He managed to get it on and check the pockets for his car keys, before continuing, "sorry about that," expecting to see an exasperated delivery man instead, he was faced with a tearful Rosalba Babineaux.

"Rosalbeen isn't it?" she nodded and without thinking, he signalled she should come in and go through to the sitting room. "This is a surprise," recognising that the woman wanted to talk about something serious. "Please take a seat. Let me just text my girlfriend to let her know I'm running late." Mills gave her a head stroke then sat next to her. There was no smiley face and no white teeth today it was all red eyes and tears.

As Andre sat down she said, "my name is Rosalba but please call me Rosa, I am sorry to trouble you, but you remember me and Michel from last week with the wine?" Andre was vigorously nodding, "well he is gone, he has been stolen away by criminals. I think these people took him away on Wednesday morning last week when he left for work. The police told me he is really called Thierry and he has a family in Marseille who want him home. They would not tell me much. I need help to find him and bring him back, he would not have gone on his own. Can you help me? I don't know where else to go. I know you don't know me but you seem like a nice person. Please help me I have only been in England for six months and I don't know anyone except at work," Rosa caught her breath then sobbed.

Andre who wasn't sure what to do declared, "Rosa the police have already been here I couldn't tell them much except that he was arguing in the car after you left here. You were there I saw you in the back." Rosa looked uncomfortable but replied; "no that was our team leader from work who was complaining that you only ordered one case from us after spending so long. She had waited in the car for us to take her home."

"Sorry, I was not so keen on the wines you were selling, I prefer the French," Andre replied feeling guilty. "I'm not sure what I can do for you," getting back on track. "Perhaps you should contact the French police," which was just an excuse to get rid of her. He glanced at his watch knowing the guys would be assembling shortly. "Do you need water or maybe tea?" hoping she would say no.

"No, yes, perhaps some water," she replied.

While he filled a glass Andre tried to reassure her by waffling on about the visit from the police, "they are all over it and will no doubt find him," hoping she would drink up so he could go.

"No, you don't understand, I know what happened to him and if I tell the police they might kill him," she said quickly looking into his eyes.

"Who the police?"

"No, I think that some French gangsters have taken him because he would not give them any wine. He told me that he had been chased by bad people before and that was partly why he had to leave France," she explained to a confused Andre.

"What you mean they have pursued him from France just to get wine from him? Are you sure, it sounds a bit much to me?" The news both alarmed and intrigued Andre. He was thinking there may be a grain of truth in what she claimed, if so they knew where he lived. "Look I am due to meet up with friends in a few minutes and I can't be late. Can we meet tomorrow morning and talk about this as it all sounds a bit extreme to me and you shouldn't be getting involved with such people?"

"I understand, but please help me," she whimpered and began to tear up.

"Let's meet at the Café Nero in St Peter's Street tomorrow," becoming more desperate to leave. "Where do you live, do you need a lift?" hoping it was close by. The French woman declined and said she would go on the train which ran close to their flat in North London. "Say 11ish is that okay?" he continued. "Why don't you give me your phone number so I can call you if necessary." He keyed the number into his phone before she reluctantly headed for the door. Andre ushered her out and told Mills to watch over the house as he set the alarm and ran to meet Avery.

"Hi, babe!" Andre said to his girlfriend as they arrived at the pub at almost the same time. Had a good day so far?" he asked.

"Busy again doing numbers for Jack, how about you, who delayed you?" she asked accusingly.

"Well la la" he said flicking his tongue for effect "you probably won't believe me, but it was the Winewoman who has managed to lose the Wineman," he announced. Over drinks, the story emerged along with her request for help. He explained he had managed to get rid of her by arranging to meet her for coffee in the morning. "Hopefully, you will come with me, then we can get some food for the weekend," which was met with an "ahem" but no words and they proceeded to dinner with their friends.

On the way home the subject of Rosalba and the missing Wineman returned. Andre explained in less colourful tones what had happened at the wine tasting and before he left home. Avery was sceptical about being able to do anything worthwhile and quickly decided it would be a huge waste of their spare time. Andre began to think he had made a mistake suggesting they meet her.

"Ave it was the only way I could get rid of her so I could come and meet you for dinner. I thought she would never leave. Hopefully, it won't take long tomorrow, but I would appreciate the help. She keeps breaking down and I find that hard to deal with."

Avery understood his dilemma, relaxed a bit and eventually agreed to the invitation. On the way home, she decided it sounded unusual and even fascinating, certainly much better than financial analysis.

The next morning Avery looked at the sleeping Andre in her bed and began her assessment of his lovemaking abilities. She thought, *he must have had a few girlfriends to learn how to satisfy me with that big circumcised penis which tastes good and feels great. Although he still needs to slow down and enjoy the build-up rather than try and get me to cum quickly, but I guess we can fix that. He has more stamina than the traitor although still has a few tricks to learn* and smiled broadly. *Still, he is fun, looks pretty and is certainly well-muscled for his age.* 'So you get a B+ on your six-month assessment,'' she murmured swinging her long legs out of bed and walked to the bathroom after momentarily holding her large still firm breasts.

She began thinking of the day ahead, part of which she thought would be a wasted meeting with the French woman. *But we could still have a good healthy lunch and a long walk,* she decided.

Andre was still asleep recovering from his exertions and dreaming about the beautiful African American who had taught him what she had called a best practice for male lovers. His previous girlfriend, Georgie, and Avery had very similar muscular bodies and large breasts. They both enjoyed making love, although Avery was probably more overtly forceful in what she wanted. He learned quickly that she prefers cowgirl while Georgie favoured spurring him on as a missionary. But he was happy either way but understood he had to stay in shape to maintain his performance. Andre woke up and smiled at a naked

Avery towelling her hair while wandering around, he was once again struck by her athletic body.

"Morning," he said while stretching and revealing he might be available for an early workout, which did not go unnoticed.

"Hi I think you need to put that away," she said pointing to his manhood. "I have just had a shower and we have things to do. It's time to get up, the shower awaits your hot sweaty body."

A shrinking Andre jumped out of bed and kissed her, "will do, then we can go and get breakfast." Although he wanted to ask her to make him a coffee, he thought it better to wait to be offered.

"Do you want some green tea?" Avery asked mischievously smiling knowing that he would really like a black coffee.

Forty minutes later they were heading for the coffee shop for their meeting. When they arrived, the shop was full; lots of children running around and lots of adults trying to read their newspapers and ignore the general mayhem. There was no Rosa. The search for a table suddenly yielded one near the entrance as one of the paper readers decided to escape and seek quiet elsewhere. Avery elected to get the drinks while Andre found a third seat and waited. Rosa appeared but she was not in great shape, her eyes were red and puffy and her shoulders slumped forward grasping her phone looking around without seeing. Andre observed her for a moment, she was expensively dressed and although shorter than Avery was a very attractive French lady.

"Rosa", Andre called she turned and with a vague smile walked over to the table and sat down where Andre pointed. He was not sure how he should greet her, so he shoved out his hand which she sort of touched with her fingers.

"Would you like a drink?" he asked.

"Just water would be good for me," she replied and Andre rushed over to update the order.

Once introductions were complete, Avery looked at Rosa and found it difficult to understand why her boyfriend would suddenly leave for no good reason. She thought of "R" and how the traitor ran off to his wife. At that moment she decided they should help Rosa to either find Michel or let him go, as she was trying to do with her former lover.

Rosa began to tell her story by explaining they met while she was working in Toulon She had gone to see the match between Toulon and Claremont with a group of friends. After the game, they got to know each other and it just grew from there. There had been a forty-five-minute train ride between them, it was easy to meet up but she had not met his parents. He said they were having difficulties and fighting a lot so he left for a job in England. After a few months, he persuaded her to join his new company so she moved to London to be with him. Everything had been going well to start with but recently Michel, as she continued to call him, had become quiet and lost interest in both the job and her. More tears flowed.

Rosa suggested that the problems started after he had returned from a sudden trip to the company he used to work for in Marseille. She explained that he was supposed to meet up with his former colleagues and explain to the new man what he had to do. "I thought it was strange that they had to get him back for that, but he insisted he owed it to them. Something must have gone wrong because when he came back he would not talk about the visit or tell me what was wrong. He has been like it for weeks spending most of his time working, and that's when we came to see you last week. He asked me to come with him as it was one of his first customer sessions." The couple listened intently to the strained narrative and did not interrupt until Rosa faltered and tears flowed once again.

"He certainly seemed alright when he came round to see me and knew a lot about the UK company," Andre said but then failed to avoid the temptation of commenting on the wine yet again. "Although the wine was ordinary for the price."

"What?" said Avery shooting a withering look, that accused Andre of not taking things seriously. "Do you know the company in Marseille, is it the head office? Have you ever been there? Do you know where it is? Could you take us there?" Avery began to fire off lots of questions, as she went into consulting mode trying to gather information quickly to assess what could be done.

"Whoa Ave, give her a chance to answer," Andre began to wonder where this line of questioning was going to take them.

Avery continued to take the lead in questioning Rosa but they kept coming back to the argument in the car. The French woman was having difficulties describing what was said as the conversation was in English. The boss lady, as she called her, spoke too quickly with a heavy regional accent like she had heard in Birmingham. She could not remember the name. The couple suggested to Rosa that maybe the boss lady had reprimanded Michel, so he ran off to hide for a while but would eventually come back and apologise to everyone. Rosa then revealed she had received a text from Michel saying he had gone home and not to follow him. The couple looked aghast at the sudden and belated reveal.

"But he must have been forced to say that, "Rosa said desperately.

"So that would be former home not current home then," Andre suggested sarcastically and was about to chide Rosa.

Avery gave him a "don't look. He watched her, could almost hear her brain computing everything Rosa had told them. Unfortunately for Andre, his girlfriend was confirming her earlier diagnosis they should help Rosa. "Andre I am going to make an executive decision. You said you wanted to see the Stones hotel in Bandol, well here's your chance. I don't think Michel has been stolen away by gangsters, I believe he went back to Marseille to hide. I suggest we go down there next weekend if he has not returned. We can look around for him, talk to his parents, visit with his old company, find him, he must be there somewhere and persuade him to come back. Does that work for you, Rosa?"

"Oh thank you that would be so good for me," replied Rosa finally smiling. "We can go to all the places where we have been together and make a visit to his mother who lives in Marseille near his old company." Although as she said all that, Rosa still believed that Michel had been kidnapped somehow.

"Are you sure this is a good idea?" mumbled Andre thinking that it was a bit of a leap to suddenly go to France. He was certain it would be a waste of time but quite fancied a few days away with his girlfriend. He concluded it couldn't hurt so started thinking about how to free himself from his work.

"If it's a waste of time then you will get to see one of my favourite places," Avery said with a big smile. We should go down on Thursday so we can do extra visits on Friday. I don't think Jack or Robbie will have a problem with me having a couple of days off." She turned to Andre, "I am sure your team will be happy to see you out of the way," she laughed while Andre offered a sort of smile. Eventually, they worked up a plan that took them to Marseille on Thursday with a return on Monday. Andre continued to think it was a fool's errand – but with a holiday tacked on the end. When Avery contacted Jack he expressed similar sentiments about running off to France with no idea what they would find. However, he did agree they could use the private apartments of Hotel La Beaux in Bandol. He even contacted Yasmeen the manager requesting her to make them welcome.

Yazmeen Maktoum, like a number of the Stones Associates, had been acquired by the company from a difficult situation. She was a low-ranking member of a wealthy Dubai family and had run into problems building a serious hospitality career after refusing to marry her father's choice. Her attempted kidnap in Amsterdam was reported to London by the US Stones protection team who intervened. To prevent her return to Dubai and probable torture, the Stones UK chief flew to the Netherlands and extracted her with a warning that he would مطارده والقضاء على anyone who dared come after her. He paid a ransom to the father for her services and the matter was closed. Many in the family still hire Stones for protection, know Sir Robbie, the Viscount and General De Vries, so took the threat seriously.

Chapter 7: St Albans, Thursday 4 am

The Radio started speaking, waking Avery from chasing a husky through the woods on one of her runs. The flight was due to leave in three hours from Heathrow. While still in bed she was thinking, *I must be out the door and on the way in half an hour and be parked by 5.30ish.* Her thoughts went to the day ahead as she built up the strength to get up. Self-doubt began to overwhelm her, worrying about what could go wrong in addition to wondering why she had agreed to help Rosa. She took a deep breath, for a moment thought about feigning illness and calling the whole thing off.

She returned to their discussions, the plan and what they would do if they found nothing useful. She shook her head, power flooded her mind and body. *It would be nice if we found the guy or maybe not, what if he is having an affair or something?* she thought. Doubt returned, she began telling herself, *if we find nothing then we can enjoy the weekend, I'm sure that's what Andre really wants,* then smiled.

"Hey, what am I doing? I have to get going I have a flight to catch," she shouted, switched off the alarm, switched on the TV news and jumped out of bed. She quickly stripped, ran to the shower to get ready for her departure quickly and efficiently. When she was going to meet "R" she would be driven on by the excitement of being with him and the naughty things they would be doing to each other. As a ritual, she always packed her carry-on bag the night before ready to go quickly in the morning. Standing in her towel she checked for messages just in case, there were none except:

CuS Axx.

Her heartbeat increased but not as much as it used to with "R", at least not yet. "What am I doing?" she asked the bedroom. "Come on stop wasting time," she quickly got dressed and continued the departure routine. It was now 4.40 am. "Okay, now off, off, off, and lock, lock, lock" as she rushed around the rooms performing the routine she had learned from a friend's father. She was ready to leave, set alarm option 1, the bleeping starts. One last look, out the door, lock the door, into the car, bag in the back and body in front, off she went.

She began to panic, thinking, *now what was the name of those parking people I put on my phone? Pinker's parking,* she remembered and called them. After they explained everything she turned up the volume on the classical music channel and headed for level 2 for drop-off and "meet and greet'. Now on the way, she relaxed while looking forward to being with Andre and helping poor Rosa to find her lost love. *Maybe it will be an adventure,* she thought.

After a very brief airport breakfast, they made their way to the plane. During the flight, they agreed on a basic plan that took them to Michel's parents" home first, then if necessary, onto the offices of the wine company near the Vieux-Port. Then they would follow up on any leads. At the end of the day, they would head off to the Stones hotel, a late dinner and plan for Friday. They took advantage of the time and dozed until arrival in Marseille less than two hours later.

It was mid-morning, the weather was typically bright and warm for early autumn. There were lots of people going about their business, they were not rushing but looked relaxed, tanned and happy. Not so the trio, after they picked up some provisions for lunch they hurried over to the car rental zone, where Andre tried one last time with Avery, "Are you sure this all makes sense?" he now believed that Michel had gone off with someone else and did not have the balls to tell Rosa. Although he was still struggling with why he would have left all his stuff behind. He thought, *there must be a simple explanation for all this. We have no real leads and we are going to look stupid.* He began to plot a way forward that ditched Rosa allowing him to spend time with Avery and turn the trip into a long weekend break. He was struggling to shake off the memory of her naked body and the desire to explore it more.

"Yes, it does," replied Avery sounding exasperated because she thought he was probably right and they would never find him. *Perhaps I was too impetuous bringing us all down here without a detailed plan of some kind. Still, a promise is a promise and we must try to help Rosa,* she thought. *After all, we have only just arrived and who knows what lies ahead.*

With Avery driving, they set off for Michel's old home hoping to find at least the mother. No one had remembered to ask for a sat nav and no one knew old-style map reading, so Rosa volunteered to be the navigator using Google maps on her phone. They headed for the wealthy Roucas Blanc district in the hills above the city. Andre sitting in the back left his thoughts on the subject of Avery's body, was instead composing an upcoming presentation on his latest income-generating methodology. The thought of appearing in front of the class, seeing them show joy brought a smile to his face, which Avery noticed in the rearview mirror and decided that meant he was thinking of work, his car or their physical activity. She smiled as he was quiet.

"Look, Andre, it will be fine," speaking to the mirror. "Let's just get this done and then we can enjoy being down here." The twinkle in her blue eyes and smirk on her face was enough to encourage him to start talking again.

"The last time I was down here, we were at the French Grand Prix with my Unk, but I can't remember where we stayed. It must be great being a racing driver," Andre continued by speaking about the F1 drivers; Hamilton, Vettel, Verstappen and some of the older generation. He turned to the teams, the constructors and how well Mercedes were doing compared with Ferrari. Then described the differences between a race on a circuit and one in a city like Monaco where he had watched the race from his hotel balcony. Most of the time Avery was not interested in what he had to say about cars and racing them and contributed nothing, but she was happy he was happy. Finally, he slipped back into silence and retreated to the e-mails on his phone.

Every so often Rosa looked up from her phone to check where they were and mumbled some directions. Where the motorways split outside the city, Rosa suggested that they should follow the route into the Vieux-Port, rather than the one that pointed to the city centre. Avery was not sure which was right but she knew the city well enough and could get them out from most places if they got lost. They passed the vast port and she wondered where the huge car and passenger ferries would be going and how long it would take. Then the super-luxury yachts parked in one of the service docks slipped by. She wondered who owned them and decided that Stones should acquire one for use by the team. *I wonder how much they cost, they must be cheaper than the planes we have.* As they continued, she admired how the old port building had been refurbished and put back to use and wanted to talk about it but no one seemed interested. "R" reappeared in her thoughts, this had been their territory, she shook her head and he vanished.

The Stones associate continued to drive into the city receiving occasional instructions from her navigator who was often confusing and slow. Sometimes asking Avery to turn left when she meant right. They agreed Rosa would point so that Avery would not have to take the left on the right-hand side but the right on the right-hand side. Suddenly Rosa's face lit up as she proudly proclaimed, "This is the avenue and that is the number," Avery stopped at the end of a long driveway.

They all looked surprised.

Chapter 8: Roucas Blanc, Thursday afternoon

The trio had stopped next to a formidable ten-foot-high iron-barred gate topped by spikes and flanked by equally high stone walls on either side. It reminded Andre of a seventeenth-century prison. Looking through the gate, at the end of the drive, they could see a four-story building that was far from a penal institution. The fortress had a modern entry phone next to a plate proclaiming it Villa Notre Blanc.

"Is this where he used to live?" Avery asked. "This is a pretty big and expensive place for a wine salesman. Are you sure? He must have been in trouble to leave here." They continued looking up the driveway at a car park decorated with luxury French and German cars. A large man wearing a blue blazer wandered around, perhaps a car park attendant but more likely a security guard, with a smart yellow walkie-talkie in hand. There was a sort of gatehouse to the right where they could see more men.

"Yes, this is Boulevard Georges Estrangin and the villa name I have on my phone," replied Rosa. Let me try the gate, she was out of the car before either of the other two could move. It was locked but the activity attracted the attention of the security guard who looked but did not move.

"Try the entry phone on the wall," suggested Andre as he slowly climbed out of the rental still thinking this must be the wrong place. However, he was impressed by it and the restaurant they had just passed displaying a big number 8.

"C'est ce que tu veux, qui es tu?" shouted the big man as he approached at a good speed for a man his size. "This is private property and you can't stop here," pointing at the car. Rosa said something in French, but the man was not listening he wanted to get rid of them, there were no visitors scheduled for the day. After a few more seconds Andre switched on his French-speaking brain and reported to Avery that the guy was telling them to sort of bugger off. The guard stopped shouting as he reached the gate and spoke to Rosa again but looked uncertain at what she was telling him. The guard looked blankly at the trio assessing the alternatives and speaking into his walkie-talkie. This unsettled Andre, it reminded him of the security guards his uncle used when they were in South Africa. He thought, *is that a weapon in his belt? something is not quite right here. Who needs a security guard at their villa in the South of France?* Avery sensed his unease but turned back to see what would happen next.

The iron gate slowly opened inwards and the big man walked up the drive with Rosa behind on foot and the other two following in the rental like a funeral procession. He pointed to a parking space next to a large black BMW SUV with dark windows. *A classic drug dealer car,* thought Andre with an ironic smile. Their rental looked like a baby alongside the others adding to the uncertainty he felt. Andre travelled back to Cape Town and their holiday villa below Table Mountain when his uncle had summoned an Armed Response Unit to deal with raiders. Guns were fired, people screamed and died, it was a frightening experience that surfaced at times like these.

Once inside, Andre scanned the large open plan ground floor as he followed the line headed by Madame Martin. She was tall with a runway model's straight back and purposeful walk. *She looks in her early forties but must be older given her son,* thought Andre. *Perhaps he was adopted.* They arrived in a large glass-fronted room which looked out over a beautiful blue and gold swimming pool, being cleaned by a young man and women. The room was pale with off white walls, wooden floors, leather and oak furniture. Then almost as a surprise, it was flooded with colour from two huge paintings hung on one wall. He looked over to Avery who responded with a look of "the mystery deepens'.

Madame Martin was speaking at high speed, Rosa responded with exclamations and hand gestures. They sat, Madame called out something in French and a young girl rushed in.

"Would you like tea?" she asked in perfect English. They all nodded and the maid scuttled out.

Avery looked around and then spoke first, "Madame Martin."

"Please call me Astrid," she replied before continuing, "Rosalba has told me of your reason for being here and I can help you. I have been explaining to her as we came in, Thierry is fine and rushed away just before you arrived. His company in London has an office in Paris where he was sent to a secret meeting by one of the senior managers. He could not say anything, it had to be like a secret agent I suppose," she forced a laugh.

"He told me he meant to call Rosalba," directing her story to all three guests. "But his battery flattened and he had to get the train. I expect he will call when he gets there. He was very angry he believed the company were taking advantage of him because he was there for only a short time." Turning to Rosa she continued, "Thierry said he had left you a message explaining that he had been told to report to Paris and that's why he had rushed off but all is well, not to worry." Rosa nodded as the other two looked on remembering her story. Madame continued, "he managed to sneak a call to me earlier using a friend's phone to say he wanted to surprise you when he gets back but because he's on a secret mission you can't call him."

Madame continued looking around again, "I also know he wants some time away from the company when he gets back to decide what to do with his life. You must know that his move to work in England was not easy and despite being with Rosalba he has some worries. We have all tried to explain that we will help as much as possible, if he wants to stay with us, here, we would welcome him, and you too, Rosalba. He has had a difficult time with the death of his older brother and my husband Matisse, his father, is also away a lot and that has made things difficult for all of us." Madame Martin looks down as emotion appeared to overcome her, "you do not need to worry he will come back soon." At least that is what Madame Martin was praying for, without knowing anything about what happened to Thierry.

Avery jumped in, "Madame Martin, sorry Astrid, thank you for seeing us at such short notice. We came to help Rosa find Michel, sorry Thierry, but now you have set her mind at rest we can enjoy the weekend." Andre looked at Rosa and her face said she was not convinced by the story. Avery looked at Andre and read the same thing. She changed tack, "what a lovely home you have, how long have you lived here?" hoping that would reduce the tension.

"Yes, we love our home very much and living up here where we can look down on the city is wonderful. We used to live near Toulon but there was such an influx of people from Africa that we did not feel safe. It can be difficult here too with several drug gangs fighting. We are a bit isolated so we keep some security men around, just in case," she continued confidently. "I am only sorry that my husband is not here to meet with you he likes English people. But he always seems to be away on business."

"So, you live here with your husband and Thierry just the three of you?" replied Avery. "It's a very big place, do you ever see each other?" making conversation while they finished their tea.

"Yes, we are fortunate to have such a beautiful home, there was four of us in the past," she corrected. We have our own import-export business which is why my son knows so much about wine and was able to work in England. It would have been very easy for him to stay in France and work with us. But the death of his brother caused him to think about the future, so left us but only for a while – we hope." Avery continued to talk about her adventures in the South of France explaining they were staying at the new Le Beaux hotel in Bandol.

Occasionally Andre joined in to comment on the beauty of the villa, the paintings, and the pool. Avery decided that the other two must be getting restless, wanting to leave. Rosa had withdrawn to sit in silence and stared at the pool worrying what all this meant for the trip. "Well we are sorry to have wasted your time," said Avery preparing to leave. "We thought Thierry had been kidnapped, harmed in some way or had come here. We didn't know he had become a secret agent on a mission for his company," she said with a titter. "Now we know he's safe we all feel much better," she said looking around for support. "So thanks for the tea and we will leave you in peace," she concluded and stood up to leave. Andre did not move he was weighing up whether he should confront her about the story. Avery felt awkward, not quite sure what to do next, while Madame Martin sat silently smiling, drinking tea and praying they would leave.

"Thanks again for the tea," said Avery. "It's time we were going," looking around using her eyes to cajole the other two to get up. She moved to shake hands with Madame Martin, the others did likewise and followed her out of the room where the security man was waiting to take them away. The trio followed him, looked back to smile and wave farewell as they walked to their car. Andre caught the change of expression as Madame Martin turned to go back into the villa it reminded him of Cruella De Ville, the women who stole the puppies.

Although it was time for the trio to regroup and decide the next steps, Avery was berating Andre for not helping her deal with the French woman. As they argued Rosa suddenly asked her to pull over as she felt unwell. Avery drove the car to the end of the narrow street so they could look down on the city to have a car picnic once Rosa felt better. She switched off the engine and waited, expecting Andre to suggest it was time to go for a drink or something equally irrelevant. She was still angry. Instead, he said, "how do you say, what a load of bollocks in French? What was all that about? That woman started by saying her son was on a secret mission for his current company who were the ones who reported him missing. Then she tells us he is upset at being in England and wants time to decide his future. We're here because we think he is seeing his previous company who need him to train a new employee. I have to say that none of this makes much sense. What do you think Rosa?" he asked leaning forward from the back seat. Before Rosa could speak, "something is badly wrong," he continued. "I looked around the villa, it must be worth five million euros at least, a villa with big cars and armed guards. Where did the money come from? There were no coats or shoes in the hallway, there was nothing. No sign that anyone lived there."

As he listened to himself Andre was curious; Avery was worried and Rosa, looking much better, put her phone aside.

Rosa spoke in a high pitch like she was choking to get the words out quickly. The other two listened carefully to the rant which was hard to follow, she kept switching in and out of French. They had never heard so many words from her, she ended with, "Madame Martin is lying about something so we should go and check at Michel's old office, see his team leader and find out where they have sent him. If he does not want to see me anymore then he should just say so," she began sobbing. Avery thought about "R" telling her he had to go back to his wife to avoid losing everything, to her that meant she wasn't worth enough for him to stay with her.

Avery joined in, "can we first agree on what we are going to call your boyfriend please Rosa? May I suggest Thierry so we don't confuse everyone down here?" A fed-up Rosa nodded agreement and Avery continued, "I know the story is convoluted and strange so let's do what Rosa suggests and go to his office and check it out to make sure. We were going to do that anyway."

Andre initiated his best detective impersonation dissecting the story to discover what they knew. He concluded, Thierry's company had some control over Astrid and she was doing what she was told, which could be a good or bad thing. He decided that Astrid did not live in the villa, it was owned by the company and she was a housekeeper. "I must be right, the company is forcing her to do things, didn't you see those paintings I am sure they were by Franz Kline and must be worth a small fortune. Where would she get that sort of money?" Andre was showing off his knowledge of art following his recent research. "The company must have done something to Michel," he concluded.

"Look if they or she can afford five million for a villa, they can buy some pictures, don't you think?" suggested Avery trying to calm him down. "Let's just go and talk to his company and see what they say" Rosa began to talk about how much she loved him and if they killed him she would never see him again.

"I am sure it won't come to that" said Andre trying to reassure her despite having no reason to believe it.

"Now look what you've done Andre, stop upsetting Rosa with your stupid theories," cut in Avery unconvincingly. They agreed they should go to Thierry's old offices, to see what they could learn.

"Okay, Rosa can you navigate me please?" asked Avery.

"We need to get to Le Panier, it says it will take about forty-five minutes," said Rosa brightening up and looking at her phone. Avery remembered driving through the busy narrow streets of the city was potentially dangerous, one lapse of concentration would bring a French guy hooting and aiming a car at her.

Andre spent most of the journey loudly going over and over what Madame Martin had said and then interpreting it differently. Twenty minutes later announcing, "Thierry is being held hostage by the French company to get his mother to work as a prostitute entertaining wealthy guests in the villa so that they would sign contracts to buy wine." Then discounted that theory, "I can't work it out, but maybe she is not really his mother and is somehow involved in his disappearance or has him locked away in one of the rooms, so he can't leave France. He has to stay with her until she dies. So where is the father? Maybe he has been murdered and buried in the garden to fertilise the trees. That would account for why there were no coats in the hallway at the villa, cus they're all dead." The other two were ignoring him as they navigated to the next location.

"At least he has not been abducted by aliens then," confirmed Avery and quietly chuckled.

"I give up, are we there yet?" he said getting bored. "Have you thought if there is anything bad going on they now know we are looking for him?" The question raised their interest and they responded.

"There must a simple explanation to all this although it does seem a muddle," said Avery. "Let's hope we get it sorted at his offices, if not then I'm not sure where we go, other than hope he comes back on his own."

"We're here," Rosa said to a hot and bothered Avery. She continued, "can I please ask the questions, I want to know exactly where they have sent him?" They drove through the open gate and parked boot out, opposite the only other vehicle, a grey transit van. As they climbed out of the rental they faced an office building with a large warehouse attached. Andre walked a few feet to his right to look behind the office building to see a row of loading bays with only two occupied by trailers both with no cabs. At the far end, he could see another gate labelled "Sortie" although it was closed. In the distance peaking above the wall was another building that looked like it was ready to fall down. As the trio walked towards the office doors they could hear the sound of people working and the noise of bottles, almost like milk bottles being moved in crates. There were voices in French some loud some just a murmur. There could be no doubt the property was occupied with people working.

Avery suddenly wondering whether they needed help, but who? She thought perhaps they should stop and ask Jack if he could whistle up some of the Stones" French security associates she had heard of. *But what would Jack know about them? He's an investment advisor with some suspicious friends who may be gangsters too*, she thought and smiled. *What about Robbie? I know he's dealt with kidnapping and that sort of stuff.* But it was too late they were almost at the doors.

"Why are you smiling Avery, this is serious stuff? Andre said as they both rushed to keep up with Rosa who ran across the car park to the entrance.

"I will tell you later," she replied at the doors to the offices.

Rosa slowed to allow the other two to catch her, "are we doing the right thing coming here?" she asked as they stood outside the building.

The door looked very old, with the glass replaced by wooden boards making it far from a prosperous head office complex. To Avery, it reeked of a company that had been in decline for many years and a long way from the place she had expected. Another surprise.

Chapter 9: Martin Warehouse Le Panier, Thursday 3.30 pm

"Don't worry it will be okay," said Avery trying to avoid confusing explanations as to why such a routine visit should feel so scary. Again she wondered whether they were getting into something that could cause them harm, with no backup and no one knowing where they were. Then she remembered telling Jack something, but neither of the other two looked concerned, so she dismissed her fears as being over cautious.

A smiling Rosa announced, "Look we are in the right place, NOTRE BLANC," pointing to the heavily tarnished company nameplate, next to an equally faded RECEPTION sign. Rosa stayed in the lead as they entered the building to look for the reception area. A few metres along a corridor she pointed to a sign, "This is not what I imagined Michel's old company would be like," she said. "He told me it was a good place to work and they have much money." The other two looked at each other, agreed in silence and followed her.

The reception was remarkably simple; a small table for the receptionist, who was engrossed in reading SARL du Vieux Port, walls decorated in faded blue paint and carpets that looked like they had been old before people were worrying about Y2K being the end of the world. The sudden appearance of the trio caused the large unpleasant looking male receptionist to look up in surprise. He seemed to be rooting around his brain for words, but instead, he raised his huge hand and rubbed his stubbly chin. *This must be another place where no one was expected today*, thought Andre. Eventually, the receptionist managed to speak in an unexpectedly soft voice, to which Rosa responded angrily. The couple could neither hear nor understand him so they stepped forward to stand at the edge of his desk. Now all three were less than a metre from the still sitting Frenchman.

"What's he saying Rosa I can't hear him?" asked Avery. Turning to her boyfriend she murmured, "He doesn't seem very friendly."

"He is telling us there is no one here called Michel or Thierry and none of the managers are available as it's nearly Friday and they all go early," he replied.

"How can you hear what he is saying?" asked Avery. Before she could get a response an argument broke out between Rosa and the man, who was almost twice her size but half her volume. The receptionist now looking like a nightclub bouncer, stood up to walk round to their side of the desk. Andre keen to avoid a physical conflict or having to intervene in some way decided to apologise as a way to stop him. The receptionist ignored him, tried to shout something but the huge scar on the side of his throat confirmed why he couldn't. Andre was momentarily distracted, wondering whether the man had been stabbed. In fact, it was the result of being shot several times in a gang battle.

Rosa continued to provoke the man, who advanced with arms raised to a fighting level. Andre backed off knowing that being the same height would not compensate for the difference in weight, something else had to happen and fast. He tried to stop the big man by switching to his best French, offering the excuse his friend was ill, desperate for help and could he please forgive her for whatever she had said. Fortunately, the man stopped but not from fear or pleadings but because his communicator was shouting at him. A man, who sounded like his superior, was asking what was going on in the reception area. The big man told the voice he had some strange English people with a French woman asking about someone called Michel and Thierry Martin. The voice said nothing for a few moments then recovered to tell him to get rid of them and quickly as the chief's son was not there and the Africans were busy working. The trio heard what was said, leaving Rosa incandescent with rage with both hands and teeth clenched.

"Vous devez partir," said the receptionist, outstretching his arms to shepherd them back down the corridor to get them out of the building. They reluctantly complied. Outside, he looked at them and spat on the floor murmuring, "*au revoir ordure and don't come back*". As they walked towards their vehicle Andre wondered why anyone would reverse park with only one space between them in an empty car park. As they approached, the driver suddenly appeared at the front of the white van, got in and moved it to the other side of the car park, well away from the grey van. As they prepared to leave, Andre walked around the car to check nothing was missing, then looked underneath to make sure nothing was added – there was nothing to be seen. Rosa still shaken asked for a few moments to have a cigarette to calm herself and everyone else. While the French woman smoked the other two loitered, glancing at the warehouse, the trucks and up at the sun with eyes closed to enjoy the warmth and let go of the stress.

A now talkative Andre suggested to his girlfriend it was now getting scary, particularly as he had nearly been physically attacked by a security guard. He concluded that it was not a normal company and the "ugly" receptionist was really a bouncer. "I am getting a bad feeling about the whole thing. We should quit now while we are STILL alive," he whispered. "This is getting us nowhere and these are not nice people. They look like crooks of some kind, we should leave them alone," advocating for a quick departure.

"I agree this does not make any sense, they don't seem like wine traders to me," Avery replied starring back at the doors that had seen them ejected. "We should do something having come this far although I am not sure what, or even why, given that Michel or Thierry is not here." Then moving towards the driving seat she suggested, "come on, it's time to leave," looking at Rosa for confirmation.

The French woman was still looking angrily at the office building while leaning against the back of the rental. She threw down and stamped out her half-smoked cigarette, the other two took this as a sign that she was ready to go. They climbed into the front seats whispering about the next steps. Rosa did not join them, she continued starring at the office. Andre put down his sun visor vanity mirror, wondering what she was looking at, Avery followed with hers. Two very big men came out of the building and headed straight for the grey van. The couple continued to watch with mild interest. Andre slid his window down to call her, she was mumbling words in French and getting angrier. She opened the rear car door ready to leave but still watched the men.

Andre was thinking how big they were and said to Avery, "you know they look like two of the front five forwards of Toulon rugby club rather than delivery men," then laughed. In case they were famous he decided to sneak a photo before they reached the van. Unfortunately, they saw him and veered towards the trio gesticulating angrily. As they got closer Andre uttered a few expletives and started to think up a cover story, like asking for their autographs. Halfway across, the smaller of the two stopped to drag the other one back on course. The angry one waved a dismissive arm at the trio even smiling before climbing into the transit.

The receptionist reappeared at the door to see what was going on but stopped as his phone rang. He hooked the door open to take the call. After speaking for a few seconds he walked to the grey van where he leant in the window to give the large men instructions of some sort. While Double-A were thinking they were now safe, Rosa bolted across the car park and straight into the offices.

"Rosa," shouted Avery.

"What the fuck," shouted Andre in surprise, the two got out of the car to follow her, as did the large men and the receptionist. The couple arrived at the office first, looked around and saw no one. The big men were only a few metres behind and puffing. More shouting and a uniformed guard appeared carrying a squirming Rosa. Andre stepped forward to free her just before the receptionist plus the two large men from the grey van, charged in to stop him. Andre changed tack, shouting in French, "arret, put her down." The guard dropped the French woman carefully avoiding her swinging arms. Avery ran to help the sobbing Rosa, the guard yelled insults demanding they leave before getting injured.

The trio retreated once again so the French men stopped, out of breath the receptionist leant against the wall, while the other men bent forward to catch their breath, they were not built for sprinting.

Andre was slow in leaving, fascinated by the butt cheeks of the two larger men, one a cavern and the other filled by an old Smith and Wesson 9mm. Avery meanwhile led Rosa away, supported under one arm like an injured soccer player, she looked back and called for Andre to hurry up. What she saw was her boyfriend still staring at the large bottoms of the now standing men. He turned away and ran to catch up. The four men argued loudly in French as they followed the trio to the outer door.

The guard said, in English, "You must leave." Then moving forward to hustle the trio completely out of the building he continued, "You must not come here again. We will not be so good with you next time. We will give you to the gendarmes to put away for trying to break into the office. GO and GO now," he shouted and like the receptionist spat on the ground as they walked away.

"Come on let's get out of here," said Avery baring her teeth. They coaxed Rosa out of the building and across the car park.

This time there was no stopping for a cigarette. Avery drove the rental at speed out of the Entrée and down the street making only one adjustment to the right to avoid an oncoming truck. Rosa wept in the back and the couple remained silent as they completed their escape from the offices. Avery announced that they were going to Bandol for the night before returning to silence in the car. The white van left the car park soon after, driving rather more slowly.

Andre spoke first, "that was pretty hairy stuff," to which the others made noises but said nothing. "Okay, then we shall have to talk about this over a beer later," trying to lift the mood. He sensed it was best to stay quiet so went back to his e-mails to discover how well the business was doing without him. Once he discovered they had signed up three new clients he forgot about their predicament and sent e-mails to the finance team to make sure they received the money before the sales guys sent out the log-ins. Everything else seemed to be in order, there was even a note from Jack asking if he had any more thoughts on the wine industry. "I will think about that tomorrow," he said out loud. Avery gazed at him said nothing carried on driving. He texted Tess to see how Mills was doing. The reply came back a few minutes later with a picture of Mills lying on Tess's couch like she owned that one too. After an hour he could wait no longer, "perhaps we should start talking now," looking at Avery then peering over the seat to see what Rosa was up to.

Rosa quiet for so long took up the invitation, "these were bad men who have no place being at the company and no reason to act as they did. There is something wrong when you get physically assaulted by big ugly men when you go to company offices. Please, you must help me find Michel," as she still insisted on calling him and started to weep. The other two agreed something was wrong but were not convinced there was any evidence these people had kidnapped the Wineman, as Andre preferred to call him. The trio passed through the toll and began the approach to the town.

"Bandol," announced Avery. "We will be at the hotel in about ten minutes. This is such a wonderful place on the Cote d'Azur, I wish I had spent more time here," but left out the 'with "R'. The other two took in the sights; the beach, the casino, the beachfront shops and restaurants. Rosa's phone chimed, she checked Facebook then WhatsApp before producing a smile at a picture showing her niece performing a backflip. For a moment the shock and anger melted away.

Avery was thinking about the trip and concluded, so far they had wasted their time, upset many people and nearly had some big fat ugly men attack them. She thought, *if we don't watch out we will finish up in a French jail for being idiots. What possessed me to lead this trip?* Doubt returned and her self-confidence leaked away as it had done in the morning. Yet she could not shake off the belief there was something very, very wrong and they should find out what it was. *I wish Andre would stop drifting back to his work and his cat and help me.*

A few minutes from the hotel Andre spoke again, "you know, there is something wrong here don't you? Did you see the gun that fat guy had stuck down his backside? That can't be right, can it? They must be French gangsters we should go to the police. Or perhaps they are police on a secret mission or something in which case we could get ourselves into the shit for screwing things up. But surely those fat guys can't be police, can they?" he continued. "By the way, Avery, did you notice there is a car following us?" he said mischievously having noticed the same car behind them since they went through the toll.

"Where, which one?" Avery asked nervously looking in all her mirrors trying to see the car and speeding up to get away with only had a few hundred meters to travel.

"Only joking," laughed Andre having recovered and returned to his normal self.

"Jesus Andre, we just had a run-in with some gangsters with guns stuffed in their trousers and you are joking, are you insane?"

"Sorry, sorry, sorry. I was just trying to cheer us up." He became serious and spoke softly to Avery, "remember we do have a choice, we could just let things go, we should decide soon. Then turning around he spoke to Rosa, "how are you feeling?"

Yves a senior member of the Martin crime family and Head of the Wine Division sat in his white van and made a call. Now in his early forties, tall, attractive with pale blue eyes was the personal advisor and lover of Madame Martin. He told her, Rosalba and her English friends had arrived in Bandol and were proceeding to the new hotel on the bay. They agreed he should watch the place for a while to see if anything interesting happened.

Madame Martin stared at the pool, illuminated by powerful coloured lights, thinking about her next move. In frustration, she shouted, "I cannot have that stupid girl and her English friends running around causing chaos." Then she thought, *but how can I stop them? If I ask the men they will simply kill them causing more trouble. No, we need something clever, something to scare them but without violence.*

Chapter 10: Bandol, Thursday evening

Rosa did not get to answer Andre's question instead they arrived at the Le Beaux Hotel. Disappointingly the car park was full of vehicles driven by late-season holidaymakers. After a huff, Avery parked boot out, in one of the multitude of public spaces opposite the building. The trio collected their wheelie bags and quickly covered the thirty-meter stretch to the entrance.

Le Beaux had been fully refurbished as a five-storey luxury hotel, complete with all the amenities including a small pool and spa with a discreet outlet to the beach for a morning stroll. The Stones architect had modified and equipped the top floor, with its superb view over the bay, for company use. The community thought of "Jack l'Anglais" as the owner because he had been involved in the difficult acquisition and remodelling. The hotel itself was considered a good employer by both local government officials and local people partly because the staff were accommodated in an old and beautiful three-story house opposite. In reality, the property, along with several other French investments, was owned by De Beaux Endroits SARL, a wholly-owned subsidiary of BloedStone Investments, whose links to a crown dependency had caused some issues with local politicians.

Once their IDs were checked the trio were directed to the company's penthouse where they would have the run of the floor. The receptionist suggested they take the rooms on the bayside to enjoy both the breeze and beautiful view. Meals could be taken in the restaurant with the other guests or in their private dining room. They were pointed to the elevator and after a few moments arrived at the top floor. There was an outside terrace at one end, four suites, a sitting room with a bar leading to the dining room and some office space including a meeting room. After a quick search, Avery picked the suite in the far corner on the bayside, it looked the most private, a place they could avoid being heard discussing Rosa or making love.

"Wow, I like this bedroom it has such a great view," Andre commented as he opened the doors to walk out onto the balcony. "This is a pretty impressive place. How did Jack find it and get it modernised?"

"As far as I know, he and Robbie arranged it with the French local authority. I know it took a long time because of local opposition with it being owned by foreigners and being partly used as a conference facility."

"Who is this Robbie guy, I think Jack mentioned him when we met at the pub, he seems interesting what does he do at your company?"

"Who is Sir Robbie?" she repeated suddenly feeling more secure thinking about him. "That's a good question, he's officially the Chief Executive of the UK Stones companies, but he is also rich, has restaurants, planes and his house in Harpenden is to die for. At first, I thought he only worked for your uncle as a favour but he actually likes his job. When I first joined, Jack told me he used to call him the "effin policeman" but now they are great buddies. Together they have made vast amounts of money through investing in companies and property. As far as I know, they have not been involved in stuff like paintings, gold or currencies. Although, there is a rumour that he, your uncle and his deputy, Nicky, have a secret stash of Bitcoins they bought for less than a dollar each and that someday they are going to use them to buy a whole country," she laughed. It was definitely a stress reliever.

"They both seem interesting guys," responded Andre planning his next move that did not involve searching for the missing Wineman. "We should sit with Rosa and talk about what we do tomorrow. Perhaps we could persuade her to go for a drink or maybe the casino so I can teach her to gamble and you too, of course," he chuckled.

"Can't believe she would be a gambler," Avery responded smiling "maybe a drink or just a walk to calm down, then we can eat here. Jack would be upset if we don't eat the food and drink the wine from their chateau. After all, it's free as I am a director of the company you are my guests," she finished carefully avoiding the difficult conversation they needed to have.

"How can we say no then?" Andre responded.

"Let me text Rosa to meet us in the lounge area and we can start talking about tomorrow," continued Avery deciding to deal with the issue. There was a quick response from Rosa, and they met up in the sitting room. Avery suggested they have drinks, eat in, then plan the next steps. They all agreed although Andre was disappointed at the word plan, he would have preferred exit strategy. He dutifully prepared the drinks before joining the other two on the soft leather chairs. Andre appointed himself chairman and started speaking.

"Rosa what do you think we should do now given what we have seen and heard?" he resisted the temptation to summarise the events of the day. Her reply was somewhat unexpected.

"I have texted Thomas about what has happened here. He knows we are looking for Michel, I told him last week when he went missing. I've just updated him about what has been happening, he still believes that Michel is not a bad person. They have met each other when he came to see us in London." She focused on the couple who looked mystified to suddenly hear about this person, but this was not the first surprise, she had form. "Oh, I should tell you, I have two brothers; Alexandre and Thomas who is a gendarme officer working on the Cote d'Azur. His speciality is co-operating with police departments that are tracking drug gangs. He sent a message saying he will call before ten tonight after he has done some investigating. He will tell me whether we should do anything more to find Michel or give up. I will tell you in the morning, or tonight if you want."

"May I suggest," started Avery we have something to eat and then Andre and I will go for a walk while you speak to Thomas, is it? We will come back at about eleven and then we can talk, would that be alright?" Rosa immediately nodded in agreement while her boyfriend, still recovering from the latest revelation of a secret policeman, gave a less enthusiastic okay. With an interim plan in place, Andre vacated the chair and opened some vintage Chateau du Carys.

Over dinner, they chatted about the South of France until it was time for a full and repetitive discussion about their day. Multiple bottles of 2014 were inspiring them and they came to firm conclusions …..`

Those terrible, no ugly big men, no rugby players, had big guns and big, no huge backsides. The weapons weren't loaded or even real, the head office was fake and the nameplate bogus. Madame Martin or "please call me Astrid" was Swedish and lied about the company in England and Paris. She didn't know who Michel was because he was really Michael. Who was Thierry? He was betrayed by his mother and father so he ran off to make his fortune. Michel is someone else entirely, with nothing to do with his mother or the company. He's really Spanish, they should go there to find him because the weather is better in the autumn. What about the guns? No, not that again.

Andre decided he'd had enough wine, Avery agreed it was time to go for a walk. The couple were about to stumble out when Rosa received a call from a withheld number. She hesitated for a moment, looked anxious but answered in slurred French. It was Yves sitting in the car outside, Astrid had decided what to do.

"Salut my name is Lucas, I work for the Notre Blanc wine company you visited today. I understand you had some trouble and bad treatment from our security men. I wanted to apologise to you and your friends for what happened." She brightened up trying to shake off the alcohol and looked at the couple, "I would like to invite you to come back tomorrow and we will make sure that Thierry is here to meet you. He will be flying down from Paris early tomorrow morning. Unfortunately, he still cannot call you because he has some unpleasant people tracking his phone so he has to keep it switched off." She smiled even more.

"Yes it was bad and I, we, are very angry about our treatment. If we come tomorrow you must be there to make sure it does not happen again?" she said struggling to be clear.

"Are your friends with you?" he asked. "If so please put me on speaker so I can reassure them too," she waved for the couple to join her and Yves switched to English. He apologised again explained that it was a mistake. He suggested that the security guards were trying too hard to protect Thierry who was on a secret mission in Paris. He repeated they would make sure her boyfriend came back to meet her in the morning. He answered their many questions including why one of the guards carried a weapon. In their state, his calm and melodic tones made everything seem plausible so they agreed to go back to the warehouse at 10 am.

After the call, Andre asked, "Are we really going?"

"Let's wait and see what Thomas has to say when he calls later then decide," said Avery. They all ummed their agreement before the couple almost fell down the stairs into the evening air for a sobering stroll.

Rosa went to her room to wait for Thomas, flopping onto the bed as the alcohol took hold of her. She managed to crawl between the large scatter cushions and pull the patterned bed scarf around her shoulders. She gripped her phone and began to think about her life so far.

I miss Honfleur so close to Calais, London and Paris my favourite place. I wish I could find someone and go back to that beautiful town where I was born. I haven't seen my mama or papa for so long. Why did they go to live down at the bottom of Spain? They go to see their English friends in Gibraltar rather than come to see me. I remember when they came to see me in Paris so wonderful so beautiful but inhabited by mysterious people from so many different countries. I miss them and some of the people from when I lived there.

But why do I always pick the wrong people to love? None of them was right for me, not until Michel. Where is he? He is handsome, kind and strong. He told me he had done some bad things in his life, that he would tell me about one day, but he had left them behind. He was good but I don't know who he is. The tears flowed freely and as she moved to find some paper towels to wipe her eyes and nose but her phone chirped, it was Thomas. She cheered up a little although her mind was not yet clear she began to tell him about what happened to them. It was going to be a long conversation!

Double-A were walking on the beach at the casino end of the town having a heated discussion about what to do next. Avery insisted on being positive, meaning going back to meet Lucas in the morning. She believed having come this far they should take the opportunity to meet with Michel or Thierry whichever he was calling himself. Andre suggested it was a trap, laid by the "front row forwards" and the "gruesome receptionist" with the high pitched voice, to do unpleasant things to them. He was still insisting they could not be good people with guns stuffed down their backside. There would be no Michel they were gangsters. Avery insisted that they ought to make sure, perhaps they could take Rosa's brother with them as insurance against trouble. Andre agreed he would be happy to go if they had a police escort.

"There's that drone again, I wonder who it belongs to? It's either that or it's a miniature alien ship," he chuckled.

"I wonder what he's like?" asked Avery

"Who?"

"Michel of course, it would be really interesting to see him with Rosa. I was trying to imagine what he looks like. You've already met him back in St Albans, Is he little like Rosa or tall like his mother?"

Andre wanted to end the conversation and replied, "normal height as far as I remember. Let's just wait and see what Rosa's brother comes up with." Then he added, "I would love to go back to his mother's house, that was pretty impressive." It worked, Avery showed no interest and quickened her pace.

The evening was warm and for Avery, it began to feel like the days of "R", she wanted to relax, regretted the arguments, and just wanted to enjoy being together. "Come on let's get going," she suggested. They started back to the hotel along the seafront boulevard, stopping to look through the occasional shop window. They slowly approached the hotel from the beach before speeding up when they saw Rosa smoking a few meters from the entrance. She saw them and turned, looking pensive, but also ready to talk. Andre glanced towards the parking spaces to check for the rental but instead saw a black SUV parked front out close by. A passing headlight revealed two men sitting in the front seats looking directly at him. A third man appeared from their side of the street and walked over to the SUV. He had been taking pictures of the bay and surrounding buildings including their hotel. Andre was concerned but the man waved as he climbed into the back of the vehicle. Seconds later the vehicle passed by slowly with all three men smiling at him. Seconds later a white van followed.

I must calm down, that was just some holidaymakers checking out the area and hotel, he decided and dismissed it, the others had shown no interest. "Just going to make sure the car is alright," he said to Avery wandering over to the rental to kick the tyres. Finding nothing amiss, he jogged back to the entrance as the other two disappeared inside. He saw the drone again this time it was sitting above the hotel. He ignored it but wondered what was the point at this time of night.

The couple joined Rosa in the penthouse sitting area to hear what she had to report. "I have spoken to my brother, he thinks we are doing the right thing. He wants us to go back to the offices in Marseille tomorrow, observe what is going on inside the building, then tell him so he can report back to his superiors. He says that they have suspicions about the place but they need more information. Before we go in they want us to put on a listening device so they can hear what is said. There is no risk, they will be watching and waiting and will come in if we are threatened in any way.

"Oh," said Andre "I was not expecting that, having to wear a wire. This is becoming like a TV movie, but it gets us the back-up we wanted."

Avery looked happy at the news, which supported her decision to continue the search but was concerned by what they were being asked to do.

Chapters 11: Marseille, Friday morning

The traffic to Marseille was busy, but it was quiet inside the car, each person thinking about what lay ahead, with at least two wondering how they got themselves in such a situation. The trio arrived at the police meeting point in good time to be greeted by several plainclothes policemen. They were escorted, one by one, into a large box van for a listening device fitting. While the trio felt even more vulnerable waiting to enter the offices of the warehouse, the police felt even more jovial as they prepared to storm it. The commander issued coded instructions that the team should avoid injury to their "stalking horse" if possible, but not at the cost of a successful operation. Thomas was not happy and was, sidelined until it was over.

Inside the warehouse Yves, Noell and Pascal were running through the plan once again. It was simple, their men would overpower "the agitators", as Madame had taken to calling them, in the canteen whilst they met with Yves or Lucas, as they knew him. The confab would not be interrupted by les ouvriers as they were forced to eat where they worked.

"So what do we do once they are bound and gagged, "asked Noell, one of Andre's "forwards".

"We take them to the lock-up and wait for disposal instructions," replied Yves. "Maybe they will be ransomed or maybe they will go to Henri for him to sell. He should do well with the women they are both very beautiful making a gesture with his hands. The man will make a special treat for our Asian friends," he joked.

"We will use the van nearest the exit to take them out at about 4 pm when we have cleared out the Africans, Noell told the other two. "Really," he continued, "we should have postponed the meeting till later so we do not have to keep them here so long."

Pascal had been listening to the conversation but appeared to show no interest until he suddenly turned to Yves, "text them to move the meeting to 11.30 am. Let them sweat, they aren't going anywhere. I want to make sure we have most of the work done and loaded before they get here, then we can give them our full attention," he produced one of his lurid smiles. "Now how about a glass of wine before we do this?" he asked. "Do you have any good stuff or is it all piss from the desert?"

"No, we have some good wine which we keep for Madame," replied Yves going to the door. "Hakim" he shouted a couple of times before a tired-looking man appeared smelling of wine. "Hakim get me a couple of bottles of that good wine I told you to keep near the cellar," the man looked vacant. "With Chateau du Carys on the label," Hakim nodded and scuttled away. Yves shouted after him, "don't take too long and then quietly "or we won't have time to drink it," he smiled again. He had an important romantic date later. The three men sat at the table and waited for the wine to arrive.

Rosa groaned as she received the text and had to tell everyone the meeting had been delayed until 11.30 am. The jovial commander became irritated, he had a lot of heavily armed men cooped up in vehicles getting hot and edgy. For him, the delay was the worst enemy followed closely by the fear of failure. This time he accepted that the gang were probably playing with them.

"Has anyone seen the son? Has he arrived or not? That will be the next delay," he shouted to his deputy and team leaders. "We will be sitting here waiting for that clown to arrive before we can do anything," the commander continued. The teams all responded with a negative. *Perhaps he is already in there*, he thought. He asked his deputy to check the area again for anything out of the ordinary.

"Everything looks normal, the gang are loading the last truck," replied the deputy in a calm flat tone. He was used to his boss getting over-excited before a raid and took it upon himself to calm things down whenever he could.

The commander began again this time with a raised voice, "we MUST have a reason to stop that truck before it leaves to have a good look inside. It's probably full of contraband, we must prevent it from getting onto the street."

"Sir, they will not be leaving before the new deadline. If they try we will block the street with a car or something, so please don't worry," replied the deputy.

"Let's just hope the gang are quick to do something to our three informants so we can execute. Have you checked the wires we don't want any screw-ups do we?"

The time ticked round to 11.05, there had been no more texts and the trio decided the meeting must be taking place so went for a short drive to ease the tension. They arrived a few minutes later and reverse parked a few spaces away from the entrance. This time there was a truck, with cab attached and a couple of vans reverse parked against the loading bays. Again they could hear the noise of people working. Andre was pleased to see the exit gate was wide open for their escape if necessary. The trio sat and waited, the police sat and waited, the three Martin men sat and drank coffee enthusing about the weekend being only moments away.

Andre got out of the car first, stood stretched and waited for the other two. They had five minutes to go, Avery locked the car they strolled through the hooked open reception door once again.

"Bonjour," said a smiley lady receptionist from behind a new looking desk, "what can I do for you?" she continued.

"Bonjour, we have a meeting with Lucas and my friend Michel at 11.30," Rosa replied. Then continued, "my name is Rosalba

Babineaux and these are my friends Andre and Avery." She looked straight at the receptionist who stood up.

"Lucas is here but I am not sure about Michel," she faltered on the last name and looked confused. Andre joined in to advise the surname was Martin. The receptionist, with eyebrows still drawn down, left through a door behind her, Andre peered through the gap as she left, but could see nothing.

"They're here, are you ready?" the receptionist asked Yves. "For some reason, she is asking for Michel Martin," she continued in a quieter voice.

Yves ignored her comments, opened the other door and used two hands to summon the six men who had been briefed on the kidnap. They were to sit until given a signal to seize, gag, tie, hood and hold them, prisoner, until it was time to leave. Pascal watched, intrigued by what was about to happen, it was a long time since he had seized civilians. The receptionist was dispatched back to the front desk where the two women were sitting waiting and Andre was wandering around looking at things on the walls. She asked the trio to go with her, they followed into the canteen and over to where Yves was sitting with Pascal and Noell. They saw no cause for alarm even though the place was awful, the men were all smiling looking relaxed. Yves stood and welcomed them in English saying his name was Lucas but he did not introduce his colleagues while politely asking them to sit.

A few hundred metres away, the commander, now on the highest alert spoke to his deputy, "I wish they would say something it's all too quiet for me."

"Soon," replied the deputy. "Get ready," he said to the men, now like sprinters waiting for the gun.

Yves began the interrogation by asking Rosa, "how do you know Michel?" Rosa set off on a long explanation looking around every so often at her two colleagues. Andre immediately felt an acute stress reaction thinking, *they are playing with us, they know there is no Michel.* He began to run through potential exit plans but struggled to find even a way out of the room without some help. He knew that with his fight or flight response triggered he should engineer the discussion to a point where the gendarmes would feel able to carry out a forced entry.

"Where is Thierry, is he here or not?" he interrupted the discussion causing the three members to look at him and lose any semblance of calm.

"Who?" replied Yves and casually waved his right hand. The discussion ended abruptly with six men exploding into action to the screams of the women and the shouts of first Andre and then a few seconds later by the gendarme commander. Within a minute; the shocked trio were subdued and dragged into the corner. The warehouse security alarm went off, the "gruesome male receptionist ran into the canteen screaming to Pascal, as best he could, there were hundreds of armed police pouring into the car park. Pascal and Yves jumped up, told the men to hold the trio until they told them differently, and ran out of the room followed by Noell.

Weapons were being fired as the Martin members were trying to fight off the heavily armed gendarmes and police. They were losing fast, many were veterans of the Marseille drug wars and would fight to the death. To their credit, the criminals managed to do enough to give Pascal and his two colleagues enough time to retreat to the back to the warehouse and disappear. On the way, the three men co-opted Hakim and Sami to drag the unpacked drugs into a secret cellar. Once in, it was sealed from the inside and very hard to find from the outside.

Down in the cellar, the angry men listened to the gunfire. They argued about whose fault it was, questioned who the trio were and asked how the police knew when to attack.

"Merde, merde they must have had wires," hissed Pascal at the other two. "they arranged for the police to raid us, merde."

They continued to discuss what happened, carefully avoiding the issue that none of them had thought to search the trio when they arrived. By the time they left the cellar later that night, the story became clearer; it was a deliberate act by an English owned French company to destroy them and take over the Martin family business. That is what Madame would be told, no one outside the cellar would be able to say differently, they would either be in custody, wounded or dead, a fate the hiding Africans hoped to avoid.

While the three senior Martin members were hiding and their colleagues were fighting, the trio were being held hostage. Their six guards initially expecting no problem kidnapping three civilians were left sharing three old S&W 9mm handguns and a total of nine bullets. On being challenged by a police negotiator, the criminals did the usual thing of threatening to shoot the hostages unless they were allowed to leave. They selected a transit van as the preferred mode of escape. The police buoyed by the success of stopping thirty gang members split equally between arrested and dead, immediately agreed to the demands. It was thought best to finish the raid quickly before anything could go wrong.

The hostage-takers trusting the police shuffled out with one captive and one gun shared between two, the weapon being pointed somewhere around the face or neck. The unarmed members walking hunched at the waist in a futile attempt to protect themselves. As they struggled towards the van the commander gave the "kill order" and the three armed criminals received headshots from the sharpshooters, so successfully deployed in recent gang battles. To the disappointment of the police commander, the unarmed kidnappers immediately gave up throwing themselves on the floor, arms outstretched.

In the feverish and almost joyful post raid activity the trio sat in the back of an ambulance in shock. Horrified at being in the line of fire and worse, being splashed by blood and bits from the now-deceased members. While being cleaned up and checked over by the police and ambulance services, Captain Babineaux arrived to thank them for their co-operation. Thomas told them he had not been allowed to take part because of his sister, but unlike most, he looked genuinely relieved rather than overjoyed at the results of the encounter. He offered to take them all back to Bandol if they wanted to leave their car for a day or two. The couple decided to take the rental while Rosa would stay with her brother and return later for dinner.

Two hours after being taken hostages Andre drove out of the car park with Avery sitting next to him. Other than for directions little was said as she navigated him to the outskirts of the city. Andre felt stressed but he had faced the "eye of the tiger" before and survived. For Avery this experience was so far outside her comfort zone she would struggle to avoid PTSD symptoms.

Eventually, Andre spoke, "after all that we still have no idea where the Wineman is or indeed, what he's really called, or did I miss something?"

Avery let her head slump forward as she received humour as medicine, blew a breath and mumbled "unbelievable."

Chapter 12: Marseille, Saturday

Martin family business summary prepared for De Beaux Endriots Sarl.

By officer 23451 Marseille Gendarmerie (on secondment).

Provides situation report after the successful raid at the NOTRE BLANC warehouse.

Martin Crime Family – a Summary.

For details please refer to reports MF1 1019 to MF10 1019 available on secure lines.

The Martin crime family is a well organised and managed enterprise. They have thrived on finding and distributing illegal or illicit product or distributing legal product illegally, without being stopped by the law or tax authorities. Their specific geographical area is the Marseille region and they are headquartered in Roucas Blanc. Matisse Martin is the current head of the family and has one remaining son Thierry – the other was killed in the recent Marseille drug gang battles.

They are much more than a simple cartel: procuring, processing and distributing US Schedule I drugs like Heroin and Schedule II drugs like Cocaine. They operate successful legal companies to hide their highly profitable illegal activities. Secrecy has been imposed through mandatory non-disclosure agreements with the membership We understand there have been several instances where the agreements have been ruthlessly enforced and the individuals are now listed as missing.

The business conducts its operations through highly developed structures capable of reaching across the world and are supported by members of a Western Europe crime syndicate. They also have connections to crime gangs in London, one of which we believe is currently under investigation by French and UK authorities. Note. You have access to details through your UK associates.

Their leader, Matisse Martin, whose current whereabouts is unknown, manages the unlawful businesses with his two assistants Pascal Duval and Patrice Barre. The two men are well known to local law enforcement for developing and executing projects to improve the business. To date, neither man has been charged with any crimes, which to us appears suspicious. The business is split into three main sections with the following team leaders; Chevy Merle - Drugs, Henri Segal – Trafficking and Prostitution and Yves Calvin – Wine Fraud. The first two activities have been in operation for many years with drugs providing the major revenues.

Wine fraud is a relatively new venture and has caused significant internal division blurring the line between their legitimate retail business and criminal activity. Patrice had a special involvement in the project and has established relationships with several vineyard owners. We are unable to provide details of how many vineyards are involved or whether the fraud extends to any Bloedstone Investments in either Bordeaux or the Rhone region.

The legitimate businesses of wine import-export, building, retail (wine, clothes etc.) and casino management are overseen by Astrid Martin, the wife and Deputy Leader. Madame is a former wine négociant and latterly a merchant from Bordeaux. We note that she has been very successful in growing their legal businesses albeit using drug profits. It seems that this may become their main enterprise in the future. The legal businesses are housed in high specification offices in the Marseille old port area near the seafront, well away from the group's main warehouse in Le Panier.

After the battles in Marseille and the recent raid on their main warehouse, the organisation needs leadership, time and money to rebuild and avoid alerting the WE Syndicate and local cartels to their problems. Earlier we noted that the Leader was currently unaccounted for but it is rumoured that both he and his son were hiding and controlling operations from overseas. We believe that they are most likely residing in Algiers at a compound they use for people smuggling. The organisation is rumoured to be short of both drugs and money following the recent police raid. However, we have no information on why that has occurred as the police have not reported any large confiscations. There is a rumour (currently ignored by the police) that there is a hidden cellar in the warehouse where the drugs and money are stored ready for collection when the armed guards finally leave. We have not been allowed access to search the warehouse or the rumoured cellar. Pascal and Patrice along with much of the senior members escaped the raid and gang battles and have been tasked with rebuilding operations.

We understand it was Patrice who was ordered to follow up on the intelligence that the raid was organised by your company, De Beaux Endroits, who they believe to be secretly working with a rival unidentified organisation.

We recommend that Stones concentrate on pursuing and if possible persuading Patrice to become a Stones agent or informer to provide further intelligence and help execute remedial activities. If they become necessary.

What remained of the family's senior members were summoned to an early morning meeting at a restaurant in the old town of Marseille. The mood was sombre, they had just lost nearly forty of their members on top of those lost in the recent drug battles. Their number now reduced by more than half, to less than 100.

They had no readily available drug product or money, both were locked away in the cellar of a warehouse heavily guarded by police. The leadership team were going to spend most of the day scrutinising what had happened, why and what they should do next. The investigation would include:

1.   What to do about the "missing" Matisse and "lost" Thierry?
2.   Who were the English couple accompanying Thierry's alleged girlfriend?
3.   Who is the Englishman called Jack who owns the hotel in Bandol?
4.   How to get their product and money out of the cellar?
5.   Where to get more product to substitute for the loss?
6.   How to calm down their band of "Entrepreneurs" who sell the product?
7.   …...and a few more.

Once the analysis was complete the leadership would create a plan to repair the business as they had done after previous setbacks.

By Saturday afternoon after considerable arguments and vitriol, they arrived at an elementary but very loose plan which might keep things going for a while.

1.   Patrice would reconnoitre Bandol and start the surveillance of Jack's team. The alternatives being considered; extort money from the French company and or its English owners to pay for the damage. Or kidnap for ransom or burn down the hotel if they found links to another gang or something else!
2.   Pascal and Chevy would make sure the drug business did not fall apart until they found a way to get their product out of the warehouse. Or they found alternative suppliers who would take credit.

3.	Henri would get on and smuggle as many people as possible and at the highest prices to generate cash for the purchase of the product and pay some wages.

4.	Madame Martin would make sure there was no blowback on the legal businesses.

5.	The missing men would continue to be reported as working in Algiers on family business.

The meeting broke up and the gang members rushed away to get started. Patrice was last to leave he was making a call to his friend Frederic who managed a French wine company that had its own chateau in Bordeaux. They were working on a secret project to generate money for themselves rather than the Martin family. He failed to reach him as usual but it was a Saturday and he decided he must be off somewhere with his boyfriend. He changed tack and started on his latest project.

"I must meet this Englishman, the boss of those three troublemakers I saw in Bandol," he said in English. "I know the company he works for. I must find out why he has started a war with us, a war he cannot win in France," Patrice announced to his driver who spoke very little English and just grunted. He switched to French, "Revo, just follow the directions on the phone there," pointing at the smartphone in a dashboard holster. Revocat grunted again, he was one of the Africans the family had recently recruited to bolster their depleted numbers. He had a lot to learn, including apparently speaking French, there was not much time to prove his worth. Failure would mean being sent into poverty in Algeria, possibly being killed by a cartel for joining the Martins.

Chapter 13: Bandol, Saturday and Sunday

Saturday arrived to find Double-A drowsy, fatigued and unable to do much more than just lie together. Friday night's dinner had been cancelled, none of the trio were mentally ready to do more than have a late supper, a stiff drink and go to bed to sleep off the horrors of the day. Captain Babineaux dropped Rosa back at the hotel at 9 pm, they all agreed to have dinner in the penthouse on the Saturday evening instead.

After a restless night's sleep, the couple did little but check they were feeling better and ordered room service. Yazmeen personally brought them breakfast to check on them. She had already told Jack about the raid, following a short conversation with Rosa's brother. He had asked to be kept informed of their progress but did not want to call to avoid having Avery think about work.

Rosa was in much the same condition without the benefit of a companion. Yasmeen took the opportunity to check on her mid-morning and found excuses to do the same throughout the day. The Hotel Manager came to the conclusion that the more time the French woman spent on social media the better her demeanour became.

After breakfast, the couple took a walk around the town, the food market was in full swing and they treated themselves to some cheeses and fruits. They bought a few trinkets from the seafront stores and generally acted like they were tourists, even the sun came out to help. But they were subdued they knew later they would return to the subject of the Martin family.

Dinner was at 7.30 in the penthouse dining suite, the couple invited, Yazmeen, Rosa and Rosa's brother, Thomas, to join them. It was to be a sort of celebration after defeating the Martin family, although the "elephant in the room" remained the missing Wineman - the reason they came to the South of France. The evening started well, they almost got to the point of laughing about what happened. Thomas promised he would ask for them to be awarded medals, however, as the evening wore on and the wine went down faster, it became statues. Eventually, the conversation arrived at the remaining Martin family and in particular mother and son. Thomas having enjoyed large quantities of wine was encouraged to unleash his English to tell them more. Andre hoped it would include something interesting about Astrid Martin while Avery and Rosa were more interested in Thierry.

"They are well known to us for much time," he began. The local police have been unable to capture them doing their drug sales. Matisse Martin is Chief, he has strong control over the men in the gang, I don't think there is any women gangsters. I am told that there has never been any member who has, I think you call it, snitches on what they do. So we don't arrest anyone. After the gunfight in Marseille, no one could find the boss we still don't find him. After the raid yesterday you helped us with, thank you once more for that, none of our chiefs want to search for him or his sergeants or captains. I don't know why, it is very strange, but I can't do nothing."

Captain Babineaux continued for a further twenty minutes on the subject of Matisse, Astrid and the son who ran off to England. When he finished, the rest chipped in with their stories about the rude men and the deceitful Lucas who got them kidnapped.

Once the conversation slowed, Yazmeen, the only sober one, announced that she thought one of her friends in London did design work for Astrid's shops. This caused a few comments, more than when Thomas suggested the Marseille law enforcement had many issues to resolve, but probably less than if they had heard him say he would like to leave and go to England too. The group were getting tired, they broke up for the night.

Sunday morning saw the couple lying in bed, with the balcony doors still open from the night before. They had enjoyed a good meal rounded off by some inspiring sex given the volume of wine Andre had consumed. This time neither of them thought about their previous partners, the relationship had moved on to a different level after their recent experience. They felt a greater bond and appeared to have recovered from being taken hostage. It was impossible not to return to the previous night's revelations to consider what it meant for the future.

Andre started, "I keep thinking about what Thomas said about the Wineman being a member of his parents" drugs gang. A gang that tried to kill us. As for Rosa, surely we should be encouraging her to go home like her brother suggested. Avery ummed while thinking about what he was saying. "I was also surprised that Yazmeen knew of, "please call me Astrid", through her designer friends in London. How can she be doing work with proper companies and still sell drugs?" Andre was speaking rapidly and a bit too loudly, "you would think they would be able to arrest her for something. It is unbelievable that not one of the gang will say anything about who is in charge," he was becoming more agitated.

"I agree but keep your voice down we don't want anyone else to hear," replied Avery stretching out and thinking about Rosa. "El Capitaine also said that he probably ran off and left the gang to live like a normal person in England. That's a good thing, besides he wasn't involved on Friday so perhaps we can forgive him for Rosa's sake." She paused then asked, "so are we going to help her or not, she still wants to find Michel sorry, Thierry?"

Andre relaxed a little then replied, "I just don't know what we can do for her or how we can find her missing boyfriend, that is if he wants to be found."

"If we decide not to help what are we going to tell her?" asked Avery. Andre mumbled something and jumped out of bed to go to the bathroom.

On his return, he snuggled up to her, "let's not think about her today we are not leaving until tomorrow. After all, we're heroes, aren't we?" he continued. "Maybe we will get that medal from El Presidente," and kissed her.

"I don't think it was so scary," murmured Avery returning once again to the previous Friday. Andre knew, just like Saturday, he had to do something to get his girlfriend away from thinking about the Martins, the missing man and sad Rosa and onto something much more pleasant.

He did the male thing, "babe, forget him and them, just think about this one," holding his manhood. "I think he would be ready to go again with a bit of encouragement from you," he said with a lewd expression.

Avery weighed the prospect of another session against getting on with her day, "keep it for tonight babe." Then in a rapid about-turn, she decided on more exercise, to Andre's surprise she took his hardening penis into her mouth to start another workout. Once complete and again lying in the cool breeze Avery returned to the Rosa conundrum she said jokingly, "we must make sure Rosa is okay and does not go on another one of her runs."

"Yes, she certainly can be a bit of a Usain Bolter," replied Andre. "I'm going for a shower," thinking, *what a nice surprise, it worked for me, I forgot about Rosa for a few minutes*, he smiled.

Once dressed and feeling good they went to the ground floor restaurant for breakfast. Their plan involved Avery doing the talking with Andre smiling and being nice. When they arrived Rosa was sitting with a coffee and phone attached. Avery called her name, she looked up with red-rimmed eyes from the lack of sleep. The couple sat at her table, ordered breakfast and smiled saying very little. Avery started by asking how she felt and tried to engage in general chat, but it had little effect. Rosa said nothing just continued to hide behind her phone. Andre wanted his girlfriend to be more forceful to get the French women to open up and talk about the previous night's conversation. Breakfast continued in silence with Andre desperate to wade in and get the discussion moving. He leant forward, Avery gave an involuntary but loud, "NO," to which Rosa put her phone down and looked at them.

"I would like to keep looking for Thierry," the couple noted the name change. "But my brother does not think we will find him, he is either hiding from the Martins or a rival gang have kidnapped or killed him and dumped his body somewhere," she became emotional. Avery moved to comfort her, "so I must forget him and go on with my life." Although the couple looked relieved, Avery realised how difficult it was to make such a decision and felt sad for her. "Can we go for that walk now?" she asked.

"Of course, let's have a look at Toulon and walk on the beach," replied Avery. They collected their stuff, grateful the city was even further away from Marseille. Andre, now the designated driver decided to inspect the rental before they left. He thought he had seen suspicious-looking men hanging around the hotel on Saturday evening but quickly dismissed it as paranoia although perhaps he shouldn't have.

The trio set off to the east along the A50, eventually leaving it to turn down into Toulon and the coast. Andre followed the line of the sea so they could explore the numerous inlets and small bays. At the Toulon beach market, they stopped to have a simple lunch of bread, cheese, fruit and coffee. Next, they took a stroll along the Henri Fabre walkway onto the beach. They chatted about their lives and whether Brexit would change anything between the English and French. They were laughing, relaxing, it had turned into a weekend break.

Avery was first to get the feeling that someone was following them but dismissed it as yesterday's leftover emotions. Andre kept seeing the same shirt that he liked, but thought, *it must be a coincidence or a very popular shirt around here.* Rosa was too distracted exchanging phone message to notice anyone. But when the shirt stopped near them, Andre had the distinct feeling he knew its wearer. He scanned faces in his mind. *It's not anyone from the warehouse or hotel,* Andre thought. Then came the realisation he had sort of met him, he stopped and pulled Avery back. "There is a guy following us, he is the guy who was taking pictures of the hotel, you know, the one who waved before going off in the car." Avery looked surprised, Rosa looked at both of them wondering why they had stopped.

Avery remembered the men, was about to say something when the man walked up to them and spoke, "I have a message for you so stay still for a moment. You three caused a lot of trouble on Friday when you called the police to our warehouse." Rosa started to speak but was stopped by the man pointing to a colleague standing close by, "we don't want to hurt you," although he was thinking, *yes we do want to hurt you or maybe just play with you for a while.* "But we will if we have to." The man spoke good English, had dark skin, not tanned and brown eyes, he was not French. "You need to pay us back for the loss you caused on Friday. We know you work for a French company and someone that is called Jack l'Anglais." This time Andre was about to speak and Avery stopped him, "do you understand?" The approach succeeded in shocking the trio and sending Andre back to a time where he was threatened by bandits on his uncle's farm. He had survived that and decided to confront the aggressor.

"What do you want," demanded Andre sternly knowing they were in the open with lots of people around. *What are they going to do here?* he was thinking. *Perhaps I should tell him to fuck off, he's not that big, neither is the other. Maybe I could make a scene, knock him down then start shouting. No doubt he would run away.*

'Don't do anything silly, I have a sniper trained on you all. He will hit you before you move," the man said as his colleague walked over to and greet them like they were close friends.

"What, you're joking," was Andre's reaction. The other two were quiet, more interested in what the men wanted rather than fighting. He continued, "what do you want from us, we don't have lots of money or anything."

"Yes you do, or your boss does, if he doesn't pay us then we will come for you, we know where you are staying in Bandol and where you live in England." They knew the first piece of information but not the second, yet.

"How did you find us," said Andre heading off down a different track, the thought of these thugs turning up where they lived was too awful to contemplate.

The man ignored the question instead handed him a cheap flip phone, "keep it switched on and charged until we call you." He started muttering warnings about not calling the police again as they had caused enough trouble already. Then he repeated, "You wait for the call and your instructions, understand?" The men stepped forward, hugged the trio as if they were family then walked off and were gone in seconds.

Good start, thought Patrice watching from his observation point behind a nearby wall. On his way back to the vehicle he told Evo, "now that Armella he's good, he does exactly what I tell him, a new boy but off to a good start. He could go far in this organisation," he smiled. Evo nodded just seeing his boss happy was a triumph after all the disasters.

The trio once again in trouble, resolved to return to their hotel and talk about what happened. The enthusiasm of the morning now replaced by a new confusion. As a morale booster, Andre suggested it was a hoax by what remained of the gang. They would never hear from them again once they left France. The others sort of agreed but without conviction.

"I think we need help," proposed an irritated Avery. "I will call Jack, tell him what just happened to warn him of the mess we have got ourselves and him into. Rosa, you should call your brother and tell him about these people to see if he will arrest them for assault or something," she was becoming angrier.

Andre was not convinced, "you don't know that anything will happen, we just had a couple of men threaten us on a beach, of all places. They were not even French judging by their accents if anything they are just trying to frighten us, to get money, after hearing about what happened at the warehouse. I am sure nothing will happen once we get home," he repeated. He was thinking and hoping, *this is just a local scam and we should not fall for it. Telling Jack would just make it worse and anyway what could he do. He's a nice guy but an investor the worst he has probably ever seen is an irate owner of a bankrupt company.*

Avery was thinking, *poor Jack, he will go mad, what does he know about this sort of thing? These people think we are in some sort of gang led by him. He doesn't know anything about gangs and doesn't own the hotel. We have landed poor old Jack in the shit. Oh god, this is a nightmare, I wish I had never brought us here,* her eyes filled with tears at their predicament. *I'll be glad when we get home tomorrow.*

Andre continued, "Avery, let's not do anything yet. First, let's get home then decide what to do. Please?" he pleaded.

Rosa silent since they started back said, "if we're in trouble I'm sure Thomas will tell us what to do. I agree we should wait before we tell anyone, we should not worry them if it is really nothing, don't you agree?" Andre was surprised and looked across at Avery who nodded and said nothing. "Don't worry I will call Thomas just as soon as we get back to the hotel and are safe."

It was mid-afternoon when they arrived back at Le Beaux and parked boot out in the hotel car park. On the way, they all agreed to stay in, eat in the private dining room, pack and have an early night.

At the hotel, now being watched by Stone's armed guards, they met together in the dining area to do normal things like answering e-mails and checking in with Auntie Tess. Eventually, Andre announced he needed a drink so he opened a beer for himself and delivered cola to the women. He followed up with a search of the wine cabinet for something to go with dinner. As he foraged, Rosa spoke rapidly to her brother. Andre struggled to make out more than a few words but got the distinct impression the call was going badly.

"Wow, there are some more bottles of Chateau du Carys 2014 in here," their downfall from the previous night. "I wonder if these are real or scam wine from the Martins? I think we should give them the benefit of the doubt and drink them don't you?" looking at Avery draped on the leather couch looking at her messages.

Yasmeen arrived to check on them and take their dinner order but stopped outside the dining area to listen to Rosa explaining the story of the Toulon confrontation. After a few minutes, she knocked on the open door and entered wearing a hotel manager's smile. Yasmeen swiftly realised the Martin issue was far from resolved. The Hotel Manager wondered whether they would ask for help from Sir Robbie the man who had saved her. She made a note to warn Jack there was a new issue and let him decide what to do when they were back home.

"I spoke to Jack," she said to encourage them to share the latest problem. "He hopes you had a good day after your horrible

Friday." They looked at her then each other, before Avery replied keeping to the agreed story.

"We had a great time but can't wait to get back to the office," forcing a chuckle. "I will be there on Tuesday morning first thing in case he calls you again."

"He also said you should not drink ALL the good wine," continued Yasmeen looking at Andre and forcing a similar smile. "Perhaps I can take your dinner order if you are eating here?" she continued handing out the menus. Once they had all given their requests and the Hotel Manager had studied their behaviour she continued, "I will leave you to enjoy the rest of the evening and see you in the morning before you leave."

Avery returned to her sad thoughts, *what should I say to Jack after all this? What about, we had a great time getting involved in a police raid, being held at gunpoint and then being accosted in the street by gangsters who want a load of cash from you. Other than that it was wonderful, oh and hasn't OUR gang got a great hotel.*

A phone rang, they nervously looked at each other, it was not any of theirs but was it the flip phone? Dread returned, Andre left to fetch the Martin phone from the bedroom. On the way, he heard Yasmeen saluting a new caller while walking down the stairs. *Panic over but I must keep that phone handy just in case it rings, he thought.*

The food arrived, the wine was opened and Rosa finished talking to her brother. It was time for a difficult conversation. Rosa slowly described what she had told her brother, while the couple sat patiently listening and eating. *I know all this, I need to know what to do,* Andre thought. When she started to repeat herself, he stopped her to ask what her brother was going to do about it, or alternatively what they should do.

The French woman replied, "the police can do nothing unless there is what he called a "creadibal threat" to health or life or they did something to us." Rosa concluded as the other two corrected her with credible. "As far as the police are concerned, those men were just asking for something, they may seem threatening but it is not enough. Thomas also said that the police believe the Martin organisation has been so badly damaged they could not go with us to England. My brother is very sad for us but he did not think we should worry because your chief Monsieur Ritchie and his organisation were known to his bosses. He told me they are powerful people who would be very angry when they found out what the criminals had been doing to Bordeaux wines and to us. Do you know what he meant?"

"I think they must have the wrong Ritchie," replied Avery. "I guess from what he said we just need to get out of here in the morning, okay," Avery concluded. Andre remained quiet thinking about what he had been told and praying the flip phone remained silent. They continued their meal and said very little for the rest of the evening. The mood was sombre they wanted Monday to come quickly.

That night when Avery could not sleep she went to the kitchen for water and took the opportunity to wander around the empty parts of the top floor. She looked out at the sea gently lapping a bay lit by moonlight, it was a beautiful place even though it was autumn. Before returning to bed she looked down at the car park and thought she saw someone near their car. It was dark on that side, maybe it was an animal. She dismissed it as nothing.

Chapter 14: North Africa, Sunday night

The Wineman, Michel Canning aka Thierry Martin, son of Astrid and Matisse and former Deputy Leader of the Martin Crime Family, stood looking out of the hotel window at the distant port. He had been there for a week and was bored with everything from the room service food to the lack of decent English and French TV channels. He had read no newspapers, had no access to his phone and his room was being kept locked to protect him from the same fate as his father. He guessed he must be hiding in Algiers town because he knew they had a compound nearby. He saw a group of Arab women dressed in matching thawb, they reminded him of the Buddhist monks he once saw at an exhibition at the British Library. It made him feel worse he wondered whether he could sneak out and pretend he was one of them to escape from this hell.

Over the previous few days, he had asked himself many times why he had ended up in this shabby room even though he had left the Martin business. He had been sent a message, which used the family's security code, to get together with someone near his flat in London for important information. When they met early in the morning the man explained he must visit his mother to learn what they were going to do about his missing father. Thierry knew this to be code for his dead father, something he regretted, but because of him, he had left the country. After an argument with the man, whom he didn't recognise but assumed to be a new recruit by Pascal or Patrice, he agreed to go to Marseille and then on to his current location. Although he thought the whole situation was strange besides being a waste of time, he still loved his mother and so he agreed. *Can this really be where I am supposed to meet mama,* he kept thinking. The guards told him secrecy was very important to keep him be safe after the gang wars, rivals would be looking for him.

Thierry felt guilty not telling his girlfriend about his journey to North Africa but was advised against it, to avoid putting her in danger. He thought, *If only I had done more than just send a stupid text*. He loved her and wanted them to build a new life together in England. He had explained to her there had been bad things in his past which he would share with her one day. He knew she loved him and was worried about his recent frame of mind following the death of his father, of which he could say nothing. He had been clear with both his parents that his days of dealing with drugs, people smuggling and killing rivals were over. He felt shame at what he had done.

Once he had arrived he wondered why his mother made no attempt to contact him and wished he had ignored her pleas to come home. He went through all the questions; *how could my mother be so deceitful? Why did I fall for it? Why did she do this to me, I am not a threat I don't want anything to do with the business anymore? Is this punishment?* Then onto, *what of Rosalba, my Babi what will she think has happened to me? What will she do now I am not there with her?* He eventually concluded they had kidnapped him, but felt fortunate at not having been tortured or killed. He was worried at not being asked to provide proof of life and knew from experience, that was a bad thing.

"What are you looking at?" asked the duty guard. "There's not much out there to look at. Those people keep themselves all covered up, you can't see what they look like, it wouldn't do for me."

"When am I going to see my mother or anyone other than you two?" Thierry asked walking the four paces across the room to sit on the bed. He looked up at a mindless quiz show which the guard was enjoying. "Morons," he said quietly.

Chapter 15: Marseille Airport, Monday morning

The trio set off early for the flight home, everything went well, traffic was light and there were no men following them. At the airport, they successfully returned the rental, checked in, and made airside with two hours left before the flight. At the gate, they sat brooding, reading e-mails or wandering around until their flight was called. As they queued to board an unfamiliar ring came from one of Andre's pockets. He froze for a moment then turned away to answer, the other two looked concerned they knew it wasn't a work call.

"Hello," said Andre after opening up the unfamiliar phone.

"Don't forget to keep it with you. We are watching you and will see you again at Heathrow," came the reply. "Have a great flight," the line went dead. Andre looked devastated, deep in thought, completely unaware that the rest of the passengers had now boarded. Avery dashed over and almost dragged him to the gate and onto the plane causing the boarding staff to think something was wrong. He was thinking, *when will this nightmare end?* The boarding staff advised the flight crew to keep an eye on three passengers who were behaving strangely.

When they were sat in a line of three Avery continued, "was that them?" Andre nodded. "What will we do if they are there to meet the flight?" she continued

On the plane, his optimistic side suddenly emerged, he whispered to Avery and managed a smile, "they are just trying to frighten us and get into our heads. Remember what Thomas said they were so broken they could never follow us to the UK'. The watching flight attendants thought all looked normal and relaxed their checks. "We need to stop this, so when we land I will call my Unk and ask him for help, he's in the security business." Andre began to feel better at the thought of having his uncle intervene. Avery nodded and they both went quiet. Then he wavered and began thinking, *he's in the US and we need help now. Perhaps Jack can do something as he is sort of involved, although he doesn't know it yet. But it's not his kind of thing but knows Unk, at least I think he does, but I am not sure how well. Maybe Unk's got some men in Europe we can borrow.*

All sorts of thoughts continued to flash through his mind preventing him from speaking with his withdrawn companions. Avery was busy rehearsing what she was going to say to Jack while Rosa was becoming anxious about her job. All three were preoccupied with the ramifications of the nightmare following them home. In what seemed only a few minutes they were told to buckle up and get ready for landing.

This is like a bad dream, how could this have happened to us? thought Avery. *I can't see how we are going to get rid of them especially if they come to the UK and start threatening us.* Strong as she was, being consumed by such doubts would make her miserable unless she found help.

Part Two - Les Martins Ripostent!

The Martins Fight Back!

Chapter 16: London and St Albans, Monday

The trio walked from the plane thinking about what lay ahead. During the flight, between bouts of silence, Avery and Andre spoke about whether they should help Rosa given what they knew about her boyfriend. Brother Thomas had managed to make things more complicated with his suggestion that Thierry had most likely been assassinated or kidnapped by a rival gang. They made no decision except Avery would ask the French woman if she would like to stay in St Albans while she decided what to do about her job and London flat. When they reached the Arrivals Hall, Andre scanned the taxi sign holders and assorted waiting people, seeking out anyone who might resemble a gangster. After a few seconds, he saw nothing and turned back to tell the others but they were standing motionless staring at a man who was waving. Andre decided to approach him but his progress was somewhat slowed by his carry-on bag. The two women were rushing to catch up. The man did not move he continued to smile and wave as though greeting their return.

"Hi, you must be Andre," said the man, "I have a message for you from your friends in Marseille."

"Who are you, how do you know my name?" questioned a hostile Andre.

"Dude, I'm just a messenger, my girlfriend's plane is delayed so I am stuck here. This other French dude rocked up, said he had an emergency so could I pass you a message when you arrived. He sent me this picture so I would recognise you." He showed Andre a photo of the trio standing outside Le Beaux hotel. The women looked on in dismay as the conversation continued.

"What was the message?" asked Andre warily, keeping his eyes on the man's hands just in case he had a weapon, something his uncle taught him.

"Oh yes, he replied, "you should call this number on the phone he gave you when you get here," the man produced a contact on his phone. Whilst Andre struggled to create "Martin" on the flip phone, he continued, "good guy, giving you a phone for nothing eh?" Then Saville said, "okay dude, you need anything else?" he liked play-acting

"No thanks that's enough," answered Andre and Saville walked away smiling. The other two quizzed him, as to what had happened, "let's go over there and I will tell you," pointing at the coffee shop. After a brief explanation, Avery was despatched to get some drinks while Andre called the number. It was answered almost immediately, he walked around outside the cafe, phone in one hand gesticulating with the other. The two women looked on helplessly as the call became more and more animated. Andre changed from waving his hand to pointing a finger. He was getting redder every minute, they were clearly ignoring his protests. The call ended, Andre looked stunned, he shoved the phone back into his pocket, blew a deep breath and walked over to the others.

"They want 20 million euros for the trouble they say we caused and they expect it to be paid by the boss of our company who is apparently Jack l'Anglais. If we don't pay they will take us or our families prisoner until we do. If we call the police they will burn down the Le Beaux hotel."

"What, I can't believe it, that's nonsense, where do they think we can get that sort of money? Did you tell them it's not Jack's company?" said a disconsolate Avery as a dejected Rosa looked on. "Look we need to do something so let's go back to St Albans and decide there," she continued. "Did they say when they want the money?" Avery asked with an ironic snigger. "Anyway we can't stay here we need to go now," she repeated, "the car park people will be screaming at us, we told them we had our luggage thirty minutes ago!"

Andre stood shaking his head not hearing any of the questions, lost to the continuing ordeal. He suddenly came out of his daze to march with the others to their vehicles. Andre thought, *but who can help us, are we going to tell the police? Besides, how do we know this is real? Maybe it's just a scam, perhaps it's only a bad dream and I'm really asleep?"* He sniggered causing the others to look.

Saville hiding behind a pillar but watching, enjoyed every moment, every despairing look, every movement, he smiled at a job well done. He was one of Henri's smugglers who were offloading Iraqis they had escorted to London. He called Patrice to tell him the trio looked to be in a panic and he should carry on with the plan. He wished he could stay involved but had to finish the smuggling operation for Sylvain. Once completed he would go to Maidstone for a new group being "chauffeured to London" as he called it, by his friend Henri. It never ceased to amaze him how many people were willing to pay huge sums of money "to sample the delights of English life", when they could live in France. On this occasion there were two groups; one coming on trucks that he would meet after they made it to the UK and the other was going for what he called "a cross channel attempt'. He began thinking, *I just hope the guys have got some decent boats, last time I was in Calais starting a cross channel attempt the crappy boats sank. I could have been on one of them*, he laughed in mock indignation. *But you got to make a profit, don't you?* He was certain he would enjoy the next trip working with Henri even if he had to put up with Un gros for a bit longer.

The good news meant Patrice would proceed with his plan on Wednesday unless the English gave in and agreed to make the payment. He decided he would continually chase Andre on Tuesday to keep him on track which meant speaking with Jack. He organised a flight from Marseille that evening with two of his men, he would stay at the usual hotel in South Kensington and eat at Sylvain's restaurant.

The trio collected their cars, Andre agreed to follow Avery and Rosa to St Albans. When they reached the M25 Avery couldn't wait any longer and called Jack. After greetings, she hesitated then decided to say nothing about the threats and confirmed she would be in the office early in the morning. Fortunately, Jack did not ask any questions he was in a hurry. It was a short conversation. After the call, Avery wasn't sure if she was uneasy about involving Jack or just panicked. She justified her lack of action by pointing to Andre's suggestion they should be certain about the Martins before calling for help.

As their journey continued, she began to wonder, *who are Jack's friends and why did the French police know them? It must be to do with the French company or perhaps something else going on. Who is Robbie? Just the CEO of Stones with a restaurant on the side and a ton of money or is there more I don't know about? WHO is the Viscount I've never met. Then there's Andre's uncle, what's the story with him? I guess I have never really thought about them as anything other than colleagues.* Avery made a sickly smile just as Rosa looked up from her phone.

Avery took the opportunity to probe the French woman about her home and job. Rosa explained that she had taken two weeks holiday to look for Thierry so they were not expecting her back. She was concerned about the apartment they shared as the rent and bills were far too much on her own, although she had enough savings to survive for a couple of months. Avery stopped the questioning, discerning Rosalba was not in the mood to talk.

The trip continued around the outskirts of the city the French woman had found terrifying when she first arrived. Being with Thierry gave her strength, she had stopped worrying about a city filled with people from everywhere in the world, none of whom seemed friendly. Rosa recalled how Thomas had offered to do a background check on him, which she rejected telling him there was no need he was a good person. *Was that a mistake?* She thought now she was alone in a place that she would never have come to by herself, but she loved him. One good thing, she had two new friends who were helping her.

In the other car, Andre called Auntie Tess to thank her for feeding Mills and keeping her safe, a word he said with some feeling given their predicament. When they spoke he tried to be cheerful, blaming a cold for his lack of good humour. He advised her he would be back later that evening after he had dropped off some stuff at Avery's place. Next, he called his team and spent time finding out how things were and when he was next due to appear at a training course. Just talking about work made him feel better, more in control and he looked forward to meeting his customers, his staff and even the accountant. Despite the current difficulties Andre's business continued to grow and become more profitable. Best of all, it was able to do that without him being there, a sign of an investable and scalable business. He knew his Unk would be pleased with what he had achieved after several failures. But first, they had to get past the small matter of a 20 million euro ransom demand.

They arrived at Avery's townhouse and decamped to the kitchen to have something stronger than tea. They spoke for a while about what they should do and quickly agreed that Avery would meet up with Jack alone, talk about what had happened and get his advice. Andre then left, he needed to be alone to process what had happened. On the way home, he felt guilty for leaving Avery after spending only a few minutes to reassure and comfort her but he knew she was strong. Avery was happy for her boyfriend to leave early, partly to reduce the tension and partly to let her house guest settle in.

Chapter 17: France, Monday

With Patrice away chasing the English for money, it was time for other senior Martin members to develop a plan to regrow the drugs and smuggling parts of the business. The chief among them was Pascal Duval, principal member and enforcer, nephew of Matisse's younger sister. After short and rather uninspired schooling, ending at age sixteen, he joined the Martins where he quickly learned the business and bulking up physically to deal with their violent activities. Fifteen years later he reached the most senior level in the hierarchy to become one of the "Deux P's" reporting to Matisse. His major selling points lay in his unflinching loyalty to the family plus commanding absolute obedience from his men, both French and African alike. While the other P, Patrice was responsible for the wine division, he controlled illicit drugs and smuggling. He was very important to the success of the Martin family.

Only a few years ago, Matisse and Pascal took the monumental decision to stop supplying high-end illicit drugs like heroin to become mid-range retailers specialising in cocaine. There had been far too many accidents and the resultant police activity had been bad for business. They left the market segment to the drug cartels to fight over which they did, often, with deadly consequences. As for the bottom end of the market, supplying Rif mountains or Asian cannabis there was far too much competition to make any serious money.

For a while, the strategy worked well and the family grew rich. The business was protected because the drug was difficult to bring into the country and needed work before it could be sold. By 2018 they were producing profits of at least 10 million euros a month from a 6X cut and a 20X end-user mark-up. This made illicit drugs the Family's cash cow.

But like all good things, it came to an end when jealous market entrants wanted a bigger share causing an armed conflict in

Marseille in early September 2019 drawing in all suppliers including the Martins. In the fight, a fatally wounded Matisse was extracted and hidden away. For Pascal, the death of his mentor changed everything. Originally he had accepted the marriage of his boss to an outsider showing her total allegiance. However, he soon realised that his loyalty diminished as he watched Madame and her son, Thierry, persuade Matisse to change the direction of the business away from illicit drugs and smuggling towards their legal businesses. He believed it was his duty to restore order. He started his mission by ensuring Thierry could not rejoin his mother and continued garnering support for a coup in which he replaced Madame Martin. But such activity was on hold until he fixed his parts in the business.

His first task was to meet with his remaining senior troops to agree on what could be done to get back to the business model of spring 2019. Pascal was keenly aware that the army of dedicated street sellers, the so-called "entrepreneurs" were short of produce. With the family locked out of their warehouse unable to get the cash or drugs, they needed to replace both quickly.

The first to arrive was Chevy Merle, in charge of the illicit drugs group. He was close to Pascal as both men had worked under the tutelage of their leader Matisse Martin in the early years. Together they dealt with many setbacks including a failed attempt to improve the supply chain by shifting from Columbia to Venezuela.

The drugs chief was soon followed by Henri Segal who had travelled down from the North of France where he conducted a number of his smuggling activities. Chevy started by reporting on the stock he believed was secured in the cellar when the raid took place and the challenges they faced getting it out. This was no surprise to Pascal, he and his colleagues had been unable to remove anything from the cellar during their hasty departure on Friday night. Chevy made it clear the money and produce could only be extracted through the entrance at the far end of the warehouse using the access from the derelict property they owned. This would need people, time and transport to succeed. The gang's lookouts reported the police had already posted a lot more guards, far outnumbering the ones they had paid to help them escape. The surveillance also confirmed that the warehouse had not been properly searched although it was being looked at by various officers. There were rumours that a full search was delayed due to manpower shortages but it would happen later in the week. Henri suggested that the longer the police were around the more likely it was that they would find their way to the cellar. He had no suggestions as to how they could extract the drugs as they had never thought they'd be in this situation. They agreed it was impossible to remove anything from the cellar so they would have to continue their operations some other way.

"We need to acquire some new product to service our entrepreneurs and their customers, or they will go elsewhere," said Pascal trying to think what they should do. "How about we buy the merchandise using money from the cellar by taking it out in small amounts. Although the more we sneak in and out the more likely they will spot us and find the entrance" he continued with a sigh.

"Perhaps they will set up cameras to catch us if they think we will go back," suggested Chevy shrugging his shoulders and gesticulating. Henri nodded but had no suggestions.

"Mes amis, we need solutions not just problems," came the irritated response from Pascal. "What have you heard from our dealers, do they know what has happened? Are they going to leave us for the cartels? We need to know that too." Addressing Chevy he commanded, "go and speak with your team and come back when you have an answer as to what we must do to avoid losing business. If we don't get a solution we will be in a bad way with the other gangs. After what we did to them last month they will not be kind, they will eat us up." Chevy sloped off to rant at his team to find something that would fix things.

Pascal was joined by Henri's men Nichol and Ynon. After their recent smuggling success, they were buoyant and talked about another two projects that were ready to go. "The first is our sold-out boating trip from Calais to Dover where we have filled twenty-five seats at 10,000 euros each," Henri announced. "Now we just need to find the boats," he chuckled. "Lena and Saville will be coordinating it from the UK where they are working with Un gros. They are staying near his place and might do some work for Patrice while they wait for the migrants to be ready," he continued. "The other is a three-truck run for ten or more Africans. This business is not so profitable, we have to pay the drivers and sometimes the migrants jump the trucks themselves. If they get caught, they get sent back, but it's not a loss to us as they pay before they leave. We have tightened up our security to avoid that happening, so we should get at least 50,000 euro."

Pascal smiled at their enthusiasm, it was a profitable but risky business and they could easily lose everything if the French or British put more effort into tightening controls and ending it. *No, we need the drugs business back,* he thought. *We have a network and must keep it working. If Patrice can get the money from the English we will be back in business fast. But he will be the hero and I don't want that. But for now, anything will do to keep us in business. I will tell Patrice he needs to get the money or help find a way for us to get back into the warehouse. We don't have much time and Madam is doing nothing to help.* As Henri left, he waited for Chevy to return, he thought about the unpaid bribes to the officials, *those whores won't care if the drug gangs get us.*

Chapter 18: St Albans, Tuesday morning

Andre woke early with sore eyes and a sick feeling in the pit of his stomach, he slept badly, disturbed by the threats. He showered, fed Mills and left for the office without eating. It was one of those wet mornings in early autumn, fallen leaves lying on the ground, blocking drains and causing roadside puddles. As he drove the strain set off an anxiety attack, something he had been free of for many years. It was a struggle to keep going, he broke into a sweat, felt sick and moisture ran down his back under his shirt. After the short journey, he stayed in the car to compose himself to deal with the cold sweat as best he could. Fortunately, always being first in meant no audience.

At the door, he concentrated hard, got in switched off the alarm, ran to the toilet and locked himself in a cubicle. He vomited into the pan then sat for a few moments with hair and shirt soaking wet but the sickness was subsiding. He tried to dry his hair with his handkerchief before emerging to squat under the warm air dryer to finish the job. He swilled his face with cold water, it felt good. He hurried to his office and closed the door to hide behind a non-existent call.

Andre's concentration on recovery was suddenly disturbed by his office manager bursting in to tell him about the good things that were happening to the company. He feigned sickness to make him leave, "sorry, Bruno, I am not feeling too good," holding his stomach and wincing. Bruno nodded, grimaced in support and left. Andre returned to his worries believing that the threat was real and the only way to handle it was to ask the police for protection. But before he did that, he would wait for the outcome of Avery's meeting with Jack, to apprise him and seek advice on how to tackle what was becoming a dire situation. He planned to keep his diary free for at least the morning so kept up the pretence of sickness. This was difficult for Andre, being an action man he was not good at queueing or waiting, but this was an unusual situation. Being back in the office surrounded by his staff did make him feel better, even inviting Bruno back into his office to talk about recent events and the upcoming Programme 34.

Avery left a note and key for the sleeping Rosa with a suggestion she relax make herself comfortable and enjoy St Albans. She thought, *don't worry about Thierry or our situation until we have made sure the threat is real.* Then she drove to the office again rehearsing what she was going to tell Jack. She felt tired, only managed an hour's sleep after her 4 am "wake up and worry" planning session for the upcoming meeting.

Avery planned to tell the story in a business-like way, leaving out everything that was not essential. She would explain that a Marseille gang were trying to extort money from them because they had accidentally been caught up in a raid. The thugs threatened that if they didn't pay they would kidnap their families and hold them for ransom. The advice from French police was that the gangsters would not follow them to the UK, so not to worry. They were only involving Jack because the criminals thought he was their boss and had lots of money to help pay, so if anything untoward happened they would involve him. She would then ask what he thought they should do, particularly given he knew the US BloedStone security company, Robbie and so on. It was still a bit sketchy, but it would let Jack make the running.

Even though Jack doesn't know much about this sort of thing he knows men who do, Avery thought, while parking. She noticed Jack's favourite space, was empty. *It's 8.30 Jack is usually at his desk by 8, where is he today of all days?* she thought. His car arrived, she blew a breath in relief, but it was being parked in a different place. Avery got out of her car ready to talk but was met by a man with a big BMW badge on his coat.

"I am returning Mr Ritchie's car, we had to keep it overnight as we ran late with his servicing, he told us to leave it here and have a Ms King sign for it. Can you tell me where her office is? I need to leave her the keys and the bill."

"That's me, I mean I am Avery King," she proceeded to answer various questions until he was satisfied that she was Ms King. He handed over the keys and paperwork then left.

Avery decided that Jack must have been dropped off by his wife and that he would be sitting in his office waiting for her. She returned to her rehearsed speech, being interrupted by the greetings of the early starters. She put laptop plus phone on her desk, took a deep breath and walked quickly to Jack's office, only to find it empty. *Unbelievable,* she thought and was about to ask one of her staff where he was when the phone rang in her office. Rushing back, she was not fast enough to get there before it rang off, it was Jack. *Why is this happening to me today,* she thought whilst calling him back. The phone rang for what seemed a very long time before he picked up. They exchanged greetings, Jack explained that with his car in the garage he decided to go to meet a client at the IOD in London. Avery could not contain her disappointment, blurting out she needed to speak to him about their recent trip.

He invited her to explain. She told him, "We accidentally got involved with a gang whilst looking for Rosa's missing boyfriend. These people sell drugs, fake Bordeaux wine and worst of all in my opinion, traffick people like you see on the news. Jack responded to her story at the right moments with verbal sounds. "Then we got caught up in a police raid which the gang blamed us for and the losses they incurred. We even got held hostage, it was scary, frightening and horrible," she became emotional while speaking quickly.

She kept going, "Just to let you know, after the raid the men threatened us and you, Jack, they thought we were a rival gang or something. We spent time with the French police as Thomas, I mean Rosa's brother, is one. When we mentioned you he said they knew of you and your friends." She was getting faster and faster, "I'm guessing that's because of the hotel in Bandol. I'm so sorry that we got you into this. We don't know what to do, we need help, we are….", Avery was now in top gear and rushing out an explanation before the expected irate response.

Jack cut in, "Are you all okay? That's the main thing." No yelling just a sympathetic response.

I must have spoken too quickly he doesn't fully understand what I am trying to tell him or how serious it is, she thought, before answering his question. "Yes, we're all fine but very worried about the gang catching up with us and demanding a ransom or something," Then she started to tell her story again, but this time more like she planned.

He cut her off again, "glad to hear no one got hurt. Umm, it sounds like you had an interesting time," he continued. He was pondering whether he needed to ask questions given Yasmeen had already been forthcoming about the unusual events. Thinking ahead he asked, "by chance do you know if our vineyard is implicated in any of the wine scams? We have a large investment in a St Emilion Chateau as you know."

"No idea, sorry, I don't think the French police know either," she responded surprised at the question. "From what Rosa's brother said they were mainly interested in the drugs and people smuggling stuff rather than the wine. In fact, I don't think Thomas knows how big the wine fraud is or even whose involved as it appears to be a new venture." *This is not going the way I planned,* she thought. *Jack is not showing any interest in the threats. Why is that? Or is it me, does he understand what is happening? What does he know already?*

To calm her he produced another umm followed by, "No worries, we, I, have a contact in the French police down in Marseille and we already have some information on what is going on there. I will give him another call to tell him what you have just told me, we can get this sorted."

Of course he could, Stones had powerful allies and friends in many countries including France. The last time a French drugs cartel targeted the company was in 2017. Nicky and Robbie dealt with the threat by assisting the French police to organise a takedown similar to the one that brought disaster to the Martins. The French Ministry of Interior were very grateful to BloedStone and agreed to provide secrecy to avoid any blowback.

Jack continued, "I will be in the office tomorrow at the usual time so let's get together first thing, you can give me more details. Take it easy tonight and don't worry, I am sure we can sort things out, I have to go."

He pocketed his phone and returned to thinking about the situation. Stones had invested millions of euros in French wine and planned a lot more. Jack had to avoid saying anything to his fellow shareholders until he had the full facts, he knew he would be grilled by them. *They don't shoot the messenger they just beat them up if they can't answer the questions, he thought.* He needed a list of infiltrated vineyards if such a thing existed. He grimaced as he imaged the look on Robbie's face when he realised that someone had dared to mess with his precious wine. *Come to think of it, such an issue might even get the Deputy Chairman out of the Napa Valley vineyards and on a plane back to Europe*, he thought. Given his recent research into wine investment, Jack knew things could only get worse if a rumour were allowed to spread.

The Stones associate now represented the first agency to understand the issue but not its scale. If only a few vineyards were affected then it would be a local difficulty, but if it involved large parts of Bordeaux it could represent an extinction event for investable French wines. Jack had to deal with the situation very carefully and went off to make his phone call and meet his client.

Avery walked to Andre's office and immediately blurted out, "Shit, I made a right hash of that, I was babbling like a child." She sat down, "He didn't understand what I was saying or he would at least have shown more concern even be a bit frightened like us. He was much more interested in hearing about the wine scam than about the gang chasing us. Perhaps he knows more than he is telling us, after all, he has friends in the French police so maybe he has spoken to them about the gang and that's why he is only worried about the fake wine," she concluded. "It will be much worse tomorrow when I tell him properly. I didn't even mention the money'. She was downcast knowing that she didn't get control of the call, her "4 am wake up and worry plan" had failed and they had to wait another day for advice.

Andre replied, "Look I was thinking about this on my way in, we still don't know if this thing is real, no one has called me. Why don't we meet up at your place tonight and go through things before you meet Jack tomorrow? Avery agreed given it was the only way forward for the day.

The two went back to work, feeling better and more normal after their latest decision. Andre recovered from his anxiety attack was in full working order preparing his next presentation, which most definitely would not involve investing in wine. Avery forced herself to get into the numbers of the prospective client Jack had gone to visit.

That evening after they had collected more of Rosa's possessions for her St Albans sleepover, they returned to Avery's morning meeting with Jack.

"I have not had a call all day, nothing at all has happened, has it? Maybe it's just a trick by those guys who didn't get arrested. Have you thought about that? So, we need to be careful we don't get everyone fired up for nothing and look like idiots. Let's agree that if they contact us, we speak with Jack, if not, we drop it. What do you think? Although I have to say I'm also not sure what Jack can do, that the police can't." Avery looked uncertain but seemed willing to follow his suggestion.

On the way home Andre wondered whether he was just avoiding the issue and he should confront it. He decided the Martins were setting the agenda and that had to change, starting the next day.

Chapter 19: South Kensington, London, late Monday night and Tuesday

Patrice plus his men landed late Monday evening then travelled to South Kensington to the place known locally as "Frog Alley" where many of the 300,000+ French people live in London. A place the criminals could hide without raising any suspicions. He was staying at a hotel close to the bar-restaurant club owned by the UK based French gangster, Sylvain, a man with no known surname and a Martin associate for many years. He used the eatery as a useful front to his criminal activities of selling illicit drugs together with people smuggling and trafficking. Patrice's men were rather less well catered for in a cheap hotel close by, happy to be away from their boss as their hotel had the benefit of a late-night bar, often frequented by off-duty prostitutes from the nearby brothel.

Once unpacked, Patrice called Frederic who was slow to answer, he was asleep. The conversation was short with Frederic reluctantly telling Patrice that Jack had his office in St. Albans, Hertfordshire rather than London or the Isle of Man. The news met with approval from Patrice who ended the call and switched out the light feeling good. Frederic was unsettled by the call, he knew problems were coming his way. He did not sleep well.

In the morning Patrice spent half an hour using Google maps to view the Stones office building in St Albans, together with its approach roads. He decided that a transit van and one other car would be sufficient to screw up their car park enough to get their attention, without breaking any laws. The senior Martin member arrived for breakfast, in Sylvain's private dining area at 9 am. It would be a simple affair involving little food but lots of black coffee. The main subject of conversation for Patrice would be getting help to deal with the Englishman, for Sylvain, it was always money, food or women. But there was a lot of boasting about nothing much before they arrived at the serious stuff.

Sylvain had been enriched by his partnership with the Martin family, they had supplied him with both drugs and people to sell in West London. However, Patrice was in no doubt that this man would show no gratitude for his good fortune, indeed he would always demand more. Fortunately, while Matisse Martin ruled, he did exactly as instructed. With the Martin leader "missing" and Pascal manoeuvring, things were different, Patrice would have to find a way to befriend and control the Kensington gang leader.

"Do you know when my good friend Matisse will be calling me again?" asked Sylvain. "I miss our talks he was always good for business," he continued. "The last time we spoke he told me of a delightful scam to import grenache and merlot grapes along with wine from North Africa, where it is dirt cheap, to sell as Bordeaux or Rhone. Such wine would sell well here in London I told him many English, god bless them, will drink anything if it's in a good bottle and cheap. He even talked about some sort of deal with those poncy Bordeaux chateaux bottling it under their name as a way to make us all rich, I love that don't you?" As he spoke Patrice was working on believable answers to his questions. "But he was worried," continued Sylvain. "Wars between the suppliers were bringing too much attention to our business. He said we needed a period of quiet to get on with making money, now you're here...." Sylvain stopped and waited for a reply.

"The boss is away in Algeria working on the project you just mentioned. It seems that the Africans are thieves and want us to pay more for their wine than they can sell it for themselves," he responded making eye contact with Sylvain to ensure he believed the story.

"Bastards, who do they think they are trying to rob us?" asked Sylvain. Followed by him ranting about smuggled Africans complaining about how much he charged them. "You would think they would be grateful to me for digging them out of those shitholes they live in. But now they want to talk to me about value for money, safety and shit like that. I had to sacrifice a couple of them, you know what I mean, to keep the rest in order. What about the lovely Astrid, is she still as gorgeous as ever?" he said while making lewd faces at one of his female waitresses.

Patrice thought, *judging by his responses I must have lied well, Sylvain does not suspect anything is wrong with the family.* "Yes, she's fine, sort of in charge while the boss is away," he told the gangster. Although he knew that Madame Martin would hate having that "sleaze" even think of her, let alone say her name. "She sends her best regards to you hoping she can come across to have dinner with you soon, especially with Matisse being away so much," he said mischievously knowing that Sylvain would be having more lewd thoughts. It would keep the man's brain focused on female parts rather than where Matisse was. "Perhaps it is time for me to tell you why I am here," announced Patrice which secured the immediate attention of Un gros.

"I thought you had come to see me cus you love me," he replied leering at Patrice, who managed a false laugh rather than gagging. "I'm all ears," he laughed flapping them with both hands. "I think that is what the English say at this point," he was in a good mood and expecting to hear about the next project to make him money.

Patrice decided that he would tell him the simple story and offer inducements for help if necessary. In this fiction, framed as a debt collection exercise, which Sylvain had great experience of when renting out his female staff to randy punters, the Martins were owed a great deal of money by an Englishman. The debtor owned a hotel plus several other businesses in the Cote d'Azur but ran his empire from an office in a city north of London The man, called Jack, was being difficult about paying so they needed to change his mind.

"We are going to see him tomorrow if he does not agree to pay us today," he told Sylvain. Patrice had already decided he would wait for Andre to call him rather than waste time chasing. He reckoned that if the trio were sufficiently worried they would speak to Jack, then they would make contact to head off further trouble. Even try and arrange a meeting, make a silly offer or something to get them off the hook. If there was no call then clearly they were not spooked enough and more pressure would be needed. The squeeze would come in the form of a visit to the company offices early on Wednesday morning. They would cause enough trouble to get Jack to speak with him or realise there would be a lot more pain to come if he didn't.

"Can you lend me a transit van?" he asked Sylvain knowing the gangster was happy to be involved so he could claim some of the cash

Sylvain agreed to provide a modified vehicle, one that had extra seats to accommodate "people cargo", plus a driver to make sure they completed the trip safely. Patrice would be able to get his two men in the back with plenty of room left over, just in case, they picked up some Stones associates to bring back to play with. Sylvain lost some of his exuberance, disappointed he hadn't been offered any kind of "finders fee'. He decided he would work on Patrice later once he knew how much money they recovered from the English. After finishing breakfast, which involved reminiscing about previous projects they had worked on together and ranting about Brexit, it was almost time for an early lunch. But before that, he called one of his men to keep checking that Jack would be there in the morning. *Even better if the other three were there too,* he thought.

Whatever opinions Patrice might have about Sylvain as a person he left them at the restaurant door. For his personal guests, the food and wine served by Un gros are legendary across London and the East of England. The gangster insisted that his chef and assistant chefs were able to produce dishes that at least matched those of his favourite restaurant Le Bouchon Provencal, Marseille Vieux Port. Paying guests did not fare quite so well, except for the French wines he selected personally for their quality. He felt a responsibility for educating the English on what wines to drink.

Over a wonderful lunch, they talked about the past with the Martin family then forward to Yves" team in Marseille before the disasters. Patrice continued with the success of the fake wine and bottling frauds. He gave only the official version of where the business was, concealing the secret project he was working on with Frederic. Sylvain suggested several times he was eminently qualified to help resurrect the Marseille production business once they had the money from the English. He sensed there may be some fine French wines to be had and some high margin fake wines to sell to other restaurants. To subdue Sylvain's interest Patrice suggested that it was merely a trial at some Bordeaux chateaux and Rhone domains. Patrice was careful not to mention any of the vineyards by name despite the many prods from Sylvain.

Eventually, they returned to what was going to happen in St Albans. A place Sylvain confessed he had only heard of because one of his girls used to meet a punter outside the Abbey. She reckoned he was religious and prayed before enjoying her company. He paid her well but last year was arrested for being a paedophile. This had surprised everyone given that she was at least forty with a plus-size frame!

"Would you like to try her?" asked Sylvain. "She's a real lady?" Patrice shook his head violently, he was more a size 8 to 10 man, standing only 1.78 metres tall at best. After a couple more hours arguing about the best way to attack the English, the wine was beginning to win out. A short break was agreed upon with expresso coffee on the restart. Finally, it was settled, the chauffeur would pick him up first at around 6 am, then his men. Bendy would drive them out of Kensington through London and up the M1, rather than go all around the M25. Patrice didn't care about the route he wanted to be there waiting at 7.30 am ready to pounce. Lena would travel in her own vehicle and meet them there.

They shook hands and Patrice went to speak with his men and sleep off the alcohol. "I think I'm going to enjoy this bit of action," he smiled, but then he was drunk!

Chapter 20: BloedStone Office St Albans, Wednesday morning

Avery planned to pick up her coffee and be in the office well before 7.30 am. She had rehearsed her story many times and was determined that Jack would fully understand the gravity of the situation. When she arrived, Jack's car was parked in its usual place. He was also early and sitting in his office with his favoured skinny cappuccino watching Bloomberg on SKY. Avery joined him thinking he looked strangely relaxed. He started by declaring the wonders of the FTSE 100, which had grown wings flying ever upwards. "But is it Icarus, will it crash and burn?" he asked her looking up, smiling. He gestured for her to sit on the matching leather couch opposite. Jack preferred to do deals in the Board Room, he kept his office as a place for thinking, planning and on occasion relaxing.

"Morning Miss, how art thou today," he said showing no hint of concern.

"I'm okay but I need to tell you everything so you know what's what. I don't think I explained myself properly yesterday," Avery looked uncomfortable. She was bursting to regurgitate the French story once again, this time slowly like she was explaining her analysis of a company's accounts.

"Okay go ahead.

Avery spent thirty minutes telling Jack about what had happened from the time they left for France until they returned to Heathrow. She finished with the kicker, the money.

"Jack, they want 20 million euro from us, I don't know what to do."

"Wow that's a lot, but I guess you make loads of dosh selling drugs, people AND faking fine wine."

"Jack this is serious, they threatened us and said they would blow up your, sorry our hotel if we went to the police." Avery finally broke down, telling the story reminded her of the hopelessness they felt. "What are we going to do?" This time she had done better and explained the predicament.

Jack skirted around the coffee table, sat next to her to try and comfort her. "These people, do you know how to contact them, other than the phone they gave you?" he asked quietly. "What about Madame Martin do you have her number?" Avery was distracted as she talked about the wonderful Martin villa and how they found it.

She came back to the question, "sorry, yes Rosa, you know the Winewoman as Andre calls her, she is staying with me at the moment, she has Madame Martin's number and address. I told Rosa about you so we can get all that information from her," she continued rapidly. "I think Andre is going to come over when he gets in, he is struggling a bit with how to fix things and whether he should involve his uncle who is a security man or something in the US. He thinks maybe he could come over and help us, of course, you know him don't you?"

Jack was thinking about an answer when they heard someone shouting outside, it sounded like it was coming from the car park. They tried to ignore it and made faces at each other, but it got too loud. They stood up and went quickly to the window where they could see two men arguing with Andre. There was a transit partly blocking the car park entrance stopping Andre from getting to his space. Sleep deficient Andre was getting angry and looked like he might attack the two outsized men who were arguing with him. There were two others in the van, one a woman. The men behaved strangely they were not attacking him but goading, stepping back and laughing. It looked like they wanted to cause a rumpus. One of the men looked up to see Avery and Jack at the window, he gestured to Patrice who came out of the car smiling. He walked into the open stood looking up and waved at the two in the office.

Avery turned to Jack and shouted, he did not hear, he was staring cat-like at Patrice and his men taking in what they looked like and the way they moved to know them in future. Avery called again to Jack, but he ignored her looked directly at the Frenchman it was difficult to lock eyes, but for a moment the Frenchman sensed he was being assessed. Jack took the phone from his breast pocket and started to take photos of the three men including a full frontal of Patrice. The leader responded by using his hand in a neck slash motion before pushing Andre onto the bonnet of his car and waving the other men back into the van.

Avery gave up screaming at Jack and ran out of the office on an impossible mission to interrupt the altercation and save Andre. By the time she had reached the car park, the Frenchmen had driven around Andre and left. Patrice recognised Jack was different from the others and would need a different kind of encouragement.

On the drive back to London Patrice received a text from Pascal telling him to work fast, they had little product so the entrepreneurs were getting difficult to control. He contemplated what to do next, *no doubt Un gros would have some suggestions*, he thought. Failure would mean working for Sylvain or his worst nightmare as an African slaver or for a drugs cartel – he shook his head to clear the terrifying images. He called Pena, to make sure she followed or tagged Jack's BMW so they could find his address. After the initial failed attack, the criminals were going to get ready to pressurise their target into submission.

"Why didn't you do something, Andre could have been killed?" an angry Avery shouted at Jack on returning to his office. He was deep in thought looking out of the window, then at the photos, enlarging them so he could see the faces better. He snapped out of the trance-like state.

"I know you have questions about what I just did and why I seem calm, but this is not the first time I, we, have been threatened by a bunch of thugs. It is something we had to deal with many times in the old days." She didn't understand what he meant about "old days" but the message was clear. "Perhaps you should take Andre home he's probably in no shape to work today? You should also think about whether your French troubles have caused some form of mental stress like PTSD, affecting your disposition, or your sleep because you're stuck in danger mode." He watched affectionately as she plonked herself back on the couch.

Avery was puzzled by the suggestion, but would certainly check it out as soon as she had a chance. For now, she was more worried about Andre who she had left sitting in his car. She was not sure how to respond other than to agree with the suggestion that they go home. "Will you call me please, we should talk about what is going to happen next," she said looking warily at her boss.

"Of course, I will," replied an unruffled Jack. "Perhaps you could do me a favour when you get home, text or e-mail me the names and numbers you have for these people. How about we meet at Costa at lunchtime to talk. That gives you a few hours to relax. Is that okay?" she nodded and said nothing.

Avery texted Andre to stay in the car park and left the office in a hurry. On the way out she met Bruno who confirmed no one in Andre's company seemed to have heard the fracas or if they did paid no attention. He asked for details so he could do something but accepted an explanation involving some errant builders. She explained that Andre was sick and she was taking him home. The manager took this as a reoccurrence of the day before and wished Andre well. Avery left pleased she had escaped without answering any questions.

For the next hour, Jack went into investigator mode writing down the information he had on the crime family noting what more he needed before reporting to his Stones colleagues. He started thinking about the way to deal with the twin threat of violence in the UK and damage to their French investments. *The guys have already fixed one cartel so what's one more, right,* he thought. For the vineyard investigations, they would get Frederic on board through his boss Robbie. Thinking back to the property they had acquired after the 2017 police raid, he already began to wonder whether the villa Avery talked about might be a great addition to their portfolio. *Perhaps there is another profit to be had here if we play our cards right,* he laughed.

The first step, he thought, *call the guv, just in case.* This involved sending an e-mail to Sir Robbie (using a super-secure and secret, purportedly un-hackable address), telling him they had some issues with a French crime family potentially targeting him, their vineyard, their hotel and demanding a ransom. Explaining more information would be coming after lunch and would be shared. *Better leave out the demand for money or he might start jumping about and ordering gunboats,* thought Jack chuckling to himself. *Hopefully, Avery will remember to send me the information so I can look up the Marseille gang. I trust Robbie's restaurant will be serving lunch so he won't read his e-mails or call me until they are finished, which will give me a bit of time. Although he may go mad if he thinks that those French bastards have been messing about with our most beautiful Chateau. I wouldn't mind moving there if we could put a bit of an extension on it and….*

He returned to thinking about the recent incident, *I wonder why that French guy was assaulting Andre in broad daylight? He must be desperate or very confident, I wonder which?* Jack put away his laptop and went to tell the staff that Avery had to go home as her boyfriend was mistakenly attacked in the car park. They were surprised and very supportive.

Sir Robson Manley-James was in his car rather than his restaurant on his way to lunch with an American client and his daughter. The client wanted him to invest in art, in exchange for donations to his daughter's charity. Robbie was intellectually interested in paintings but sceptical about the way arty people spoke. "Almost as if they were fine wines," he would say. He liked some renditions by Franz Kline but secretly preferred representations such as a big old fashioned Constable. "Not sure about investing in art, who knows what will make money," he had told Jack on several occasions. He was, however, willing to give it a try if he found an advisor who inspired confidence. On the way, Robbie was stopped by roadwork traffic lights and after a quick look round to avoid being caught by police for a second time, he checked the list of e-mails on his phone. It was most unusual to get one from Jack who usually called or texted, even more so through the secure mailbox, he pulled over on the other side of the lights to read it.

"Ummm that's interesting," was his response to an empty car. He began thinking, *I wonder how much ransom those bad boys want. I bet it's something stupid like that other bunch of nancies. Whatever it is, no doubt they'll be willing to settle for 10% when I have spoken to them. Once we have sorted them, we'll take it back along with the rest of their shit. That said, we don't negotiate with terrorists or with French,"* he laughed. *I wonder what this is all about, I bet it's because we have just finished the place in Bandol and they want a share of the profits.* "No chance of that mes amis," he said. He looked at his watch he did not want to be late for lunch even though he would not be able to indulge in a good Rhone.

Robbie would call Jack later as the e-mail didn't suggest imminent danger and he knew "Miss always early Elizabeth", would be waiting.

Chapter 21: St Albans, Wednesday lunchtime

It was a warm afternoon and inside the coffee shop, the heating was still on high after the recent cold snap. It was stuffy but the smell of coffee made the place tolerable. Jack was slumped in a worn chair starring at his coffee cup sitting on its odd-shaped saucer. He always arrived early, checked the room for entrance, exit and potential threats, training that followed him from a previous life. His wife hated his routine but would include something similar in one of her novels with a former special forces hero. He relaxed, all his systems went to inactive like almost everyone in the place. He was waiting for Double-A as he had taken to calling them, out of earshot of course.

The peace was disturbed by a young woman dressed in a gothic-like uniform sporting rings and studs from all parts of her face. She was shouting at her phone, Jack was shocked awake and scowled like his fellow customers irritated by such an intrusion. She was carrying a shoebox-sized package covered in newspaper, "sorry I can't hear you, I said dad has booked in for an autopsy tomorrow morning. What? No sorry, I mean that's a test on his dodgy liver or is it kidney?" The audience smirked and quickly lost interest, going back to their own lives, no one listened. Jack studied the strange creature, fixing his gaze on the strange red and blue snake curled around her neck. She headed in his general direction still shouting. He vaguely wondered how such people could manage their lives to earn a living. She stopped in front of him, took the seat directly opposite and leaned forward. Steel-blue eyes staring at him, she pushed the package across the table towards him. Jack looked up in surprise and was about to tell her she had the wrong person.

"Hello Jack," she said in perfect English, this was no longer that creature this was something different. "You need to look in this box when your friends get here, do you understand? They are just parking across the road. You met my friends this morning, they are very unhappy with you and your colleagues. Jack glanced down at the box still trying to speak but held by those eyes. "We will be in touch shortly to make sure you do what we want," she continued. "Don't forget we want the twenty million you owe us or there will be trouble, DO YOU understand?"

"But what? Who are you? What is this?" Jack asked, but all wasted questions.

She stood up pulled out her phone became the creature again, walked away continuing to shout about what was wrong with her dad. "Yes, he always has a massage on a Thursday. Yes, down there." No one paid any attention they would not remember much about her except she was noisy with tattoos and piercings.

Jack stared at the package knowing that the last sixty seconds must be bad news. How did they know he was there? *Who are they and why the charade?* he thought.

"Hello Jack," he flinched and looked up to see Avery. "Are you okay you look worried?" suddenly thinking, *Jack, must be realising the mess they were in.*

"No just deep in thought," he replied jumping up to welcome Double A. "Did you see that girl leave, the one with the tattoo?" he asked. Both arrivals shook their heads and looked puzzled at the question.

"What's in the package?" asked Andre. "It looks like a shoebox or something wrapped in newspaper."

"Some strange women just dropped it off to me for my neighbour but I think she has the wrong person," he lied. "I will drop it off on the way home," he continued moving the package to the floor to avoid disrupting the meeting. "So, what do you have for me?" he asked.

Andre began with replaying a short form of the story, starting with "lovely Astrid Martin" which got him a nudge and a scowl from Avery for misplaced humour. He continued through the raid, raised questions about how they were followed and then harassed. He finished on the 20 million euros and the car park confrontation. "So we need a game plan to deal with this, I was wondering whether I should be calling my Unk to ask him for advice and perhaps some help from his local guys." He went on, "I now realise those bastards in the car park were simply playing with me."

"Just count yourself lucky they did not hurt you," interjected Avery. "What are we going to do Jack? Do you think we should get his uncle involved even though he is in the US?"

Andre jumped in, "he runs the US BloedStone which does security not investments like the UK company you and Robbie have. He sends people to Iraq and other places to work with the army. I think they call them contractors or something. Perhaps he could call the gangsters to frighten them into leaving us alone," Andre began to believe that was a viable option.

Jack had considered it but wondered whether Robbie had enough resources in Europe. "Whoa, let's think about what we want to achieve. We can't just bring in some grunts to bust up places in the UK or France. Also if we go off half-cocked at professional criminals some of us will get hurt." The other two were not quite sure what grunts were but agreed they needed a plan first. "I know the guys in US BloedStone very well, your uncle is also Chairman of the UK business. True the US company is in a very different to ours and very secret squirrel, but we have worked together on various investment and security projects in the past." He changed the subject, "do you have the information I asked for so I can get working?"

The couple spent the next hour eating sandwiches, drinking coffee and giving Jack all the information they had. They were working on a plan which would make Double-A feel good – assembling security personnel from all over the world to control the Martin's activities. The couple were happy with what they thought had been agreed and went off smiling.

Jack's real plan involved Robbie working alongside the French Army and Gendarmerie to destroy the gang. He thought it best to steer clear of the US, if possible, to avoid having "military-style" contractors operating in Europe outside the control of MI5. To start, Jack would phone Astrid Martin to ask her to call off the guys in the car park while Stones worked on a deal and secretly a method to eliminate the group.

As he got up to leave, his foot caught on the package stuffed under his seat. He sat down again tore off the newspaper to reveal a shoebox. It was leaking some sort of red liquid which made him hesitate before wiping the table with the newspaper. He broke the sellotape at one end, flipped off the lid, leaning back slightly, half expecting something to happen, nothing did.

"Shit" he exclaimed at the contents. Adrenaline pumped into his bloodstream as his fight or flight, response kicked in. For a few seconds, it was difficult to grasp what he was looking at. It was his wife's latest thriller covered in blood stuffed inside a leaking plastic freezer bag.

He worriedly called Cass, as usual, there was no answer the call went to message. He tried again, she picked up. For a moment he could not speak she sounded so normal, there was silence.

"You alright Jack, you sound a bit odd?" she said. "Where are you?" the writer began to worry her husband was usually so business-like, totally in control of his emotions.

Jack recovered himself and tried to sound normal, "I'm fine just shocked that I managed to get through so easily, it usually takes me three calls, he forced a laugh. "Are you having a productive day?" he continued. The writer wasn't convinced, she waited for him to tell her why he had really called, it came, "sorry to interrupt your day but a few issues came up at work, I need to make some calls to the US so could be late home." Before she could ask why he didn't make them from his palatial home study he continued, "I have to get with Robbie, he needs to be on the calls as well."

It sounds like something bad has happened, she thought having lived with him for so long. She decided against pursuing it, preferring instead to assume it was a business issue. He or Robbie would tell her what was happening if it involved their safety and then she knew they would call in the cavalry. "Be careful, see you later," she responded. "Love you."

"Don't worry, lots of love," then he was gone and she was left holding her phone and feeling uneasy. The doorbell rang.

Jack rewrapped the box and left the coffee shop for the car park. Out of the corner of his eye, he noticed someone waving. It was the snake creature and she was smiling at him. He weighed up the possibility of running her down. She made the slit throat gesture so he set off after her but was stopped by a van crossing in front of him. He hesitated for a moment, but when he looked up she was gone. Jack was now shouting and cursing, threatening terrible retribution, in the middle of the main city street. He stopped, realising he was doing just what they wanted, they were getting inside his head. He felt stupid, went to his car to call Robbie. He kept getting the message centre, his boss was busy learning about art.

For Jack, the situation had changed, he would now do whatever was necessary to protect his family. He left Robbie a message then went home explaining the meeting was cancelled because his boss was busy with a client. That night he tried to act normally but was too attentive making Cass nervous.

Chapter 22: St Albans, Thursday

It was mid-morning, Jack was hoping he could get Robbie on the phone then have him come over to the office. "Hello Robbie, it's Jack."

"Hello, Jacky, how the devil are you?" "I am guessing you are calling me about those nasty French gangsters you met up with," ventured Robbie who was relaxing with a coffee and current best friend, Antony, at his restaurant in St Albans. "I hope they did not mess about with our new hotel or I will be very upset with them."

"Bit pissed off really and yes we need to deal with the French thugs, they turned up at my offices and caused a ruckus. Do you have some time now?"

"I do, fire away," smiling across at his companion. The pretty man indicated he wanted another coffee so set off for the bar leaving a trailing hand to make its way along Robbie's leg.

Jack proceeded to relate the whole, now much longer, story of the Bandol trip and the events that followed. He lavished the story with as much detail as he could while leaving out the snake creature and the shoebox but finished on the 20 million euros.

"Wow that's a good story, Jackson," he always changed to the full name when he sensed trouble. "I am amazed you didn't just go and sort them out yourself, are you getting too old or were there too many witnesses?" he laughed. But his demeanour changed quickly as his military police training took over. He waved away a returning Antony, "seriously, Jack there are several things we need to know and quickly. Let's start with, have these people been messing about with our chateau or hotel? Secondly, are any of our wine investments affected? Thirdly, are any of our people involved? Fourthly, which other chateaux have been compromised and who knows about them, and fifthly, how do we get in touch with these shits and disabuse them of their chances of shaking us down because they got caught by the local police?"

He continued, "I can't imagine any circumstances in which we would pay protection money. They should be paying us they're so useless." Robbie was getting worked up, Antony took this as a sign to find something else to do. "For Christ's sake Jack we should ignore them they will go away. I will call the Stones guys in France and tell them to get the gang arrested by the local police. Jack reminded him they were also in the UK but agreed the best way forward must be to totally destroy their remaining people and operations in France. "Jack, do you really want me to have a squad of Stones guys go down there to shoot them up like they were in Iraq? Are you insane? They may be criminals, but we can't slaughter them in their own country."

Jack told him about the recent gang wars in Marseille suggesting they could pretend it had started up again. "Stop, this conversation is getting ludicrous we need to be sensible. I will get some UK Stones people to guard you and deal with the French guys if they come around again. Or we can just tell the police as normal people do."

"Robbie, I hear what you are saying, but if you won't help me then I will have to give them money to go away." A remark he knew would fire up his boss even more.

"Jack, what's wrong with you? Why are you behaving like this? Let's just say for a moment you paid them to go away, do you think they won't come back. Anyway how much would you give them, they want 20 million, even you don't have that sort of money to give away, do you? You would be financially wrecked, that is, if you survived Cass and the girls tearing you apart."

Jack continued to argue either they "smash" the crime family in France or negotiate a financial settlement. "Anyway Jack, you can't sell your shares in UK Stones for a least another twelve months. Don't even think about selling your shares in the US company to give the money to a bunch of cartel guys in France. If the US customs people found out they would put you in jail for at least a thousand years. Forget it, let me handle it my way. I will let our police friends know what we need and get some of our people to protect you and our stuff. Calm down, this is not like you."

"What else can I do Robbie?" he used his ace, "they threatened my family. They gave me one of Cass's books in a box dripping with blood, I think we understand the message."

"Shit Jack, why the hell didn't you say something earlier," he replied slowly, surprised at the revelation. "That makes a big difference, it tells me we are up against some dangerous and unpredictable people prepared to do anything to get their own way. We must talk about this, I will ask Miss Elizabeth to come and get you and then over an early dinner, we can decide the best way forward. Does Cassandra know anything about this?"

"Okay I am at the office and no, Cass knows nothing although I think she suspects something is wrong. I will let her know I am having dinner with you although I think she may be out until later this evening," replied Jack.

Robbie continued, "while you wait for Miss Elizabeth why don't you send me the information on the Martin gang, the warehouse, police involved and the rest of it. I will set some hares running after I call Cassandra to apologise for taking up your time. She is like a sister to me," he finally managed a smile, which Antony took as a sign he could return. "Sorry, Antony you may have noticed some problems have come up. Can we have lunch tomorrow or dinner?" Antony murmured a yes and briefly kissed Robbie before leaving.

Robbie despatched Miss Elizabeth with instructions to make sure Jack had sent over everything before collecting him. He was proud of how much his daughter had achieved in the last few years, if someone was threatening her he would bring them carnage. Next, he called Cass to tell her a story about hiccups in France that he needed Jack to help him fix. It seemed to reassure her that it was his fault Jack was not his normal self.

Robbie opened his laptop to scan the information from Jack, he took another drink of Bandol wine and decided to alert the Stones Chairman that all was not well in Europe. He would need permission to use resources on an internal project, they would have to come from outside the UK because all his teams were deployed on profitable work. In anticipation of approval, he called the Head of the Stones group in Paris to ask him to get some men to start on an investigation as soon as they received the details. An initial report was requested by lunchtime the following day in time for a call he was going to try and arrange with the General.

The Stones Chairman was sitting in his Maserati 4x4 having just left his palatial home in the hills above Tiberon, overlooking Richardson Bay. The General was on his way to the Richmond Bridge on the 580 hoping the trip would be a forty "minuter", a good day. His thoughts were interrupted by a ring. He saw the name, accepted the call and spoke first, "Hey Sir Robbie, sawubona thobela."

"Unjani, I'm good General how are you?" replied Robbie in their usual African greeting.

"Wonderlike, but it is still early, nothing has gone wrong yet, hoping for a good trip in today. We have a difficult job coming up in Iraq and I am not sure we have the right people available to get it done right. We made up a team from different offices, which we don't usually do, associates from different parts of this country are very different in the way they think." He was worried and talking too much.

"Understand General, but I have to ruin your trip. We have some gangsters threatening our people and assets in both France and the UK. Can we call you back on Friday morning your time, I will have more information then and Jack can explain things?"

"Can't you just use the security guys you have, the people on hire from us? They are the best people we have, aren't they? They have weapons?"

"I would if I could, but this is more than just commercial stuff. I don't think the police will be interested in our problem until something bad happens, why would they? I only have security guards with those stun guns they're not supposed to have, let alone use. We sent the rest off to your old place to help the government sort out some of the locals if you remember? I think we will need a few old military guys as the problem involves an armed French gang and we believe some British mercenaries. These crims have already threatened Jack's family, to blow up our new hotel and may have screwed up our Bordeaux vineyard."

"Ja I see, you certainly are doing a great job ruining my morning. We don't have anybody left on the bench here in the States, as far as I know, so you'll have to look again in Europe." He paused then continued, "oke call me at about ten my time, six yours, I will be in the office. You will have plenty of time to give me the bad news in detail and tell me what you're going to do about it. I have to say, this all seems a bit strange, especially after what you and Nicky did to those other French gangsters a couple of years ago."

"Thanks, that will give us enough time to work up some ideas and a plan for dealing with this, as you say, strange state of affairs. I have already asked our French guys to investigate the gang they will report back ready for that meeting. He paused before taking the opportunity, "one other thing, we will need a qualified project manager to come and run things, there are none here. I don't think either Jack or I are field commanders anymore, do you? Please think about who can do the job even if we have to shuffle people around."

Before the General could speak Robbie said, "by the way, it's not all bad news, the investment in Penedes wine, is agreed, the opposition has gone away." Hoping to brighten up his day, "we managed to persuade those gangsters to piss off and they went to Ukraine, not sure why they went there, but they were on that plane that was brought down by the Ruskies. The guy we signed up from Mexico, the one suggested by JD, is in place and will take charge of the assets soon. Nice tip from our old boy eh?"

The General grumpily reiterated he had no one to give them but felt obliged to congratulate Robbie on landing a difficult deal. They ended the call with their usual Zulu farewells. Robbie blew a breath of relief as he sat in his private dining room awaiting the arrival of Miss Elizabeth and Jack.

Chapter 23: Kensington, Thursday evening

Having returned to Sylvain's restaurant, Patrice was explaining his problem to the disappointed gangster who insisted, "you must do something big, or he will make a fool of you. Go to his home threaten him and his family, break his resistance, only then will he give you everything you want." Patrice nodded in agreement, it was imperative to take control of events by doing something violent in Jack's home. But he had no idea where Jack lived unless Lena was able to find out. His intelligence gathering was weak, they only found out about Jack's wife, for the book and pigeon blood stunt, from the helpful Bandol hotel staff. The precise location of the St Albans offices came courtesy of a hesitant Frederic. "How many men do you have because I can lend you some more if you want?" Sylvain asked becoming frustrated at the lack of progress.

Patrice was getting ready to explain it might be a waste of time when his phone rang. "I must take this call it's Madame Martin," Patrice wandered off to get into a heated discussion. When it was over, he muttered to himself, "it seems she cares more about her shops than the business we are over here fighting for. He told Sylvain, "I have to go to a house in John's Wood by a cricket place. Madame is texting me the address from which I must get some designs for her clothes. She said I can go by underground train, but I have never been on one in London before," he declared uncertainly. He continued to relay what she had told him about the location.

"Patrice, it's a place called St Johns Wood near Lords cricket ground, it would be better if I have one of my men take you there and bring you back. We don't want you to get lost now, do we? We want you to look the part going to such a fine place." There would be no argument from Patrice who preferred being driven, it felt right to him. Sylvain disappeared for a moment to inform his chauffeur to make sure Patrice was not up to any "funny" business. An hour later Patrice was sitting in the back of a black Mercedes driven by Dave Bender to a house in Hamilton Drive to meet a designer for Astrid Fashions.

When they arrived at the exclusive row of townhouses in St John's Wood, Patrice texted Madame for confirmation he was in the right place. She replied;

Chiara Prinzi my designer, has been contacted and will be waiting for .you. You are one of my store staff on holiday and doing a favour. Be good and nice, don't upset her she is also my friend. AM

The deception was necessary because Chiara and her husband knew nothing of her unlawful activities. Definitely nothing about her husband's drugs business - at least that's what she thought. As he approached the door, it was opened by a young woman wearing a uniform that reminded him of an expensive hotel. He was led through a high-ceilinged hallway to a large room where he was encouraged to sit on a yellow and gold sofa. The room was decorated in white, yellow and gold, like the furniture. On three walls hung large pieces of modern art which Patrice never understood, but the fourth, the largest wall, was almost completely covered in books. Not old books like in French chateaux, but a mix of books resembling something from a public lending library, entirely out of keeping with the rest of the room.

Patrice's room inspection was interrupted by someone calling his name. He turned to see an alluring Arab, with light-brown hair, yellow-green eyes and plump bright red lips, complemented by an animal print dress. He immediately stood to take in the outrageously beautiful women looking directly into his eyes. She held out her hand to introduce herself as Chiara. He responded by holding her hand rather than shaking it, telling her he was Patrice, a colleague of Astrid. He let go of her hand, looked into her smiling eyes and unnecessarily confirmed his mission. He was smitten at first sight.

"My ladies still have a couple of things to do before I let you have the designs, perhaps you would like a drink?" He agreed that was an excellent idea and ordered a Ricard, a speciality from his home city. The maid who had been waiting by the door scurried off to get some fresh ice and water. Chiara assembled his drink in the traditional French way whilst her admirer had difficulty in keeping his eyes off her, which was her intention. "How long have you known Astrid?" she asked.

"Since I left school to work with her and her husband Matisse." In an attempt to increase her interest in him, he claimed to be a specialist in their fine wine business.

Chiara looked impressed and continued, "we must ask you what to buy, my husband has no clue, he will drink anything but I like silky Bordeaux don't you?" she continued as her eyes moved over his body.

A face appeared at the door Chiara said, "I must go, I saw you gazing at the books," she continued. "I know they look strange in this room," waving her hand at the wall. He smiled. "My husband is a publisher, he insists on keeping copies of ALL his books and some of his competitors. Feel free to look at them while I get things ready," she said out loud "and take them if you want," she said quietly to herself and chuckled. "I will be back shortly." Next Patrice was disturbed by a man's voice calling him. He turned to see the husband walking over with his hand outstretched. After introductions, the very English publisher talked enthusiastically about his books to a bored Patrice who hated listening to men who had drunk too much. The publisher asked him if he had seen any books he liked. Patrice noticed a hardback version of the book he had recently covered in pigeon blood. The Frenchman explained he had seen a copy of the book in a hotel in Bandol where he had met up with the owner. *Perhaps he knows Jack,* thought Patrice. The publisher announced that she was good but not yet one of his clients. As Chiara returned her husband left.

"We will be ready in just a few minutes, can I make you another drink?" She refilled his glass whilst the publisher returned with a glass of red wine in hand. Patrice thought he sensed some tension between them, which he liked, he wanted to get to know her a lot better. The publisher began to talk about books again, this time to both of them. He announced to his wife that Patrice liked the book by Cass. Chiara claimed she did not know her and had never read it. The publisher strongly reminded her that she did.

"I don't know her, let that be an end to it," said Chiara showing anger. Patrice thought it was going to get ugly, he would of course console the beautiful lady. The publisher would not be stopped.

"You know her husband Jackson Rich or something he is the one who got the money for this house or at least his company did. Something like Bloody Jones it was called. We went to his house in Saint something. Neots that's right because you wanted to move there. You fancied him just because his house cost a gazillion pounds. Remember, we went there for dinner and we smoked those glorious Cuban cigars that you hate so much," he said now laughing. The publisher continued to provide more and more reminders. Patrice was now very interested and hoping he could get Jack's address before the two of them started fighting.

Chiara shouted, "enough, I'm not stupid, those cigars were frightful, they made me cough for ages after we left and the smell." The tension between them was increasing Patrice intervened while he still could.

"I met Jack in Bandol recently at his hotel and I agreed to come and see him. I know his office is in St Albans, but I can't remember where his home is. I guess I can call them in the morning although I do need to take these designs back to Astrid. The publisher was now becoming wobbly and in danger of a spill. Patrice tried one last time to get the address, "can you remember the street where Jack lives and maybe I will remember the number he gave me?" Chiara left the room promising to bring the designs so he could leave.

"Yes, I know the street. We were talking at dinner about the cowboy and western films we liked, and we decided that our favourite hero was Matt Dillon of Dodge City. He's dead now you know, the actor, he died in about 2011. We joked that Jack was the Matt Dillon of Dodge Drive where they live in St Neots, top of Hertfordshire. I have no idea of the number all I can tell you is that the house is huge with a giant back lawn and a tennis court I think, or was that next door?" Chiara returned with a large cardboard tube and a memory stick for Patrice to take. "I must away, nice to chat to you, cheerio" said the now very wobbly publisher as he left the room.

"Sorry about my husband he drinks far too much," Chiara apologised to a happy Patrice. He thanked her for the drinks and told her he loved her home, but he really wanted to say what an idiot her husband was. "Perhaps when you are here again you can tell me more about the fine wines you export," she hastily thrust her business card at him. "Call me if you want anything else," smiling as her eyes flicked down to his waist and lingered. Patrice wanted to play with her right there and then, but fought the urge. He thanked her again gently clutched her hand and he told her he would be in touch about the wines very soon. He then skipped off to find his driver.

Better make sure I get her the real thing and not that stuff we're shipping, he thought and laughed. *Wow, I am in love again.* He bounded over to the car and they left for Sylvain's restaurant to plot an attack on Dodge Drive. He decided that after he had taken care of Jack, he would go back to John's forest for some recreation. On the way back Pena texted to say that she had fixed a tracker to Jack's car and would send him access details. He slapped the seat and shouted merveilleux and laughed as he explained to Dave what he had found out. The driver lapped up the information for onward transmission.

"How was that, do you think he bought St Neots?" the publisher asked his wife. Maybe Jack will find out from Bendy what your new boyfriend thought of my performance.

"'Not enough for an Oscar, you would have had to fall down drunk for that," she giggled. "But I think he wants me, although I couldn't see anything happening in his pants" she continued giggling.

"Never mind, why don't you come with me and try again you bad girl!"

Chapter 24: Alameda, California, Friday morning local time

It was a beautiful autumn morning in Alameda at the Marina Village, Yacht Harbour Offices of the BloedStone Security Corporation. The company logo of green with red blood spots sat shining on top of the glass building. Behind it, the moored boats swayed and clinked in a slight breeze. They were part of the bay area community of northern California. The Chairman and Chief Executive Officer Gendrie de Vries lay back in his executive chair with feet on his desk worrying about the Iraq mission after arguing with his deputy the Englishman, former NATO Commander Viscount Hatfelt Manor. Matters remained unresolved as the conversation was cut short, Nicky had to leave to meet with the CIA Director about a West African project. Gendrie knew there was a good chance of casualties in Iraq to add to the ten associates they had lost since the company started military projects. Fortunately, there was no shortage of people willing to do such dangerous work.

The General, as he was mostly called, left South Africa in 1993 soon after reaching the most senior rank. He had been fearful of reprisals at the end of the apartheid era that brought Mandela to power. The General had known the Madiba from the work he had been doing imprisoning his so-called terrorist followers. But that was a long time ago, since then he had become a valued US citizen who supported US military activities and protected corporations from theft and violence. With the help of former military friends, an injection of cash from the UK investment business and some unsavoury projects, he had grown a multi-billion-dollar organisation. He named the corporation after the virtues of protection and nurturing that came from bloodstones.

The investment company under the stewardship of Sir Robbie and Jack had grown into a medium-size company with high-grade assets in Europe, Southern Africa and the USA. At times like these, the General wondered whether it was time to sell BloedStone and live on the riches they had accumulated like JD.

He made a mental note to speak to Robbie about having a look at what could be done. Finally, the video call came through, the General moved to sit on his couch and look up at a large screen with two smiling faces looking down at him. He spoke first.

"Gentlemen how are you today?" speaking only in English this time.

Jack and Robbie acknowledged they were fine and ready to talk about the French situation. Rather than waste time, Robbie told him, the predicament came about after a weekend trip to Bandol by Andre, his girlfriend and a French woman. The three had gone there to find the woman's missing boyfriend. For various reasons, the police were involved which culminated in a raid of the gang's warehouse and a loss of a large part of their business. The boyfriend who was originally part of the gang is still missing. The problem definition is:

1. A French crime family, based in Marseille; involved with illicit drugs, people smuggling and faking fine wines, possibly including the Stones Chateau du Carys, want Jack to pay a 20 million euro ransom because of the raid at their warehouse. There is a connection between this group and the one in Kensington that our Miss Elizabeth is assigned to.

2. Failure to pay will result in them blowing up Le Beaux and/or injuring Jack, Andre, his girlfriend, the French woman, Jack's family and any or all of their friends.

3. The criminals believe a) Jack known locally as "Jack l'Anglais is head of our French business; b) the others work for him; c) he has lots of money; d) they are probably involved with a rival gang plotting a takeover.

He went on to suggest that they had a few things to consider before they decided what action to take. The conversation was business-like and lacking any sort of humour – very military.

"Ja Robbie, while I appreciate your clear definition of the predicament we find ourselves in, I wonder if you would indulge me for a moment. Can we go back to the start of this to understand how my nephew goes away for a weekend, gets into a strijd with a French crime gang and brings the fight back to the UK?" an agitated General asked. "It's not something you see that often, in fact, I have never heard of such onzin in my life," he continued with the occasional Dutch word. "Can you explain this to me please Jack?" Before he could answer, "you're supposed to be watching over him making sure he doesn't get into any more trouble and instead you let him get into an oorlog." The General continued the outburst culminating in, "you know I told his mother that I would take care of him. If my brother was alive now, he would be incensed." Robbie interrupted the General trying to get back on track, but he was not finished complaining and started to yell at Robbie for not fixing the problem locally. Then he threatened to send Nicky to sort them out. Jack's attempt to reiterate the story received similar treatment, the Chairman continually interrupting seeking clarifications. Finally, Jack yelled back he wasn't there and was telling the story second hand.

"If you want the story first-hand then we need to get Andre in here to tell you himself."

"Look we are getting off the subject here," said Robbie, deciding they were taking flak because of the problems with the upcoming Iraq project. "We must decide what to do," hoping that it would stop the shouting.

"Okay I am sorry, it's just that I have tried so hard to keep Andre from messing up again and now he's doing so well….," moaned the General as his anger and frustration dissipated.

"Gendrie, Andre did nothing wrong," replied Jack and if you speak to Olivier he will tell you that the three of them are heroes. They could have run away but they stayed and risked injury to help. I gather that when it came to the shooting they had the blood of gangsters splattered over them. They are not part of our military business, these are ordinary young people who are not like us, it must have been terrifying for them. They proved the rule that no good deed goes unpunished and could have proved the rule that the good mostly die young." He felt emotional being reminded of the conflicts they had been through and their deceased friends.

As the yelling dwindled Robbie took the opportunity to propose the initial findings of the French associates. He went through the information they had assembled on the Martin's business, its owners and key players, ending with, "so it seems that the crime family are treating us in the same way they would any other rival. That means, stealing money from us or taking tradable assets from our business. They need cash at the moment, if they get desperate they can pawn assets with the crime syndicate they belong to. Not much difference to the way legal takeovers happen I guess, other than the level of violence involved in the negotiations. So we think in the short term, we have to tell them we are raising money and offer our assets like Le Beaux and Chateau du Carys as collateral if necessary, whilst we work up a plan in the next week or so. Fortunately, we have the protection of the local Gendarmerie and if it comes to war, both Bandol and Bordeaux, unlike Marseille, are difficult places to mount any sort of attack and get out afterwards. As I said earlier, we know they have three illegal businesses but we are only interested in the phoney wine because it affects our investments. The legitimate businesses they have may be of interest to us, they include; building, property and retail, plus a cool Marseille villa which we photographed."

"How and why did you do that?" asked a surprised General.

"I had our friend get his police officers to put up a chopper and tell the gang there was slippage below their property line and that they should leave," Robbie informed him. "They photographed everything including, I believe, a naked lady who jumped out of the pool," he was joking it wasn't true but he thought it might reduce the tension. "It looked like the gang were hard at work and did not appreciate the interruption. We did it because we wanted to see if the gang leader was hiding there as it seems he has gone missing. There is a rumour that he is either hiding out in North Africa or dead. We don't know which but know he was not there as we "heat checked" the building when we got them all out. We did manage to photograph several of the senior villains who managed to escape the warehouse raid.

We have to assume that the troops are now reporting to Madame Martin who is being instructed by her husband or working on her own. Originally she was working with the legal businesses and unbelievably, one of her vendors is the lovely Chiara and husband Pubs, who live here in St John's Wood. Anyway, Chiara called me after chatting with Yasmeen about what had happened and mentioned that she knew an Astrid Martin. One of the gang's enforcers, sort of a hitman, a fellow called Patrice, visited them yesterday on behalf of Madame Martin. From what he said to Chiara he is involved with their wine business so we will definitely keep an eye on him."

"We have Frederic plus a couple of French associates finding out more, especially WHO if anyone is involved from our side, but the money is on the Chateau Manager, Claude. I don't think Chiara knows much about the gang's activities unless she got it from Yasmeen, but I did ask her to be extra nice to the gangster in case we needed a place to pick him up. I told her it was a French tax thing for the moment." He finished with, "I believe we should proceed on the basis that Astrid Martin is in charge, plus the gang is in turmoil and vulnerable to a takeover by another gang or indeed anyone with resources."

"Excuse me Sir Robson, but are you hinting we do some gang takeover of our own as you did in 2017?" asked the General and laughed.

"Yes, I believe I am General, a sort of reverse takeover it would seem," agreed a smiling Robbie. "But we only want certain pieces of the empire, the rest would be left to the French police to close down or sell on. But there is more to this issue," he continued. "We must find out how far the wine scam has progressed and who is involved. There could be some wealthy people or a certain government who will reward us for dealing with this matter quietly. If the news goes public we could be looking at a meltdown in the French fine wine industry, then we'll all have to drink Spanish, Italian, American or even South Africa wine," which brought a chuckle. "It turns out that your nephew may well have done us and indeed the whole world a favour by accidentally revealing the wine scam," suggested Robbie becoming animated. "This presents us with the opportunity to save the wine world. Superheroes ready to get the job done," he continued laughing with Jack joining in with the change of mood.

"Now you are getting ahead of yourself, even a bit dramatic," replied the General. "I'm not sure I have seen you this excited for a long time. What do you think Jack? Should we be saving the world from American wine?" he laughed. He was warming to the project especially as his nephew had been a hero rather than a villain.

Jack spoke again about what had happened and identified some of the pitfalls of getting involved in such an unusual enterprise. He led with how messy it could get if they didn't have sufficient forces to neutralise key Martin members. Then followed up by reminding them of the perils involved in keeping assets in good working order during a forced takeover and finished with referring to some sort of strike in France, where some Stones associates might have gone rogue.

"Okay so let's do this," said the General. "First draft a plan when you have sufficient information and get back to me on Sunday, I mean Monday?" He looked up at the smiling pair and continued, "our MINIMUM strategy should be; securing the continued investment credibility of the French wine industry, including our vineyard, while ensuring the destruction of the Martin gang. I will leave you to develop a best-case scenario. But, I must add, without causing a mess which makes the French government unhappy, and dead bodies will do that. If any of our people are involved in this business, I want them dealt with quietly in a fair manner. I don't want to see any unfair dismissal cases in a French or UK court that might lead to the release of sensitive information. Are we clear?"

"Okay understand," the two said together.

"By the way, did you tell me whether they found the missing boyfriend, what's his name, Michel?" asked the General

"No, it was Thierry Martin the son of the gang leader whom we think has been killed by a rival gang and is buried at sea or something equally unpleasant," replied Robbie.

"Okay, I think I understand or maybe I don't," the General thought about how bizarre the whole thing had become. "Is the girlfriend alright, is she on our side or one of the gang? You will need to find out and deal with her accordingly," he continued almost while shaking his head. "Let me know when you want to talk on Monday."

"We'll be in touch, have a good weekend," Jack said. "By the way, we don't think the girlfriend who attacked some of the gangsters, is anything but a regular person."

"Well, that's something I guess." They ended the call with the General waving to them. He went back to his desk to worry some more about the upcoming Iraq mission. The other two breathed a sigh of relief in unison and went to call their French team to find out what else they had discovered.

Chapter 25: Kensington and St Albans, Saturday

Patrice's phone call persuaded Madame Martin that now he had Jack's address their ambition of acquiring at least 20 million euro would be fulfilled. He left her thinking that with a little bit more pressure, the Englishman would hand over cash and properties. The French leader believed the news, she wanted to. But was it just a case of groupthink, a fantasy causing her to start planning what to do with a beautiful hotel and lots of money? Such thoughts brought her feelings of exhilaration, *after all, this is France the Bandol hotel would be better owned and run by French people. The English have many other things they can enjoy,* she laughed. For Astrid Martin, it was one more step away from the world of drugs and desperate people.

Jack and Robbie set up their weekend operations centre in the luxury flat on the third floor of the Stones CEO's restaurant building. The bedrooms had been replaced by a standby BloedStone security operations centre, equipped with the latest technology for use in Europe, the Middle East and Africa. The flat had its own entrance, seemingly in constant use by strangely quiet humourless individuals bringing in and taking out equipment. Stones always had at least one person on call to operate equipment and that person agreed to make the system fully operable for use that weekend. Fortunately, being over a restaurant and getting free food made that individual more amenable.

The second floor was often used by visiting associates or Robbie when he wanted to continue the evening into the night rather than go home. He usually had all the people, food and wine he wanted in St Albans. His house, a private compound, designed and built by an architect friend, stood close by in the affluent town of Harpenden.

Robbie budgeted for Stones to spend up to a hundred thousand pounds deploying French-speaking associates or renting agents to investigate the Martin family. Robbie issued an instruction that none of the De Beaux Endroits associates could be involved to ensure nothing was accidentally or deliberately hidden. It had taken a lot of cajoling and negotiation for the resources to agree to work over the weekend at such short notice. Holidays, nightclubs and some very unsavoury gifts were offered and accepted. Robbie would remember those that were most costly and unhelpful. They needed to act fast and did not rule out agents using violence to extract information from the Martins or other gang members. Robbie emphasised that the success of the mission rested upon finding the key players, especially those involved in the wine scam, and monitoring their activities for the next week.

Patrice rounded up his two colleagues and driver Dave for a sightseeing tour of St Neots and surrounding districts. He told Sylvain he wanted to avoid driving so he could observe everything in the town, but in truth, he didn't want to drive on the left. As they passed Stevenage he received a text from Lena giving Jack's address as Marshal's Drive, St Albans. After a few expletives, he ordered Dave to turn around and go back to St Albans. He started thinking about the publisher, *that dumb imbecile who gave me the wrong town, I will get my own back for wasting my time.* He updated the satnav and his phone while Dave quietly drove them back down the A1M. *Time to have another look at Jack's offices, the town and Jack's home before coming up with a plan,* he thought. *I will deal with that irritating merde and force him to give us that hotel and the pretty vineyard in Bordeaux. That reminds me, I must call Frederic and give him an update, so the faggot does not foul up.* He already planned to call Madame Martin early on Sunday evening to get her agreement to whatever they decided to do. Once she agreed, they would execute the plan immediately.

For the Saturday morning stint, Robbie equipped the ops centre with a mixture of desserts, pastries and coffees provided by bemused staff from the restaurant two floors below. The large wall was set up like in a police crime room with photos, papers, words and connecting lines. It took Robbie back to his former life, he felt comfortable. The two colleagues manned the phones, calling their people in Marseille, Bordeaux and then the UK. As they received fresh intelligence they wrote it down, printed it out and put it on the wall. Very soon they had added substantial data to the initial reports and had built up a detailed picture of the crime family businesses, its leaders, people, associations, those who it bribed and most importantly the members they wanted to question about the wine con. Progress was good so they congratulated themselves and went to Robbie's house mid-afternoon.

Cass and Jack had agreed their family would stay with Uncle Robbie for the weekend to help cheer him up after the loss of a boyfriend – a cover story the two men dreamed up. The girls loved spending time at his home and being with Miss Elizabeth. The Stones CEO's compound was a veritable fortress, including safe rooms and anti-explosion shields on top of the usual cameras and alarms. The local authority had been very difficult regarding setting such precedent, but his previous position won him authorisation for such safeguarding measures. Once Miss Elizabeth had collected all three girls, as Jack often referred to them, she took them to Harpenden. The property boasted not only many rooms, but an indoor pool, spa, a ten-person cinema complete with new movie releases from Stones US friends, and a huge garden with a tennis court and a separate luxury lodge for use by his staff. It was like staying in a luxury hotel complete with staff including a chef, who rotated through the St Albans restaurant. Cass likened it to living in a holiday resort without any other guests.

After a playful telling off for carrying their luggage, the women almost pranced to the main reception room. *How could you not love this place even when you have your own wonderful home?* thought Cass. Every time they visited she would ask Jack why Robbie was still working rather than sailing around the world with his boyfriends. Every time she asked that question, Jack smiled and

159

told her, for the same reason they weren't sailing around the world – it just wasn't fulfilling enough.

They spent the evening eating, drinking, watching movies and playing a couple of games. Everything seemed agreeable but it wasn't. Cass noticed that not only did both men drink less than usual but when the conversation lagged they looked preoccupied with something. She decided it must be something that happened in France they were not telling her about. *They'll be fine they always are,* she concluded. When Cass and the girls had gone to bed, Jack and Robbie went to enjoy a brandy and cigar in an old fashioned smoking room which reeked of stogies.

Once the cigars were clipped, the drinks poured and bodies slumped into armchairs it was time for a bit of business. It was Jack who started the conversation.

"You know they have or had two hundred men from what the guys are telling us. I'm not sure how to go up against such a large number without causing slaughter, something the General warned against." He tried blowing smoke circles while thinking, "neither would it go down well with our US army buddies or the French government?"

Memories triggered, he continued, "do you remember that trip to Congo when you spent the first few days on the loo after eating street food. Lucky for you the Doc had that stuff for your stomach and your ass," Jack laughed.

"I thought I would have an arsehole twice the size after all that crapping," replied Robbie suddenly remembering the trauma. "What a man the Doc was, shame what happened to him, terrible way to die, I liked him. Why are we talking and recounting that terrible time after such a great evening?" asked Robbie settling further into an armchair to enjoy his favourite Cuban friend, Bolivar Belicosa.

Jack continued, "do you remember the story that Yankee MP friend of yours told us about JD when he was in Iraq?"

Robbie looked mystified for a moment, "no, YES I remember, we were in my restaurant. JD was trapped in a cave surrounded by jihadis," he smiled as he remembered.

Jack continued, "apparently he wanted to get his boys motivated and said something like, it's not the quantity but the quality of men in your team that matters and if we lose, we lose with honour. I always remember that because it sounds so strange coming from a guy who thinks he's an Aussie."

"That's right I remember, he started telling them about the charge of the Light Brigade," Robbie responded. "Before they knew it he was shouting through the loudspeaker they'd been using to direct traffic, "FIXXXXX BAYYYYONETTS. The troopers wondered what he was talking about, most of them didn't have one or couldn't fit one to their rifles. Then like idiots, they followed him out of the cave and down the hill like it was an old fashioned bayonet charge," Robbie laughed as he recalled the story and thought of the image.

"It put the shits up the bandits, they ran away rather than be stabbed to death by the end of a rifle," Jack laughed. Then becoming serious, "We'll have to do the same thing with these French guys and hope they run rather than fight."

"All two hundred of them?" Robbie asked also becoming serious. "I thought you were going to tell me again that we should pretend to be a gang and have a big shootout like they had a couple of weeks ago. It's something we should think about tomorrow, although it might prove difficult quietly cleaning up having shot two hundred thugs in the sunshine down in the South of France," he joked. "I think I hear your Mrs coming to take you away." Cass appeared in the doorway to be met by, "hello miss just working with your husband to sort out the world," he said putting out his cigar in a cloud of smoke.

Cass and Jack left for bed, Robbie took a last drink, before making a call to Antony to wish him a good night's sleep.

Patrice spent Saturday evening with Sylvain's Eastern European lady friends. They were mostly in their late teens, too "magnifique" to traffic to wealthy clients, so Sylvain kept them for friends and family. After about three years of abuse, they were usually considered worn out and sent overseas to a life of slavery or early death. This was of no concern to Patrice, he did not work with the traffickers he thought himself above such grisly work. But he was having problems enjoying the female company which was mostly due to the constant texts from Sylvain's St Albans stakeout team. The interruptions caused him to think about the next day, there was a lot at stake. There were not enough men to be certain of success, but he did not want to cause a delay by sending for more. He decided to leave, turning down Sylvain's offer of a partner for the night explaining he needed to sleep and have a clear head in the morning. On the short walk back, he thought about the recent gunfights in Marseille, *we had more than two hundred men on the streets that day, we were top dogs.* He went straight to his room.

He continued to recall, *those were good days. God knows how we managed to lose Matisse in that fight, but we will be proud again when we defeat these English bastards. I still believe they are working with the Toulon mariners because we stole their load at the port last year. But how would they know that? The English must be in it for themselves. They caused us a lot of trouble, now we have nowhere to store our stuff or do the wine conversion.*

But WE WILL get everything back and grow again. Perhaps with a new handsome leader like me to help the delicious Astrid, he laughed and decided to call the stakeout crew. They reported only one person had been there, an older woman who left with some sort of package after fifteen minutes. The house was empty and in darkness. "Merde, merde," he said out loud, "but it's only Saturday, calming himself." He lay still and asked God to make sure one or more of Jack's family would be at home the next day.

He thought about Chiara's face and going back to see her, but fell asleep.

Chapter 26: Kensington and St Albans, Sunday

Patrice arrived for breakfast at nine after speaking with the stakeout crew. The news was not good, there was still no sightings of Jack l'Anglais or his family.

"You don't look so happy my friend," Sylvain said as he joined him. "What is wrong?" he continued waving for one of the waitresses to take their orders.

"I may need more men to carry out my plan," Patrice told him. While pointing to the fixed breakfast of coffee and croissants with honey.

"No problem," Sylvain replied while he pointed to an omelette then ran his right hand over the rear of the waitress. "She has such a splendid arse, don't you think?" he said making a two-handed gesture, wearing a pervy smile and thinking about what he had done to her the previous week. She returned a fake smile which unfortunately encouraged him more. He spun around to face Patrice to continue, "I have many men and what's mine is yours, my friend." Patrice doubted that. "What are you going to do?" he continued while making suggestive faces at one of the other waitresses.

Patrice had no intention of sharing his plan with someone he couldn't trust. Someone, he considered a low life thug to be eliminated if he got in the way. "I have not yet completed the plan but as you know we will do whatever is needed to get our money. Perhaps three of your men to add to my two would be sufficient." He could not risk having more as it might encourage Sylvain to have his men take over or set a trap. "No that should be enough, if I need more to move the money then I will give you a call," Sylvain smiled and gave a slight bow of acknowledgement as he thought of a house in St Albans full of cash. Patrice continued, "perhaps you could change the guys who are watching the house as they must need sleep. We need to know who is going into the house, although we will wait until it's dark before we strike."

Sylvain agreed but would secretly speak to the replacement guards so they knew it was partly HIS money they were guarding, and they should not let anyone take it anywhere but his restaurant. They were to call the minute the raid was over to tell him what they had acquired.

Patrice thanked Sylvain for his help, indicating he would be greatly rewarded when the whole thing was over. Sylvain claimed it was a privilege to serve the family and that he should be remembered to Matisse. Patrice left to meet with his men to go through what they were going to do that evening. He hoped he could rely on them, promising to take better care of them in the future if the project was successful. Sylvain told the chauffeur, Dave, that there was a raid in St Albans on Jack's house and he should drive Patrice. Dave would relay this message to Jack and Robbie when they called later.

Robbie was admiring the good weather, looking out over his rear lawn, "I would like porridge with blueberries and a bacon sandwich please Chef." The bacon started to sizzle, he continued, "that smell should get the others down here pretty sharpish." Sure enough, Jack appeared then the girls and they all ordered a cooked breakfast despite having eaten a large dinner the night before. Robbie explained how difficult it was to keep himself fit in the face of such temptations offered by Chef. After breakfast, the Stones men went back to St Albans to the temporary ops room. Neither said very much, each thinking about the chances of being able to overcome the Martin family. Before climbing to the third floor, Robbie insisted on greeting his restaurant staff and arranging a regular flow of coffees.

Once settled in, they returned to calling their associates and agents to complete the data collection. They not only wanted confirmation that all key players had been tagged but welcomed any ideas that would help put a virtual ring around the Martins. With the call to the General only a few hours away, they pressed their people to use any means necessary to find and extract information. The total focus was on how to meet the General's strategic demands through developing viable objectives. Once they could build a plan it would be executed without any emotion. Recent experiences had told them there was little difference between winning a war, taking over a company or eliminating a criminal enterprise.

They called time on collecting intelligence to start the analysis. The first thing they identified was a problem with the Stones wine business if only because the agents could not find Frederic Arsenault, its chief. He was supposed to be working with them but no one, not even his partner, seemed to know where he had gone. It was not clear whether he was missing by choice or had been kidnapped by an unknown party. Further information provided evidence that Frederic had been working with the Martins, after setting up a new home only a few minutes from their Marseille villa. The exact activities were not known but there was talk of large shipments of wine unaccounted for in both Bordeaux and the Rhone vineyards, part-owned by the Stone's French business. The more they looked the more it pointed to fraud as a minimum, more likely theft as well. The facts clearly pointed to the Stones wine business being involved in the fraud.

Robbie was devastated, the French wine business was part of his managerial domain. He had appointed the missing Frederic, a former lover, believing him to be totally trustworthy. He had even given him such benefits as access to one of his smaller planes so he could travel between Marseille and Bordeaux easily. Now, the two Stones executives had to treat the wine business as compromised, potentially under the control of hostiles, possibly requiring retrieval by force.

"I can't tell you how I feel about letting you all down," said a shaken Robbie. "I can hardly believe this could have happened after all the years I have been with you guys. It's heartbreaking. But you should know I have done nothing except be a complete fool and trust in a friend who is a fucking traitor," tears formed in his eyes. Jack looked at his friend in horror unable to speak. Robbie had worked loyally with the Stones team on some of the worst projects in the most terrible places around the world. Now he would be under suspicion and treated as a potential hostile party until proven innocent. That was the way it had to be in their world. "I shall have to leave," he continued. "You will have to work up a plan on your own, I'm so sorry," he repeated turning to leave the room. Jack worked through the options quickly but still in shock shouted.

"Robbie, stop, come back. I know you have done nothing wrong, you have saved us many times and we all love you. I know the General insists we follow YOUR rule that if you have people above or below who are dishonest, you must step aside until you're cleared of involvement. But look, the way to solve this problem is to find Frederic and have him tell us everything so we can clear your name. From what we know, the French property investments which I look after have not been infiltrated, that means I don't have to stand down and can still work on some sort of plan," although he knew it would be difficult doing the whole thing on his own. "You go and find Frederic by whatever means necessary. It would be great if you could find him by this evening, if not I will work on a way to keep things flexible. Robbie looked happier starting to work on a way to get to Luton and use one of the jets to fly directly to Bordeaux. "But to cover us, I must put someone with you to report on what is happening. I will get a couple of our French police friends to meet you when you arrive, hopefully, they won't get in the way. If you leave for Luton in the next hour or so you may be able to get there by mid-afternoon."

"Thanks, Jack," replied Robbie brightening up, "I will rouse Miss Elizabeth and have her take me to the airport, while I sort out a co-pilot and file a flight plan down to Bordeaux. Just give your men my number, I will meet them when I land. I will find Freddy and sort this out I promise. Jack, why don't you and the girls stay at my place tonight, you still need to be kept safe." Robbie bade farewell and rushed off to get his bag for his sudden trip to Bordeaux.

"Cool," Jack replied still struggling with the turn of events. He began to think that maybe it would be a good thing to have Robbie in an operational role. Jack took a deep breath and thought about phoning the General. Instead, he called the French agents, who also happened to be gendarmes. Fortunately, two of them agreed to meet the Luton flight and work with Robbie. They were the best available armed officers, maybe they would be helpful, but more likely a constraint. His next task was to work up a plan for the General. Normally this was one of Robbie's strengths, Jack was far better at analysing than creating them

Jack knew he would not have enough information for the call with the General, so would have to come up with something else. He spent the rest of the afternoon either looking for inspiration from the ops room wall or checking his watch hoping Robbie had landed and was hunting down Freddy.

"Shit this is not going well," he told the room and was hoping that the problem with Freddy was not an omen of a disaster to come.

Chapter 27: Bordeaux, Sunday evening

Robbie piloted the ageing Learjet 31 at full speed to land at Merignac Airport, Bordeaux in ninety minutes. He left his co-pilot to complete the paperwork and get the plane back for leasing on Monday morning. After rushing through passport control and customs he jumped into the waiting SUV to drive at high speed, ignoring the protestations of his two helpers, to arrive in Saint Emilion in under an hour. A few minutes later saw them parked at Chateau du Carys. It was dark as they burst into the main building to wake up the terrified Estate Manager and his wife. They dragged them down to the customer wine tasting room where it took a little over three minutes of looking at a furious Robbie and into the barrel of a police issue Sig SP 2022, for the man and his wife to confess to being involved in defrauding the company. They claimed that it was all under duress from Frederic who was in league with a gang in Marseille. Frederic had told them that if they did not co-operate they would be killed and their grown-up children trafficked.

"Before we decide what to do with you, I want some information, then you need to do something for me." The couple continued to apologise, cry, profess their allegiance to the company, hatred of Frederic and that they were only following orders. *How many times has that been used as a defence?* thought an angry Robbie. "Stop apologising, it's just making me angrier. I trusted you like I trusted Freddy and you all screwed me over. Just keep quiet and answer my questions," he was not good with disloyal people. It was fortunate for them he had handed the Sig back to one of his helpers or he might have been tempted to shoot the manager. They sensed he was close to the edge, stopped their remonstrations and waited for the interrogation. "My first question, I want to know the names of the gang members you met or saw. Just so you know, I can't, I don't know or something similar is not acceptable, it will instead cause me to ask these two fine gentlemen to beat you until they are satisfied you're not lying. I'm not sure about you, but to me, they don't look particularly friendly." The helpers gave their endorsement with one of those intimidating police smiles. The couple nodded to agree they would do as he asked.

Robbie called Jack and after a quick introduction, he asked the Stones associate to record the answers given. The terrified couple gave several answers which are best summarised as:

- First, they claimed not to know the Martin members except for Patrice who they declared to be the leader, the one who dealt secretly with Frederic. They suggested he mostly worked with them from his house close to the Martin villa. Freddy would not have done the detailed work or moved the produce.

- Second, they explained how the scam worked at Chateau du Carys but did not estimate how much money had been made or where it was, that was a question for Freddy - especially now he is missing.

- Third, they suggested at least fifty highly rated Bordeaux Chateaux might be involved. The vineyards were spread widely across Bordeaux's 7,000+ locations, to allow the criminals to operate in secrecy. They could not or were not willing to name more than a handful of owners involved. Potentially just a negotiating tactic.

- Fourth, they identified so-called respectable people who they suspected were helping in the illegal scheme. They did not give any corroborating evidence to support their accusations. Neither did they quantify how much money these people were supposedly making. Perhaps these were people they disliked or had a grudge against.

- Fifth, they said the work done by them at Chateau du Carys was under duress to save their family. They received no money whatsoever, swearing on their children's lives, as criminals often do. Then suggesting they were glad it all came out so they could live their lives and return to church – or something similar.

- Sixth, they had no idea why Frederic had gone off or why no one could contact him, nor explain who told him Robbie was on his way?

Both Jack and Robbie were appalled at the story and even if only part of it were true it could be devastating for Stones and the rest of the French fine wine business.

"OK, so where is Freddy now, why has he not returned?" Jack shouted to the couple.

Claude described his departure in more detail, "he was here and then poof he vanished before the police arrived here earlier. They looked just like those two," pointing at the helpers, one of whom pulled up his windcheater zip to completely hide his blue-collar. "We called for Freddy and there was no reply anywhere in the house or outside. The police thought we were hiding him so they searched the place but eventually left," one of the helpers nodded. He finished with, "even his car is still here, so he must have walked or someone drove him, but we did not hear any vehicles."

"Please have another look," Robbie said turning to his helpers. "Okay Jack, I think we have everything under control here except for Freddy and I will go and find him tomorrow morning."

"Robbie pick up the phone will you?" asked Jack. "I've been thinking, when I call the General, I will tell him we have found out about the wine fraud in Bordeaux and that you are staying there to sort out what we should do about it. Besides that, you're going to search for Freddy who is missing or might have been kidnapped. I will avoid telling him the rest of the story until you have more information. Are you okay with that?"

"Great, I will get things sorted here then we can talk some more to decide what else needs to get done. Thanks for believing in me."

"You're welcome Sir, it was nice to be able to help you for once. By the way, how were your helpers? They cost a lot of money so let them go as soon as you can, I will send you some replacements when we are straight."

"Big, very big, they frighten everyone including me," replied Robbie.

Jack continued, "I am now almost certain that the guy who has been threatening us is the same Patrice who is running the wine scam, so we must get him." Jack felt happier that the pieces might be falling into place.

They agreed to speak the next day and rang off.

Chapter 28: St Albans, Sunday evening

It was seven in the evening, Patrice plus the new team were on their way to St Albans. An hour earlier the lookouts had called him to announce Jack had arrived home, driven by a woman they assumed to be his wife. The house was well-lit and there were no children as far as they could see.

Patrice fully equipped with a UK communication system, complete with a wire coming out of his ear, was able to speak directly to his seven-man gang. *I have an army,* he thought. One of them was equipped with an old sawn-off shotgun to frighten, another with a revolver to force compliance. The rest carried a cosh, Sylvain hated knives after his cousin was stabbed to death. The group were travelling in one Ford transit dressed as a gas service van, one black SUV and a superfast black BMW 535 driven by Dave the chauffeur. The Frenchman believed he had overwhelming force but felt troubled it might turn violent.

His men knew they had to kidnap whoever was in the house and hold them for ransom. Sylvain's men thought it was a robbery, they were there for the cash, only resorting to kidnap to get the money later. Patrice knew it was unlikely that there would be a stash of money in the house but he had to encourage Sylvain to help. He was expecting to abduct Jack and possibly the wife. More likely he would take Jack and leave the wife to make arrangements to pay. He told them loudly NO SHOOTING whatsoever, the guns were for show and pointing only.

Once they arrived in Marshal's Drive they met with the lookout crew and together created a formation around the house. The BMW sitting up the street to protect the exit, the SUV set down the street alongside the surveillance vehicle, blockers in case of interference. The transit containing the assault team parked across the exit side of the horseshoe drive. It was quiet, everything was ready, no cars on the public street all on owner driveways. Patrice gave the order and the assault commenced. The transit reversed into the driveway entrance and four men jumped out dressed as gas company workmen. They were carrying various props, including flashing yellow lights and signs warning of a gas leak, which were put across the driveway exit. One of the men wearing a cap and glasses strolled forward to ring the doorbell. He looked awkward trying to keep his face hidden from the camera.

"Hello, who's there?" came a female voice from the house. "I'm just getting out of the bath, but I can speak to you through my security camera. I can't see your face very well can you look up please?"

He ignored her request, "gas company madam there's a leak, we need to get into the property to fix it."

"I'm sorry but you will have to wait while I get dressed, is that okay?" she continued.

"I'm sorry but you need to hurry up," replied the gas man, worried about being filmed.

"Won't be long," she continued leaving him standing under the camera getting more and more nervous. He turned away from the house while responding to the questions Patrice was shouting in his ear. He jogged on the spot watched casually by the other men who were getting bored waiting. He turned back nothing was happening, he rang the bell again, he thought he could hear movement, but everything stayed the same.

He was receiving instructions to get on with it and spoke to the house again, "if you don't open up I will get my manager to come over to talk to you. You do realise there is a terrible danger to you and the community?" something he heard in a disaster movie.

"I can't smell any gas," the voice replied. "Why don't you get your boss to come over so I can talk to him while I get dried off," Miss Elizabeth continued stifling a laugh while sitting in Robbie's car in the drive opposite. She was accompanied by a fellow BloedStone associate who was also working on the Anglo-French team tasked with breaking up the trafficking network run by Sylvain. "Where's Dave do you think?" she asked the associate while waiting for the criminals to make their next move. Before he could answer, they heard a voice and looked up at the dashboard-mounted phone. Patrice was standing wearing a baseball cap pulled down to hide his face. He had just finished supervising a flanking manoeuvre so that they could simultaneously enter front and rear to prevent anyone from escaping to raise the alarm.

He started speaking to the house in his best English, "Madam, I understand you are reluctant to let us in but I assure you that there is nothing to be worried about. If you don't open the door we will need to call the police as you cannot obstruct the gas company. So please open up," he repeated getting angry but wanting to avoid using a ram to break in the front door. "I will go away and give you a few minutes to open the door as I understand you are not properly dressed." The Frenchman walked towards the transit listening to the men at the rear of the house who thought they could gain entry through a slightly open lower window.

"Are they really going to go ahead?" the associate asked Miss Elizabeth who was now avidly following their every move on the rear cameras. "Have these guys not heard of alarms?"

Patrice instructed two of his team to enter the house to find out who the woman was and if Jack was there too. As they looked around the alarm went off and a deafening noise echoed around the house. *Why did they have the alarm on?* wondered a surprised Patrice. The answer came when the criminals confirmed the property was empty. Patrice told them to get out as the noise was becoming unbearable and the police would arrive soon. The men wasted more time in a futile attempt to follow Sylvain's instructions to find the safe before giving up and trying to escape through the deadlocked front door. When that failed, they decided to retrace their steps, go out the rear window, over the side gate onto the drive and into the transit. That failed because their teammates had already driven off leaving them and everything else behind. The two gangsters, still carrying large shoulder bags one containing a shotgun, told Patrice they would escape by running down the street away from the house.

They were stopped by a searchlight and a loud shout from a Stones associate, "armed police drop your weapons, get face down on the ground."

There was a loud shout in their ears from Patrice, "what's happening, where are you, we will pick you up."

One gangster responded with "merde" and the other babbled about the police. Neither man fancied their chances so threw their bags a few metres in front and dropped to the ground.

Given these might be Sylvain's men the Stones associates were allowed to arrest them. Miss Elizabeth holstered her weapon to cuff one while her associate did the other. The watching police, unaccustomed to receiving such assistance from MI5 authorised NGO, insisted on officially arresting the men before taking them away.

"Those guys were lucky, if this had been back in the US we would probably have shot them there in the street to save the paperwork, "the associate informed Miss Elizabeth without laughing.

"Right," said Miss Elizabeth turning to look at her colleague thankful they had not reached such a remedy in the UK. "Let's go check the place over before we leave it to the police and tell Uncle Jack he's a lucky man there was no messy shoot out," she smiled as they walked over to the house. After taking a few pictures they left the Ritchie home being sealed off for further investigation, of the alleged "attempted burglary'. An hour later all the police had left and Marshal's Drive returned to a normal Sunday evening.

On the way back to South Kensington Patrice was fuming. He kept repeating, "they knew we were coming, they played us, there's a traitor," his men agreed Sylvain must have an informer. Sylvain's men disagreed mumbling, he was useless at leading a robbery. In the end, he decided to take Jack in a raid on his office early in the morning. This time there would be no messing about, they would use their weapons if Jack did not do what he was told. The Englishman would be made to pay for this humiliation. It would have to be Tuesday morning to give them time to plan the attack. He called Sylvain to tell him about the traitor causing things to go wrong.

The conversation went badly there were angry words exchanged and several threats were made. Once the call was over Patrice decided to delay his call to Madame Martin preferring instead to work on an excuse involving a traitor. Sylvain continued to sit in his bar thinking how he much preferred working with Pascal, a far better class of villain, after Matisse of course.

"Hurry up for Christ sake get me back to my hotel," Patrice yelled at Dave who was chuckling to himself at the way Stones had humiliated the error-prone Martin member.

Jack was on his way back to Robbie's house when he heard from Miss Elizabeth that the kidnap attempt by Patrice ended in a disaster and two of the Kensington traffickers had been arrested carrying guns. She told him there was no damage as the gangsters were only in the house for a minute or two.

"Glad we all stayed away from St Albans then," Jack replied. I guess you guys have locked up and are on the way back. I will explain to Cass and the girls that there was an attempted burglary but you were there to stop it, so be prepared to be lauded as a hero."

"Yes sir," said a very happy sounding Miss Elizabeth. "I'm going to dinner with this rather smart man from the US of A and he has promised to tell me all about the adventures of BloedStone associates across the world," laughing loudly.

"Now you be careful with those pretty boys, well that's what Robbie told me to tell you anyway," replied Jack to laughter from the car. "I am about to call the General who will be wide awake and full of questions. Just so you know, your dad is searching for Freddy. Our French friend has been a naughty boy hanging out with that bad boy Patrice, the one you just screwed up. Between them, they have caused a mess at our chateau."

"Oh," said Miss Elizabeth becoming serious, "that's bad news, I know you guys are very attached to Carys. I worry that dad will dish out some punishment when he finds Freddy. Will he be okay? You know he can be very nasty."

Miss Elizabeth, muscular like a young Grace Jones, was adopted by Robbie in 2000 aged ten. Her parents, good friends of Robbie and opponents of the Mugabe regime, were murdered in Algiers, allegedly by French traffickers. The young Essien had escaped the attack only to be sent to an orphanage where Sir Robson found her. After a lengthy legal battle, he adopted her and brought her to live in the UK. When Essien came to England she insisted on adopting the name of her queen. After private schooling in Elstree, Elizabeth Manley-James studied modern history at London University before joining Stones and graduating as an associate. She specialises in Crimes against Persons and is currently on assignment in Europe. She lives at home in Harpenden as much as possible.

"You saw what he did to that huge Russian guy acting stupidly in the restaurant. He just stood up, walked over, struck him and had him dragged out in a terrible state. He would have done the same to the friend if those Stones guys had not stepped in to stop him. He might kill Freddy for what he has done, especially as they were once so close. Did you know they talked of marriage at one time?"

Jack interrupted her, "yes I did know and he was upset it did not happen. But please don't worry, Robbie has a couple of rented French police working with him, they have been told to make sure he doesn't do anything stupid. They are even bigger than the Russian," he joked. "I am here now so I will have to ring off. Have a great time tonight, I will see you tomorrow," Miss Elizabeth mumbled something, the call ended. Jack was in a hurry.

First, Jack, met up with his girls to explain that a couple of burglars had been arrested in their street after trying to break into their house. Fortunately, Miss Elizabeth had been there checking the property so stopped and arrested them. They sort of accepted the story as Jack sounded so relaxed. After a catch up on their news, he apologised and disappeared into Robbie's study for the call.

The General started in a good mood and listened to Jack explaining:

- What they were doing in France.
- What had happened so far in the UK.
- His views on how they should handle the project going forward.
- Some objectives to begin work on.
- Reiterated what he thought they would need from the US company.

"Ja I'm sorry to hear about the events at your house but would love to see Miss E in action. Anyway, you have a pretty ambitious plan given how many men they can put in the field. But I see a certain beauty in what you are suggesting. You say ALL you want from me is a field commander to work on the detail now that Robbie is in Bordeaux, plus an attack team to execute it, with permission from the French to shoot some undesirables. You say the French will be happy because you will save their wine industry, break up a massive crime family and bring to an end a people-smuggling ring. All of this at OUR expense. Do I have it right?"

"Yes, I think so. But I do believe you are understating the benefits to Stones as we could also make a small fortune, don't you think?"

"Or get us wiped out, jailed for life or both," a now exasperated General replied. He paused it suddenly struck him, *this could be helpful. It would give Shamir time to work with the team before they go to Iraq. Surely it can't be hard to do this without casualties on our side.* He returned to Jack, "Here's the deal. You can have the team going to Iraq for a week or so, I will arrange it with the army people. The team are meeting up in Las Vegas at the Cosmopolitan

Hotel so you need to get there tomorrow or Tuesday and brief them. They're being led by Shamir for the work in Iraq, but she should not lead in France. May I suggest you get JD as your field commander then you, Robbie and Shamir work under him to get things done? Get to France on Thursday and do the work at the end of the week. Shamir can then take the guys onto Iraq the following week. That luie wespen, JD, is messing about down in Mexico, he needs to do something worthwhile instead of playing around on a beach. I will text you his number and don't you take NO for an answer. Tell him to get his sorry ass up to Vegas on Tuesday to meet with you and the team, he continued mixing African and American slang. What's worse, he's living the life we should all be living, with the money we've made. Oh, and for God's sake no casualties."

"Okay, I will call him when we're done. I'm sure this will work even though there are several of the Martin bandits we have to get in the right place," Jack replied enthusiastically. "I will go to

Vegas on Tuesday after I have met with our French friend on Monday night. I will chat with Andre and Avery tomorrow as well."

"Now, do we need to talk about Robbie or is he is alright? queried the General. Let me know if I need to talk to him, if not then just fit him into the plan for Bordeaux. I bet he's pissed by what happened. I'm certain, I wouldn't want to be in Frederic's shoes," concluded the General.

"I agree," replied Jack happy that Robbie was almost in the clear. "He will do just fine when I tell him his role. He is also best placed to tidy up after we are done and to make sure it works to the benefit of Stones. I think that's it for now Sir unless you have something else, I need a drink and get some sleep."

"Good luck, I will speak to Shamir today and our friendly Minister tomorrow. Keep in touch," the General signed off and went back to his garden to enjoy the rest of Sunday.

Jack went to get himself a drink before he called JD, it would be a difficult call. Who wants to exchange living in luxury on a beach, surrounded by senoritas, for fighting with gangsters in Marseille, even if only for a few days.

Chapter 29: Puerto Vallarta, Mexico, Sunday

It was late afternoon, JD was almost skipping along the white sand dressed in swim shorts, a faded polo shirt and an old Aussie baseball cap. He loved the ocean smells, the gentle splash of tiny waves and the squabbling sea birds fighting over discarded food. He fled the Stones New York office three years earlier with more than a lifetime's supply of cash. Plenty of sleep had left him feeling well and he had enjoyed the lunch of a Mexican king. He looked across at the horizon and watched the sun sliding towards the sea.

Like most days he was thinking, *how lovely and warm it was* and *that dinner was looming. Perhaps just a snack after my grand lunch,* he chuckled to himself. *It's great to be alive, no problems, no sweat, what a cool decision to come here.* Well-being was flooding his senses, *it's nearly as good as the time I spent in Melbourne learning to play cricket and Aussie rules footie while drinking the golden nectar. How sensible was I coming here? Money and lots of girls who love me for having it,* laughing out loud. His phone burst into song, he had his irritating ring tone turned up too loudly. *Must change that shitty noise,* he thought. The call showed as an international number which immediately raised his concerns. *Maybe I should leave it, it can't be good news.*

"Hey," he responded.

"How are you?" a friendly voice replied in a serious tone.

"Oh, it's you, I was…," John Wayne Davies was struggling to come to terms with the unwelcome intrusion into his late afternoon stroll. "That is not your number, whose is it? Where are you?", he was concerned something was wrong dropping his usual friendly demeanour.

"I'm at Robbie's house in the UK while he is in France, I am staying here with Cass and the girls. A moment of silence which JD did not fill, he was waiting for the bad news, it came. "We've had a few problems here, we need your help to fix them."

"What kind of problems?" still searching for the bad news to match Jack's serious tone. A moment of silence, but this time he stepped in, "what do you want?" hoping it was going to be a simple request for advice but fearing the worst.

Jack decided to start with the ransom threat which was easy to talk about. "We are under threat from a Marseille crime family. They have already attacked our French business and are demanding twenty million euros, or they will take one or more of us for ransom. It's a long story, they are a big outfit into drugs, trafficking and stealing fine wines including ours, it's a mess," Jack could hear JD's heavy sighs. "The General is going to lend us a team from Stones US, but wants you to manage things in France."

"Oh shit, is there no one else? Gendrie must have loads of people he can send," JD replied hoping to avoid the mission but knowing it was going to be difficult.

"There is no one else we can use, the other ops leaders are with the US army in places like Iraq and Afghanistan. Look it will only take you a week or so to get it done. But you need to go to Vegas on Tuesday, the team are assembling in the Cosmo ready for another Iraq mission, they may welcome a little detour to the South of France."

"I bet he said don't you take no for an answer from that lazy bastard and tell him to get his sorry ass on the plane," JD continued. "He thinks I have nothing to do here but drink and enjoy the locals. I do have things to do, I've got a trip planned starting tomorrow. Indeed, I am taking a business partner on a buying trip." He continued, "if I don't go, she will be well pissed as her husband is coming back from Chile next week." He quickly realised what he was saying would not help and stopped.

"Come on JD this won't take long, you can see your friend Black Cat as she is running the Iraq trip," changing tack and appealing to his senses. "You two were close once, isn't that right?" Jack continued, he could hear the sounds of the ocean and seagulls growing louder as JD held his phone in the air while he thought.

"Jack, I have given up that sort of thing, I live a quiet life now," trying one last avenue.

"Come on, you know that's not true," tell me about that Mexican cartel guy that went missing. I heard from the Stones people that he was the husband of one of your girlfriends. Unfortunately, he also happened to be the local Mayor and he threatened to have you thrown out of Mexico unless you did him a big favour. We heard that they have a new Mayor now and the cartel has put a price on your head if you go back to that part of the country."

"It wasn't like that."

"Which part? The girlfriend, the Mayor, the favour or the contract on your head that no one will take up because the General has sent a message to the gangs that he would be muy enojado."

"I really can't help you, Jack, I'm sorry I must…. anyway, the job I did in Costa Rica was my last I thought we agreed?" JD was getting ever more desperate. "I am ill, I have a serious illness I have LIV, no I mean HIV, I have to stay near my local hospital. Some terrible woman gave it to me last month."

"You're not ill and you don't have HIV, the local Stones guy told me he can see you walking and running around the beach as fit as ever, with a great tan."

"What, you got someone spying on me? Where is he, I'll sort him out" JD looked around dementedly trying to spot them.

"Just joking JD, but I could have. So, are you going to help or not? You know the General still loves you, is missing you and wondering what you are doing with all that money. He believes you are wasting it, you know how religious he is. He would not be happy to know you are spending it on many senoritas. Are we going to keep arguing or what, you know you have to do this if you want to continue to live the way you do, we don't ask you for very much do we?"

JD started to think about doing yet another last job, "I'm getting like one of those old rock bands doing just one more tour. Where is Robbie in all this? I bet he is pissed with the gang for stealing his wine. I'm surprised he didn't hire a bunch of contract killers to get rid of them all," JD continued laughing at last. "Course he was in the police, I guess he can't forget that. But Jack why are you not leading the mission you are well capable?"

"Not so, unfortunately, I have become old, slow and a little knackered, whereas you still have a few years left in you," replied Jack realising that he had his man on the hook and he needed to be nice to bring him in.

"You will have a young and keen team led by the lovely Cat to do the work, all well trained and former military. Your biggest problem will be keeping them under control, they will be hyped up as they're on their way to Iraq for some action." He left out the bit about them not knowing each other. "Once you're done, you can go back to the beach and ponce about in the sun enjoying your money while we continue working to pay for it."

"Okay, okay, I give up, I guess I am in then for my last mission, for now."

"I will e-mail you details in the morning my time. I suggest you pack your bags for a week, I will have Stones UK plan your trip and let you have the details. In the South of France the weather will be changeable but around 12-18 degrees, mid-fifties to mid-sixties in your speak. As I said, this is a very short assignment and for you, pretty easy peasy."

"Shit, I've heard that before haven't I?" JD remembered the one-week project in San Salvador that took nearly a month and a "million" mosquito bites to finish.

"Bye for now, love you JD."

"Hate you, Jack."

Standing looking at the sun halfway into the sea, he was no longer hungry. As he grew older he tried to avoid this kind of project, it usually meant death for some people. But he also knew that because of these projects he kept himself in great physical condition to help make the rest of his life simple. He trudged back up the beach to his villa to pack; *I wonder why God let me fall into this way of living, I just wanted to be an artist or a cricketer or any other fucking thing. Perhaps if I had prayed more as a child I would have been an actor. Of course, on the positive side, I will get to drink some great wine and take down some bad people. Maybe I will see some beautiful French maidens and I'll see my Cat again. Who knows it could be interesting and fun! But somehow I don't think so, it's never been fun before.*

Chapter 30: Kensington and St Albans, Monday morning

Patrice woke up feeling bad-tempered. Stupidly he had gone for supper with Sylvain to assuage his anger but ended up having the gang leader moaning at him all night about the failed robbery and loss of his men. The Martin member moaned back about the informer who had made sure Jack had escaped through the back garden, after setting off the alarm. To make things worse there was a late evening call with an angry Madame Martin. She warned him not to mess up again if he wanted to keep his job. Then told him to pick up more designs from Chiara which helped him sleep.

At breakfast it was evident that not all was lost, Sylvain still fancied some of Jack's loot. He eventually agreed to lend Patrice more men to get the cash or take a hostage to get the cash. That meant an "old fashioned" armed raid, on Tuesday morning. The only remaining question was where to strike, the house or the office. Sylvain thought it should be the house as they would not expect a second attempt. For him, it was about getting the money rather than a messy kidnap and ransom. Patrice just wanted to get Jack, his family, his friends and anyone else he could get his hands on to make up for the embarrassment. Finally, they agreed to the same approach as Sunday, on Tuesday morning but under a different disguise!

With the mood improved the next order of business for Patrice was to call Chiara to go and collect more drawings. After a flirty call, Patrice brightened up and began to look forward to his lunch at Cote at 1 pm. He decided to text Madame, he could not bear another call.

Plan to get cash or agreement from Anglais tomorrow morning. No probs this time plans secret from traitor until we get there. Will get the drawings today. Anything else you need? Pat

He was hoping that would be enough information to keep her quiet until later on Tuesday after everything was done. Before he managed to put away his phone a reply arrived

MUST speak with you at 4 pm French time today as something serious has come up. DO NOT fail. A

"Merde," he said out loud and put his phone away. To make matters worse a spiteful Sylvain declined his request for a chauffeur to take him to lunch and told him to Uber or get a cab. *This may be my last lunch,* he thought walking to the main street to flag down a cab.

Chiara and Patrice met at the restaurant, they began flirting and touching across the table, he was like a boy with his first love. When they finished the main course, Patrice was sure he had seduced the most beautiful woman ever. However, both the dream and the lunch suddenly ended with the appearance of the Publisher. He was standing over the table flanked by a couple of drunken colleagues. *Merde, it's that stupid drunken fool who sent me to the wrong place. Why, how did they pick this place?* thought a crestfallen Patrice. The three men took over the lunch, had the staff join two tables and demanded more drinks. Next, they decided to speak to Patrice in French but kept asking each other "what is the French for'. A frustrated Patrice wanted to hit the Publisher very hard, but resisted the temptation and made excuses to leave. The only good thing, was the naughty smile from Chiara as he struggled past the drunken handshakes, clutching the designs. His bad temper returned, deciding it was all Jack's fault and he would pay.

"We didn't overplay it, did we?" the Publisher asked his wife seeking his usual reassurance.

"No, I don't think so, but you upset my boyfriend, I think he still loves me though," she giggled.

Their acting parts over the men sat with Chiara to finish their diet cokes and water.

Patrice arrived back at Sylvain's just before 3 pm UK time and began to fret about the call he had to make in a few minutes. Once again he considered what it would be like to be fired by the Martins. There is no government legislation to protect against unfair dismissal in his business. If she got rid of him, he would most likely be hunted down and eliminated unless he could hide. He shook his head ready to make the call.

Jack had arrived for work that morning at his usual time, thinking about what he had to do in the next 24 hours. He knew Patrice would want to attack again soon, today or maybe Tuesday. He had one of his associates follow Patrice. His instructions were clear if the Frenchman looks like he was going to assemble a team to go to St Albans, call it in, if not just keep following and recording. Jack wanted to delay any further activity by the Martins for the rest of day so he could carry out his initial scheming. He hoped for further good fortune like delaying Patrice at Chiara's lunch date. He was gambling the Martins would plan to wait until dark before hitting the Stones office or his house. His greatest concern was Patrice knowing about Robbie's restaurant or home, attacking one or maybe both or perhaps dummying one then hitting the other hard.

Perhaps they know that Frederic had run off and Robbie was searching for him, he thought. *How would they respond to that news? Would they even care? They might just consider it a meaningless distraction.* Jack continued his preparations while pondered the intriguing alternatives available to the Martins.

Double-A arrived together in the black Porsche, Jack waved for them to come up to his office. Rosa had remained at Avery's house joined by Miss Elizabeth, who would provide both company and security. Ten minutes later the couple were drinking coffee listening to Jack talk about the attack at the weekend and hiding out at Robbie's place. He told them that Stones now had a complete dossier on the Martin family and were ready to execute on the plans they talked about in the coffee shop.

"So, what we want is for you two and Rosa to go to our hotel in Bandol for Thursday this week." He continued, "that means being there on Wednesday night I'm afraid. I know you can probably do that Avery but what about you Andre? I know it is a bit short notice, but we must work fast to avoid another attack against any of us or our properties in the UK or France. We are exposed at the moment, we won't have the right people in place until Thursday morning. I know Rosa is staying with you Avery can you call her and check if she is willing and able to go. Tell her we are trying to find her boyfriend. We have an idea where he is but it would be easier if she's there in case we need proof of who we are. Perhaps you could call her now?" he continued turning to face an apprehensive Avery.

She made the call to Rosa who jumped at the chance to go back to find Thierry but only if she did not have to go to the warehouse. The Stones Finance Director had the feeling that Jack was holding something back.

During the call, Andre asked, "are you sure you want to do this? There must be better ways. Can't we just phone the police?"

"We have agonised over this situation but agree that this the only way to prevent casualties in the UK and keep the situation contained in France where it belongs," replied Jack being partially truthful.

"Why do you think that Madame Martin will agree to do what you want when she has so many men? She may just want the cash NOW," Andre continued with conviction. "Avery and I feel partly responsible for this whole thing as we were the ones who took Rosa to France and got involved with the raid and now you are paying for it. Frankly, it doesn't make any sense, until you factor in the wine scams affecting your investments. Can't my uncle do more to help us?"

"I spoke to him and he will be helping us, but we need time. Until we're ready Stones will have to take the hit. You mustn't blame yourself, after all, it was the police who carried out the raid. It's just unfortunate that we got caught in the blowback. Hopefully, we can negotiate a smaller settlement that will protect us all." Jack was hoping he did not sound too matter of fact when so much money was at stake. "All okay Avery?" he asked. She nodded to confirm Rosa would be joining them on the trip. Looking once again at Avery Jack asked, "can you ask our PA to take care of all the tickets for you three and tell Yasmeen to expect you all on Wednesday night? Thanks." The two looked uncertain as to why Jack seemed so in control and upbeat in such circumstances. Avery reasoned that he must be in his analysis mode, running on facts rather than emotions.

"Oh by the way," he continued. "I have to go to Las Vegas tomorrow first thing to meet up with an old colleague who is very ill and needs to talk about his investments, in case he dies. I will be back on Thursday morning to meet you down in Bandol."

"Okay," replied Avery even more uncertain as to what Jack was up to, but there would be no point in trying to find out, Jack was a master at the poker face. "Do you need me to do anything before you go?"

"Yes please, can we go through a few client things? Then I have to pack before going to a meeting in North London that could run on for a bit."

"Well, best of luck to you Jack," offered Andre along with his hand. "You have a lot to get through this week, we will see you on Thursday," he nodded to Avery, left for his office and the warmth of his staff and customers. He looked troubled as he left but trusted that Jack would fix things, after all, he had spoken to his Unk who was a security professional.

At around 2.00 pm UK time Jack left his office for home, on his way he called Madame Martin. "Time to end this," he said and then proposed a solution.

At 3.10 pm UK time Patrice finally summoned up the courage to call Madame Martin. After some surprisingly friendly greetings, a little admonishment for not keeping her informed, she came to the purpose of the urgent call.

"Jack has agreed to pay us a great deal of money so that his company can continue to operate in France without interference from us or any other family or gang. The exact amount is to be negotiated and they want to meet with you tonight to start the process. Well done, it looks like you may have saved us," she laughed. Patrice searched for the words to describe how such an unexpected victory would cause an about-turn in his fortunes. "Are you there Patrice, I can't hear you."

"I am glad we pulled it off, it was very difficult," replied Patrice trying to sound cool when he was close to exploding with relief. Where am I meeting with Jack?" he asked still recovering from the surprise.

"At Chiara's home it will be neutral ground, of course, you know where it is," replied Madame Martin. She asked me to apologise to you for your lunch being cut short by her husband and his drunken friends. She seems to like you, I wonder what you were planning for that lady, be very nice to her she is my friend," laughing again. "The meeting is at 7 pm UK time so don't be late and make sure your men behave. We can't get our hands on his money if you shoot him. You never told me everything about Sunday, Jack kept pleading for you to stop attacking his family and work colleagues he seemed very upset. I thought he was going to break down at one stage," she continued. "He didn't seem to be the sort of man who would fight against us. I told him I understood what happened, it wouldn't happen again while we are talking, but that we must have the money or the property soon. He was very happy for us to protect their business in the future, or should I say, that part we don't own," she was in a winner's humour, laughing at will.

"I agree he is weak and very frightened by us, he will do what we want," replied Patrice with a mixture of disappointment and relief. "Madame I will call you after I have been to the meeting."

The French women was not used to this humble, quiet and respectful sounding Patrice. She ignored it to consider a reorganisation that did not include "those horrible men" that her husband had employed. *Maybe I can even encourage Thierry to come back and work with me,* she thought.

Chapter 31: Bordeaux, Monday

Monday morning arrived in St Emilion to reveal dew-covered vines shorn of grapes. Today Robbie ignoring the pleasures of the countryside instead waited for the return of his two men and the "hunters'. He was told the search team only worked for eight hours with a lunch break included. That forced him to start at nine rather than first light. Finding a runaway was going to be an interesting challenge for the former Military Police Chief now a specialist training advisor to the French government. He was becoming techy wondering how much further Frederic would get. The search team had received instructions well in advance so he was expecting them to know what to do and give him their full co-operation, or there would be trouble.

The gendarme officers were amused at the instructions, which amounted to a game involving searching for a Frenchman hidden somewhere in the St Emilion area of Bordeaux. They did not mind, it was easy work, a game to amuse their chief, dreamed up by a "mad Englishman" who was offering a prize, which they all wanted to win.

When they finally arrived to start the hunt, Robbie's assistants were two senior members of the Gendarmerie. They were surprised to see Robbie wearing a holstered Glock 20 under his jacket, which he did not attempt to hide and they did not attempt to challenge.

Frederick Arsenault, head of the wine division at De Beaux Endroits was huddled in a corner trying to think, keep warm and deal with pain. His coat, with smartphone, was draped on the back of a chair in the chateau office. *How stupid is that?* he kept thinking and shaking his head to clear the thought. One of Patrice's men told him about the raid in Marseille suggesting that captured members might try to save themselves by revealing details of the wine scam. *The police must know I'm involved why else would they come*, he thought. *I ran just like they always run*, a favourite saying of his boss and now former friend.

The unexpected prison was cold and dry with an overwhelming smell of wine. He had broken in the night before by opening the wooden side door, a former delivery chute. Unfortunately, he forgot it was halfway up the inside wall and in the darkness had fallen fifteen feet to land amongst the wine. The bottles, all with different labels, were packed in cases and neatly stacked on pallets, supervised by him the day before. This store was as far as he had managed to run to evade the flashing blue lights charging towards the chateau. But where else could he have gone on foot and in the dark?

Evading the police was only the start of his problems. *Robbie will be searching for me soon, God knows what he will do when he finds me*, he thought. Frederic had been Robbie's friend, his lover, a valued part of the Stones empire before all was lost because of his greed. *What will Emile do when he finds out what I have done?* he closed his eyes. *He will leave me, shit*. Frederic had been with Emile since leaving Robbie to return to France.

He was trapped, there was no way out of the main doors, they were locked on the outside by him the day before. The key was sitting in the coat he wasn't wearing. During the night he had tried to build a ladder with boxes of wine but it kept collapsing as it was too unstable. Using pallets had been better but there were not enough to reach the door. His climbing endeavours ended with a fall on an outstretched hand causing the limb to swell and become useless. He was left sharing the underground storage unit with counterfeit wine, waiting to be shipped to unknowing restaurants and wine drinkers. *Shit, I must have broken some bottles, he thought. I need to get out of here soon, the smell of wine mixed with dirt is killing me.*

The choice of what to do suddenly became critical with the arrival of a vehicle outside. If he called out for help it might be someone he knew or someone picking up wine. In which case he would explain he had lost his key, and ask them to get another from the chateau or get the manager. But it could be a gendarme or worse still Robbie, in which case he would be hauled out and thrown into jail or worse case beaten to death. The choice was made for him, a bang on the main doors, a voice called out, "Frederic are you in there, the police and the chief have gone." It was a familiar voice. "I thought you might come here, it's a good place to spend the night, are you there, can you let me in?"

"Oh, great it's Claude," he said quietly. "Mes amis, can you open the door for me?" Frederic shouted as he struggled over to the main doors clutching his swollen wrist. "I don't have the key, it's in my jacket."

"We, no I, don't have a key either, can we get you out by the side door?" It's not that high, I can get some rope," the Estate Manager continued.

"No, I broke my wrist or something when I fell," he replied, "can you get the keys they are in my coat pocket, the black one in my office, you know it? Who have you got out there to help?"

"There's only me, I had to send the rest to look in other places. I will get the key and be back in about ten minutes. Don't you worry we will have you out of there very soon."

Frederic heard the vehicle leave and began to feel he might escape from his dungeon. To celebrate he thought about a glass of wine but then realised that probably would be a mistake given what was there. After a few minutes, he heard the van return, it stopped outside the main doors. The Estate Manager called out to Frederic, told him he was going to unlock the doors and to stand back because they opened inwards. As the doors slowly parted Frederic ran out shouting for Claude to get back in the driving seat. There was no response only Robbie and one of his assistants leaning against the front of the van.

"Salut Freddy, going for a run are we? You know they always run," said Robbie. "This man," pointing to the gendarme officer, "likes people to run because he has his big bad dog who hates the name FABOUSSE." The word caused a loud bark from a dog desperate to get out of the van. "FABOUSSE," he said again to create more excited barking, "likes to chase and bring down runners." Both men leaned forward to look at Frederic, "well, what are you going to do Freddy, come with us and talk about what you've been doing or run? Why not take the risk that you can outrun our Fabousse hater here, I'm sure you fancy your chances? If you get away, we'll let you go, won't we?" he turned to the officer who nodded uncertainly. "I can see you have injured your arm, so we can give you a bit of a start if that helps. Although I have to say, it would be interesting to see how much damage the dog will do before my man here can stop him."

The gendarme officer began to wonder whether this was the British humour speaking, it sounded real enough. *At least,* he thought, *the Englishman has not drawn his weapon.* Silence from Frederic who looked pale and shocked, it was his worst nightmare come true.

An enraged Robbie stepped forward and pointed into the distance shouting, "GO ON Freddy, run, you cheating bastard, run." The gendarme looked on at the desperate scene, wanting to stop the humiliation but reluctant to intervene. Frederic slumped to his knees with tears of disappointment and pain, "shame on you, you coward," said Robbie. "I'm glad to be rid of you, Emile needs to get a proper man not some cheating, lying shit like you."

The gendarme officer realised this was no game, it was a real manhunt and the man on his knees might have been killed. He cursed under his breath as he helped Frederic into the back seat of the van. *Who are these people in my country?* he thought. As they set off he replayed what happened convinced if the fugitive had run Robbie would happily have set the dog on him. *Who does that?* he thought. He turned to lecture the Englishman about his unacceptable behaviour, but Robbie gave him such a hostile look he changed his mind. *What can I do*, he thought. This Englishman looks like he would be pleased to kill me if I try to interfere. The gendarme was left hoping Robbie would at least take the injured man to a hospital, but he doubted it

At the chateau, the gendarme told his colleague what had taken place but was pleasantly surprised to see the local doctor load Frederic into his car and wait. Then, as if nothing unusual had happened, the Stones Chief thanked both officers, told them they were the winners of the Le Beaux dinner and requested they call the hotel manager to arrange dates. He wished them well before climbing into his SUV and leading the doctor's car away. The Estate Manager, equally nonchalant congratulated them before handing each a bottle of chateau wine, "something for you to celebrate with." The officers left, one thinking how easy it was to win, the other feeling uneasy about the Englishman's methods.

On the way to Frederic's Bordeaux apartment, Robbie called Jack to tell him they would soon be extracting information from a slightly damaged Frederic. His associate cautioned against further harm until after the Frenchman gave up the intelligence they wanted.

Jack switched subjects by updating his friend on where they were, confirmed everything would commence with a bit of chicanery, followed by a workable plan from JD and his borrowed team.

"So Robbie, you and JD will probably be in Bordeaux on Thursday and Friday to take care of the main event. We will let you know about the other stuff as it happens but nothing will start until we have a deal or a breakdown."

"Sounds good to me, it could be fun," responded Robbie. "By then I will have all the information Freddy has on the chateaux and domains involved in the scam."

"Now I must get ready for kick-off," said Jack before he rang off.

Chapter 32: St John's Wood, Monday evening

A very different Patrice sat in the corner of Sylvain's bar, one brimming with confidence, a hero to the Martins, waiting for Jack to confirm his triumph. Shortly after 5 pm, UK time, the Englishmen called to confirm the details of the meeting:

1.   It would take place at 7.30 pm at Chiara's house in St John's Wood.
2.   Neither Chiara nor her husband knew anything about the reason for the meeting.
3.   No need for weapons or bodyguards.
4.   It would be like a normal business meeting with Patrice acting for Madame Martin and Jack for De Beaux Endroits.
5.   The main agenda item, payments/transfers to the Martin family for providing security to the BloedStone's French company and its assets (hotels, vineyards etc.).

Patrice agreed to the terms but would still keep his two men nearby ready to act if anything went wrong. He was desperate to humiliate Jack. Once they finished talking, Patrice waved for Sylvain to come over to sit with him. A moaning, cursing man shuffled over but on seeing a beaming face held off making his feelings known. Patrice explained that the English guys had given in and were paying them. Sylvain sensing a share apologised for underestimating him, told him how great it was and to be working with him. The champagne was summoned, poured and toasted. When it was time to leave Patrice had no trouble acquiring the chauffeur who was happy to listen to the bragging!

Dave arrived early and waited close by. Patrice instructed his men to stay alert watching their phones, in case he pressed the panic button on his GPS tracker. He rang the doorbell at nearly 7.45 pm. *Fashionably late, I think,* smiling to himself. The maid answered the door and seemed impressed by his all-black outfit of shirt, jeans, jacket and Nike Metcon trainers. He followed her into the sitting room, Chiara was waiting with a smile and a glass of his favourite drink.

"It is good to see you again, how you are?" she asked. For a moment he forgot about why he was there, preferring to think about what it would be like to enjoy the company of this woman. "You are especially handsome tonight with your gangster look," her eyes wandered up and down before she giggled.

"I am very well and you are especially beautiful tonight," Patrice responded smiling at the irony of her last comment. "Thank you for the drink," smiling again. After a few more exchanges he asked if Jack had arrived, ready to create an angry scene if he hadn't.

"Of course, he is in the library waiting for you. I hope all goes well for you negotiating to buy wine from him," she said with a big naughty smile. "Let me take you to him, Jack seems very nervous about this meeting," she continued. "He seems a nice man but very unsure of himself I think." She was telling him everything he wanted to hear. Although that was not his recollection of Jack in St Albans, *but then it's different face to face, he thought.*

"Jack this is Patrice," Chiara said as they walked into the library. Jack stood up, went to shake hands, but the Frenchman avoided him to sit in the seat opposite. Chiara smiled at them both before she left, closing the door to return to the study.

"I think the video is working now Gendrie," Chiara announced.

Jack started, "first, let me apologise for what has happened, but you must understand, it was an accident, as I explained to Madame Martin in some detail." He kept his eye contact to a minimum and looked down to show the right level of deference. "We were not trying to interfere in your business, it was simply Thierry's girlfriend Rosalba searching for him with the help of my people. We are sorry about what happened," he repeated hoping that Patrice would believe him. "I have not been able to make contact with Monsieur Martin to explain, his wife is not sure where he is at the moment. Perhaps you know? Also, where is his son so I can apologise to them both?" Jack asked looking up and straight at Patrice. The Frenchman physically flinched as his mind was diverted away from triumph and back to a disaster. He briefly wondered what Jack knew and whether the man was deceiving him. He quickly recovered to provide a suitable response rather than an answer.

"You don't need to speak with Monsieur Martin about anything we say today. He is too busy to waste time talking to you, he is away in North Africa in Hautes Plaines," he lied. Patrice knew the place well, they had been suppliers of cabernet, merlot and syrah grapes in the past. "Even if I wanted to, there is no way to contact him as the telecoms are useless. We are here to arrange payment are we not?" he queried to regain control of the meeting. Jack took the exchange as corroboration that something must have happened to Monsieur Martin, *perhaps he has departed the world rather than just the country, thought the Stones associate.* He noted there was nothing said about Thierry.

"Yes quite," Jack responded while Patrice readied himself for an angry scene in case this was delaying tactics. The Englishman continued by sliding some papers across the table, "the deal on offer is as follows:

1.   "Property from our French business (which includes hotels, vineyard and wine investments) which can be cashed in when required, no questions asked. That is worth more than 10 million euro at the current valuation.
2.   We also agreed on a contract for you to provide security to our French locations at an annual fee of 1 million euros with price rises of 3%.
3.   Before agreeing to the deal, Madame Martin will have our books reviewed by M. Labbatt. They are going to our hotel in Bandol to do that.

4.   You are to evaluate our St Emilion vineyard Chateau du Carys later this week after the deal is signed.

5.   We have police contacts who will help you to get back your Marseille warehouse."

Patrice's face softened at the victory, "that is not as much as we wanted, I would not have accepted it," he lied. "But if Madame Martin has, that is good enough for me. When do I have to go to Bordeaux?" he asked just wanting to shout out in triumph. "I would like to go this week when I am in France."

"We are arranging everything for Thursday and Friday, so we will pick you up from Marseille airport on Thursday and fly you to Bordeaux. We will let you know the details and perhaps you can tell us how many of you will be going." Jack realised he was getting too excited now the Frenchman was hooked, "but only if that is alright with you?" Hoping he had returned to the right level of servility he continued, "I was also hoping that you would be able to forget our previous transgressions so that we could work together."

"Yes, it will be acceptable for Thursday and Friday this week. As far as working together, we shall see after everything is concluded. In the meantime, I trust it will be a comfortable plane and not some small piece of trash," continued Patrice now beginning to enjoy himself. "Now if there is nothing else, I will leave," standing up to try and emulate the celebrities he had seen on TV. Jack walked around the table to offer his hand, Patrice ignored it again and said "I will see you on Thursday."

The Martin member left the room to find Chiara waiting for him. He smiled, "thank you for letting us come to your home it was a short but good meeting." He kissed the back of her proffered hand and continued, "I hope we will see each other again." After she agreed they should meet soon he left to re-join his men.

"Thank you, Chiara, I must go now I have an urgent meeting. I will ask Yasmeen to arrange for you and Pubs to use the penthouse, she will be pleased to see you both," said the General.

"Thank you too, it was my pleasure to be able to help after all you have done for us. Please enjoy the rest of your day," she ended the video call.

Jack rushed into the room to be told the General had to go. "But he did suggest you may have a new career in acting," producing her infectious giggle once again.

"Not too wussy was I?" asked Jack looking serious. "I think I did enough to flatter his ego so he plays ball. I deliberately did not mention the attack on my office or house as I guess he sees that as legitimate tactics." She nodded in reply.

"I must say you did alright too with your flirty bit," he continued "or did you fall for his French charms?"

"Yes, he has a big ego that will certainly get in the way of his brain, at the least the one he keeps in his trousers," this time Jack joined in the laughter.

Part Three - Resources and Strategy

Chapter 33: Paris, Tuesday

Inside the Ministry Headquarters at Place Beauvau, Hugo tapped twice before entering the palatial office. The Minister looked up from his huge ornate desk. It was standing on a French Savonnerie style rug, surrounded by neoclassical furniture and large 18th and 19th-century paintings of the Republic's heroes. It was an office best described as "dressed" to match the architecture rather than furnished for comfort. It would seem entirely normal for the Duc de Richelieu to be sitting hard at work, had the scene not been spoiled by the 21st-century technology and dress. He waited for the Minister to speak.

"Oui Hugo, what is the problem? We agreed on no disturbing me this afternoon."

"Mes excuses Minister, but I have received a call from a company in Amerique called Hoodston, I believe," the Minister looked vaguely interested. "It was difficult to understand the man I think he said he worked in security and sounded like a Dutchman, but I could not be sure."

"So why have you disturbed me with this?"

"I am so sorry Minister, but he did come through on your private line, he said that he needed to speak with you urgently about some trouble investing in wine."

"Ah, Hugo could he be from BloedStone perhaps?"

"Oh, oui, oui, that is possible Minister."

"In that case please put him through," said the government official smiling but still feeling tense.

"General."

"Minister, I trust you are in good health and HE is treating you well?"

"Yes I am well Gendrie," he continued, "you know it is always a pleasure to speak with you, but do you think that this is the right place for us to discuss our private business."

"Olivier, it's great to talk with you again, I am sorry to disturb you, but I have some bad news and it relates not only to our business but also to your country's business."

"How so my friend?"

The Minister remained silent while the General, using plenty of hyperbole, recounted the now much-travelled story about what took place in the South of France. He even described how the crime family had gone to the UK to attack his friend, Jack, before finishing with the apocalyptic scenario for Bordeaux fine wines.

"Gendrie, my good friend, I can see how these criminals would pick on your business but it is hard to believe that they have infected, I mean affected, significant parts of the Rhone region let alone Bordeaux,'. replied the Minister. "This is only one small crime family we are talking about, the one that your people helped us to, how do you say… bring down, only a few days ago. Why don't you just call your contact man? The one I gave you, he will deal with the rest of the criminals if that is what you want. Or is he still in the UK with that trafficking gang problem we are working on? That is a real problem we must solve or it will be a stain on the reputation and the soul of France."

"Ja Olivier, unfortunately, OUR wine chateau has been compromised but we have plans in place to deal with that and our other investments in your country, said the General hoping that would soon be true. We believe that if any of this information finds its way into the press then we will not be able to save Chateau du Carys and many others from collapse. You do not need me to tell you that this could be a really bad problem for France. You have I believe, around 2000 companies making some 8 billion bottles of wine each year. What would happen if that was halved or that people started to think that Petrus or Romanee were fake and not worth 1,000 bucks anymore? No, we need to do some work to eliminate the threat quickly and quietly or we will all lose a lot more than money, don't you agree?"

If it was possible to hear a brain computing the noise would have been deafening at that moment. The Minister was weighing up the situation from all angles, considering the political impact, the potentially catastrophic effect on the French fine wine industry and finally what could be done to resolve the situation. He could not find anything of comfort, other than his good friend had the motivation and skills to make the problem go away with the minimum of fuss.

"Gendrie, I am struggling to believe all this can be true, it is as unlikely as one of those Chinese SARS causing a pandemic and the closure of everything. But I agree we must take precautions and since you have to deal with du Carys we should have you start the process. What are you suggesting should be done to prevent the cat from jumping out of its bag?"

The General smiled at his French friend's attempt at English sayings and replied, "to bring this to an end, we need to find all those people who are or have been involved wherever they are. When we do that we must make sure they don't tell anyone what they have done. It's the last part that could get a bit messy, as you know, people will say anything to save themselves."

"How should we do this? I cannot just send the Gendarmerie or the Police to collect up these villains and make them quiet. They will need clear orders and instructions about how it should be done. This is not what they do well, they know how to stop criminals and terrorists and bring them to trial. Unfortunately, as you say, these people will say many things to save themselves, the press will report it. That will not address the problem, we do not want rumours created that will damage France or our wine industry, nor do we want to hide the truth from our authorities. But we will need to control what we tell them and only at the right time. You understand this from your work with the Americans I'm sure. Truth is a weapon that can be used against us, we must be vigilant to ensure, we only tell people what they need to know and only when they need to know it. To do anything different would only cause the French people unnecessary anguish and pain and we don't want that."

"Olivier, we are planning to fix our problems using some of our UK and French people supported by a US security team on their way to Iraq. We will have the Americans stop off in France and maybe the UK for a few days just in case we need a bit of muscle against this cartel gang. You should know they are demanding something like 20 million euro from us on account of the raid in Marseille we helped you with. If we have to pay that money to stay in business, we would have to sell a large chunk of the French company and we don't want to do that do we? Of course, if you gave us the cash we would not have to do anything," suggested the Stones Chairman knowing it would cause a big reaction.

"Merde, such a choice you give me, I cannot ask HIM for this money he will not pay, he does not make talk with gangs or terrorists who want to blackmail France. He always wants to do the right thing as his teacher tells him," he continued with a snigger. "So I must agree for you to bring in your American cowboys to shoot the bandits like in the wild west." The Minister laughed at his joke and then carried on. "We must find a way to protect the wine industry and Le Beaux from damage. Tell me what you will do as you say, to make it go away in quiet time."

"It may be that we need some money to buy silence or maybe none at all. Perhaps we can make them see sense, persuade them to stop fooling with the wine industry and to go sell drugs like the rest of the cartels. But it could get ugly if they won't listen hence the need for my cowboys as you always call them," responded the General.

"I agree, but I am not sure we want them to do drugs again, as you know they are always fighting each other and upsetting the people who live there. I also worry when I think of your soldiers. You must also remind them that they are coming into France and not Iraq or the wild west," the Minister became serious. "You cannot go around and be shooting up people in the street. They must remember they are only criminals, not terrorists to be shot dead like wild dogs. Can you make sure of this or we will have HIM screaming at us?"

"Olivier, my people are professionals, not cowboys as you know. They will deal with the situation under the guise of protecting Jack from the Martin crime family, who want to extort money from a successful Englishman who owns hotels and property in France. All I want from you is to make sure that the Gendarmerie and Police don't interfere but help us. We need you to watch our backs, help with expenses and make sure we get help if we need it. If it all goes wrong we can say we got into a battle with some terrorists and destroyed their group in France or something similar, it will make you look like a hero, how's that? Or we can put it down to another flare-up of the drug gangs that took place in Marseille recently. By the way, how is the fifty-five-point strategy HE came up with working out?"

"Not so good, but we are still thinking about it. You must do one of those things you call black books to make sure no one knows it is you."

"You mean black ops and off the books."

"Yes, precisely, how many are in your team?"

"There will only be six or eight and will be led by JD and Shamir."

"Ah, the Chat Noir, will I see her when she comes here? I have not seen her since we met in Lebanon some years ago. She is so graceful with such wonderful muscles and skin and those eyes for me to swim in."

"Olivier, she is one of the team, we don't think of them like that, only as associates."

"Gendrie, you cannot yell at me just because I am a man, I cannot help that." The Minister was suddenly transformed as he imagined his short time with Shamir.

"Maybe when the job is done you will be able to see her, but not before."

"You are right we have much to do," the Minister switched back to his official self. "I will find you a contact who you can work with while your team is here. He is one of my special forces and he will get you what you need."

"Thanks, Olivier, we will start work and keep you informed as we progress. Goodbye for now my friend."

"Good luck and be careful with France," the Minister returned the phone to its cradle and began to worry. *Should I have allowed this to happen? How I will stop it if it goes wrong? Merde.*

Chapter 34: Las Vegas, Tuesday morning (local time)

The US BloedStone security associates arrived at the Cosmopolitan Hotel at various times over the weekend. They had instructions to have some fun before assembling on Tuesday morning for an operations session. They were then due to fly to Iraq on Wednesday. This all changed following a text from the General, sent after Patrice accepted Jack's proposals. He requested Shamir delay the meeting until he told her about some changes he wanted to make to the posting. The team members were unconcerned about the delays, "this shit happens all the time", their leader had told them. They went off to do more Vegas stuff even though it was just for a morning. *How much trouble can they get into now?* thought Shamir knowing partying had already taken a toll on their fit bodies and pockets. *Perhaps they'll be smart, go to the gym to buff up. Nope, they'll just keep partying like it was night out there. They know they can sleep on the plane. I wonder when the Gen will get back to me?*

It was in 1987 that Shamir Ruslana Tehrani was relocated to the USA from Iran by her absconding parents. Her father was a notable academic, author, Christian and supporter of the deposed authoritarian Mohammad Reza Shah. On the winning side and increasingly persecuting his enemies was the equally authoritarian ruler of the new Islamic State, Ayatollah Ruhollah Khomeini. To avoid prison or worse the Tehrani's fled Iran and made their way through Iraq to claim asylum with a sympathetic America. She was five years old at the time, with the aid of some secretly transferred cash the family went to live close to friends in San Francisco. The young Shamir perfected her Persian to indulge a fascination with her heritage country, hoping one day to return to see the "Garden of Eden" to see paradise. Educated privately, she became fluent in English, then French courtesy of her aunt. To thank America for her rescue and to avoid her father's selected suitors, she joined the US military. Going on to serve in both Afghanistan and Iraq reaching "Designated Ranger" grade.

The General recruited her in 2014 to become a Project Commander with expertise in communications. The extra money and benefits allowed her to buy an apartment close to her ageing parents, who accepted she would probably never marry and they would never have grandchildren. Like all parents, they worried about her travelling to places like Iraq even though she deliberately misled them as to what she had done in the military, or did in her current security job. She thought it might be difficult to explain to her devoutly Christian family that she shot US-designated "bad people" for a living.

Mid-morning the call came just as Shamir was becoming accustomed to the comfort of the reception suite. She did not even have enough time to pray the deployment would not be extended or moved somewhere riskier before he spoke. "Hey, Shamir how are you? I'm sorry I didn't get a chance to speak to you before you left and now I have screwed up your planning session."

"That's okay sir it was partly my fault, I had a few last-minute things to do that kept me out of the office. You know the stuff you have to do when you go away for a while," she replied. Her thoughts returned to Sahba, her Iranian model girlfriend, who had taken the deployment badly and threatened to leave her.

"There's been trouble in Europe with a criminal gang and we've been asked by the French government to help sort them out," manipulating the truth to keep it simple. "That means we need to divert your team to Marseille in the south of the country for a week, maximum," Cat gave a big sigh at such unexpected news. He continued, "at this stage, we don't know if you will have to do anything but we need you there just in case the French can't find enough people to help us. To explain more JD and Jackson Ritchie are on their way to meet with you and your team. That's why I asked you to delay your session. I think you know both of them is that right?"

She knew JD very well, following a brief, but highly charged affair, a few years earlier when she favoured men. Jack less so, they had worked together on a previous mission. "Yes sir," she replied. When can I expect to see them?"

"Jack is likely to be with you at around 2 pm as he left the UK early morning, their time, on a direct flight from London. JD will be with you about now as he has come up from his place in Mexico. He can start to tell you about what we have in mind while you wait for Jack. Their plan means that we have you all on a private jet on Wednesday morning, US time, as we need you in place for Thursday morning French time. You will all need to sleep on the way to be ready for action, or maybe you don't, having spent a few days in boring old Vegas," he joked. The General asked the crucial question, "are you going to be okay with this change? I know it's a bit last minute and on top of a team who don't know each other, but..," he tried to continue but she cut him off and he let her talk.

"Yes Sir I am okay with the change, it will be interesting to meet the old guys again," she said lying convincingly. "More importantly, who is going to be in command?" she continued fearing that she would be put in a difficult situation.

"For France, JD and Jack are there to explain what needs to be done and control the mission objectives but not the people, they still come to you for guidance. I should also tell you that there may be a specialist job for you as part of the mission." In Stones terms that meant capture or removal of something or someone. She had become comfortable with being a specialist. "Once it is all done then you are back being the commander of the Iraq mission. Given that JD is an old trooper I have asked him to help you unify the team so when you get them back they should be easier to manage. This is NOT a demotion for you, it's an opportunity to see a couple of old-timers at work. A privilege I would pay a million bucks to see." Shamir was considering the instructions and decided that on balance it was probably to her advantage.

"Sounds good to me General, I will get with JD and Jack and then work with the team. I look forward to watching two old boys on a caper," she smiled as they ended the call.

He was not sure whether she was serious, knowing her wicked sense of humour, but was happy to finish the call unscathed. Now it was down to, what did she say *old boys doing their caper,* he thought and had to laugh as he imagined her watching them. *Shouldn't laugh really, but it's not life and death like Iraq is it?*

Chapter 35: Vegas, Tuesday late morning (local time)

JD arrived feeling sad, he had abandoned his lady friend but happy he travelled in style on a shared private jet. The flight had taken less than three hours, the majority of his fellow passengers were business people on their way to conferences. Most would sneak some time at the tables, slots or take in a show or party with someone they just met. He sat next to a British former Vice President of Human Resources, for an obscure US software company. The man had morphed into a motivational speaker and became more irritating as the flight progressed. Nigel was forever talking about taking control of your life, managing your time, and building a REAL team to make REAL money. His message to JD, who accidentally mentioned he was meeting his new team, "get right into bonding sessions to build a team that will die for you." Nigel then drank his way through several repeats before falling asleep. JD wondered what the irritating man would say if he knew that some of his teams had already died for him and his fellow shareholders. *But methinks I might just try a bit of bonding it might work, who knows?* thought JD.

After decamping the plane, he made his way through the multitude of slot machines littering the Arrivals Hall. Many of them in use by people who could not wait to get their baggage before losing money. After collecting stowed luggage he passed more flashing machines and occasional joyous shouts, to stand in the taxi line. The sight of the Strip away in the distance brought a smile to his face, he had been there many times and done many crazy things over the last thirty years. It was a place he once thought he could make his home, but the sand with the ocean won out in the end.

While he waited he remembered the strange city stuck in the Mojave Desert. *We put up crazy hotels with cowboys and flamingos hanging off them. Fill them with a seemingly unlimited number of people who come for conferences, gambling, the weather, sex and oh yes, good cigars that you can smoke indoors whilst gambling and drinking free beer.* He shuffled with the queue, *but I just love it and you have to smile when you see it, La- la- land, a place for having fun. Unfortunately, I'm here for business and in a couple of hours, I will be meeting with the lovely Shamir and her pick and mix US team. Maybe Nigel my boy, we will use some of your ideas on cohesion to help her.*

The cab took JD past the old familiar landmarks of the Strip on Las Vegas Boulevard to the Cosmopolitan Hotel and the assembled BloedStone team. For once, the check-in queues were short, he picked the third line hoping it would be the quickest. It was composed of happy, noisy and mostly large Americans dressed in a uniform of shorts and polo shirts for men, shorts and white T-shirts for women. He was wrong but eventually reached the front desk.

"I have a reservation, John Davies," he announced to the receptionist.

"Yes sir, only the one night, leaving on Wednesday, is that right?" asked the receptionist like it must be wrong. JD expected him to say, who stays for only one night are you some sort of cheapskate? But the man responded, "that's a shame, although we do have your room ready early. Have a great time while you are here." Then he continued by reeling off all the delights of staying at the Cosmopolitan for two weeks.

Administration complete, JD made his way to a room on the thirty-first floor, unpacked, showered and made ready for the team meeting. He had been told not to contact Shamir until she had been briefed by the General. The light came on his room phone and the message told him it was time to go to work.

At 12.30 pm Shamir and JD stood in the reception suite and embraced after a gap of nearly two years. They had been good friends who became lovers while on a stressful mission. But the passion died away when they returned to normal life, both were fine with that especially with Shamir's fluid sexuality. JD spoke first as he held her, "Shamir it's great to see you again, how are

217

you? You look great." A huge smile spread over his face and before she could speak, he hugged her again.

She broke free and replied, "JD I am great and you, just look at you, tanned, fit, I think you look even younger. Mexico has made you well, very well" she kissed him close to his lips on both cheeks. I have missed you and your funny jokes." She stepped back to ask him what he would like to drink from amongst the sodas and introduced the food set out for lunch. A few minutes later they were sitting close to each other, eating and talking about old missions. Eventually, they reached the French mission. JD told her as much he knew suggesting it would be a complex operation. During his explanation, he took a call from Jack.

"I believe the plan is to take down a powerful French crime family who have many troops because they are threatening the French wine industry. I believe that the French government are with us and so is Robbo. She looked at him suggesting she did not recognise the name. "Sorry, you know him as Sir Robbie," she nodded several times. "This is going to be serious shit," he continued, "it could get hairy, which is why we are part of the deal."

"How hairy can it get in Paris, come on? she replied. "When you consider where we are going after. I'm guessing we will be working on the Sir Robbie principle, the one he taught us, you remember. There is no need to worry, only professionally trained soldiers stand and fight when faced with an overwhelming enemy ordered to DO or die."

Together they finished it off, "most enemies don't DO, they run and die." They laughed loudly together.

"You say this is a criminal gang with lots of thugs to throw at us," continued Shamir seriously. "These are bad people who know about waving guns around or beating up unarmed people, but they won't know jack shit about how to fight soldiers. I guess that must be why there are so few of us, to make it a fair fight," she lightened up and laughed. "So we take them down and then we can go shopping in Paris."

"Shopping again? Some things don't change," replied JD. Unfortunately this time we are not going to Paris, so you can forget about shopping in that place that has just reopened after a hundred years of work. What's it called?"

She jumped in with "La Samaritaine, can't we even go there for a day, for lunch or anything."

"Sorry, you're not going to be one of the 5 million Paris tourists I am afraid," he made a pout as he laughed. "But you are going to see the Mediterranean, perhaps you'll get time to paddle in the sea when we're done."

"Shame," she replied I was hoping for a few hours in La Sam, I can't believe it took 15 years to fix, maybe on the way back then," she carried on knowing that it probably would not happen this trip. "I also wanted to take a look at those yellow vest people you know the ones burning down their own city, how dumb is that?"

JD continued, "another thing we should talk about is the instruction from the General to develop team spirit. Apparently, your guys come from all over and haven't worked together before. May I suggest we start with a corporate bonding exercise? I had one suggested by a drunken Brit. I know it sounds bizarre, but we have only tonight to get them comfortable with each other."

"Okay if you think it will help, but it must not take more than an hour, we need the bulk of the time to sort out what we're doing," she said thinking it might help if that's what they did in big companies. "When's Jack going to be here?" she asked.

Jack's flight was early, he only had carry-on so was able to rush to the front of the immigration queues and through Arrivals.

The Englishman also had many memories of time spent in Vegas but today he would pay them little attention. He was a man on a mission, with a team to brief, a plan to make and a flight to catch the next day. In the cab, he called JD and they agreed that he should proceed directly to the reception suite to meet Shamir and the team. He would check in later for a few hours of sleep.

Jack knocked gently on the door and walked into the suite to embrace the other two. Shamir took his luggage. Big smiles all around.

"Jacky, great to finally see you, did you have a good trip?" asked JD

"Yep, pretty good, the flight was early for a change and I got here quicker than I thought," he replied before turning to Shamir. "Hey, how are you Cat, you look better than ever, much better than this beach bum," pointing at JD. He gave her a hug with a back rub as a sign of real affection and laughed. "Great to see you both again, it really is," Jack continued. He was presented with cola and went to sit down. It was a reunion of the Stones warriors who had fought engagements under the leadership of Colonel Robson.

At 2 pm Shamir and the old boys took their seats around the boardroom style table. They would be using their intensive training and practical experience to quickly develop a viable proposal containing the objectives needed to meet the General's strategy. Then they would work with the team to turn the agreed objectives into an action plan. To be successful they would have to make sure the actions were clear, efficient and adaptable. The team required a mixture of mutual belief, respect and a firm grasp of the actions each one of them had to undertake. Time was already short, the team would be arriving in 90 minutes and they should only work through until 10 pm.

For the first thirty minutes, Jack explained the background to the mission and the problems they were going to address. The next hour was spent talking through Jack's outline proposal for the three, or worst case four, locations involved. They would use the team in Vegas, a Stones associate known as Texas who would be co-piloting the flight, and whatever resources Robbie had in Bordeaux.

They decided:

1.　　　To brief the whole team on the strategy and associated objectives for the mission, to help them develop the programme of events.

2.　　　Create one group for each objective.

3.　　　Task each group to produce an action plan to achieve their part of the mission.

4.　　　When the plans were ready have the group quality assure them.

5.　　　Make changes, and then re-review if there was enough time.

"Okay, shall we wrap up and get the team in?" Shamir asked still digesting what was being proposed. After a moment she continued, "I think we need to keep it simple. We must not confuse anyone about who is UK Stones and what is the French company. We should just tell them that this is a BloedStone mission to be executed like any other, agreed?" she asked looking at the others who nodded. "If we tell them too much they will ask lots of questions about why they are doing this and who is paying for it. Much as we love you, Jack, using one of our teams to deal with some guys who want to beat you up is hardly what THIS team does." She kept going, "we should stick with, we are taking down a drug gang and saving France. They will be happy with that," she laughed. Both acknowledged her message.

Shamir received a text telling her the team were outside waiting and could they come in. She asked her colleagues, they nodded in unison. She sashayed towards the door, both men watched to admire the view – she knew they would, she smiled and strutted even more.

Chapter 36: Cosmopolitan Hotel, Vegas, Tuesday mid-afternoon (local time)

At 3.40 pm the team entered the suite looking like they had just left the poolside club. Most stopped for a moment to inspect the two older men sitting at the table. Instinct told them their demeanour marked them as officers from some military organisation. JD and Jack would have preferred to get up shake hands and welcome them individually but there is a certain military etiquette to be observed during first contact for a mission.

Shamir walked over to Jack's laptop, ready to present the agenda. There was silence, everyone watched her, sitting at attention in case they were in the presence of ranking officers. The agenda appeared in four parts, some items were unfamiliar, non-military, it kept them wondering who the men were although they knew who they weren't.

BloedStone Security

Agenda

1.   Introductions – JD
2.   Strategy and Objectives for the mission – JR
3.   Sessions for action planning – groupings by assigned location
4.   Presentations for QA – Group Leaders (ST, JR, JD)
5.   Questions and observations

The team listened in silence as Shamir walked through the agenda. When she arrived at item 5 the two men were hoping to see an early reveal of an influential personality, who had comments to make. But they were to be disappointed, the silence continued. Shamir decided nothing was going to happen so looked over to JD, as did everyone else, except Jack, who could not help but smile at the symmetry of the collective movement.

"Any questions at this stage?" she asked. Nothing, so she turned to JD, "this is John Davies a BloedStone associate who operates out of Mexico, he is going to take us through the first item on the agenda." There was an audible murmur while they considered the announcement and Shamir sat down close to Jack. All eyes switched to JD.

"First thing, relax, we have a lot to get through, you are all going to be involved very soon I promise. I understand that most of you are strangers to each other, although I suspect you may have been doing some partying together already." He could see a very slight relaxation, "well, we are going to fix that by introducing ourselves to each other here and now. I also want to know some unusual facts about you as well. Just to help, I will introduce myself first, then give you 10 minutes to make a few notes on yourself. Is that clear? In case you are wondering, you should keep questions about the mission until later." He started wondering if this was such a good idea, but if nothing else it was the fastest way to get to know them and help decide who goes where.

"Yes sir", came the loud response almost in unison. Jack smiled as he recalled the military way he had forsaken so many years ago.

"Okay, no "sirs" please let's use given names from now on. Okay?"

"Yes sir," came the response again in unison like in a movie.

"Right then," began JD, who is caucasian, an inch or two over six feet, muscled, fit, very tanned, blue-eyed and has a slight limp caused by bullet damage to the muscles of his right thigh. "I am John Wayne Davies aged 49, known as JD, a former US Army Ranger with tours in Iraq in 1991 and again in 2003. My last rank was Major. I am working as a contractor for BloedStone and live down in Mexico in a place called Puerto Vallarta. I have worked with Commander Shamir on projects in the past. I love cricket which I learned about while in Aussie and wine which I import by the gallon." There was a trickle of laughter, it was a start, but he wanted a guffaw by the end of the evening. "I will be in overall command of the mission's objectives which means that if something goes wrong, I get to make the call on what we do. I will also be leading the project in Bordeaux, in the west of France alongside Robbie James the chief of our UK and French businesses. Any questions about me?"

"In that case, why cricket? that's British and you're American aren't you?" asked the tall associate sitting at the far end of the table looking happy to speak at last.

"I spent a lot of time working with Aussies who are the true kings of cricket, they have the Ashes. Does anyone else know about cricket?" Lots of no's and head shakes. On another day he would have spent hours going on about how great Australian bowlers and batsmen are.

"The what? Why do they want ashes?" continued the associate.

"Never mind, it's a trophy let's move on." *At least one of them is now involved,* he thought. "Okay take ten minutes to make some notes."

After a short break, JD broke into the silence, "Shamir, would you go next, please?"

"I am Shamir known as Black Cat or Cat," she said. Standing at five feet ten ripped from hours of boxing and weights. She looked like an underweight wrestler. Possessed of disturbingly pale green eyes she had become a deadly fighter and competent Project Commander.

"You're not very black," commented the tall associate at the end of the table.

"And you're not very yellow," Oohs all around. "Perhaps I can continue? I am from the San Francisco office where I live in the city. I left Iran with my parents back in "87. I spent time in the US army and have worked for Stones for five years. An interesting thing about me; I know all the words to the Beatles songs. Oh and I've had the pleasure of working with JD and of course that gentleman over there," pointing at Jack. The news prompted sighs and knowing smiles from the rest of the team.

"But that stuff is really old shit," said the tall associate. They ignored him and looked at the beautiful fighting machine in front of them. Baby Bob was captivated, but he had met Sahba, the even taller and more beautiful Iranian, Shamir had stowed in a hotel suite a few floors above.

She ignored him. "As you all know I will be in command for the Iraq mission," she continued turning her eyes towards the talkative associate. He began to wonder what happens when you upset your boss. Shamir did not want to tell them too much about herself, she was their commander so wanted to keep some distance between them. "We will talk about the Iraq mission when we meet up after the French work is done," she continued. "Questions?" There was no response just a few headshakes.

Jack was thinking they had found the joker in the pack but had to make sure he made the team happy rather than antagonise them.

"Okay Bob you're up next," said JD.

"My name is Robert Lee Parker and they call me Baby Bob because I am new to the company. Baby Bob is caucasian, six-four and bulked from his time as a defensive lineman in football and physical work on ships. He has a very young face for his age and his head looks small in comparison with the rest of his body. I come from a small town in South Dakota where I was hoping to play football but got injured and so they cut me loose. I spent five years as a navy engineer down in San Diego, cus it's a lot warmer there," he looked up and chuckled, but no one said anything. "I drive and fix stuff." My main interest, other than football, is monster truck driving. You know those trucks with giant wheels," he put out his arms out to demonstrate and revealed some ugly underarm stains on a shirt struggling to stay together. No one said anything to him but there were mumblings in the background. Finally, the conferring stopped and the tall associate jumped in to comment yet again.

"How did you get that name? It's a good old boy name from the south, are you sure that you did not come from Virginia? That name has bad karma for some people."

"No, my dad loved the Dukes of Hazard, they had a Dodge charger called General Lee and he named me after that beast of a machine," misunderstanding the comment.

"So you're named after a car, I guess that must be why you're a driver," said the tall associate laughing, while the rest of the team smirked. Bob just looked on with a sort of grin nodding his head unsure why they were laughing. "Me next?" he continued.

"No, let's have the Newtons go next, you go last," said JD who was ready with his plan to stop the tall associate upsetting proceeding. The guy on the plane was very clear; you cannot have just one person doing all the talking it will eventually alienate the rest and that's not good for building YOUR team.

"My name is," they said in unison and stopped. Unfortunately, that was standard practice when they were working together.

"STOP one at a time please," they looked at JD for guidance. "How about you go first Lavender and tell us a little about yourself," he suggested with a smile. As the female twin made herself ready, JD took the opportunity to look at Shamir.

He thought about their brief but intense desert affair, which could have cost them both their jobs. He had heard rumours about Shamir having girlfriends, *I wonder if that makes her bi-sexual or perhaps ambisexual,* a word he picked up from Nigel, *or uncommitted or something else? Whatever she is definitely making herself even more interesting.* His thoughts were interrupted.

"Hi my name is Lavender Anne Newton and I am usually called Lannie." The associate is in her late twenties, looks like a long-distance runner has short cut blond hair, bright blue eyes and lots of smiles. "We have been at Stones since we were eighteen when they sent us to army training to get skills. We live in Ridgewood, New Jersey about thirty miles from New York. We share a house which is convenient as neither of us is married... Umm, interesting things about me, none really but I do like to go horse riding and of course love photography." *She has at least one fan in the room,* thought JD looking at Shamir. The Cat watched her intently assessing her every word. "Your turn Richard," she said to her brother. "Oh yes, I work with a long gun as a shooter, a sniper, with Richard as my spotter most of the time." Before he can start she continues, "he is not too shabby a shot himself, sometimes we swap to make it more fun."

The male Newton smiled at his sister and announced, "hi, I am Richard Ethan Newton and I get called Hockey Stick." This news caused a mummer of surprise. He is around five feet ten, thin and blond like his twin. "Unfortunately, it was you John who started the name about five years ago when we were drinking in Sausalito and you started calling me Dick. I think you were trying to insult me at the time as I was not drinking much and you kept inserting an "a" before it." JD made a face and mouthed "sorry" wondering what would come next. "Then I introduced my girlfriend, who played for the US women's hockey team, you were so drunk you said I must have a dick like a hockey stick and then everyone started to call me "hockey stick dick'. Fortunately, only Hockey Stick stuck," at this point, everyone was laughing as JD feigned another apology and asked everyone to stop to allow Richard to continue. "My interests, other than hockey," more laughter, "are hunting and of course the Dodgers. My job is in reconnaissance and a spotter for Lannie."

"Thank you Dick" said the tall associate, "I'm hoping the French don't need too much of your services eh," he started laughing at his own joke. JD felt he was becoming tiresome and would soon have to deal with his behaviour. But first Jack stood up to introduce himself.

"Hi my name is Jackson Ritchie, called Jack or Jacky and I am a Director of the UK and French Stones companies along with Robson Manley-James who some of you will meet soon. He left out the title to avoid jokes about knights and armour. Jack, now 56, smaller than the two big Americans but looks only a few years older unless you get up close. "I was born in the 60s, so I am getting old now, I spent most of my working life as a Banker before moving into investment and helping set up Stones back in the day. I am not a big military man but served in the UK army when I was younger, a family tradition to do three years at least. Went to the Falklands to help the rebuild. Interesting things about me; I drink lots of red wine and my wife is a best-selling author of crime novels. I am going to be looking after our negotiating team in Bandol then I am going back to my day job in the UK." The tall associate wanted to say something but was cut off.

"Now it is time for Mr Jackson to tell us about himself," said JD.

"Nothing to tell I have worked for Stones for three years out of the Chicago office, that's it," replying with much less information than the team wanted to hear.

JD remembered Nigel had told him, "to keep things in balance, make sure you follow the other golden rule of team building, those who give shit must be able to take shit. "That is not enough, what about your names?" he said.

"Tyron Jesse Jackson," came the reply from a six-foot-five, African American built like a small, 230lb heavyweight boxer topped off with a "number one" haircut. "I specialise in heavy weapons."

"Before you finish Tyron why don't tell us why you are called Chinaman. I will give fifty bucks to anyone who can guess." The team were surprised at the offer and jumped at the opportunity to talk about him. JD hoped this would be enough payback to show he could take as well as give humour, thereby making him part of the team.

"He used to have a ponytail," said Cat laughing and making slant eyes with her fingers.

"Eats Chinese meals all the time," said Lannie.

"Not bad, but no to both," replied JD.

"Eats Chinese herbs to make him such a big boy," said Cat having another go. Chinaman makes faces at her this time.

"I know," said Baby Bob. "He used to live in China."

"No, good try, whose left?" said JD.

"How about he married a Chinese woman," said Hockey.

"Wow he's a bit big for them don't you think," said Lannie looking at him intently. They all looked at her in surprise not quite sure what she meant.

"Good try" said JD.

"Okay, no one wins, shall I tell them or will you Tyron?" JD said.

"Man, you go ahead you know you want to" said Chinaman sheepishly.

"Yes I do, I really do." They all looked at JD smiling in anticipation, "well, when Tyron first came to BloedStone he was persuaded by the General that he should drink herbal tea to help his digestion, so he did. One day Jack meets him in the coffee room and persuades him that to get full value from the tea he needed to drink it from a china cup and saucer which he then bought for him to show how it worked." Jack started to laugh as he remembered what happened. "Tyron picked up his cup like this," JD proceeded to demonstrate the use of the pinkie finger, "one of the guys took a picture and circulated it. So Tyron here became the pinkie man. Unfortunately, we had to drop the pinkie bit because of the political correctness brigade who said it was borderline racist against the English." At this point, everyone was laughing and waggling their little finger at him. "So we had to call him Chinaman because of the cup and saucer and because we did not have any Chinese in the office." JD hoped that a little bit of humiliation would help bond the tall American to the rest of the team for the French mission and beyond. He took it well. JD looked over and mouthed thanks to him, he returned a smile, to confirm he was part of the team.

Later, Jack, JD and Shamir would build on the introductions, walk the room, talk to each individual to get to know them better and make them comfortable with the mission.

"Okay take 10 minutes, get a soda and we will get onto the next item" said JD. He looked around the room happy to see the group talking amongst themselves. *Thanks Nigel, your team-building advice seems to be working,* he thought. Then he joined in by attempting to apologise more fully to Hockey, but the man exhibited no angst, the opposite, in fact, he thanked JD for making him a bit of a celebrity. Bob seemed to be on a mission to speak with Shamir, but it was not so much an infatuation more interest in how she worked out. Chinaman was in conversation with Lannie about her shooting ability, on account of him wanting to be a sniper. So far he had failed to be inducted into the Stones sniper group on account of his inability to stay still for long enough.

JD shouted, "okay everyone please take a seat it is time for me to tell you what we are up to. Starting with strategy, objectives and resulting projects for the mission in France. No need to write anything down, we will send everything to your phones."

"The first thing you should know, this is not a military operation, we are not going to storm a building or engage or charge the enemy," murmurs around the room as they looked at each other. "Strictly speaking, it's a policing operation that requires us to perform activities that are outside the normal remit of both the French regular Police and the more military Gendarmerie. Given the size of the criminal gang and their methods to date, it is likely we will go beyond our normal rules of engagement, "use of force to defend" to "use of force to stop armed hostiles'. However, it will vary depending on your project and who you are working with. The ROE will be confirmed by the individual team leader when you arrive on-site, determined by the latest intel." There were lots of facial expressions because JD was articulating a posture, more usually associated with special forces supporting police operations.

"That's why you guys are here, these are not Mexican gangbangers, this is a business that operates inside a European country, it may be criminal, but its people are much like you and me. Our activities must also include the imposition of a blackout not only on gang members but also the press and civilians."

Jack took over and started by telling the group they would be working with, or for local consumption supporting, the French National Police forces. The mission strategy involved:

1.   Saving the French wine industry from ruin by fake wines.

2.   Destroying the viability of the Martin crime family – the gang responsible.

3.   Maintaining a strict silence over what was being done and to whom.

4.   Where possible, repair the damage to BloedStone's assets in Europe.

He told them the objectives, or how they were going to get things done. This involved getting key criminals and their leaders to three or four separate locations where they would be made to submit to Stones or law enforcement officers. He shared where the locations might be and why they had been selected. Then gave examples of what would have to be done at those locations.

"Any questions or comments so far?" Jack stopped to ask the group.

"So looking at the agenda, I'm guessing we are going to fill in the blanks on the how and what in groups, suggested a studious Lavender unable to contain herself.

"We will come to the actions later but essentially that's right, thank you Lannie" answered an impressed JD.

Jack resumed by explaining that the mission would be difficult for two reasons; first, the gang had lots of trained members who might decide to fight rather than give in. Secondly, they must avoid gun battles on the streets in France, unless they had local law enforcement officers with them, in which case it would be classed as just another drugs gang being brought to justice. He cautioned that the French involvement may be an issue, no one could be sure they would all be committed to an American led mission. Some may even be on the payroll of the crime family and therefore an informer. There had already been feedback on adverse comments made by the gendarmes assigned to assist Robbie.

There was a knock on the door, Jack stopped while Shamir allowed the dinner buffet to be brought in and laid out, it smelt great. It was 5.30 pm, time for the team to be split into groups and given their tasks. *The food will no doubt help our brains to function better,* thought Jack.

"Any questions?" he asked again, there was a collective shake of heads, they were hungry. "In that case, we will break in a moment, then restart in thirty minutes on item three. You will have a couple of hours to get to the point where you can present back your initial thinking, but I should warn you now we may need to run past 10 pm to get this done, so be prepared. We will take another break when you have your plans sorted," Jack continued. He raised his hands and pointed to the food, "please eat."

The team got up to speculate on what they knew so far and attacked the buffet. The leaders picked up their share and returned to the table to talk about the way forward. The team lounged around looked at phones and made calls. Shamir managed to break away, whisper into her phone and wave her hand as Sahba demanded her return.

Just after 6 pm, JD called them to order. They returned to the table to see the teams appear on the TV screen.

1.   Team Alpha – Bordeaux, JD (Leader), Robbie, Lannie, Chinaman and gendarme officers.
2.   Beta – Marseille, Shamir (Leader), Hockey, Texas and police officers.
3.   Delta - (location TBA) Shamir (Leader) and Texas.
4.   Gamma – Bandol, Jack (Leader) and Baby Bob.
5.   Zeta – UK, UK BloedStone/UK govt.

JD talked about how they matched the projects with team members and specified what each group had to achieve, with more background intelligence being sent to their phones. "We need an action plan for each of the projects, how do we get them there and what to do to them when they're there, as Lannie suggested. Tonight we will focus on Bordeaux and Marseille as we are short of time. Baby Bob, you will help the Beta team and

Jack will help Alpha. Shamir, you should start work on Marseille, then look at the e-mail you have on Delta and think about what you would do if we go ahead. Oh yes, I just remembered you lucky people will be will be travelling by private jet courtesy of the French, co-piloted by John Huston, our very own cowboy from the Texas office."

"John or Texas as we call him, is a solid guy served with the cavalry for ten years I think, left in 2005 after the shit storms at Sadr City. He went back to Texas and learned to be a pilot with one of the oil companies and now contracts for us. He is available for a week and will be given the plans once we have signed them off. I also had a message that the General is going to call us at about 9 pm to see how we are progressing, so no pressure. Okay please get with your groups, let's make some plans," JD breathed a sigh of relief seeing the teams assemble to start work.

Initially, the groups thought the process of identifying alternative vaguely suitable actions to fulfil a single objective was easy, especially given their many years of practice in different theatres of operation. However, it soon became clear that picking the right ones, thousands of miles from the locations, was going to be almost impossible. There was only limited intelligence, they had no feel for the locations and little chance of further information until they arrived in situ. Once they realised the difficulties the arguments began, some noisier than others, they struggled with what to do. It was an unusual situation, the associates had more say in what to do than in a conventional project where they would mostly follow military orders. But it was a good test for them all and would help mark out the future leaders. JD thought Chinaman, when in business mode, and Lavender did especially well, even pushing herself into an unusual role.

Eventually, they arrived at the subject of weaponry and the ROE. In their role as private contractors, Stones associates were generally the best equipped in the field and would want it to stay that way. BloedStone assault team members were normally equipped with sidearms and rifle, selected from the alternatives used by the US or UK Special Forces. This could prove an issue for the teams working closely with the less well equipped local law enforcement officers. A list of requirements would be sent that night to the designated British Special Forces armourer, who would arrange for the equipment to be transported to Marseille ready for collection on Thursday morning. Once the mission was over, the weapons would be left for the French Stones armourer to return. Fresh equipment would be supplied to the US team when they reached Iraq. As for setting ROE, always a contentious subject, the group leaders were non-committal preferring a promise to be flexible in approach given the huge difference in numbers.

The absence of Robbie and Texas caused only minor concerns, they were considered seasoned professionals who would be able to pick up their roles quickly.

At around 9.30 pm the Bordeaux and Marseille groups were ready to present their plans to the full team. JD started by asking Shamir to run through her Marseille project before adding a warning they would pause when the General called. They were making good progress until a video call came through at 10 pm from their CEO. He gave them a 10-minute motivational speech covering the importance of the mission, how the French were depending on them to get the job done and his great faith in their abilities. *All good stuff to get them fired up and on board to do a great job for the company,* thought JD.

Speech over the team went back to their peer group reviews and were able to sign off the plans with only a few changes. Although they registered concerns about the lack of intelligence on the strength and weaponry of the opposition – they always did that. The groups identified the remaining tasks as follows:

1.   Fleshing out the activities to improve the chances of success.

2.   Memorising what they were going to do.

3.   Envisioning how the venture would most likely play out.

4.   Developing a Plan B in case there was a serious change to the operating environment.

5.   Memorising photos of the key players in the Martin crime family.

It took another two hours for the groups to feel confident they had a chance to execute successfully. To reinforce that conviction, introduce flexibility and prepare some Plan B scenarios, they would run through their intentions a few more times as individuals or in groups, before they landed in France.

JD brought the session to a close, "we are done, for now, it's only one in the morning so not much of an overrun," bringing a few sniggers. "Thanks for all for your hard work which looks great to me, give yourself a round of applause," which he and Jack started. Another thing Nigel had taught him. They all hooted, laughed, and joined in the celebration, while JD quietly wished Nigel success for the return flight for some other unsuspecting passenger.

"One last thing," he said loudly, picking up his phone. "Before you all go and play the tables, let me tell you about the flights then I will send them to you.

•   Depart Vegas, tomorrow at 11.00 all teams.

•   Arrive at London Stansted airport Thursday 06.00 British time– re-fuel and pick up additional passengers.

•   Depart London for Marseilles 07.00 – all teams.

•   Arrive at Marseille Provence Airport – 09.00 - Teams Beta and Gamma disembark for projects in Bandol and Marseille. Plus maybe Delta.

      o   Pick-up Martin family members 2-3 in number.

- Depart Marseille airport for Bordeaux – 10.00 - Alpha team and Martin members.

- Arrive Bordeaux-Merignac airport – by 12.00 Team Alpha disembark with Martin members and head for Chateau du Carys in the St Emilion region.

"You all need to be at the airport in the private departure lounge at around 9 am for final clearance. Any questions?" he asked and once more there was silence. "Don't eat too much for breakfast," he continued "there will be plenty of food on the plane and remember you will get dinner after breakfast and no lunch so that will save you calories," he joked without much response. He finished with, "okay everyone GO and don't stay up all night." They were out of the suite in record time.

JD was tired having slept badly on his last night in Mexico. Jack, was ready to collapse from lack of sleep and jet lag, but would still wake up by 6 am. A beaming Shamir looked at the two men.

"Hey, not bad for two old ones," she said. "I learnt a lot today, I'm grateful, thanks. Let's hope the Iraq mission goes as well," she made a tiny bow and left the room. They looked at each other and JD pulled Jack to his feet laughing.

"Still got it, right?" said Jack.

"Let's hope so, replied JD. "I did enjoy the meeting and watching the next generation coming through, especially our Shamir. You know, she still makes me shiver every time I look into her eyes."

"Let's go, old man, she would kill you now!" and they both laughed.

Chapter 37: Marseille, Wednesday morning

Madame Martin looked out over the city from her office in the family villa, she was having a difficult time controlling her husband's empire and its misogynist members. Despite what they said, none of them had taken kindly to being managed by a woman, let alone one who had never worked in the illicit drugs industry. But news the Englishman had agreed to settle their dispute buoyed her mood while she waited for the 1 o'clock meeting with her direct reports. *Perhaps that's a good omen,* she thought watching the sun appear after another heavy shower. Over the next few days, it would be essential for the business that she effectively directed the activities of her men while she completed final negotiations with Jack and the owners of De Beaux Endroits. She would use skills acquired during her twenty-year business career to both encourage and coerce the members to do what she wanted. They would be working on projects in at least three if not four different places in France. She knew this was going to be difficult for several reasons, not least because she had agreed to Jack's tight schedule for Thursday and Friday. Yet she was convinced she knew exactly what to do, *I will focus them with fear,* she thought. *If they don't do what I ask and we fail to get the money, they will all be out of work. Most of them will never get another job as good as this, they are more likely to be killed or finish up in prison.*

She remembered her lover's observations that one or maybe both of the "two Ps" were planning to engineer a takeover of the business and dispose of her. *One of them has taken Thierry, but which one?* She wondered. *For now, I must avoid conflict, act as though all is well and ensure everyone is working together to boost our, NO my, fortune.* A sudden attack of nerves jolted her she began to feel stressed believing only success would save her and Thierry if he was still alive. She reverted to yoga deep breathing exercises to regain her calm. For a moment she was captivated by the sun's rays reaching through the dark clouds to light up the harbour water, then they were gone. Madame Martin shook off her torpor it was time to get going, adrenaline surged through her. She checked the mirror, gathered up her papers, paused to sit and await confirmation her men were assembled. "Waiting, WAITING FOR ME, their Mistress," she snarled then shushed herself.

To anyone watching, the arrival of the gang members looked like a scene from an Italian mafia movie. Top dogs, the "two P's" arrived in separate cars, just before the allotted time, each with an escort. Pascal had been driven by one of Chevy's men, while Patrice drove with Cyrano riding shotgun. They both wore suits, left their cars slowly and looked around before walking up the driveway. Guards were looking on from all the vantage points with sidearms hidden and assault rifles out of sight but ready to use. Henri was nearly late so had to run up the drive nodding apologies to the guards as he went. The "two P's" scowled at him when he arrived in the sitting room where they had congregated prior to commencing proceedings.

Meetings of this nature were always held in the imposing dining room, which doubled as a meeting room and would perhaps be a board room for a large successful business. Madame took up her usual seat at the near end of the 20 seater table and commanded her assistant to have the "guys come in'. She welcomed them, they took up their usual seats, which saw Pascal and Patrice to right and left of Matisse's old seat at the far end. Mid-table saw Henri, Chevy, Cyrano, Yves and Harbin, who was considered just below Chevy in seniority. Madame Martin's right side was empty while M. Labette took up a new position to her left. The unexpected attendee was the Family's Chief Accountant, Company Secretary and official record keeper of what needed to be kept. Twenty-five years of service had made him indispensable, a man who knew where all the so-called bodies were buried, a man kept in a gilded cage in a nearby guarded villa. To make the arrangement work, he was supplied with whatever he needed or wanted including on occasions, a female being traded by Henri. Indeed M. Labette liked his living arrangements so much he had sworn an oath of devotion to his new leader. He was one of the few outside this inner circle who knew the fate of the former leader Matisse Martin. He was conscious they needed a deal quickly if he was to maintain his self-indulgent lifestyle.

There was no laptop or technology in use at this meeting, the only record kept by M. Labette would be of the actions each member "agreed" to undertake. The attendees knew that failures were never brought up on these occasions usually because the person responsible would be unable to attend the next meeting. The reason for their non-appearance depended mostly on the criticality of the failure. A minor infraction would mean some unpleasant task like piloting a boatload of illegal migrants across the English Channel. But a major transgression would probably result in an unpleasant meeting with someone like Lena Peja.

Madame began, "before we speak about the next two days we must talk about our revered former leader my husband, Matisse, and our missing son, your colleague and friend, Thierry. We agreed at the last meeting not to tell anyone about my husband until our business has been secured. That means we must now get through the next few days without any outside interference. Are we still in agreement?" she looked at the faces around the table. These meetings required everyone to state their position in public, nods were not enough, there was no secret voting. Any opinion that dissented from the majority, was a cause for a debate in case it had merit. Most of the time it was purely preference rather than fact-based and would be quickly discounted but not necessarily forgotten.

While the men called out their vote, Madame Martin drifted back to past meetings where few, other than her son, had been willing to disagree on anything of importance. Matisse had indulged Thierry's dissent, even when he argued that 21st century STP (smuggling, trafficking and prostitution) was getting too risky for the limited returns. He suggested the Family should get out of such a degrading business by selling their contacts to another criminal gang. He advocated "going legal" as the best way forward. His behaviour had made him enemies within the group not least

M. Labette, an avid supporter of STP. Matisse had kept him safe, but with him gone she now realised too late, it was only a matter of time before he would be attacked in some way. *No doubt taken by one of his so-called colleagues,* she thought. It was silent again after a round of "Oui", unsurprisingly there had been no dissenters to her request, at least not yet.

"Next, has anyone heard about or from Thierry or know where he might be?" she asked hopefully but with no expectation of a positive response. "I haven't received a ransom request or anything like it. Does anyone know where he is or how we might find him?" she asked again. "We will need to search for him in a few days when we have more time." She knew that securing the business was the top priority for now, although she would have preferred to send them all out immediately to look for him. "Please answer today, one word will do if you have heard nothing or have no idea," almost spitting out the words. They ignored her increasing emotion and replied with a "non" that sounded like they just declined a coffee. *Not a surprise,* she thought. *But at least one of them knows something, I'm sure.* Yves started to tell her, supposedly on behalf of the group, how sorry he was about Thierry and how sure he was they would find him. When he finished, most mumbled something except for Henri and Pascal who spoke loudly about how upsetting it was and they would do terrible things to whoever was responsible for such a heinous act against the Family. Madame Martin smiled at the two men while being reminded of the often misquoted Shakespearian dialogue from her school days "...*doth protest too much methinks.*

"We WILL find him, but in searching, we must not arouse suspicions amongst other families and gangs or we will have difficult questions to answer," Madame cautioned. Perhaps we should stick to saying father and son are away working together. Fortunately, the search by that silly girlfriend of his, that caused us so much trouble, is over and she has returned to England. I hope we won't be seeing any of them again," this time lots of nods of agreement around the table.

Madame continued, "now let's talk about our current businesses and what we must do to save them after the attack on our warehouse." She called upon the three most senior members to report on their domains, knowing this would cause them some embarrassment. The assessments were downbeat. A shortage of cash, saleable drugs, migrants to traffick and stricter controls on prostitution. Supposedly there was little to be done to improve things but the situation was not yet desperate, even though their cash was locked up in the warehouse cellar.

When it came to her turn, Madame Martin enjoyed talking about the profitability of their legal businesses which had been facilitated by the high level of funding from drug sales. Now the companies carried considerable amounts of free cash which she would not be sharing with this group. The team showed no interest in her success or even worried about it. This was mostly because her business did not generate a ton of cash that could be stacked on wooden pallets. No one bothered to ask M. Labette any questions, so he said nothing but gave an admiring nod at the end of her presentation. A smiling Madame Martin ignored their indifference, instead, she called for a short break to enjoy lunch.

The meeting restarted at 2 30 pm, Madame Martin explained that restoration of their fortune required the successful completion of several activities in the next two days. She looked at the worried men and tried to motivate them one last time. "The money we are getting will substantially strengthen our legitimate businesses" she beamed, before remembering to say, "and our drugs operation of course." The incentive missed the mark, now they believed she intended to get rid of the other businesses and probably those members who were not in Chevy's drug team. Which of course was her real objective.

"To do this we are going to split our team into three groups each with a single job to do," she said confidently while looking around the table. The men perked up at the thought of some action, "I will start by telling each of you where you are going and what you must do when you get there. Then you must give your acceptance." This was the way Matisse operated, it had usually been successful even though it lacked the "top-down" meets "bottom up" planning favoured by the Stones team. Ironically it bore similarities to the way police create special-purpose teams for specific projects. The men in the room were Martin family veterans and knew what it took to lead their team and get things done. That made it easier for Madame Martin, she only had to tell them what to achieve then leave it to them to decide how.

She started, "Patrice you are already booked to go to Bordeaux with Jack who is representing the owners of De Beaux Endroits, or "DBE" as I will call it. You met him in London on Monday to accept their surrender, following your activities to encourage DBE to compensate us for the losses they caused us. We must congratulate you on that," she started to tap the table. Most of the others joined in, banging on the table, cheering their colleague while Patrice was bowing and smiling. Pascal was far less ebullient, he clapped slowly while thinking about what this would mean for his future. She raised her hand, they stopped. "You are to inspect the DBE vineyard, Chateau du Carys. I am told the property is worth many millions of euros. You should make sure it is real and as good as they claim, we will probably own it, once the deal is concluded."

Patrice looked surprised for a moment, struggling with how the Martins could own one of the vineyards where he had implemented the wine scam for his personal rather than the Family's benefit. He decided to call Frederic right after the meeting to agree on a plan for the next day making sure the Stones executive did not did speak to anyone especially Yves - who had the Martin's official list of vineyards being scammed.

"Are you alright?" Madame Martin asked. "You look worried, is there a problem?" by this time everyone was looking at the silent man.

"Yes, no, I'm fine, I was just running through the details for my trip and remembered I did not have the flight times and so on," he improvised. "I'm happy to go to St Emilion with Jack and look at the property," he continued still looking confused. His mind was searching for a course of action while his mouth was talking about something entirely different.

"I believe you are to being collected at Marseille airport at 9 am tomorrow, is that not true?" she wanted to make sure he knew the arrangements. "Remember they sent you details about where to meet, I think they are using an executive jet, so enjoy it." His behaviour set off alarm bells in her head, *this is not the annoying boastful Patrice I'm used to, he seems distracted, I wonder what's wrong? What will I do if he decides not to go to Bordeaux?*

'Sorry yes, I forgot I have the details or just received them," Patrice produced a weak smile and waggled his phone. He was still reeling from the surprise and knowing he would not survive the discovery of cheating the Martins.

"Is there anything you need?"

Having recovered enough to answer Madame's questions, he told her he would take two of his men to help with the inspection, to ensure the English did not play the fool with him.

"D'accord, what will you inspect."

He told her he would go through the buildings, the vineyard and the books, something he heard you did on these occasions. He would demand that Jack follow him everywhere just so he would be like a dog, doing as commanded by his master. That way he could humiliate him for what he did in St Albans.

"D'accord, you can tell me later about St Albans," she smiled, happy the man had returned to his irritating self. Patrice had already suggested to her nothing happened in St Albans, it was Jack wasting time and for her to forget about it now that the Englishman had agreed to their demands.

She turned to the other side of the table, "Pascal, you are going back to our warehouse with your men to get the drugs and money hidden in the cellar." He looked surprised. "Don't worry, as part of the deal we'll get some friends who will let you in." He looked happier but would still need to be convinced. "You will be contacted by your new benefactor, on this phone," she slid the box across the table. "Someone from DBE will call to meet you on Thursday afternoon where they will explain the arrangements for getting in and out of the warehouse and show you where your trucks will be parked. Our friends will remove the guards so you can get in through the old building next door, once it starts getting dark. You will have a couple of hours to collect our money and the stuff," she hated using its name. "You will then take it to a new location they show you and guard it until I get there on Friday morning. Once that is done you can work on a plan to get the business up and going, which we can start on Friday. Happy?" she asked adrenaline driving her on.

"Ca a l'air bien, can I tell our entrepreneurs and their customers we will resume supply next week," a happy-sounding Pascal asked, delighted at the thought of being back in business.

"From Sunday would be acceptable," said Madame Martin to an admiring Pascal momentarily forgetting he wanted to replace her for being incompetent. He was intrigued to know how she pulled off such a smart deal. Anticipating his questions, she told him the assistance was part of the compensation she agreed with the English company. "They have some police officers on their payroll as they are connected to an offshore company who can do things the rest of us can't."

He nodded with admiration, thinking, *she would be a good assistant when this was all over. Perhaps Matisse would be happy for me to make his beautiful wife useful for more than business.* He smiled to himself.

Madame turned to Henri, regretting it was necessary to carry on with his business, but Stones had encouraged her so she could get the cash. "You are going to catch a plane to Lille, then drive to Calais to take charge of the operations there." He perked up. "You must get the Africans we have, more if there are any with cash onto trucks or boats and send them to England where they want to be." He nodded thankfully. "For those going over the water, we have arranged for boats and there will be some "life things" available which they must wear," she did not know the name for the preservers. She comforted herself by saying, "the boats only have to get out into the channel and the English will pick them up and look after them. They never send anyone back after that as far as I know." Then deluding herself by saying, "this is a service we provide for the Africans who have family in England and the local French people who don't want these people in their towns."

For those Africans who will go in trucks, our local man will give you the names of the drivers you must use. Go with one of them, drive one of the trucks if you want," she smirked at Henri who she disliked intently for loving his job. "Meet with Saville in Dover port or close by, he will tell you where and help you with the trip. You will take two of your men with you to make sure everyone follows these instructions. Is that clear?" Henri gave a smiley nod. "It is all arranged for Friday morning so you must go tomorrow. When you arrive you must make sure that everything is in order and if not you must call me."

"Thank you, Madame Martin, I will do as you wish, it will be my pleasure," he said having expected to be sacked, but now with an important task to get done. Henri was very pleased.

"M. Labette, Yves and I will be going to Bandol to finalise the remaining payments and arrange for a security contract to protect DBE in the future. One that will stop other families or cartels from interfering with our business in France. It's getting dangerous here, it will be a very expensive contract," she sniggered and everyone joined in, including the accountant who was happy to be allowed out for the day.

Pascal was bored, the discussion was not about him. He was considering whether Matisse was a cuckold and Yves was the lover. If that were true then who knew about it, he decided it didn't matter when he took her for himself, he would get rid of Yves.

Madame Martin smiled and thanked them for their loyalty and reinforced the message that next week they would be getting back to their best. They replied by slapping the table and shouting allegiance to the Martin family. They were fired up and ready for action, she had done well. She stood, grinned in triumph, bowed slightly and left the room for her office. Out of sight she felt sick with the strain of dealing with these men and closed the door to recover. Back in the meeting room, the members were happily chatting with each other, promising to keep in touch and to be successful in their endeavours. They embraced each other wildly and left the room delighted to be getting back to work.

It was 5 pm French time and Madame Martin had done her job well now it was mostly out of her hands.

With the meeting over and the members on their way home, messages were being sent and received in Algiers, Bandol, Bordeaux, Calais, California, Dover, Las Vegas, London and St Albans - everything was on schedule.

Chapter 38: Bordeaux, Wednesday afternoon

Robbie had spent the morning having breakfast and drinking coffee with a repentant Frederic still fearing for his life. The Stones CEO was prepared to indulge him while they waited for Madame Martin's lunchtime meeting to finish. Frederic had begun by recounting how he was forced to co-operate with the Martin family. He described how he was groomed by a stunning male dancer who seduced him in the washroom of a club in Marseille. The resulting pictures were sent to him and at least one posted on the web to make sure he agreed to do their bidding. The Martins wanted him as a way to make contact and prepare the chateaux and vineyard owners for criminal ventures. The seduction story was credible, Frederic was beautiful for a man but the excuse paled when Stones forensic accountants found he had been trying to hide cash payments in French banks. *I think it was cash rather than blackmail that turned our Freddy,* decided Robbie. *How pathetic to try and hide money from us, a company that knows more about hiding money than anyone.* Becoming emotional he continued thinking, *how many times did I warn him not to treat the company as a chocolate box for his personal enjoyment?*

Frederic still in pain from his sprained wrist, interrupted Robbie's thoughts by talking about his current lover causing him lots of stress, apparently because he was so untrustworthy when it came to other men. The Stones CEO knew this to be a lie, he had secretly spoken to Emile on several occasions to reassure the young man that Frederic was a good guy, despite his occasional erratic behaviour.

The rest of the morning was consumed with gathering intelligence about wine fraud. Robbie had asked Claude to join them and help catalogue the locations involved. The listing would be divided into those vineyards entangled with the Martin family and those that were somehow improperly involved with other parties. The Estate Manager immediately offered a third category; those places like Chateau du Carys that were not known to the Martin family but had been ensnared by Frederic and Patrice for their benefit only. *Well done Claude*, Robbie thought. *He must be hoping to keep his job, who knows maybe he will? That said I'm not sure yet about this third group or what it means to be part of it.*

The morning progressed slowly for Robbie but to keep up the momentum he asked Claude and Frederic to draw up a list of the three groups. He provided them with his laptop to produce a spreadsheet. Nothing much happened, one did not know how to and the other did not want to. Robbie built it himself to store data in an organised way, it would be swapped to other database software later. The other two men watched making no contribution, Robbie demanded they complete the three groups containing:

- The name of Chateau/Domaine/Vineyard.
- Owner/Manager/other contacts.
- Financial information (columns for revenues, bottle price range, case quantities and anything else they knew).
- Contact details. (address, phone number etc.)
- Notes on the location.

That proved to be the easy bit, however, Frederic suffered a serious bout of amnesia leaving Claude in command. The Estate Manager then completed what little he claimed to know while Frederic sat in silence. After he finished, the spreadsheet still looking empty until Frederic agreed to type in a few vineyards but claimed not to know much about them or their contact details. With such limited progress, Claude fearing for his future turned informer and like a child, told teacher that Frederic wasn't doing anything. The Englishman asked Claude to go and make some coffee and he sat down in the still-warm seat. "Freddy, it seems that you fear the Martin family more than you fear me, is that right?" he asked slowly and menacingly. There was no response, it looked like the younger man had gone into a trance brought on by fear.

But he replied, "if I tell you anything then Patrice will kill me and Emile, I know that you would not do such a terrible thing to us. You will forgive me and we can still be friends," he continued gambling Robbie still had some feelings for him.

"Freddy you are right, I have calmed down since you attempted the great escape. However, some people trained to extract information in the most unexpected ways are on the way here. I suspect they are far worse than Patrice would ever dream of. Once they are done, they will no doubt have to get rid of you to avoid any questions. Why not give me the information now and save yourself all that trouble. Then we will get Emile here and you can spend time with him. I still have your phone so shall I call him for you?" No response, Frederic sat sulking. Robbie called for Claude and they went through what little information they had.

When Frederic stood up to leave the room, the Stones CEO pushed him back into his seat suddenly cuffing his undamaged wrist to the arm of the chair. "Courtesy of those nice police officers you saw earlier," he said. Frederic looked surprised at the unexpected aggression. Robbie was irritated but knew it was too early to get violent, he still had until the end of Friday to produce the details needed. If it wasn't coming from Frederic then they would get it from Patrice or his men, or Jack would get it from Madame Martin or one of her people. But they would get it, either the easy way or extract it, the painful way.

While the Martin family continued their meeting in Marseille, Claude decided it was time for his special tea, Frederic was still refusing to speak and Robbie was impatiently waiting for some action. He called Miss Elizabeth but just as they started to speak another call came through. He apologised explained he had to take it and promised to call back.

"How are you, my friend?" Robbie said to the caller and looked happy by the reply. "They managed to get you off the beach then?" he continued. "When will you be here I understand we are the last stop?" he said extra loudly, for Frederic to hear. After some more conversation, he said, "no, I haven't got all the information from Freddy, he is being difficult." After another reply from the caller, he walked over to Frederic. "Okay, I will give him the phone but he can't move as he's attached to a chair. It's for you, Freddy," Robbie handing the phone to the Frenchman's free hand.

"No, no I can't they will kill me, I told Robbie," replied Frederic to the caller. The Frenchman could hear the man speaking to someone in the background about bringing some of his tools to do some work on an un-co-operative Frenchie. Then he heard another man agree and laugh while saying he would bring a shovel for afterwards. In normal times perhaps this would be a joke, but for Frederic, this was not a normal time.

"Okay, okay," shouted Frederic. Turning to Robbie he continued, "he's worse than you, he is that JD man. I know of him, he would kill me while eating his lunch." In past times Frederic had heard a drunken Robbie tell frightening stories of JD and mad Jack. Such stories grew in the telling, but they are stories that men only tell men they know, because they are so appalling. Frederic became more anxious when he thought, *this man was for real and is coming here to punish me.* "He wants you back," said Frederic and handed the phone to Robbie who spent the next twenty minutes in earnest conversation. After the call ended it was 7.30 am in Vegas. JD pocketed his phone and decided it was time to have a big American breakfast before leaving, something he missed living in Mexico.

Robbie called Claude back into the room and watched as they restarted work on the spreadsheet. He looked at his watch and thought, *must call Miss Elizabeth.* The next forty-five minutes evaporated as he spoke with his daughter. He cautioned her about avoiding unnecessary risks and keeping herself safe. He told her he was proud of the support she had given with the events in St Albans and the continued help with the company's mission in West London. He knew it would break his heart if anything happened to her, especially while he was here in France. He went back to reviewing the work of the other two, checking how productive they were being.

Wow, that is a lot of fine vineyards the Martin's have messed up, thought Robbie, but not quite as good as the *list of places that Freddy and his mate Patrice have procured for their own misuse. I'm guessing there must be more. To fix this, it will take a lot of time and money, as will trying to keep it quiet. Hopefully, there will be a large fee involved to make it worth our while,* he thought with a smile.

Robbie was becoming impatient, his Breitling ticked around to 5 pm and still no call to action. Ten minutes later a phone rang, he didn't pick it up, it is was Frederic's phone. He looked at the caller ID which showed "Patty'. He let it ring off.

"Who is Patty?" he asked Frederic who was still sulking and sucking down a soda. The Frenchman ignored the question, Robbie moved forward aggressively, "I said who is Patty?" Turning away he picked up the phone and studied recent calls, then messages and very quickly identified it was Patrice. He thought, *shit I should have checked all this before now, aargh, I must be getting out of touch.* Turning to Frederic he said, "I bet your friend Patty is calling you to check if everything is good with your little business on the side. You are going to call him back tell him you're fine and all is quiet here, do you understand?" He shouted for Claude who appeared with phone to his ear. He mouthed the question "Is that Patrice?" Claude nodded. "Drop the call, make a noise and ring off" he said. The Estate Manager responded by announcing they had phone problems again today and he could not hear him but not to worry he would find Frederic and have him call and rang off. *Nice, I am definitely warming to our man Claude,* thought Robbie.

"Now we have a little more time let's make sure we are all on the same page," he said to the two men. The Stones CEO continued, "Freddy, where is Emile? Call and tell him to stay away, we don't want anything silly to happen do we? If we can't contact him then we must watch out for him," looking at Frederic again. The man was confused, started shaking and then nodding his head. This time Robbie's phone rang, the caller gave him a message. "Ok, we'll be ready, thanks for the call," he replied and rang off.

He returned to their preparations by telling them that everything must be NORMAL at the Chateau. He continued, "tomorrow afternoon a meeting will be held at Le Beaux to settle any differences between Stones and the Martin family. Nothing must be done or said that would put that negotiation in jeopardy. That means that you Freddy will not speak to Patrice or anyone else until after that meeting. Do you understand? We are going to play the broken phone and no service game," Frederic started to protest but gave up when Robbie gave him a withering look. Claude nodded enthusiastically.

"Claude please inform Madame," who had forgiven Robbie for the rough treatment, "we would like an early dinner, an early night and an early start in the morning. Plus watch out for Emile we don't want him screwing things up." Claude went off to make the arrangements and uncork the 2010 vintage he kept for best. Frederic was allowed to use the toilet then take a stroll outside. Robbie nodded to the rented police officers as they left the building to walk along the internal road towards the vines. Frederic looked around for a way to escape, saw no one and suddenly bolted towards the far end of the vineyard, hoping the darkness would be his friend. Robbie watched him... *Why do they always run?* he thought. Frederic made about two hundred meters before a searchlight picked him out at the far end of the field and the large officers rushed after him in the vineyard's 4X4. They jumped out and unnecessarily pointed their Sigs at him. He dropped to his knees as one of them shouted to lie down and put arms behind his back so they could cuff him. Foiled by a fat wrist, the officer threw Frederic into the back seat and sat next to him.

After a few minutes, the vehicle was parked next to where Robbie was still standing. Frederic was dragged out and presented to his boss who pointed inside, "why do they always run?" He clipped the runaway on the side of the head as he was dragged past him on the way to a locked room for a night of solitude.

Chapter 39: South Kensington, Wednesday afternoon

In West London, Sylvain had just finished lunch and was struggling up the staircase to the gang's meeting room. *Must find somewhere downstairs for this*, he thought, rather than he should lose weight and drink less at lunchtime. The gang boss had built up an eclectic but generally reliable team of European ruffians. Today he had summoned his senior people to an after-lunch meeting, which they knew meant 2.30 pm. Sylvain rarely fed his troops, he thought of them as total philistines, only capable of carrying out orders, eating fast food and abusing his women. The exception was the exotic Lena Peja introduced to him by Patrice. Sylvain had no idea where she was from and so far the Martin member had avoided telling him. He fantasised about her, what he hadn't seen was the bottom of her snake tattoo and the genital piercings, what he had seen, was her being a psycho, feeling no guilt, when executing his enemies or "worn out" women. He even admired her for it, she liked doing it and that made her even more desirable to him. He believed she would have been a much better choice to lead the attack on the Englishman's home rather than Patrice who was pleasant enough but une mauviette.

The Kensington team plus Saville, from the Martin family, strolled in and sat down. They listened while Sylvain continued to berate someone on his phone. They had all been on the receiving end after making mistakes. It sounded like one of his girls had failed to find her customer or lost him so he was threatening all manner of retribution. Fortunately, he rarely carried out his threats although when he did, Lena made sure they were never heard of again. Some of the team stayed because they were too frightened to leave, but others tolerated his behaviour because he rewarded them so well.

"Men and Pen," he said chuckling to the assembled team. "Today I will tell you what you must do in the next two days." He explained the agreement with the Martin family to transfer people, as he called it, from Calais to Dover and then onto London. He reckoned because so many were trying to get across the channel the odds for success were high but regretted the fees were getting lower. He set about telling each of them where they should go, who to take with them and what to do with the people they smuggled. One difference on this mission would be the use of Saville as the leader rather than one of his men. "Do we take orders from Saville on the way down to Dover or just when we get there?" asked Dave Bender acting as a professional idiot, the gang's main getaway driver, Patrice's temporary chauffeur and the MI5 agent in residence.

'Listen wanker, I said from when you leave here," came the reply. Sylvain had expected a stupid question from the fool, *If only he were not such a good driver,* he thought.

Dave just tutted and looked vaguely into space. There followed a short discussion with only a few questions, they had done this so many times before - they were professionals!

"One last thing," he said turning to Saville. "You must let me know if Henri does not arrive. He is supposed to text you which truck he's in. You are to meet at the services place at Junction 11 on the M20 when you get across."

"Cool no problem," he responded.

"That's it, no fuck-ups, now get going and I will see you when you get back. Not you Terry," he said to his executioner in chief and former east end gangster. Although past his prime and not great on his feet he was still a deadly shot with his American made weapons of choice either a CT M200 or BM82. "I have a special job that needs doing and it pays a big bonus. The sort of thing you love and in the sunshine too." Terry Lamb liked the sound of a little trip it could be so cold in London in autumn. "You need to take two of my boys with you to help." Before Terry could speak, "how about the Albanians they're good workers and have some British papers. We know where their families live so they won't run off and leave you."

"Yeah Jon and Kot, are fine for me," he replied. "What can I do for you guv and how much is it worth," he continued. "I'm guessing you want someone to go away."

"Yes I do and I will pay two for expenses, five more as a bonus for you and one each for the Albanians when the job is finished. I need it done by the end of Friday this week."

"Sounds good to me," Terry replied. Sylvain explained the job in more detail than normal, occasionally breaking into French when he could not find the right English word. Terry listened intently and understood most of the abusive French words. He was surprised at the target whom he knew but was persuaded it was necessary and would lead to an increase for his pension fund. When Sylvain had finished Terry nodded and asked, "who do I get the tickets and hotel from guv?"

Sylvain looked at his watch it was nearly 6.00 pm, "I'll let you know more when I get a call in the next few minutes." His phone rang almost straight away, "Oui, bon, text me the name and I will call you back in a few minutes. Terry, you must do this job soon, I will let you know who has the items you need. Go and talk to your men and make sure they say nothing to anyone. Don't tell them who they are going to remove until you get there. Any problems let me know, but you must go tomorrow."

I like Terry, he thought, *he does what I want, just like Lena. I must arrange for her to come over to dinner tomorrow night and then have a… what is it, ahh yes a sleepover.* With an odious smile on his face, his mind contemplating the pleasure he would get from handling her body. A noise outside the room caused him to exit his ruminations. It was his early evening double expresso being delivered by one of his favourites. He reached out to fondle her rear as she put the saucer down. Lucky for her he had to answer his phone. He exchanged salutations with the caller before explaining arrangements were made for the two tasks and saw no reason why they would not be successful.

On the call, Un gros moaned about everything including Patrice hiding the demise of his friend Matisse. Pascal, with other things on his mind, listened, sympathised and gave him a contact who would provide travel details and weapons for his men. They moved to the next task.

"To take over the Family we must get rid of her son," Pascal said. "Or he will cause problems for us."

"I agree," replied Sylvain. "I should've told Terry to deal with him at the beginning or put him over the side of your boat. But no, we were nice and went through all the trouble of getting him to go to meet his mother," they laughed. Sylvain insisting on continuing, "then using one of your boats we took him to North Africa to stay in a hotel like he was on holiday." Pascal listened to his humorous ranting and waited for him to stop. "I must be going soft in my old age" he finished.

"Do you have any other men I can use if I decide to go to Africa and get rid of him?" asked the Martin member.

"I have Dobo one of our Bulgarians, the other got arrested in St Albans after that farce with Patrice and one Albanian left, called Ton. They are good at taking orders and have taken care of some problems for me. But they don't speak French and their English is only just passable but you must just speak slowly. But you should be alright with them if all you're going to do is get rid of the boy. I will get my forger to make some visas for them tomorrow. He's good at making documents despite being English. It is the same man who provides the travel stuff and weapons."

"Merci, that's good," replied Pascal and they wished each other the best of fortune. Both men were looking forward to the next couple of days, believing the activities would be an exciting diversion. They enjoyed the evening with their chosen women and stayed up late, for them, the night came and went as usual.

In the Mojave Desert, the door of the Gulfstream jet closed for yet another on-time departure to London, Stanstead airport.

Chapter 40: Las Vegas and in transit to London, Wednesday afternoon (local time)

More than an hour before take-off, the BloedStone associates, this time looking like a group of WWF wrestlers both in size and dress, walked to the plane arguing about the win percentage in Vegas. Given the routing, schedule and stopping places the General had provided an executive jet. On this occasion, their French sponsor's concern for his country meant he agreed to help with the cost before the Stones Chairman resorted to the "valiant men and women on their way to Iraq" speech. The team were impressed with their "kite", it was fitted with tables to work and beds to sleep.

Once seated JD gave another much shorter motivational speech ending with everyone should be careful. He reminded them where they would get their weapons and restated the ROE would be given by the team leaders at their locations. He continued with providing the latest intelligence and ended by saying after eating they should sleep as much as possible on the way to Stanstead. Then once they left London for Marseille they should get into their groups and work on their plans.

Texas sitting in the right-hand seat of the cockpit gave instructions for everyone to prepare to leave, while the Captain completed his routine and obtained permission. A few minutes later Flight STE 044 trundled along a taxiway.

Chinaman who never gambled was still arguing that punters get back 95% of their stake. Lannie who did, was getting angry, she told him he was delusional it was much less and only a statistical measure as most people lose all their money. Shamir ignored them, instead preferring to install her earpods to listen to the 2018 Anniversary White album and singing along quietly. Eventually, they stopped talking, to the relief of JD and Jack, it even went quiet for a while as the attendants served aperitifs and then lunch.

Things seemed to be going well until Chinaman decided he wanted to talk with his new friend Hockey.

"Hey man."

"Hey," replied Hockey grudgingly looking up from his Robert Reich book.

"Hockey or should I call you Richard as Lavatree does?"

"You mean Lavender."

"Oh sorry, Lavender. Just wanted to say that I don't understand why you're called Hockey Stick just because your old girlfriend played hockey."

Richard thought he should reply to clear things up, "originally the name was longer because it rhymes with dick and the guys thought it was funny. But they shortened it to hockey stick and now hockey to make it more acceptable. Look, you can call me either it's not a problem," Hockey said finally wishing he had ignored him.

"I was sorry to hear about Lavatree's cousin being involved in a drugs group and not being able to go to school and got thrown out. Where I come from in Chicago, drugs were the ONLY thing that kept many people going because of the shit we lived in."

"Not sure what you heard, but OUR cousin is not on drugs, he is involved in a chat room that keeps him up all night, so he sleeps during the day. That's what got him suspended from school" replied Hockey clarifying the situation.

"These kids, they need a bit more discipline don't you think? Can't go to school because he's chatting all night. What's wrong with his parents why don't they do something or are they liberal jerks? They need to get him sorted out. I bet he is like that kid who keeps going about global warming, what's her name? She should be back in school learning, not shouting about catastrophes she knows nothing about," Chinaman finished his rant.

"Look there is nothing wrong with being worried about the climate and it's Trump who is causing all the strife in the world," Hockey got louder and angrier.

Chinaman continued, "look the problem with you guys is that you always have to have a cause to worry about instead of just working hard, making money and living. Under "Obamee" you seemed to go quiet and spend all your time worrying about climate change and healthcare. Man, it was peaceful apart from the occasional demo. Now we have Mr Trump in charge you're wasting your time again doing nothing but complaining."

'There is a climate problem, look at the fires in California and now Australia, these places are so dry, then we have floods in England and India because they have too much rain. We must do more to save the planet for our children. We must cut down on carbon gases and stop using plastic," Hockey responded with passion. Although he knew he was wasting his time trying to convince Chinaman.

"You're talking about two different things," replied Chinaman, climate change is the result of the planet fighting back against us having too many people doing too many things on it, and plastic waste is caused by stupid people."

"Don't you think that's too simplistic, you are not taking things seriously are you?"

"Hockey, I am not going to cut down on my driving or flying or anything else just so those guys over in China and India can have loads of kids. We should start there. From what I can see you guys just want to share everything rather than earn it. I bet that if there were ten of you liberals on a raft with food enough for four, you would share it out so that you all died together. If it were me, I would throw four overboard and take a chance on saving six."

'You're insane, I can't talk to you," Hockey turned away in frustration.

"I am going for a piss" said Chinaman.

"I hope he's not going to work out how much carbon he can save by shooting people in Iraq," laughed Jack, popping up to see what the commotion was all about. "How are you getting on with your new best friend?" he said jokingly but also worrying about conflict.

"He's a crazy bastard," replied Hockey.

"Agreed, but he is a great man to have by your side when things get difficult. There is no one better, even if he won't stop talking while he's there," Jack laughed again.

"I don't doubt it, I will be okay and learn to love him especially as he is going to be taking care of my Lannie while I am in Marseille. She heard her name and looked over at Hockey who gave a little wave but she decided to ignore them. "Now can I read my book?"

Once left alone Hockey thought about the previous week when he was in South Carolina, line dancing with his lady friend, as he called her. A beautiful person he told anyone who would listen. The evening started well, uniformed in check shirts, blue jeans and cowboy boots they danced and stamped like they were ace. But it ended badly.

Why wouldn't she listen to me? Why did she say such terrible things? he thought *I would not let anyone hurt her. The guy was drunk, he insulted her, or at least I thought he did. Perhaps I was a bit rough. Perhaps I should have just told him to apologise, then it would never have happened. How was I supposed to know he was her boss and that they were just having some fun imitating their colleagues? He looked like a lightweight boxer or maybe a little wrestler but I didn't mean to break his jaw, after all, I only tapped him once. Although to be fair, it was a peach, as good as the fruit down in South Carolina,* he grinned at his joke. *Then it all went mad, there must have been at least ten of them in cowboy hats attacking and trying to kick me with their pointy boots. Thankfully they calmed down after I apologised and my lady agreed to take her boss to the hospital. Then she told me she never wanted to see me again. I kept apologising, begging really, but she didn't want to know, and went off to the hospital and left me.*

Once they were gone those cowboys got all rowdy again. I could have dealt with them all by myself, but NO Lannie had to get involved. She said she was trying to calm things down to avoid the cops being called. She used some of that Californian slang to praise the big ugly guy. She called him "AF" and "savage'. I am not sure what she meant but he was insulted. Unfortunately, he tried to slap her and then she went into that routine of hers, pointing her hands like in karate. She went mental and whacked him with a bottle, a barstool and anything else she could get her hands on. I had to pull her off him before she killed him. Then it all kicked off and we had to run. Such a rush I love my Lannie.

I hope my lady doesn't forget me while I'm away on this mission, it's only for six months. Maybe I'll write to her. He knew he wouldn't and decided to follow JD's advice to get some sleep.

The attendants finally cleared everything away and the lights were turned down. JD stood up checked his team were asleep or at least resting. He ended with the Chinaman who was silent apart from his lips blowing on outward breaths.

"Oh what a little beauty, thank God for such comfort," said JD in a whisper. He then turned to the difficult task of getting himself to sleep while worrying about the mission. He read that the best way, apart from a high dosage of melatonin, was to think of something nice, preferably something you are looking forward to. *Now if that is true let me think about Gabriela,* and he closed his eyes. In less than a minute they were open again. *That doesn't work, it just makes me feel sad that I had to leave her behind for a week.* He closed his eyes again and went back to the 90s and some good times.

We used to have a great time playing around at the Burswood casino. We flew down to Perth whenever we got leave from the fighting in Iraq. He opened his eyes, Christ these guys will still be fighting in Iraq after Paris. Eyes closed again, *Herbie and I would act like a couple of horny muscle-bound Aussies to try and attract the local talent or some holidaymakers down there. We learnt how to speak with an Aussie accent and how to play cricket, so they didn't think we were a couple of yanks on the prowl. It worked for Herbie with that cougar Pamela. She reminded me of Demi Moore. God, she was a beauty and that gravelly voice. Herbie loved her right off the bat. Actually, I think Demi looks best in that Angels film when she was that baddy woman. Come to think of it she was great in that film with Douglas where she had her evil way with him.* He chuckled which was not helping his efforts to sleep. *When we went back to Iraq, Herbie was all loved up, but those evil bastards captured him and cut him up. I should have been there with him. He should not have gone off with that stupid A troop guy. I told Herbie he was useless and would get him killed. Well, he did. They sent him back in bits, so horrible. I miss him even today, who knows what he would have been if he had lived. Shit, this is not helping me to sleep it is just making me angry.* He closed his eyes again and woke up three hours later still wondering how to get back to sleep. He looked around, nothing moved and went to sleep.

Across the plane, Baby Bob had fallen asleep quickly and was running through several dreams before he reached the one from his last trip to Iraq.

He was standing at the door to a mobile treatment room looking at a gurney. The patient had tubes going into his arms at one end and a monitor at the other. He could not quite make out who it was, but he could see it was a man wearing a field protective mask. The patient was sweating heavily, and the pillows were soaking wet. His helmet was by the door, Bob would take care of it for him, but when he tried to tell the patient there was no sound.

"He has a fever, his temperature is 49.8 degrees we need to bring it down and fast. He's in bad shape let's hurry," he heard the chief medic say to the other soldier.

He wanted to help but they rushed past him to get to the bed. The doctors started to shake the patient like a rag doll, they were still wearing their combat gear. Bob wanted to tell them to get changed and stop being so rough as they were probably hurting the patient. It looked like his arm had come off, but he could not be sure, but the room was messed up with wet towels.

"His BP is now starting to fall and fast."

"More oxygen, he is struggling to breathe."

"We need to get the temperature down NOW."

"Call ICU he needs to go there he's in trouble."

"Going to lose him if we don't stabilise him, call the crash team."

The ICU team arrived and ran past Bob to the patient whose arms were now back by his side. The soldier looked familiar to him, one of the guys in our unit, I better follow them and make sure he's Okay.

At the ICU there were lots of medics all wearing fatigues covered by blue and green gowns. They were rushing around, and he lost sight of the soldier.

"He is still struggling we need to give him…." Bob could not hear the rest.

It looks bad for the soldier thought Bob who was now lying on the gurney next to him.

"This is Corporal Robert Lee Parker goes by the name of Baby Bob," he has some sort of infection. If he gets any worse, we will have to ventilate him," said the chief medical officer. A nurse started to move the equipment.

Baby Bob woke up in a sweat, looked around at his sleeping teammates and decided to go to the toilet to rinse his face. As he looked in the darkness he couldn't remember if it was up or down the aisle until a hand waved him to the back.

It was JD on one of his wake-ups, wondering whether the rest of the team were worried about the mission. *Maybe they'll be overconfident and foul-up. I bet it's only me, Jack and maybe Shamir because of her extra mission, who will be concerned at this stage. The rest of the guys will only start to worry when the plane leaves France for Iraq in a few days. I wonder if they will be safe?* They were now well over halfway to London, he closed his eyes for another short sleep.

The Captain, assisted by friendly tailwinds, had made better than expected progress when he handed over to a well-rested Texas at 3 am London time. Later as they approached the UK, flight control gave them permission to arrive early and the Gulfstream duly landed at Stanstead airport in Essex at just before 5.30 am UK time. The plane taxied around the dark and quiet airport until they reached the embarkation lounge for private air traffic. Here they would remain airside for the next 90 minutes taking on fuel and four passengers for the onward trip down to the South of France. Onboard, everyone was waking up, using the toilets, stretching, talking and generally getting ready for the next stage of the trip. Most felt good, mainly because of their body clocks, it was much earlier than bedtime, especially in Vegas. They would need to take a good long rest on Thursday night – if that was going to be possible.

The team assembled in their groups to revise for their upcoming activities when they were interrupted by the new passengers. The team eyed the newbies with some suspicion as they looked around for vacant seats. Jack decided he should introduce them;

• "Avery King works with me at Stones UK as an analyst." He told the group a little about her including she was one of the three people held hostage by the crime family in the fight with the police. The team smiled at the English woman while taking in her face and body so they would recognise her again. Shamir wondered what her speciality was, analyst meant specialist in BloedStone. Cat decided she looked fit, tough and not unattractive if just a bit old for her.

• "Andre Devries, Avery's partner another of the three. He runs a successful personal wealth business. Yes," said Jack as they all looked at him in anticipation, "he is the nephew of the boss."

Chinaman never one to waste an opportunity, "this wealth thing you do, is it in the US, cus I might be interested in getting involved?" The others hooted at him, "don't listen to them," he shouted. "They just lost their money in Vegas but me, I've got it all to invest," more hoots.

"Maybe you two can talk later," interrupted Jack with the team making faces and jeering. Chinaman gave them all the one-finger salute but grinned. The Englishman continued;

• "Rosalba Babineaux is the girlfriend of the missing gang... sorry son who is missing and was also caught up in the battle at the warehouse." The twins looked intrigued, *was she Bonny without Clyde? How interesting,* they thought and would definitely want a word later. Shamir simply smiled and welcomed her in French and thought, *what a little sweetie.*
• "This is Tyndall Jones or Tinny – one of the Stones guys based in the UK." He certainly looked the part being only a little smaller than Chinaman. He continued, "Tinny looks after the northern part of the country and is coming with us as part of his training."

Jack explained it was okay to speak freely in front of the new passengers who would be going with him when they arrived in Marseille. Introductions complete the team went back to work while the four new passengers sat near Jack.

JD called for Texas to join him and Shamir for a quick chat before they left. "Texas we need you to go with Shamir for the special project if we get the go-ahead," said JD. He continued, "I just don't think Tinny is ready to do what we want, he hasn't been around long enough. All I can tell you now is that you will have to take the plane after you have dropped off the rest of us.

That means you will have to sort out the pilot and the attendants to work with you. Money is not a problem if you need it. Just so you know, you will be in an armed conflict, potentially the most dangerous of our tasks. Your main job will be to protect Shamir with a long gun, I know you are a great shooter and you may well generate casualties. Are you okay with this?" he asked.

"It would be an honour to protect our Black Cat from the evil dogs," he replied and they all laughed. "I have brought my man with me just in case." They all looked and smirked, his man did not have two legs but one barrel, a Glock .45 GAP.

"We'll get you something bigger when we get to Marseille" replied JD chuckling. Then thanked Texas for helping out at such short notice. JD felt much better having made the decision and went to tell Tinny.

Shamir felt better too, knowing she would be in safe hands. Texas and Shamir fist-bumped and went their separate ways, until later.

Chapter 41: Marseille city and airport, Thursday morning

While the BloedStone team were sat on the tarmac at London Stanstead, fifty-five miles away Sylvain's men had taken one of the first planes out of London Luton to meet up with Pascal in Marseille.

The Martin member was in the kitchen of his spacious fourth-floor city apartment, making morning coffee. Today he was using beans from the Ganja mountains on the island of Sumatran, a gift from his co-conspirator Sylvain. Drinking strong coffee was one of his favourite pastimes and as a man of habit, it would be consumed with local fruit and croissants. He lived alone, kept his home spotlessly clean and allowed only an occasional visit from his sister. He was a loner who took his enjoyment from visiting brothels and doing his job well.

He believed it was time to fulfil his dream of running the Martin family business. *After all*, he thought, *Matisse called me "my adopted son" he meant for me to control the business when he was gone. It just came earlier than we expected. His biological son is such a poule mouillee. Once I am the leader, I will consent to marry Astrid, she is smart and will make a good wife for dealing with the paperwork.*

He was feeling pleased with the progress so far as he thought:

* *Step one; Thierry is in Algiers awaiting execution.*
* *Step two; getting the coke and money back from the warehouse which will happen tonight. Thank you, Patrice I could not have done that without you. He chortled.*
* *Step three; remove the remaining competition, later today or tomorrow once I have agreed to the plan with Sylvain's men.* "How GREAT will that be?" he said out loud. *They had better be good or they will never go home.*

With that final thought, Pascal looked at his new and expensive DH designer clock and realised he should be on his way. He picked up the case of props and ran to his car hoping for a swift ride out to the airport. Unfortunately, a heavy shower slowed up the traffic and made him late. Pascal cursed all the way but smiled when he entered the Arrivals Hall to see all five men standing waiting for him, the plane had been delayed. They looked relaxed already drinking some passable coffee. It was 9.00 am French time.

"Bienvenue messieurs, he said shaking their hands while they were introduced by Terry. He switched to English, "let's sit over here." Driton, Dobri would you mind taking a short walk, I have to talk to these guys before they get on another plane. Please come back in thirty minutes. Thank you." The two men left to find better coffee at one of the other cafés in the terminal. He turned to speak to the Bordeaux team, consisting of Terry, Erjon and Mergim. Pascal told them there were traitors in the Martin family, so he had borrowed men from Sylvain because he did not know who to trust. He explained that the main traitor was going to be in Bordeaux for the next two days doing a deal with a rival group. Their job was to eliminate him and anyone with him. He gave them two phones to be used to contact him. The devices had only two numbers and if they used either it had to be destroyed immediately He instructed them to go to the phone's gallery to study the photo of the man they were after. They knew the name but he meant nothing to them. There were no questions, these men had done this many times before and were dismissed to get the 11 am flight to Bordeaux. There they would be met by a man who had driven through the night with their equipment.

Pascal beckoned Driton and Dobri to come over to sit with him. He ordered them another coffee and some cake. He was feeling good and announced, "right guys you're with me. I have a couple of stops to make before we leave on our trip. While I do that you two are going to relax and wait for me. Do you have your visas?" he asked jovially, knowing Sylvain would not fail him. They both nodded and he continued boisterously, "well let's go then." They left in his BMW for what he hoped would be a better trip back into the city. As they approached the ferry port Pascal detoured off the main road and deposited the two men in a nearby hotel from where he would collect them later that evening.

The next stop was a café near the Vieux Port to meet with the team Chevy had assembled to "get our drugs and money back'. Milling around the café were nine members noisily drinking coffee and talking. He entered, they cheered as he walked through the tables, the older ones embracing him, the younger high fiving. They believed in Pascal, he was their leader, the son the boss should've had. Their good cheer came from Chevy leaking Pascal had negotiated a way to recover their hidden riches and get them back to work. *Nothing like good lies to make you popular,* he thought as he enjoyed the acclaim. With the café doors firmly locked and the team sitting down, Pascal started his address.

"Bonjour mes amis, it's great to see you all again and so happy," they cheered. "We are here to finalise the project to regain the powder and money we hid from Les porcs," they cheered again. "Everything we say today is only for this room, nothing must be written, understand?" he looked around the room at nodding heads. I have spoken to Matisse," he lied and would tell them the truth later when they were back making money. "He sends his best wishes for our success," to avoid questions he informed them, "as you know he is working in Africa with Thierry where I will be going after this meeting. They didn't but imagined he must be searching for new places to get the drugs they needed

Chevy was confirmed as the leader for the return to the warehouse project, which brought more cheers and back-slapping. The two leaders spent the next two hours running through what they had to achieve, how it would be done and assigning tasks to members. As usual, there were several disputes about the undertaking of specific tasks with some individuals preferring one job to another, but nothing serious. They all

273

agreed to a straightforward plan that could be executed by the nine of them. They would use the Africans, some of whom were still missing after the recent battle, to do the carrying and loading work. Pascal thanked them, wished them good luck and with much applause bade them farewell. Chevy followed him out of the café to be told, "later this afternoon I will confirm when you can get the job done. Most likely it will be later today when the English get here. You must let me know if anyone fails you and we will deal with them," they hugged and parted. It was now 3 pm in France.

While Pascal was enjoying time with his men, Patrice was worried about his. He could never properly trust anyone, a character flaw he was willing to admit. Despite all the public bravado, he was dreading being collected by Jack and taken to Bordeaux. He was struggling to find a way past his anxiety, which had already led him to despatch four of his best men to meet him. They had driven for six hours the day before, arrived at a modest hotel close to St Emilion at midnight, slept and were awaiting further instructions. On the plane, he reckoned it would be safe, although they had no weapons, he would have Cyrano, a mountain of a man but surprisingly agile when he needed to be.

The two men met in the international terminal for the final leg of flight STE 044. Patrice texted Jack asking him where they should meet the plane, it was not listed on the Arrivals or Departures board. While they waited for a reply the men strolled around the terminal talking about the future of the Martin's business and how it should be managed.

"Me and many of our men agree with you Patrice, it would be better if you were working more closely with Madame. She is a fine lady, but we do not know if she has la savoir-faire to make enough money to keep us all safe from the cartels."

Chapter 42: Marseille airport VIP Arrivals and Departures, Thursday morning

While Pascal was meeting Sylvain's men in International Arrivals, other passengers from London disembarked flight STE 044 and walked quickly to the car rental area. They fist-bumped and wished each other well before the Gamma team, now consisting of Jack, Baby Bob, Andre, Avery and Rosa set off east. Shamir and Hockey, of the Beta team, left for Marseille centre in a Japanese SUV which the team leader wanted to road test as a prospective next purchase back in San Francisco.

Surprisingly none of the arrivals from Stanstead met any of the arrivals from Luton – that would come later.

Back in the cockpit Texas, the remaining member of the Beta team, was speaking with air traffic control advising them he had become the flight Captain and would be ready to leave for the final destination of Bordeaux on schedule at 10.00 or before. He would of course return if the team Delta project was authorised.

"Affirmative flight STE 044, we do not often see you here in Marseille, you are like what the English say, you wait all day for the bus and then two come along," he laughed. Texas laughed in reply not wanting to upset the man by pointing out he was an American and had no idea what he was talking about. "Thank you, Captain, let us know when you are closed up and ready to go."

"Affirmative and thanks," he responded and went to check that everyone who was leaving had gone, so he could have the Martin members come aboard. Before that, he had to speak with the attendants who were tidying up after the overnight flight, "please make sure no BloedStone materials are lying around and whistle up some provisions for our new friends." They nodded and worked quickly.

"Hey slick how goes it with you?" he asked JD. "I didn't get time to speak earlier with so many of the guys onboard." JD smiled at him and said nothing. "Just to let you know, we will be ready to go when you have the Martin boys on board."

"Texas," came the response. "Please sit, we need to have a chat before we bring the bad boys on board." He also turned and called Lavender and Chinaman forward to join them.

JD told them that this part of the operation could get unpleasant. He reminded them, "all of the projects must take place at roughly the same time so that we can keep control. If we arouse their suspicions or if they think we are up to something then it will get chaotic and a lot of people on both sides, including civilians, will get hurt. They have a lot more guns than we do and this is their home territory. We may have the government on our side but we don't know if the local police will stand with us or not. May I also remind you that when we stopped in London Jack told us that we can only execute our plan once he gives us the go-ahead? If that means we delay until Friday so be it. We have a hotel arranged for tonight and tomorrow just in case."

"Weapons?" asked Chinaman who had switched into operations mode. In this condition, he listened carefully, did what was required and stayed alive in some difficult situations.

"Okay, taking things in order, our ROE will be "shoot to protect yourself," no one flinched. "However, some of us won't be equipped with armour and those that are will be French police issue. So please don't get hit. If we do get fired on by a lot of gangbangers I will take things up a notch or two. But if we do things right, it shouldn't happen. That said, if things go wrong we will go on the offensive."

"Are you sure about this?" replied Lavender. "Back in Vegas you said we would use more aggressive ROE, why has that changed?" she challenged concerned about her forthcoming role.

JD continued, "look we must try to execute our plan without violence as much as possible, but if we do have to fight, Robbie has the weapons at the vineyard. We will collect them before we get together with Patrice and his colleagues for the showdown on what is going to happen to them. For now, we must stick to the script as they will be joining us in a few minutes."

"Are these the guys who might try and shoot us?" said Lavender appreciating for the first time they were the same men.

"Yeah I guess so, but we can start out being friendly, there will only be two of them after all. We agreed we would treat them like kings and be humble. Lannie please make sure you get extra friendly with Patrice in your air attendant role, so you can provide answers to their questions should they want to check us out. Any more questions? He looked over to Chinaman for sarcastic comments, but no response. He continued, "the guys joining us are expecting to meet Jack, let's hope they don't mind meeting me and Robbie instead. Are we ready for the first act?" JD asked theatrically. They all responded with a yep, "okay then my fellow thespians let the show begin," and they all laughed. "Texas if you would do the honours."

"Certainement monsieur," replied the Stones pilot, he left the plane to get the passengers.

Patrice and Cyrano were called to the VIP check-in where they were subject to the normal pre-flight inspections before being escorted to the plane by a friendly Texas. They were welcomed at the bottom of the steps, by a cheery JD who lined up with the attendants and the co-pilot. He immediately apologised for Jack's absence telling them Madame Martin required his presence in Bandol for final discussions.

"Please come aboard and have a drink," said JD "it is good to meet you both. I'm your host for the trip" and stood back while they went up the few steps. "My you're a big boy," he whispered as Cyrano passed by without hearing him. *Bigger they come the harder they fall, or is it the harder they hit?* he thought mischievously. Once the men had taken their seats, JD stood to continue his cameo role and introduced himself and the other passengers. "I am John I work with De Beaux Endroits on the marketing side, you always need us don't you? Don't worry about these two, pointing at Chinaman and the defrocked attendant, they are just a couple of Americans who hitched a lift. They're going somewhere in Bordeaux to help with security at one of the chateaux owned by a Saudi Prince, there are lots of them I believe. Those two," pointing at the other flight attendant and Lavender, in uniform, "are your flight attendants. They will get your drinks and snacks when you want them. They both speak French so that will help I hope. If you have any questions before we get to Bordeaux I will try and answer them. We should be taking off soon, landing at about 11.00 am so sit back and relax," he stopped and sat down.

"Quel trou du cul, are all the English like him?" Cyrano whispered to Patrice who smiled hoping that would be the case, but he had his insurance waiting just in case.

Un verre monsieur?" Lavender asked Patrice and Cyrano in French, both requested a Ricard. When she returned as anticipated Patrice took the opportunity of asking her about his fellow passengers and crew, starting with her. Using a husky voice Lavender told them she was a French Canadian applying for an international experience visa so she could stay for at least a year and get a proper job. Patrice continued with questions about the other two men and she complained that JD was a stupid marketing man who was constantly touching her but she could not say anything or she might lose her job. As for the black guy, he never said please or thank you. Finally, she told him that while the other attendants were resting, she had worked all night taking care of a bunch of noisy gamblers travelling from Las Vegas to London. Patrice gave her his phone number in case she needed help before thanking her with a broad smile. He turned to Cyrano who suggested that his thoughts on the English must apply to the Americans as well. Patrice responded by sharing what he would like to be doing with the small but athletic Canadian flight attendant if he had more time.

When the plane landed, JD had a car waiting to take his guests to the Grand Barrail Hotel where they would be staying for the night if the inspection did not take place that afternoon. Patrice called Frederic again, for what seemed like the twentieth time, to agree on a stratagem to avoid discovery of the double-dealing the three men were involved in. Each time Robbie took pleasure in listening to it ring out. "Merde, that bastard never answers his phone. You're going to have sort him out when we find him," he said to Cyrano. His colleague produced a smile thinking about the opportunity – he hated gay men.

The remaining Stones associates, including Texas, left separately after being directed by text to an address near the E70 two miles from Chateau du Carys. The group would meet with an armourer sent by Robbie, wait for further instructions and stay the night if necessary.

The US pilot and the flight attendants would vacate the jet for the cleaners to do their work and then wait at an airport hotel. They were on standby for any unscheduled trips.

Jack far away in the Le Beaux penthouse looked at his watch, thinking about what his fellow associates would be doing at that moment and where they would be going to start their activities. Everything depended on him being successful with his part of the plan. He thought about it again:

• *Step 1 - Getting Madame Martin to Bandol - looks to be about to happen.*

- *Step 2 - Negotiating the deal, the bit we investors love and hate in equal measure. This will be especially hard, getting her to agree to a deal when she is expecting to receive a pile of cash from a wimpy Englishman.*
- *Step 3 - Getting the deal done. Any little thing can cause a deal to falter before signature. If that happens it will be a real problem.*

He shook his head dreading what a breakdown would mean for her and perhaps for the Stones people. To help things along he had set in motion something that might encourage a reluctant gang leader to accept a deal she didn't know was on offer.

Part Four – Saving French Wine?

Chapter 43: Bandol and Marseille, Thursday afternoon

Team Gamma had checked into Le Beaux Hotel mid-morning to get ready for the crucial negotiations. Baby Bob immediately set about creating his listening post come armoury on the fourth floor immediately below the meeting room. From there he would hear and record everything that went on and have access to the Chief Negotiator's ear. Jack was not expecting any trouble but even so had taken up residence at the head of the table, spread out his papers and located his Glock in a hidden drawer. The others favoured coffees or taking a short walk before assembling for one of Yasmeen's superb lunches.

Whilst Jack was preparing to give his final briefing Avery asked, "can we just go through what you want us to do again, I'm not used to this?" The Stones Director was getting nervous about the role she may have to play later. As he was explaining, they were interrupted by Andre and Rosa followed by Yasmeen and Chiara who were all expecting the same instructions. Jack stopped his personal tuition and addressed himself to the group. He started by explaining what normally happened during this kind of negotiation and indicated where it might "blow up" or run into difficulty. If and when that happened he would select one or more of them to assist him. The most likely requirement would be for them to help persuade Astrid Martin that the right thing to do was to take the deal. When he finished the group were silent for a moment before asking a few questions to clarify dos and don'ts but soon everyone seemed satisfied with what they might be called upon to accomplish.

Astrid Martin was late, they had expected that, but was it because she wanted to revel in her victory or because of some Stones mischief? Chase-up calls were met with voicemail. Jack was not sure whether this was good or bad. Anxious associates tested personal comms links several times before growing bored with the wait. At 2 pm Jack began to wonder whether there would be enough time to execute the plan that day. Ironically his bit of mischief might have been too effective.

Thirty miles away at the Marseille villa, Madame Martin was sitting in her office, angry and yelling at M. Labette. The Accountant was trying to explain why they had received a large number of "mis en demeure" debt letters and two court summonses. She was demanding to know how it could have happened knowing her businesses had plenty of cash. She insisted the invoices must be paid immediately. M. Labette suggested it must be something to do with the Matisse "standing instructions" in particular the one which required Martin members and drug suppliers to be paid first. That would account for the company bank accounts being drained without being replaced by the drug money languishing in the warehouse cellar. What he did not have to explain, because she was too stressed to ask, was how the banks would know how to do this, without her explicit instructions.

"Why now?" she asked him rhetorically. "Bills are always paid late, it is normal in France."

He shrugged his shoulders, "perhaps it could be something to do with the negotiations we are having with the English. Maybe these companies have heard you are to receive money so they want theirs early. Then he continued mischievously, "have you noticed one of the demands is from your design company in London, the place where you sent Patrice?"

"What, Chiara is one of them? What does she know? I thought she was my friend. Am I being treated as a fool by her or Jack or maybe Patrice? I will call her and find out why she is doing this." M. Labette nodded sagely while remaining seated. Madame Martin yelled to her maid to bring more coffee. The Accountant also wanted food it was past his lunchtime, he had an abundance to fill.

She used the speakerphone to call the designer's mobile.

"Hello this is Chiara," she answered in English so everyone in the room looked over to see if it was the missing Martin family leader.

"Bonjour mon ami," the caller replied. "This is Astrid, do you have a moment to speak? I have some problems that I wish to discuss with you before I can go to an important meeting," trying to sound friendly rather than angry, as she felt.

"I am well," Chiara replied slowly and quietly. "I meant to call you to catch up and talk about some more business if that is possible," she replied. Then waiting, not speaking during the momentary silence, forcing Madame Martin to make the running on the call.

"Chiara I am in my office, we have just received a letter from an Advocat asking us to pay your invoices. We have not had that before, they are not very late."

Chiara continued to torment Madame Martin by simply explaining to her that it must be the financial people who don't understand the French ways and she would deal with it. The Martin family leader pretended to be glum, moaning that companies were ganging up against her, seeking to find if her friend knew why. Chiara countered by suggesting that maybe there had been a mistake in a credit rating review that caused the automatic trigger of such actions.

"Best to call the man Matisse uses to find out what has happened and get it fixed. Probably it is just a mistake as I said before," advised Chiara. "By the way, how is Matisse I haven't spoken to him for ages, is he there? Please send him my best wishes. You must both come to dinner when you are in the UK again." Chiara was enjoying playing her part. She looked over at Jack who was frantically using the "end it" hand signal.

"He is away on business, but I will tell him when I see him next week," Madame Martin lied. "I have to go now I am already late for a meeting, we will speak later," she ended the call. A listening M. Labette suggested that maybe Chiara was right and could he have some food. She looked at her Luce clock realised she was very late, had not dressed for the meeting and it was an hour's drive. Yves was summoned to call Jack to tell him they would be arriving at around 5.00 pm, they would stay at a nearby hotel if they had to work late. Unfortunately, that meant a further delay while she selected an outfit for the following day. Yves booked a suite for the night hoping that Astrid would be in a playful mood. M. Labette wandered into the kitchen and attacked a baguette.

Jack called JD in Bordeaux to explain the meeting would not start until at least 5 pm and with the time required to complete, it would finish late evening or worst case in the morning. JD sent a text to the team telling them to stand down and be ready to execute the next day. The team were unfazed welcoming the delay to allow more time to acclimatise. As they relaxed JD received particulars from Dave Bender, to strengthen negotiations, the Delta Team project could go ahead. Shamir and Texas were sent details and requested to prepare for action starting on Friday morning, subject to final confirmation from Jack.

At 5.20 pm Madame Martin arrived at Le Beaux, the Stones associates and allies took their positions. Baby Bob returned to his suite, briefly showed Tinny what he did then made ready to record the negotiation. The French leader's SUV following a BMW saloon stopped outside the hotel. Two Martin members left the escort vehicle to wander around the immediate area before briefly searching the hotel car park and signalling all clear. This caused Lucian and Senet to leave their vehicles to go into the hotel, wander around the Reception area for a few seconds before giving Yves the go-head. Yasmeen smiled, bowed and welcomed Madame Martin, M. Labette and Yves Calvin, before escorting them to the penthouse suite.

The party entered the room to be met by Jack and Tinny. The visitors were introduced by Yasmeen, they paused before taking their seats. Jack started with some small talk about the weather, the trip over to Bandol and what they wanted to drink. He suggested dinner would be about 8 to 8 .30pm so they had a good couple of hours to talk. Madame Martin smiled a lot but said very little. She was simply enjoying their squirming. After a while, the conversation turned to the subject of the Marseille police raid. Jack apologised for becoming involved in the Martin's business, which of course they did not approve of. Madame Martin let the snipe go but began to wonder how much longer Jack would be waffling on about nothing. She was getting bored and wanted him to move onto the real reason for the visit. She returned to thinking about her lack of cash and looked over at M. Labette who was staring intently at Jack. She was surprised, but her mind returned to finding solutions to their problems using the money they would soon be receiving. It was the moment for the experienced negotiator to strike and for that, he suddenly switched to French.

"Madame Martin, it's time to tell you that Tyndall Jones and I are from BloedStone a multi-billion-dollar US security corporation that is employed by both the US and French governments. The sudden change caught her by surprise, similar to the first of a one-two punch combination, she stared at Jack. "We know your husband Matisse was killed in the Marseille gang fights, your son Thierry has been kidnapped and is being held at a location in Algiers and your long-time lover is sitting over there," pointing at Yves. She looked at the Frenchman with her mouth slightly open as if she was going to speak but stopped when he looked down at the table. "We know you have no money in your legal businesses because we've taken it. Our company knows everything about you, what you do, legal or not and your people, good or bad." He paused looked straight into her beautiful but narrowing eyes like he had done so many times before, "that said, we would still like to make you an offer. The arrangement would allow you to live in comfort anywhere in the world you wish." The French lady was clearly stunned. "We have prepared a document setting out the proposed deal," he stood up and walked around the table to present the bound agreement.

He returned to his seat, no one moved or spoke. The leader of the Martin family replayed what had been said to her and decided she would leave. Jack continued, "I realise this must be a surprise for you, your first instinct is to curse me and storm out, but I assure you it is well worth your time to take a look."

She turned to Yves for help, they had men downstairs, but he looked away again. She felt betrayed realising her lover must be a turncoat.

She swivelled to face the family's long-standing accountant, but M. Labette casually asked, "Jack, shall I leave now or would you like me to stay and help with the discussion?"

Madame Martin became more anxious and felt vulnerable. Yves walked around the table and sat next to her. She looked at him with a mixture of anger and despair, *they are all traitors,* she thought. The French leader went to stand but Yves held her hand to keep her in the seat, she did not struggle. He asked the others to leave so he could reassure her. As they left she sat composing herself. She felt betrayed, deceived, stupid even, but most of all she felt the fear of a painful death, similar to the ones Matisse had meted out over the years.

The Englishmen left the room alongside M. Labette who went to the bar to find a sandwich to tide him over until dinner. The Accountant was a happy man, Le Beaux had one of his favourite restaurants and provided he did as he was told Jack had promised he would be able to enjoy the fine food and wine for free. He sat with Andre eating a baguette, drinking coffee and discussing South African wines like they had been friends for years. Rosa was rehearsing to Avery what she was going to say to Madame Martin about Thierry.

The couple spent the next hour arguing about what he had done. Yves won her over by asserting they could not win this fight without going to war and if they did that, she could not rely on her troops being loyal when they found out Matisse was dead.

"That was the major reason I had to change allegiance or we would both be killed and I love you too much for that to happen when I can stop it," he declared. "Also, you must know that both Patrice and Pascal are plotting to take over from you, they will kill you. I do believe that one of them has kidnapped Thierry and the English are the only ones who can bring him back."

Both Astrid and Yves were in tears, it was time to think about making big changes, it was time to go through the proposal.

He left the room to fetch Jack. She decided to call Patrice before remembering she could not trust him, then she thought about Pascal and knew him to be worse. She settled on getting advice from her friend Chiara. She called her designer but it went to message, then her friend strolled into the room. Madame Martin began to wonder who else had joined the other team. "Are you with the English too?" she asked. Chiara smiled and suggested they sit, "are they going to kill me?" she asked with tears in her eyes.

Chiara still smiling told her friend, "of course not, the offer from Stones is the best option for you. It means you can escape from your husband's gang, get away from the men who want to take over what you have built and then destroy it just to sell drugs. Why would you want to stay when you can manage your own business away from all of that chaos. You are going to be wealthy and protected by a security business." She pressed on, "if you stay, I have no doubt both you and Thierry will be murdered by those horrible thugs, except you of course," smiling at Yves.

"Astrid, you must understand BloedStone are serious business people, they may have paid you off had your men had not threatened Jack's family. After that, they decided to devote resources to finding out all about the Martin crime family and dealing with it, especially as you interfered with the Stones Chateau, their most prized possession. They may not have the number of people that you can call upon, but they have your government as a partner and almost unlimited funds. Who would you bet on?"

"But I thought you didn't know what my husband was involved in, I kept it from you," Madame Martin was dismayed her friend knew so much about her. She stood and walked to the window, "I built a great business which you are part of, now I am going to lose it all and probably my life." Tears welled in her eyes, she was struggling to accept what had happened in the last hour.

Chiara continued, "I knew about your husband and always hoped you would leave him. Astrid, I strongly advise you to sit down with Jack and his team to look at the offer. These people may be tough but they respond to honesty and good sense. For them, you have only one option, to take their deal. Anything else means a terrible outcome. Right now I must tell you they have military personnel waiting here in France. Yves and his men have already changed sides alongside your Accountant who has met with their financial representative, Avery King, whom you know."

"In that case, why do they need me?" she asked angrily. "Are they going to turn me over to the Gendarmerie and bury me in prison or just dig a hole and throw me in?" tears of anger continued.

"You might find it hard to believe but they appreciate what you have done," replied Chiara. "Shall we call them back in and let Jack go through the deal?" she continued before blurting out, "they know where Thierry is, they can get him back."

"Is that really true you're not just tricking me as they did?" Madame challenged her friend.

"It is, I wasn't supposed to tell you," replied Chiara now with tears in her eyes. They both went to the restroom to freshen up and continue the Thierry conversation. Yves secretly sent, or so he thought, a text to the two P's telling them nothing had happened yet. Baby Bob intercepted the message but released it as helpful.

Before the meeting resumed the hotel staff took the opportunity to set up for dinner. When Madame Martin was re-seated, Jack, relieved to see her return, went through the agreement. He described what they were prepared to do for her, how much they would pay and what they wanted in return. He told her it was a one-time offer, in the traditional negotiating manner, it had to be done today or the deal was off, they would proceed without her. If that happened, she would be treated as hostile, which would be hazardous for her.

Astrid, as she now wanted to be called, seemed to be negotiating in good faith while enjoying the hotel's fine food and wine, which they assured her, with some sarcasm, was the genuine vintage. She managed an apology for threatening Jack's family and friends, suggesting Patrice was just doing business gangster style. The financial component of the offer had to be increased twice to a level where Jack could do no more, or so he said. He refused to reveal how they would implement the deal but assured her they had much experience with such projects. Once they had finished, Jack felt she had engaged fully and secretly liked the way she had presented herself after the unsettling start. It was little before 11 pm French time, Astrid agreed to send a supervised text to the "two P's" telling them that negotiations were ongoing, and they should stand their troops down until the morning.

The Martin leader agreed to give them her answer before 8 am the next morning. Yasmin organised one of the hotel's deluxe rooms and Astrid agreed not to make or receive any calls until after the deadline. Baby Bob would monitor her compliance while she slept alone. Yves, his men and M. Labette were accommodated on the first floor and were not a concern, their phones had already been swapped for BloedStone encrypted equipment. The room emptied apart from Jack who had one last job to do.

"Nice work Jack" said the voice in his ear.

"Thanks, let's hope she does the deal in the morning. I thought Chiara did us a great service, in fact, she was wonderful," he replied. "Anyway, good night see you in the morning."

"Agreed, we will look after her and Pubs for that," came the reply "and good night to you."

Next, Jack updated JD and the rest of the BloedStone team on where they were with the negotiations. He told them that so far they did not have to make any changes to their plans but there was only a 50:50 chance she would agree to the deal.

"We ambushed her at the start to get her attention and it went badly, but later she started to negotiate which went well. She was impressed that we had recruited her team. But who knows these guys are all villains with little in the way of ethics, they can swap back at any time. In the end, it comes down to first whether she believes she will lose everything by not accepting the deal, and secondly, whether she believes we can protect her and prevent retaliation stopping her from enjoying the freedom we are offering"

The team members gave short updates and JD finished by saying that there seemed to be some sort of gangster build up in Bordeaux which Robbie was looking at and would report back on.

"It could be nothing but we will let you all know," said JD and continued "Let's stop now and get some rest."

Jack signed off and immediately began to worry about what would happen if the Martin men became unmanageable. *They could revert to violence to defend their interests causing us to retaliate with maximum force. What a mess that would be, shit,* he thought and shivered.

Chapter 44: Marseille, late Thursday

Pascal received the text from Madame Martin at his favourite bar in the Vieux-Port de Marseille. He excused himself to read it, cursed under his breath then explained to Saloni and her boyfriend that the talks had not finished and would continue in the morning. The BloedStone couple shrugged indicating they would soon receive a similar call to tell them the same thing. Minutes later it arrived, Pascal heard the beeps and waived them away to read their texts. The associates wobbled away whilst listening to Jack and pretending to read a text. On the way back they whispered about what it meant before theatrically slumping back into their chairs.

Earlier in the afternoon, the two BloedStone associates together with the Martin team members secretly visited the area around the warehouse and the building next door. The reconnoitre was used to explain how the group would enter and leave the warehouse carrying the cellar booty. The unusual group even met the police officers who would allow them access. Pascal was impressed as he listened to the tall and muscular American woman giving them instructions. But he still wanted to carry out his own checks by calling the police department and asking for the officers they were talking to. The station sergeant apologised explaining they were away on police business and not available until Monday. Scrutiny over, the team was primed and ready to do the recovery work just as soon as they got the go-ahead from Jack.

For most of the evening, Shamir appeared to be drinking heavily, keeping Pascal interested by telling an imaginary story about how she used to live in Provence with her brother. She explained she loved him but they had a terrible argument so she had to leave. Shamir shared that she wanted to see him again and if she could find the right job perhaps live in Marseille. She told Pascal how dull it was working nights for a security company or doing jobs like the one they had at the warehouse. When Hockey responded to his bladder's call, she revealed they were having a secret romance that could cost them both their jobs. She suggested he wanted to leave the company and go back to the US and live near his parents. But she hated them because they were fat stupid and they hated her because they were racist and wanted their son to marry a nice white girl. Pascal normally showed no interest in such drunken bellyaching, but he began to wonder, then wish, that this beautiful woman was flirting with him. He did not care if she was dark-skinned after all, he had slept with many African women. It would be no trouble getting rid of the weak boyfriend to keep her for himself.

I must stop this now, he thought. *It will all have to wait, I still have a lot of things to do tonight and an early start in the morning. I can have her tomorrow night, she will appreciate me more when she is sober. For now, those two need to stop drinking to make sure they get my men into the warehouse tomorrow, whatever time that might be.*

'Saloni I think you and Lee should go and get some rest, you have a big day tomorrow, we don't want any mistakes, do we?" he said to the BloedStone associates.

Shamir protested, suggesting one more drink for the road, just to enjoy the evening a little bit more. Pascal called over one of his men to escort them the short distance to their hotel.

"See you in the morning," she shouted with a lecherous look and wiggle of her backside as she staggered away berating the escort, with Hockey followed some distance behind. When they were out of sight Shamir pulled the escort close to her, ran her hands over his lower body and asked where Pascal was staying so she could visit him. The man pleaded with her to stop, his growing erection was becoming uncomfortable. Finally, he pushed her away announcing his leader was not staying with them because he had to go to Toulon later that night. Realising what he had said, he tried to backtrack. Shamir ignored him, then pushed him away in exchange for Hockey who then took her to the hotel with the escort trailing. They went to Shamir's room in case they were being watched, after a few minutes Shamir said,

"Sounds like Pascal is going to be somewhere else tomorrow, I wonder where?" laughing. She thought, *I did enjoy that, but I hope we don't run into him before we're done tomorrow.*

"Fancy him do you," replied Hockey and smiled as she scowled. "It looks like it's me and what's his name tomorrow? Chevy, that's right, how could I forget a name like that?" He continued, "I wonder if he was named after the cars. What time are you leaving?"

"I'll skedaddle, I love that word, at about 6ish in the morning to meet up with Texas at the airport," she smiled. "Should be in and out by early evening to meet you all again."

"Good luck and take care, we need you," they embraced and Hockey returned to his room looking around carefully for lurking gangsters.

Once the Stones associates had disappeared into the distance Pascal called Terry Lamb, the leader of his borrowed Bordeaux team, to tell him of the delay caused by "the bitch" not agreeing to a deal with the English. It would be done by mid-morning so they should be ready for Patrice and his giant guard. "Best not to tangle with him eh," he added with some forced humour.

The English gangster remained business-like and confirmed they had carried out recognisance of the area and knew how they were going to get in, do the job and disappear afterwards. "Shame it's taking so long, I wanted to get back to see the Blues," he added jokingly. The Frenchman gave a loud "ummm" to show he was not amused. "Pascal, don't worry we have all the gear we need and have done this sort of thing many times for the guv. Just as soon as we are done and away, I'll text you."

"Bien, I will wait for your call and no fuck-ups," Pascal responded then rang off. "Merde," he shouted, realising these men were not frightened by him, they were mercenaries, he had little control over them.

Terry pocketed his phone and turned to the stranger "Sorry about that Jock, I think it's your round," Robbie stumbled over to the bar. Terry continued softly, "what a fucking poofter he is for a Jock."

Pascal turned his attention to his away team of Driton and Dodri and rushed over to collect them from their hotel. It was after midnight and they had to change locations to be ready to pick up the Toulon flight. He explained to them what had to happen, but they did not seem to care much, shrugged their shoulders and did just as they were told. *They are so much better than the Englishman*, he thought, feeling happier.

Fortunately, the journey was good and they were in bed by 1.30 am ready for an 8 am departure.

Pascal lay in bed thinking that Sylvain's men were nothing like his own who feared the pain of retribution if they failed to meet his standards. Then he ran through the plan again; stopping at weapons and immediately texted the Martin armourer requesting confirmation that weapons had been transferred by the regular car ferry the day before. Next, the beautiful Saloni entered his mind, which immediately stripped her and began to imagine handling her naked body. Unfortunately, he did not get very far -he was tired.

Chapter 45: Bordeaux, late Thursday

Patrice and Cyrano had been hanging about in their five-star hotel all afternoon. They were bored having done nothing more than send texts and make calls to friends and family back in Marseille. There was still no response from either Frederic, who continued to have "phone problems" or Madame Martin who was having negotiating problems. At around 6 pm they received a text explaining nothing had happened yet, things were running late in Bandol. Patrice called the chateau again to speak with Frederic about getting their story agreed upon before the visit. Claude answered and asked him if he was still coming to visit the chateau. Patrice explained the visit was on hold until an agreement was completed and asked to speak with his other co-conspirator. Claude informed him that Frederic had not returned from his trip and they were getting worried, although they had received a brief telephone message that he would certainly be back by lunchtime tomorrow. Claude continued his playacting by asking the Martin member if he knew where Frederic might be. The response was negative, he rang off. *Where has he gone, is he hiding, or has he been taken like the Martin boy?* Patrice wondered.

"They can't find Frederic," he said to Cyrano. "Something is very wrong, any ideas?" he asked hopefully. The big man just shook his head, did not care or was not prepared to say what he thought. Patrice carried on thinking about where Frederic might be or who might have taken him and drew a blank. His next call was to the leader of his protection team stashed in a hotel nearby. He told him he did not think anything was going to happen tonight, so they should at least eat. He would not be coming to see them unless things changed significantly.

At 8 pm Patrice and Cyrano went to dinner and were soon soothed by the good food and excellent wine from, an un-scammed, nearby chateau. After dinner, the two men took up a corner of the bar to wait for a call from Madame Martin. They sat in silence with nothing left to say. In the quiet Patrice reflected on why the people over in Bandol still needed time to talk when Jack had already agreed to pay them money. *Is there more to this business, am I missing something?* he thought.

A short distance away, Patrice's protection team, were happily drinking copious quantities of local wine whilst loudly playing their version of Belote with Robo, their new Scottish friend. Although the men had been told not to do anything that might get themselves noticed.

At 11 pm the text came to stand down but to be ready for action at 9 am the next day. "Merde, they are still talking," Patrice said to his colleague. "Tell the guys to be in their vehicles ready to go at 8.30 am tomorrow" Cyrano nodded and went away to do his work. Patrice went to his room to call Frederic again but it went to the message centre. "Merde," he said and threw his phone onto the bed. He lay for a while thinking about how he could discreetly move his men to the chateau to ensure sure he was safe.

Chapter 46: Bandol, Friday 8 am

It was a normal day in the South of France, sunny with a blue sky and no clouds and Jack arrived for breakfast well before the 8 am deadline. The room was empty and silent he was hoping, almost praying, Astrid would be realistic. His past dealings with buyers and sellers had taught him that there was no such thing as a "no brainer." Even the best deals failed for the most unexpected reasons. He thought back to the day when they had bought the hotel, a deal which almost collapsed because the owners" youngest daughter liked playing on the beach below. *Christ, she was only four.* In the end, the only way to change the seller's mind was to buy up his debt and threaten to bankrupt him. *What a total…,* he thought and stopped himself. His thoughts continued, *if she screws up then it is going to get even more difficult for her. Behaving rationally means signing up, taking the money and living in luxury. Even though she will be handing over her assets at just over half their value.* He helped himself to cereals and sat in his usual spot looking out over the Renécros Bay.

A few minutes later Astrid arrived, took up a place at the far end of the table before rising and helping herself to her first expresso of the day. She said nothing, Jack could feel the adrenalin pumping, preparing his fight response.

"Bonjour Astrid, did you sleep well?" he hoped she was in a good mood.

"Eventually, I slept," she replied. Then started to drink her coffee saying nothing but still thinking. Despite her desire to leave the criminal world, she had spent hours wrestling with questions like; how could she abandon what her husband had created? How could she survive as a traitor? Would she be hunted down and killed? Would BloedStone kill her and her son after the deal? Plus many more. She was still struggling with these issues when an older man came into the room and helped himself to a coffee. He sat down near her and smiled. Astrid looked at Jack for an explanation. The man spoke slowly in French with a sort of Dutch lilt, "this must be very difficult for you." She looked at him as he walked towards her with his hand outstretched. "Bonjour Madame my name is Gendrie de Vries, I am the Chairman of BloedStone. I thought it was important to meet with you, to ask that you work with our company and to assure you that we will keep you and your family safe in the future. I hope you will believe me when I tell you that we admire what you have achieved with your part of the family business. We would like you to have the opportunity to continue without the encumbrance of the other, shall we say, less salubrious activities."

Gathering herself she started, "please call me Astrid." He nodded and she blurted out, "Jack has explained that you want to take over our business, which you helped to ruin. The fact is, your offer is far too low for our businesses, they are worth much more. If you want them then you will either need to pay more or fight for them." She looked into his eyes and saw a power far greater than she ever experienced. "You are robbing me of what I have built," she said quietly.

"I must say, it is unusual negotiating to take over a criminal enterprise but in this case, we want some parts of it kept intact for various reasons which I won't bore you with. To keep things friendly we are prepared to up our offer to 7million euros. For the extra money, you will work with us for 2 years in the UK or US and we will throw in your son for free when we find him."

"Do you know where he is?" she asked not quite believing what Chiara had told her.

"Yes we have a pretty good idea of what happened to him, we think he is still alive but it will take some effort to get him back safely. So Astrid, do we have a deal?" asked the supreme salesman who said nothing in the silence that followed.

The seconds ticked by as she weighed up, *staying alive, plenty of money, a job with a security business, protection for me and Thierry or being a traitor and fighting these pompous foreigners to save my husband's legacy along with his remaining men.*

"DEAL," she almost shouted. It was an easy decision, security for them came first followed by not being involved in a criminal business with "horrible men who hated her". Jack looked surprised for a moment then rushed to open the champagne mumbling something about *maybe there is a no brainer.* They celebrated with the grape over breakfast where they were joined by Tinny. "So what happens next?" she asked.

The General suggested they finish breakfast, run through some last-minute details and then announce the deal to the troops on both sides. While they did that, Tinny completed the draft agenda ready for the discussion. The General describing the deal as the purchase of assets from a business rather than buying the business itself.

Jack thanked Tinny as he put up the agenda on the huge TV screen.

AGENDA

1.   Agree deal to buy businesses for 5 million euro plus 2 years at 1 million a year for Madame Martin. Papers prepared by M. Labette and ready for signature.
2.   Businesses to be included:
      a.   Wine Import and Export.
      b.   Building and Design Company.
      c.   Casino Investments.
      d.   Property – Villa and all other properties.
3.   Gang members on the "keep" list – agree on deals.
4.   Sylvain in the UK, an operation planned - any connection to worry about?
5.   Inform the Martin troops and then initiate actions as noted below and complete by the end of the day.
      a.   Retrieve son – operation ready to go ahead.

b.   "Take-down" illegal businesses France and UK (excluding wine) - operation ready to go on orders.

c.   Take control of the illegal wine business.

6.   Anything else?

"I think we have done number one except for the official signing," said Jack looking at the other two. Astrid nodded and smiled at the General who had done his bit. "Do you want to go through the details AGAIN before we move on?" he continued. "We can get M. Labette in to help if you want." She shook her head looked at the key sections of the contract again and surprised both the General and Jack by signing it there and then. Yasmeen was called in to act as a rather late witness and it was done. Astrid told them both that she trusted them - she had no other option at this point. Jack continued, "our constraints are we must get through everything by noon to get the job done today."

For the next three hours, they ran through the agenda to arrive at item five, no one wanted to add any more. There had been some arguments about staff retention as there always are in a merger. Astrid was acutely aware that going on the "leavers list" would be far worse. They kept Yves whose retrospective job interview on wine scams would be conducted by Robbie. M. Labette would be taken to another part of France where he would be properly interviewed about Martin's finances. If he became a "good leaver" by telling them everything they wanted to know he could stay wherever he decided was safe. A "bad leaver" would be handed over to the police as a rapist or something similar. The rest of the gang, excluding Astrid Martin's escorts, now security guards, did not make the cut. That meant taking their chances in the failing illegal business, owned by a dead Matisse. Astrid would make the call on Thierry later.

Jack left the room to broadcast to the BloedStone associates that the deal had been done and Astrid Martin secured. He also confirmed the keep list had NO ONE on it, except for Yves and his Bandol team.

JD ordered the teams to make ready but not execute until Shamir confirmed her location and Hockey was ready to enter the warehouse. The leaders confirmed they were ready and would soon be in place, the Stones associates in Bandol could do nothing more except wait. The weather had been friendly all day, it would still be light when the operations began.

The deal would be announced to the members via a simple text from Astrid Martin. She felt guilty that she was ditching men who had been with her husband for many years. But they were career criminals, they hated her, hated Thierry and would happy to kill them both in a heartbeat. Fortunately, the members would never know what really happened, they would be told she was kidnapped, double-crossed and fed to the police by traitors. They would empathise with her, maybe feel sorry for her from their prison cells. All the while she would be living comfortably, in a sort of witness protection scheme, where she would never see them again.

They agreed on the texts:

To Pascal it read:

"Deal agreed with Jack. Proceed with the warehouse job. Will call you later today to explain the details but for now, you should recover our stuff. Make sure everyone knows we have a great victory."

To Patrice:

"Deal agreed with Jack proceed with the inspection of the chateau. Will call you later. Tell everyone we have a great victory."

Chapter 47: Calais and Dover area, Friday morning

Henri Bain, who heads up the family's human smuggling and trafficking division arrived in Calais. He is in his early forties, unremarkable in appearance, medium-sized in everything except his tan which is extra-large. A Martin member for many years, has committed many crimes, served eight years in prison, spends most of his money on Gauloises, prostitutes and poor-quality wine.

As instructed, he met his colleagues Nichol and Ynon at Marseille airport for the Thursday afternoon flight to Lille. On Friday morning they started their excursion to Calais port and would travel to Dover as co-drivers of three trucks "unknowingly" carrying twelve illegal immigrants. The smuggled Africans would be paying a fare of up to 4000 euros each for the Martin "premium service" that would take them into the East End of London or close by. Some might change from being smuggled to being trafficked, which meant being sold to Henri's UK contacts for onward transport. The three trafficking prospects for this trip being, female, healthy and young, would be located together.

Being transported in trucks is awful enough, but slightly better than the "economy service" which involved the use of a flimsy boat, a dodgy life preserver and a chance of being run down by channel shipping or turned around by coast guards. The service is generally used for family smuggling because there was plenty of room on the open decks and the ride was short - one way or the other. The passengers were constantly being told they only had to make it about 12 miles out, then they would get picked up and "chauffeured" to Dover by the UK coast guard.

When the three Martin men arrived at Calais port the early autumn weather looked just about okay for the "boating trip'. The first job was to check their local agents had everything organised and money collected. The agents tended to be African immigrants themselves who spent most of the day in and around the migrant camps touting for business. Normally the job would be controlled by the absent Saville who ruled them with "a rod of iron" to make sure they did not steal any of the Martin's money. Fortunately for Henri, the Africans were also familiar to Nichol who had learned how to deal with inconsistencies. On the last trip it seems, the local agents had difficulties with basic arithmetic of;

Twenty passengers @ euro 2,000 per person =35,000 euro.

Like most criminal enterprises "sorry I made a mistake let me make up the 5,000 difference" rarely worked. The agents involved were found drowned a month later.

This time everything was in order, the police nowhere to be seen, so they waved goodbye to those departing on the waters. The Martin men drove to the lorry park for their switch to being truck drivers. Of the three, only Henri lacked an HGV licence but he was content to sit in the cab and listen to heavy rock music. The other two would do some driving "to keep in practice" should they be needed in the future.

Henri checked his phone for the trailer names and registration numbers. He called the lead driver who told him where the three vehicles were waiting and he allocated them to his men on the way over. The members challenged the individual drivers to make sure they were as expected. One failed the test, Henri summoned Ynon to explain what was wrong. It seemed that the driver was not as originally specified but was the brother, Jean, who lived in the UK. Henri called Saville to explain the problem and asked what he should do. The phone was handed to Jean who apologised profusely to Saville before agreeing he should call his brother who was ill and at home with his wife. A call was made and answered by Miss Elizabeth, with the wife plus the missing driver whispering close by. The Stones associate, used her best theatricals to explain her husband was now in hospital in mortal danger, so please let his brother help as they needed the money. Saville let her go with the usual warning that they knew where they lived, plus a 25% cut in the fee. The missing driver was being recruited by Miss Elizabeth as a future informer.

"Saville is okay with the guy he knows them," Henri told Ynon who was happy to accept the news and get into his cab. Henri joined his driver, while Nichol gave a thumbs up and they were all good to go. Ynon's vehicle would lead as it contained Jean who spoke the best English and could deal with or relay any questions that came up. Henri did not care, he put on his music and relaxed while they pulled away. They passed French customs quickly before being stopped a short distance away on the UK side. One of the customs men ran out of the office and waived for all three vehicles to go to the inspection bays. Jean's vehicle was directed to the customs shed. While the Frenchmen waited they could see the Englishman talking on the phone. Henri and his men began to suspect treachery by the stand-in driver and began to consider what they would do to him and his family if their passengers were discovered. Ynon was scrutinising proceedings while fending off Henri's demands for an explanation. To their surprise, Jean emerged laughing, joking and shaking hands with the customs officers. One even patted him on the back as he climbed back into the cab. He smiled and waved to the officials before leading the other two trucks towards embarkation.

As they travelled towards the queue for loading Jean told Ynon, "the customs man is my brother-in-law. He knew we would be passing through here today so took the opportunity to stop us to hold a three-way call thanking me and the wife for donating clothes to their charity. He apologised if that caused any problems, "I had to play along to keep our cover, but I was shitting myself all the way through." While it was true the caller thanked Jean for his donation, it was for providing the French smugglers" plans, rather than clothes, in order to arrange for a welcoming committee in the UK.

Ynon laughed with relief and called Henri to explain the unusual situation. "Nothing to worry about, our driver here has a customs officer for a brother-in-law who apologises for holding us up," laughed Ynon getting a tiny bit hysterical. Jean was happy to hear Henri laugh besides making rude comments, at the other end of the phone. The two Martin members took the opportunity to talk about what they were going to do in London especially, the entertainment at Un gros's bar. The discussion continued once they had parked the trucks on the ferry and bought some coffee.

Down in the trucks inside the belly of the ferry, the passengers were lying or sitting uncomfortably eking out what few provisions they had brought with them. It was only made bearable because of an open hatch and the fair weather producing a temperature in the mid-teens centigrade. The immigrants spoke few words while holding onto the hope that their suffering would be worthwhile when they made it to England. In contrast, the smugglers dined well for a ferry, their only concern was getting to Essex as early as possible to unload. Not once did they think about the welfare of their human cargo. Why would they? The Africans were not going to die in the next few hours. Besides it would be too much hassle to open the doors to give them food, they might go crazy and run away.

Once the ferry docked, the smugglers departed for the M20 and Maidstone services to meet up with Saville to get instructions for the delivery. In the services area, they parked the trucks in a formation that would allow them to leave in convoy. Once they dismounted the vehicles, Jean urged everyone to use the main services rather than the truckies hut to drink more coffee. They agreed and walked off leaving Jean lagging behind in the spitting rain. Eventually, he managed to lose them so he could walk over to the supermarket truck parked in the corner near the exit. The driver jumped down to meet him.

"Everything ready John?" asked the lorry driver aka customs team leader.

"Yes sir," he replied. "They are in the main services so your guys can set a trap for when we mount up to leave. I must go and catch them up or they will get suspicious."

He ran off to complain they had left him behind and he couldn't find them. They just laughed and carried on waiting for the arrival of Saville. Thirty minutes later their fellow Martin member arrived with a big smile and jaunty walk. He hugged his colleagues and then asked about Jean. They told him he was one of Sylvain's men and was driving Ynon's truck. The criminals sat together, continuing to talk loudly about nothing much until they arrived at the task at hand. Progress was slow, they were being distracted by an older man trying to keep his dog under control. The man ended up close to their seats before the dog stopped and lay down. The man apologised to them but Henri whispered insults and gestured before turning back to continue the conversation.

"We need to take the trucks to a warehouse in a place called Goodmayes near Ilford town centre," Saville informed them. "We offload the African men when it gets dark. Sorry Henri but Sylvain wants the three girls to play with before selling them. I could not say no, you know what he is like when he doesn't get his way, he would threaten us all." In reality, only a small bribe was needed to gain Saville's co-operation. "Did any of you see what they looked like? The more beautiful the longer he will keep them and the more unpleasant it will be." They shook their heads saying they were all covered up with headscarves. He was hoping they turned out to be worth the money he received or he would have to avoid Sylvain for a while. Saville could see the men wanted to know more, "it's a long story, but one of our

Calais Africans took their pictures when loading and sent them to Sylvain by mistake, the stupid bastard says he thought he was sending them to me. Christ knows how he got hold of Sylvain's number but I will deal with that shit when I get back." He rapidly changed the subject, we let the men go in twos or threes before we transfer the women to a car that will be waiting for them.

"Are you sure they are actually in the lorries if none of us has seen them?" asked Jean looking around the group.

"We saw them not their faces," the other drivers replied almost in unison. Henri blew a breathe thinking how stupid he would look to the rest of the Martin family if he turned up with office supplies rather than people.

"What if one of the men owns the girls and starts a row?" asked Jean trying to be involved and helpful. "What do we do then?" working on the principle the more he said the more they forgot he wasn't part of the crime Family.

"That nearly always happens and we have to get rid of them somehow," replied Saville. "Sometimes we chase them away but this time we will have Lena waiting to take the girls. She will tell their family we are looking after the girls until the morning when it's safe to let them go and we give them a phone number to call. Lena will answer and agree on a meeting place where we never turn up. Most times, however, they don't argue for long and run away to avoid being caught. We have even pretended to be police to make them run away," he laughed. "By the way, do you have that little present for Lena?" he continued pointing a "pistol hand" towards Henri.

"Yes I do, I have it in my rucksack, I completely forgot about it. Merde, what if the police had searched me at the port, I should be more careful." He reddened as he thought of the calamity such carelessness could bring but he rallied to ask Saville, "so what route are we taking then?"

"Right," said Saville and read from his phone. "We are going to continue on the M20 autoroute to the M25 autoroute and round to the A12 then onto Goodmayes. I will send you these directions and you can use your phone to navigate. "What's your number Jean?" he asked and then included him in the text. "If you break down or get lost, call me so we can arrange to meet up, we don't want to have the Africans die inside the trucks. Clear?"

"Yes," said Jean turning to Henri. "There are seven of us, two drivers plus me, Saville, Ynon, Nichol and you, we only need three or four, does that mean I am done and have to hitch a ride home from here?"

"Yes, no, of course not," replied Henri. "I have already agreed with Nichol that he will take Saville's car back to London. Saville will stay with us and replace Nichol. You will continue to drive Ynon's truck and my driver will stay with me. Anything else?" Silence. "Time to go," said Henri. The old man stood up and started to leave getting in their way. Jean being his helpful self, suggested they should all "take a piss" they nodded and followed him leaving Henri whispering more insults. Once outside, the old man was transformed running with his dog to the supermarket truck to receive further orders. While he waited the dog conducted an elaborate smelling exercise.

The customs team had listened to and communicated Saville's plans to their controllers and the field commander awaited instructions. The original intention had been to arrest them all at the services but, with trafficking a possibility they were revisiting that decision. Central Command was weighing up whether or not to accept the loss of illegal migrants and/or gang members in order to capture Sylvain in possession of trafficable females. The latter would be a bigger win.

Henri led his team back to the trucks and ordered Jean to continue at point in case anything unforeseen happened. He would be in the second truck, with Saville bringing up the rear. Jean led off driving slowly in a semi-circle towards the exit with Henri's truck in formation, carrying out the same manoeuvre. As Henri approached the exit the supermarket truck reversed and crashed into the cab just behind the driver's door. Both trucks stopped instantly, the driver of the supermarket vehicle dismounted from his cab and rushed around to see what he had done. Saville ignored the situation and squeezed past the second truck to follow Jean who had stopped to look. An exasperated Henri climbed out of the cab, waving for his colleagues to leave without him. Within a few minutes, they had left the services and were heading west towards the M25 motorway.

At the services, the two trucks were separated but causing traffic problems while the drivers exchanged details. The police arrived to help out and reroute the traffic. Henri was looking forward to leaving when the driver of the supermarket truck started yelling at Henri's driver telling him it was all his fault. Quickly one of the police intervened while the other started to inspect the supermarket truck. He began by tapping the side of the vehicle then made a call on his radio. In less than a minute another car drew up and two more police climbed out, one joined the radioing officer and the other just stood, looking formidable in body armour with a sidearm strapped to his upper leg. After a few seconds, he walked behind his vehicle, opened the boot and left it open, as if he was preparing to remove something.

The radioing officer then continued with his plan to look inside the supermarket truck, even though it was a solid trailer and had not left the UK. The driver was summoned to open the back.

With the police distracted, Henri suggested to his driver that they should get going as there was only superficial damage and they had already exchanged details. They were immediately stopped by a police officer standing halfway along the trailer. The officer asked them to stay put and be patient while they dealt with the other truck. He strolled over to stand next to them. Henri started to moan that he was late but felt conscious of the watching armed police officer. Suddenly there were several shouts and what looked like two illegal immigrants jumped out of the supermarket truck and tried to run, but were brought down and restrained. The driver was escorted to one of the police cars. The Martin member watched the police summon a van to transfer the illegals and decided to call Saville to describe what was happening. The officer next to Henri looked at him and said nothing as the call turned into a running commentary.

He switched to English briefly to speak to the officer, "just talking to my colleagues," the officer nodded looking relaxed as he had obviously seen this many times before.

Then for the Martins events took a turn for the worse, the police told Henri they would do him a favour, by checking his truck to make sure no illegals had snuck in. Henri tried to protest but they told him it was no trouble and reminded him of the fines for transporting illegal immigrants. Henri began to panic as his driver slowly opened the rear doors and the modified transit van arrived to stop between the two trucks. The cuffed illegals from the supermarket truck were helped into the van, while the police climbed into the back of Henri's truck. Within seconds there were shouts as the four illegals were discovered. The exhausted men were encouraged not to resist, to get out slowly, not run and accept water. The police officer next to Henri said nothing as the Frenchman continued talking to Saville - now suggesting he was doomed.

Henri pocketed his phone and looked around for an exit, he was fighting an urge to run. The supermarket truck was driven off as he watched the illegal immigrants being taken from his truck and loaded into the van. His driver was then escorted to a police vehicle which left him standing unsure what to do next. Fleetingly he wondered whether he could just walk away, he was not the driver. He turned to look for the coffee shop but faced a black unmarked police car, complete with flashing blue grille lights and two armed police officers. One walked towards him, then past him and climbed into the cab while the other stood by the car holding an assault rifle in both hands. The policeman standing next to him stepped back a few paces before the word GUN was shouted by an officer emerging with Lena's "little present" in his gloved hand, a brand new two-colour Glock 43. Before Henri closed his eyes and dropped to the ground he saw a long gun pointing at him, he knew the drill. He was cuffed, taken to the unmarked vehicle where he was joined by his driver and they were taken away in silence. Henri was thinking how unlucky he was to get caught during a freak accident. Exactly what the Martin men were supposed to believe.

On the way to the Dover detention facilities, the illegal immigrants from Henri's truck had plenty of time to tell their story to the "pretenders" from the supermarket truck. Intelligence gained in this unstructured way would help to identify the Calais based Martin smugglers. Getting information that way often proved more effective than formal interviews where the illegals would refuse to speak unless heavily incentivised. The Field Commander reported to his superiors that thanks to a rather elaborate plan, four of the twelve illegal immigrants and two smugglers had been detained. He hoped that the gamble of letting the remainder continue on their way would lead officers to a West London criminal gang known to be behind a sizable smuggling and trafficking route.

The remaining two trucks travelled around the M25 towards the A12, none of the men spoke. Saville was struggling to process how a senior Martin member could be lost in such a freakish way. He tried to call Pascal to share the pain, but his phone was off. He avoided contacting Madame Martin or Patrice as he thought it would be a waste of time. *They would just blame me and insult me even though I could do nothing about it*, he thought. As they proceeded along the A12 he asked Ynon if he should take over. The Martin member, still in shock at losing his friend, declared he was happy to have his older colleague run things while they were in the UK. Saville then spoke to Jean to explain the tragedy and his new position. With a tiny smile, Jean professed sadness at such a fine man being arrested in such an unfortunate way. To lighten the mood he told Saville they would be arriving at the warehouse at about 4 pm.

Saville summoned up the courage to call Sylvain to tell him about the disaster. The gang leader true to form responded with a tirade of abuse until Saville was able to tell him that his girls were safe in the back of a truck. The gang leader switched to commiserate about the loss of such a great man as Henri. Then went back to yelling again when Saville explained they had lost Lena's "little present'. Eventually, Sylvain stopped yelling to give him more instructions.

"Lena will be over to pick up the girls at about 5 o'clock depending on the traffic. Do you think you can avoid losing my girls between now and then?" Sylvain said sarcastically.

"Merci Sylvain," Saville responded quietly hoping Un gros would be happy once he had the girls and he could go home to Marseille. *God, I fucking hate that man,* he thought as he pocketed his phone.

The remaining two trucks arrived at the almost empty Goodmayes warehouse at around 4 pm. As the noises from their diesel engines died away, the men stayed in their cabs waiting to see if anything bad was going to happen. After all the drama they felt strangely calm, they thought the worst was over, only the local traffic made any sound on this late Essex afternoon. The next job would be to get rid of the African men and put the girls into Lena's people carrier, but that could wait until she arrived.

For Saville and Ynon it was just another day in the life of crime family members, they would quickly forget this setback to be ready for their next mission. Such disasters would no doubt happen again and again until they finally met the same fate as

Henri or worse. For Saville's driver, it was just cash for his family.

For Jean, it was the excitement of being on an undercover mission and the satisfaction of stopping people smugglers. But now he was uncertain what to do, *should I be stopping the trafficking?* he thought. No one paid any attention when he announced he needed to have a piss and a smoke, after all, he was one of the team, right? He took the opportunity to get instructions.

The rest of the team took the opportunity to rest before the arrival of Lena had them working again.

Chapter 48: Marseille, Friday afternoon

Chevy and his team sat in their vehicles and waited two streets away, while Hockey walked to the entrance of the warehouse office. He was challenged by three police officers, who subsequently escorted him into the building. Once inside, the Stones associate conferred with the officers who agreed they were ready although expressed serious reservations about the American's plan. The senior officer made a call, then there was a short pause before a marked police car arrived stopping outside the main office. The two occupants climbed out, chatting to each other and went into the building. With this activity, Lamarr, a member of the drugs team, wandered over to the front gate and watched while pretending to make a call. Chevy moved to take up a position at the far end of the complex, close to the old building with the secret entrance, which was being guarded by two gendarme officers with H&K assault rifles. The officers looked bored having nothing to say to each other. Chevy, a US television addict, smiled and thought, *the family must be really badass if the pigs have to use those bad boys.* Hockey left the warehouse after ten minutes and shook hands with the officers the members had met on the previous night. The senior officer using a beckoning motion caused his colleagues to get into their vehicles and leave. Chevy watched the armed officers leave surprised at the power the American had over the Gendarmerie.

With the police gone, confirmed by a search of the area, Hockey notified JD they would be in position in a few minutes. He was advised to proceed and jogged over to the members'' vehicles. He jumped into one of the cars, to some celebration by the criminals, they drove the short distance to the property next door to the warehouse.

Hockey was at the front of the group of eight men vying with Chevy to be first in. Two of the smiling members whispered the American was enjoying himself so much perhaps he should join the family. At the first door into the warehouse, they came to a stop, the lock seemed to be jammed. Chevy put it down to operator error and nerves as it opened easily at the second attempt. The men proceeded through the second door into the gloomy warehouse and stopped to check for a trap. It was silent, they scanned the area with torches halting every few seconds to look at the battle damage and areas of dried liquid. Chevy wondered how much it would cost to fix the place or whether they would bother once they had recovered the money. Seeing the place in the semi-darkness made them feel angry but appreciative of the efforts made by their colleagues. They continued to creep along the inside wall using it as a guide to the cellar, nothing untoward was happening.

For one final check, while they still had a chance to turn around and get out, Chevy sent Hockey into the open space with a bulletless gun in his hand. Nothing happened, so he returned to tell them it was fine there was no one around and to stop being a bunch of wusses.

"Come on man let's get some stuff so we can do it," suggested Hockey pressing a nostril and trying to be Californian. Although struggling with his accent they got the gist and laughed. Before they could move any further one of the three sentries texted Chevy that a porc was wandering around outside and what should they do about it. An angry Chevy turned to Hockey threatening death if they failed now. The Stones associate shrugged, cursed and asked for the number to call the guard. Chevy grabbed his arm then told him to get out there and get rid of the officer. They agreed to wait until he had dealt with the situation in case they had to leave and come back another time.

Hockey approached the gendarme officer who took up an intimidating stance. The sentry called Chevy to begin a whispered commentary on what was happening. The conversation started well with the officer shouldering his rifle. Then there was an argument and the officer drew his sidearm while allowing Hockey to make a call. The police car returned and the two "friendly" officers got out to explain what was happening. The gendarme holstered his weapon apologised, laughed, shook hands and got into the car with the other two. The sentries missed the wink from the American and told Chevy it was now all clear, Hockey was on his way back to them.

Chevy and his men continued deep into the eerie echoing warehouse leaving Hockey to catch up. They stopped on reaching the wine bottling area, now strewn with broken tanks, bottles and wooden boxes. One of the men shone his light on the crates, home to spiders now weaving giant webs, grateful for the ongoing feast brought about by settling dust. The men eventually arrived at the hidden cellar door. They unfolded jumbo laundry bags and began forming a chain ready to take away their loot. This was going to be hard work, they had forsaken their team of Africans.

Chevy removed the cellar cover to descend the stairs to the entrance. It was closed but opened when he turned the handle, it should have been locked. He remembered it usually took a shoulder to open when it was properly shut. *Must have been fixed and they forgot to lock it,* thought Chevy.

He switched on the lights, walked towards the pallets at the far end of the cellar where the money had been stashed under a tarpaulin. Pascal had instructed they remove the cash first and get it shipped to a secure location near the Martin villa. Lamarr and Harbin joined their leader, the three men surrounded the pallet ready to slowly lift the covering to avoid spreading the money on the floor. Chevy first peeked then tore back the tarp to stare, along with the other men, at empty boxes stacked neatly on top of each other. Chevy looked around, *maybe it was the wrong pallet,* he thought. But there were no others. "It's gone," he said. "The fucking money is gone it's been stolen." Lamarr ran across to the drugs cage, it was empty. He fell to his knees and screamed, the others ran over to join him. They were struggling to process what they had found. There was a note on the cage door, "Tous partis, merci'. Chevy shouted to bring him the American. The men outside the cellar unnerved by the noise replied he was not back from seeing the gendarmes. He rang his sentries, one after the other there was no reply. At that moment he realised they had been sucker-punched.

"What do we do now?" asked Lamarr. "We've been robbed, we must leave," he continued in a high pitch voice. Then went berserk and ran out of the cellar shouting RUNNNN, leaving Chevy and Harbin behind. He sprinted across the warehouse floor towards the exit collecting panicking members on the way. Once the first three appeared in the building next door, the gendarmes stepped out of the darkness, pointed assault rifles, demanded they stop, drop their weapons and get on the floor. The men were so startled they ignored the officers and continued to run to avoid capture. In a reflex action, one member tried to retrieve a weapon from his waistband but failed, as several shots took him to ground. The deafening sound, reverberated around the building, causing the remaining men to freeze, before complying with the instructions.

The captured Martin members were cuffed before being thrown into the back of a police wagon to join their two colleagues who were acting as sentries. A third sentry, also too slow on the draw, was awaiting an ambulance to deal with his gunshot wounds. After wishing terrible retribution on Hockey, Chevy and Harbin debated whether to behave like Butch Cassidy and the Sundance Kid, charge out guns blazing shooting the pigs on their way to the van or simply give up. Chevy suggested they go through the warehouse office, then sneak out the front gate. The plan might have worked but for the gendarmes who were there having a quiet smoke. The two men surrendered and ended up in a transit van reportedly destined for the local Commissariat.

The men known to be leaders were purportedly being taken to a separate location for questioning about what people and which vineyards were involved in the Martin wine scam. Neither of them was aware of this special treatment nor that they would be held as terrorists to avoid any leaks. They spent most of the journey moaning about the American traitor, taking comfort in what Pascal would do to him and his "bitch" girlfriend when he got back from wherever he was.

Someone changed the plan, they were not going to be asked about wine but something apparently more important. The operation that had been meticulously planned was now considered a failure by the gendarmes and someone would have to explain what went wrong to their boss the Minister.

Once they arrived, the Martin members were hustled from the car to the interrogation rooms and made "comfortable" before the inquisition could begin. The gendarmes practised their questions, they would focus on the "small picture" as Stones had suspected they would.

Questions like:

• Why had they gone through the farce of pretending to recover drugs and money from an empty warehouse? Who told them to do it?

• Where were the drugs and money now, who was concealing them or who would know where they are?

• What did they know about the location of gang leader Matisse Martin and his son Thierry both of whom had not been seen for more than two weeks?

• Why is Matisse's wife spending so much time with the associates from BloedStone?

• Did she do a deal with BloedStone so they have the money, if so where is it?

• Who else knows anything about the drugs and money – name them and give contact details.

Unfortunately for the police, Chevy feared Pascal more than them and Harbin knew nothing.

After the excitement died down, Hockey was charged with making sure the French authorities did not connect the warehouse incident with the deal in Bandol or any pending activities. They were to believe that the Stones associates were only there to organise a deception to allow the gendarmerie to capture both loot and criminals. It was a favour to the French government.

Hockey declared he had no idea what happened to the drugs and money nor did he care. He was in tears, gesticulating wildly and stumbling along the street.

It was 5.30 pm.

Chapter 49: Algiers town, Friday lunchtime

It was lunchtime as Pascal's small executive jet was arriving at Houari Boumediene airport in Algiers after a delay due to an engine problem. The faulty plane had been provided by Sylvain's brother Benoit, who traded in drugs and prostitution from his comfortable offices in Nice, southeast France. Pascal still wanted to be in and out of the city no later than mid-afternoon but feared now they would not leave until after dark. He was a nervous flyer and a return trip at night in such a small plane made him feel uneasy.

Although he was descending into a foul mood the family enforcer was thinking positively about the afternoon meeting. He believed that rescuing the Martin boy would significantly enhance his chances of becoming the next leader of the business. He was sure that Thierry, overjoyed at his rescue, would be happy to persuade his mother, who he probably thought had kidnapped him, to step aside and leave Marseille or better still France. If Thierry agreed to that, then they would take him back to Marseille, *if not he would have an unfortunate accident or go on a fishing trip where he will become the bait,* thought a smiling Pascal.

As the plane readied for landing Pascal thought about the previous night with Saloni. He had become fascinated by both her beauty and size, but could not understand how such a "salope d'arabe en chaleur " could be with such a wimpy American. He fantasised about her being naked and on her knees, even got himself excited as he wondered if she liked it "dans le cul'. He decided she wanted him, then wondered when he should call her. Mid thought the plane's wheels bumped the runway bouncing him out of his daydream, but not before he made a note to reconnect with her once he was finished in Algiers. *After all,* he thought, *that dirty bitch would now be with his guys at the warehouse getting their money back. As much as I want "chatte", I want that money more, enough for me to take over the family and get rid of that Martin whore.*

Once the plane had come to a halt, he instructed the pilot to be ready to leave by late afternoon or early evening. He left no doubt that they would be returning that night probably with an extra passenger. Pascal hurried through Arrivals followed by Driton and Dobri. The two French Africans had been smuggled out of Algeria to labour in the family wine business. However, through a series of promotions they had become members of the people smuggling team, before being transferred to work with Sylvain's gang, where they had become very useful no-fuss assassins. The three-man were met by Vedatsie and Uranie, from the local team, who were providing the transport. First stop, the Martin's local premises to collect some weapons.

It was a compound of sorts; high walls, heavy gates, a large partly enclosed courtyard. Inside it was equipped like a normal house plus an enormous cellar to store pre-trafficked people, being used for either entertainment or the gratification of Martin members. Pascal loved the place wishing he had one in Marseille.

The three men stood in the kitchen talking about what they were going to do to retrieve the Martin boy. Pascal explained that he was acting on a tip that Thierry was being held by a rival gang at a nearby location. He needed help to rescue the boy but did not know who he could trust because there were traitors all around, so he sought help from his friend Sylvain. The men accepted everything they were told, even praising Sylvain for allowing them to help the Martin family. They quickly agreed on a not too subtle extraction plan involving breaking into the property, shooting the kidnappers, removing Thierry and taking him back to the compound in a truck. Apparently, they only needed the three of them as their intelligence had told them there were only four gangsters and the Martin team would easily overwhelm them. Pascal failed to mention that it was he and Sylvain who actually stashed Thierry in the nearby hotel, with only two new hires as guards.

As they were finishing Pascal's phone rang, it came up as an international number he ignored it. The phone rang again he ignored it, the caller kept trying. Finally, with a curse, he took the call and heard shouts and gunfire at the other end. The caller identified himself as one of the men posted at Thierry's hotel, they were under fire and needed help.

It had been a while since Shamir and Texas had broken into Thierry's room to brief him on the rescue. Their arrival was a shock when the door was unlocked and instead of the boring and unpleasant guards, two people wearing masks and carrying assault rifles entered. He wanted to shout, but they both put a finger to their lips urging him to keep quiet. He stayed still, they showed no violent intent, one removed a mask and spoke to him in French. She explained they were American security agents acting at the request of his mother, to return him to France. When he looked sceptical, they assured him that she did not have him kidnapped.

Shamir explained, "I'm afraid it looks like someone in the UK, a guy called Sylvain and some of your mother's men are responsible for you being stuck here."

When Thierry started to speak they tried to shush him again but he managed to demand proof of who they were, threatening not to co-operate. While he watched the associates contact Jack, he thought, *it makes perfect sense, Pascal and that bastard Sylvain arranged everything.* He wanted to shout out but remembered he had to stay silent. Texas lifted his mask to tell him how they could prove who they were, but the Frenchman was immediately distracted by the voice which reminded him of Hollywood westerns. Shamir left the two talking and waited by the door listening, hoping that the guards did not return.

"We can't let you phone your girlfriend or mother as it might be tracked," said Texas. "But I think we can have you use my comms system, provided you speak quietly." Texas quickly attached it to Thierry who spoke to Rosa and his mother. Tears flowed as they whispered to each other. "That's it, dude, you have to stop we need to explain the plan," said Texas taking back his device. Thierry recovered and listened sceptically to the risky proposal pitting two Stones associates against the numerous local Martin members.

"We are pretty sure this Pascal guy has not come here to execute you, a local could have done that," said Texas. "You should be safe provided you agree to what he wants and definitely don't piss him off," he continued. Thierry agreed and continued to nod as the rest of the plan was unveiled. Texas insisted they would be following his every move to make sure he was safe. An exaggeration that caused a slight flicker to the left eye of a stony-faced Shamir. When they were finished, Thierry was encouraged to take off his trousers so Texas could insert a tracker in the rear waistband.

When he was fully dressed he asked, "so I must pretend that I am still a loyal family member, is that right?" he hated the idea but was resigned to it as a means of escape.

"Yes sir, that's about right but don't worry, if you play your part right we will have you home tonight," replied Texas. "Everything okay?" he asked Shamir, she nodded. "Then I'm history," he walked to the door holstered his sidearm took Shamir's rifle and slung it over his shoulder. He tapped her on the shoulder whispering "be careful," she smiled and he left the room for his exit on the ground floor. His next task, wait near the hidden rental car for Shamir to complete her antics.

"Pret a jouer?" she asked Thierry. "Just follow the script and you will be fine, probably best to hide behind that heavy wardrobe, to make sure you don't get hit by anything when I get going," she continued smiling

"Oui" he replied pondering how such a beautiful woman was about to reign down chaos on Pascal and his men. "Good luck and I will see you soon. I hope," he continued.

"Oui pretty boy," she laughed and disappeared.

A few minutes later, Thierry heard gunfire and snuck a look out of the window. He stared down at Shamir in the car park using a rapid-fire handgun to pin down his guards. The two men returned fire by holding their weapons in the air and pointing them in her general direction. She stopped firing, they showed themselves, she nicked them in the upper arm and skipped out of the car park.

The Stones associate ran to the rental car to grab her kitbag, reload and get a lift to the Martin compound, for the next part of the mission. When they arrived at the compound she jumped out of the car, Texas told her to be careful, again, before he rushed back to a building near the hotel, to watch Pascal and his men.

Pascal's pretend rescue mission had suddenly become real. He rushed into the courtyard shouting for Uranie to assemble the men to rescue Thierry, who was being held in a nearby hotel by a rival gang. Although happy for Martin junior to die, going this way could ruin his plan. To make sure the rescue was a success, he was taking no chances. That meant, as the Stones associates had hoped, he took fourteen men assembled in four cars using two different routes to avoid any police interference. It would take about twenty minutes to get to the hotel depending on the traffic, which was chaotic in the city at the best of times. On the way, Pascal kept telling himself how lucky it was it happened when he was here otherwise it could have been a disaster? *This must be a rival gang*, he thought, *but how did they find out where Thierry was?*

Once they arrived, the scene was reminiscent of an FBI raid gone mad, with men jumping out of cars brandishing illegal weapons swarming over the hotel grounds front and back, looking for someone to shoot at. Thierry's guards, both sporting a bandage, thinking it was more of the same group started shooting out of the windows at anyone who looked armed. The Martin men returned fire but most struggled to see the opposition. Pascal managed to reach his new hires and pretended to offer them assistance, which they welcomed. Since it was his men outside, Pascal realised the unknown gangsters must have already left, which meant the existence of the two guards had become a problem for him. He did not hesitate, shooting both men from behind to put them down, then again from the front, to claim he won a shootout.

With no one shooting at them the Martin members slowly lost interest and wandered back to the front reception area where they saw Pascal talking with the hotel staff. "What the hell happened?" he demanded to know. The staff were in a state of shock, nothing like it had ever happened before. Their condition worsened when the dead guards appeared having been found and carried out in sheets. A confusing story began to unfold from the manager;

"Two people, a man and a woman, I think, came into the hotel, we thought they were guests or meeting someone for a drink or a meal so we paid them no attention. Then we think they tried to get into the bedroom of one of our guests who is, was, next to those two over there," said the manager pointing at the dead guards. "We don't know why they started fighting but one of them climbed out of the window and those two started shooting at him. He started shooting back. One of them was very tall," using his hands to demonstrate height. "He ran away first carrying some big guns like you use for hunting. The other one must have run away as he is not here now. At least I don't think so but you had better check. We don't know exactly everything we all hid in the kitchen. Then you all came and started shooting at those two."

"I thought you said it was a man and a woman, was there really three of them?" asked Pascal running through what he had been told. *They must have been assassins, which means there must be another gang after Thierry,* thought Pascal waiting for a reply.

"I don't know much, I'm sorry, it was terrible, I thought we would all die. Maybe they were terrorists planting bombs here. We must look for the…," mumbled an even more frantic manager.

As if suddenly remembering why he was there, he ordered two of his men to follow him upstairs to complete the rescue mission. He arrived outside the hotel room hoping nothing bad had happened to the Martin boy, at least not yet. After considerable encouragement, Thierry opened the door to welcome his rescuer. They embraced as though they were long lost, friends. While Thierry gathered up what little possessions he had Pascal questioned him about who tried to break into his hotel room. Thierry explained he was baffled by the whole episode.

"I think I was being held by one of the drug gangs from back home in Marseille who said they were going to ransom me." He then explained how they tricked him into coming to Algiers knowing Pascal already knew. "Then another gang said they had come to rescue me but only wanted to take me for themselves like they were going to traffick me or something equally as bad," Thierry continued before waffling on about how terrible it was. "I have no idea who they were, but I'm so grateful that you are here to rescue me," he concluded following the Stones instructions to play nice.

"Thank God they failed," Pascal said sounding genuine. "You will be safe from now on, the men holding you have been killed and we are getting rid of their bodies. Are you sure they never said who they were?" he asked again. Thierry shook his head which brought a smile to the enforcer, he could carry on with the plan rather than an execution.

"No idea they just locked me in and had the hotel deliver shit food with crap wine," sounding equally genuine. "Thanks again for saving me," Thierry replied trying to show real emotion.

Pascal described how he found out where he was being held from a corrupt member who was taking bribes from a drug cartel. The rescue had to be planned and carried secretly, at great personal risk to avoid traitors. He named Patrice as the one who hated Thierry and had worked with his mother to orchestrate the kidnapping to make sure she stayed in control of the family money. "She wants to waste money on her stupid schemes, rather than use it for the good of the whole family," he complained. Thierry joined in suggesting his mother hating him was part of the reason he had left for England. On the way out of the room, Thierry thought how depraved Pascal had become.

The two men arrived in the hotel reception area ready to go once Pascal's men had completed their search for the mysterious attackers. The gang enforcer was disappointed to leave without a chance to persuade Thierry to support his prospective leadership but encouraged by Thierry's dislike of his mother. Pascal decided they would leave early and have a more nuanced discussion on the plane.

Texas missed Pascal's men storming the hotel, he arrived on station as the criminals were gathering in the car park to wait for the ambulance. Through his scope, he determined that neither of the bodies lying on the concrete was Thierry and assumed the men had been killed in the attack. "Okay go ahead," Texas suggested to Shamir. "I don't think they're in a rush they're just milling around. There are two crims down, I missed the shooting, so not sure how it happened. I count twelve of them here, we were told sixteen after their latest shipment. So there maybe three or four waiting to greet you," he said chuckling.

"Roger that Mr Ranger," Shamir responded smiling to herself after remembered a television programme she watched as a child.

Chapter 50: Algiers, Friday afternoon

Shamir entered the compound through the unlocked front gate to begin searching for the guards with her Glock out front and her South African Baton in the seam pocket of her fatigues. She moved like a hunting cat, focused, graceful, almost silent, green eyes searching for prey. Upstairs nothing, back downstairs nothing, searching each room, all clear, all clear until she pounced on the first guard who was enjoying a wrap in the kitchen. The fight was brief but too noisy, she held back being firm rather than destructive. The second guard came running, shouting and waving his pistol. He caught a glimpse, aimed but then lost her behind the kitchen centre island. The momentary lapse allowed her to skirt around the furniture emerge behind him and strike a double-handed blow with her baton. He crashed face-first into the centre island badly hurt and unconscious. She collected their sidearms thinking, *these are pretty shitty,* then emptied the magazines. Unlike in Iraq, she resisted the temptation to shoot the guards, instead applied plastic handcuffs plus a gag. She returned to the now clear downstairs office, to search for papers or equipment that might contain incriminating information. She found two laptops along with something that resembled a ledger and stuffed them into her backpack. She flinched at the increase in weight.

"This is your Texas Ranger speaking, how's it going over there? The bandits look like they are getting ready to leave town so you have about thirty minutes maximum before they are all over you."

"Roger that, two bad boys down, now about to free the prisoners. There should be plenty of time to get things done then meet up. I just hope when they run out of the building they don't cause too much of a ruckus."

"Please be careful, I would like to fly you home in one piece if that's okay" he replied in a very non-military manner. He had grown fond of her in the short time he had known her.

"Roger that too, don't you be late either Lonely Ranger," she said chuckling. Shamir decided to call him that rather than Texas Ranger, he was a lonely old shooter. She loved the cowboy drawl, his superficial laid back attitude along with his very high hit rate.

The Stones Commander ran quietly down the staircase to the cellar where she was confronted by a large wooden door originally intended to keep sound in, but today it kept sound out. She managed to open it with a small squeak hoping to catch the third guard unawares. He had heard nothing, he was preoccupied with raping one of the younger women and rapidly approaching the "money shot'. Shamir crept in, the women saw her first and suddenly jerked up causing the guard to lose his momentum. He withdrew, let go of the girl's hips and turned to see Cat's eyes staring at him along with a handgun pointing at his lower body. He looked ridiculous with his trousers around his ankles and holding his shrinking manhood as though he might use it instead of a weapon. Shamir stepped forward and struck him just above his left ear. They blow left him lying face down on the dirty slab flooring. While the girl ran away, the Stones commander dragged him to the waste pipe, where she secured one arm with a plastic cable.

"You DIRTY LITTLE bastard," she sneered at him wiggling her little finger. He was badly concussed as he looked up, blood ran down the side of his neck, he tried to speak but instead spat blood at his attacker. Shamir had already stepped back having previously learned getting close could get mucky. She made a note to forget he was there as she hit him on the right shoulder to cripple his arm. He was now a mess.

Shamir was about to release the prisoners when she glimpsed the girl cringing in the far corner. Although she was short of time Shamir ran over to hug her while explaining she would be free to go once the other prisoners were set free. Fortunately, the cell keys were hanging on the right hooks which made the release easy. Once they were all out of their cells she asked the prisoners, speaking in both English and French, to follow her into the courtyard and wait quietly. Eventually, there were thirty women in addition to a handful of men waiting to leave. Most of them looked in good physical condition even though they had been abused in one way or another. Shamir implored them to be patient while she completed her final task, to set charges to blow up the building. To do that the Stones associate placed explosives on all three floors working quickly to avoid Pascal's imminent return. She avoided the kitchen, to give two of the guards a chance of rescue, but not the cellar. Job complete, she commanded a group of prisoners to open the courtyard doors and like the start of a marathon race, they all made a run for it.

"Prisoners have been released am on my way out," she announced to her Stones partner.

"Roger that, move quickly they're nearly there" shouted Texas getting worried. The Commander ran out of the building mixing with the freed prisoners as they left en masse. *Shit, this is heavy*, she thought as the rucksack bounced around on her back. She hoped most of the escapees would run towards the main square to safety. How they would get away from there was not her problem. The mission was to release them and destroy the compound.

Shamir ducked into a side street, entered the designated safe house and nodded to the owner who pointed to a chair. She climbed into a maxi dress, to hide her fatigues, then donned a hijab to become an Arab woman, which looked a bit odd with the rucksack. She waved to the owner and left to meet Texas at the rendezvous point for the final part of the plan.

The Martin members arrived at the compound a few minutes after the released prisoners melted into the background. As they reached the gates the explosive charges went off, producing a spectacular sound with a tremor that shook them and the surrounding buildings. Although the compound was strong enough to contain the detonation the massive destruction rendered the building unusable. The resulting fire was adding to the destruction by slowly destroying those parts of the building that had remained standing. Shamir smiled and picked up her pace.

A few of Pascal's men rushed to look for their colleagues, in what had quickly become a burning shell. They eventually found and recovered two of the guards but the third remained missing and would have to be left in place until the building cooled down. No one was able to reach the office, it was destroyed along with many important records. After a few more minutes an underequipped fire brigade arrived. The firefighters tried to put the fire out but only succeeded in keeping the fire from spreading outside the compound whilst it burnt through the rest of the building.

Pascal sat in his car next to Thierry feeling dispirited at the turmoil being inflicted by someone he knew nothing about. *No one knows we are here, who is doing this,* he wondered. He rubbed his forehead.

"Who is doing this to us we must find them and quickly?" said a supposedly angry Thierry.

He did not need the boy to tell him that. For a moment he thought about hitting him but relented and instead produced a sickly smile. "Don't worry we will," he replied while Thierry continued talking. The Martin enforcer wasn't listening he was thinking about who would be capable of such a thing. He wondered whether the raid on the hotel was just a diversion to get them away from the compound. The two compound guards were in bad shape and would not be able to talk sensibly for a few days, if ever.

Thierry continued to follow the Stones advice to be nice, so he told Pascal there was nothing he could have done. "It was the damn traitors, together WE will find them. Do you think it's the same people who kidnapped me?" he asked Pascal knowing the truth. "We will find out who did this when we get back?" he continued enjoying feigning loyalty to the Martin member.

Pascal ignored him again and got out of the car to survey the damage. *Perhaps,* he thought, *if Thierry believes it was the kidnappers who wrecked the compound I will be able to get away without too much hassle.* He leant on his car, wanting more time to strategise about how to find the culprits and where to find a new base in Algiers. He decided to send for Henri to fix things in Algiers. He got back into the car. "We need to go," he said. "There's nothing for us here let's get back to Marseille".

Thierry was relieved he was ready to go home and see Rosa and his mother. "By the way, thank you for rescuing me. You did a great job and you are a great leader we need you in our family more than ever," he continued.

Pascal nodded and remembered he had not yet heard how the smuggling project had gone. He called Henri reckoning he should be on his way to someplace near London. No answer. He called Saville, no answer. He switched to the team he had in Bordeaux and called Terry Lamb surely he had done the job, no answer. He rang the other men he borrowed from Sylvain, no answer.

He called Sylvain and could not make any sense of what the gang leader was saying because of poor phone reception. *I will call them again when I get to the airport or on the plane,* he thought. He rang the pilot and told him to get ready to leave within the hour then took one last look at the compound before getting back into the rental to drive to the airport. Pascal thought about Saloni, he would call her when he landed in Toulon. He fantasised about her body, which he could have seen if he had turned around.

It was 4.30 BST

Chapter 51: Bordeaux, Friday lunchtime

Over lunch at Chateau du Carys, JD introduced Chinaman and Lavender to Robbie, who reciprocated by introducing Claude and his wife Maria. During the discussions, with Chinaman on his best behaviour, the group were distracted by the sound of angry voices from deep in the building. Robbie explained that Frederic, their former head of wine, had been arrested for working with the crime family and was being held in the cellar. "He will remain out of sight, while we get the Martin people secured inside the tasting room. So don't worry if you see a couple of police officers wandering around, they're guarding him."

"So you were a police guy, an MP," Chinaman said to Robbie. "The Brits call you Red Hats don't they?"

"Yes, I was, but we are called Redcaps," he replied. Feeling the need to justify his involvement in the project he continued, "during my term, I spent a lot of time overseas in war zones like Bosnia, the Falklands and Iraq before getting a nice office job."

"What rank did you get to by the time you finished, you must've been an officer?" continued the inquisitive Chinaman.

"I finished up a full Colonel and Deputy Head of the Royal Military Police," he replied feeling proud. It meant more to him than the mountain of cash he had built up in the last ten years. The rest of the table looked suitably impressed. "That was a former life," he continued. "Now I am retired from all that stuff and work for BloedStone finding suitable investments and running my restaurant."

"Well sir," Lavender jumped in after returning from the bathroom and a quick nose around. "By the look of things, you are going to be back in action very shortly judging by the weapons and armour you have laid out in the next room. It looks like an Alabama redneck gun shop in there," she continued with a giggle. "You must have kept your hand in to use that kit," she said with genuine admiration.

Robbie smiled at her and replied, "why yes mam."

"Arresting Frenchie gangbangers is going to be much worse than busting fun-loving troopers," suggested a smiling Chinaman. Robbie did not reply but joined in the group chuckle.

After a while the atmosphere began to change, it was getting near game time, they were contemplating going up against an unknown and potentially prodigious enemy.

JD began final preparations for the meeting due to commence at 3 pm in the main tasting room. He started by explaining what Stones had agreed to do as part of the deal with Astrid Martin and they would be told very soon if anything was to change.

Robbie took over to explain what Frederic and the Martins had done to the French wine industry and to Stones investments including the vineyard they were in. Before Chinaman could quip JD told him they were not a 70's pop group. The American smiled at the catch.

Colonel Robbie launched himself, "we need to know EXACTLY where the wine scams have been operating and by whom. We must gather up all the people who have been involved and take them out of circulation. That includes the men coming to the meeting today, they were certainly involved. It is crucial for France that you tell no one about what you do and see here today. We must do this work well and prevent news of the scam, or the scam itself from spreading like a pandemic across the French wine industry. After France, it could move to Spain or Italy and then the rest of the world. Millions of people will lose their livelihood. There are lots of citizens in your country and mine heavily invested in wine, a collapse of the industry would damage their financial security. We must bring this to an end now and you are the people to do it."

"Phew, no pressure then, not much of a wine drinker myself I prefer a Jack Daniels," said Chinaman. "Do you think they are faking that as well, some nights it seems different, kinda weaker?" he continued.

"No that's you losing your senses when your drunk," Lavender threw in to get a laugh. They all joined in, which helped to reduce the stress, Chinaman grinned revealing his big white teeth.

"Thank you, Robbie, that tells us how important it is to get this meeting right," JD cut in to get the discussion started.

They had several issues to deal with before the meeting began, it went like this:

State main problem: Patrice thought he was coming to inspect the chateau as it was being offered as part of the deal. Verses Astrid Martin had sold him out and there was no chateau for the taking.

Make suggestions: The best; offer freedom and some "go away" money in exchange for information on the rest of the scammed vineyards plus their silence.

The consensus of the group: That was a pretty poor deal and any self-respecting gangster would fight rather than take it. If he took it he would blab anyway.

Expected outcome: JD hoped, rather than expected, that the big guy would fight and Patrice would give in. Or they would have to eliminate both.

Potential complications: Robbie discovered a lot more gangster types lurking close by and they did not have the firepower to deal with them without significant violence and more gendarmes to help out.

A short story: Robbie said he deliberately met the two groups, reported by Claude's network. He was pretending to be a (drunken, effeminate and lovable) Scottish tourist to avoid conflict. "One group seemed like they could be part of the Martin gang and were here to provide back-up if anything went wrong. They let slip they lived in Marseille and that they had driven over here supposedly for a stag night. But there was only four of them, they did not drink much and went to bed early. They are in a hotel about two miles from here almost within touching distance of Patrice. The other group of three were more difficult to make out and had a Brit with them. It seemed they were waiting for someone or something. They were a very closed group who would not talk much and are located about two miles away from the others. I am almost certain they did not know the others existed. This mob disappeared soon after we got the message from Jack. Can't make out whether that was just a coincidence."

"That makes it a bit tricky," said JD replying to Robbie's story.

Decisions by JD: "First, we need to watch out for both groups but concentrate on the one closest. I guess the group of four are closest but maybe they will stay away unless Patrice whistles them up. The other three who knows? Perhaps the police can watch over them for us. What we do know is that once we kill the phone signal Patrice won't able to call his buddies so we will be left with just him and the big guy. Secondly, it's prison for those two, along with our Freddy, OR loads of useful information. Freddy will come in handy as a witness when they start arguing with us. Thirdly, it's impossible to tell, if things will go well or get messy, so we must be ready with weapons to hand."

Robbie interjected for clarification, "so for the unpleasant Brit, Terry I think they called him, and his merry men, we keep an eye out for them but we think they are part of another gang acting on orders from elsewhere. It feels uncomfortable though," he declared.

"Yeah, we will have to work on that basis unless something changes," agreed JD also feeling uncomfortable at not knowing the strength of the enemy.

The discussion moved on with Chinaman asking, "are we going to keep the same dispositions, or do we need some outward-looking protection, what do you think?"

JD couldn't help thinking what a great guy Chinaman was on the job and what an ass, off it. They reviewed deployment while enjoying the excellent chateau food accompanied by only soda. JD made a mental note to make up for the deprivation when the mission was over. They decided Chinaman would swap to roof level facing the front to watch out for any unexpected potentially hostile visitors. JD would take up a position facing down into the courtyard to protect Robbie and Lavender, who wore no body armour. Once the Martin men were inside and seated JD would join them while Chinaman would remain in position on the roof. The two gendarmes in the chateau would call their colleagues to set the roadblock and maintain it unless summoned. The two officers were then to wait for instructions to bring Frederic to the meeting to sit with Patrice. JD's only concern was whether the Martins would react to Lavender helping out at the chateau after being a flight attendant. *I'm sure it won't matter why should it? It should be an advantage they seemed to like her,* he *decided.*

JD reminded the team they only had a short time to make calls. Once the Martins arrived he would initiate a cellphone blackout to prevent the release of information that might prejudice the other Stones activities. No one made a call but the twins exchanged texts wishing each other good luck and urging safety.

Patrice had woken up that morning feeling worried but didn't know why. Maybe it was a bad dream he couldn't remember, or more likely because he still hadn't spoken with Frederic. He was becoming desperate to tell him not to say anything to

341

compromise the Martin deal or their ability to continue their private business. *Why would he do anything stupid like that?* he thought. He threw off his concerns, all he had to do was visit the chateau, inspect it and leave. He reckoned he knew the place better than the owners having spent so much time enjoying its best wine. *But just to be sure, I will get two of the guys to come with us in the car The others can hang around close by,* he thought and then pronounced to the empty room, "we will all go together to show strength and leave just two guys outside the gates." He summoned his team and made the arrangements. The second car would join them after he and Cyrano had finished lunch. That gave the men plenty of time to go to a local bar.

The two senior Martin members were enjoying an early lunch at a friend's brasserie. The restaurant had grown in popularity since Frederic and Patrice had become its wine supplier. However, today the friend served them from his private stock of Champagne and Chateau de Vaudieu. Unfortunately for Patrice, the text came just as they were deciding whether they should have a second bottle of the Rhone wine.

After a few curses followed by farewells, the team assembled and drove to within a mile of the chateau before stopping for a final run-through. They checked their comms were working and weapons loaded. Once again Patrice described a simple visit, his car of four would drive into the courtyard while the car of two would park to the left of the entrance out of sight. The two men outside would quietly inspect the area for any kind of ambush. He would then conduct the internal inspection involving a walk around the chateau asking unnecessary questions. The exit would involve the first car leaving, the second falling in behind and both vehicles driving directly to the airport to fly back to Marseille. If they had to inspect any other part of the estate, they would reveal the second car and confess to lacking trust.

"Any questions?" he asked his team, they shook their heads. To them, he had made it seem very simple with far too many of them involved. They set off slightly drunk and very happy to have another opportunity to humiliate the English.

Terry Lamb along with his small team were using their smartphones to monitor the progress of the Martin vehicles. The three men were chatting about football and their weekend plans. They thought it was going to be an easy mission, their targets had not even checked their vehicles for bombs or bugs. Terry regretted not bringing some sort of IED to blow up the cars so they could avoid going to the chateau and get back early for the Blues match. Although he was uneasy about not knowing exactly what force they would encounter at the chateau. He estimated it as beatable unless reinforcements unexpectedly poured in. Only the day before he used his gaming skills to send a small drone to visit the chateau and surrounding area. No one paid any attention. He was particularly interested in the opportunities afforded by the large courtyard where the cars would arrive. They expected Patrice's two cars to be parked next to the vehicles he thought belonged to the manager, Frederic and the English guy who was meeting Patrice. The drone missed Robbie's vehicle, it was sitting alongside the police car in Frederic's recent hiding place. They replayed the video a few times to enable Terry to pick out the right positions in the nearby hills to fire down into the courtyard. A final quick aerial check taken from the firing locations did not change the decision. His two men would go in on foot and set up to instigate a crossfire that would take out everyone standing in the courtyard including anyone who came out to help them. Terry would cover the front of the chateau with cover fire then join his men once they had gained control of the building. He reckoned the estimated 3:1 odds they faced would be just fine.

Terry gave the order to move, the three men drove within running distance of the chateau, left the car out of sight and took up their assigned positions. As expected, Patrice's team were still sitting and waiting to make a grand entrance. That gave Terry's men time to settle into their grandstand seats, with H&K assault rifles at the ready waiting for orders. The lead gangster scanned the area through the sight of his favourite sniper rifle searching for his next victims. Although the place looked deserted he saw two men, both with long guns, concealing themselves on the roof. He alerted his team to keep an eye out for the men on the rooftop who he assumed must be waiting for Patrice, as both appeared to be looking down the road he would come. For a moment Terry wondered whether they were going to do his job for him and ambush Patrice, or were they just watching them arrive making sure they didn't do anything stupid. Either way, Terry was fascinated and a little worried, the odds were climbing, *they could be as much as 4:1*, he thought *unless I can do something to reduce their numbers*. He whispered an order to his men, "stay still and do nothing, there may have to be a change of plan."

Finally, Patrice set off for the chateau approach road. Two hundred metres out the second car, containing Cormeline and Evodie, slowed to stop in a grove outside the entrance. His car slowed but drove through the arch into the courtyard and parked as expected. The four Martin men slowly climbed out to stand for a moment as Robbie, Lavender and Claude came out to meet them. Just as Terry was about to give the order to shoot the new arrivals, one of the rooftop shooters disappeared. The change affected him.

"Hold your fire," Terry told his men "there is more going on here than we realised. We need to wait for a bit to find out who is here before we decide how to deal with Patrice. We can always hit them on the way out just as easily." Then to improve the odds he told Erjon to go and "QUIETLY" eliminate the two men Patrice had outside the chateau. Terry went back to observing, the one shooter still covering the front watching Patrice's men. He began to wonder if someone else was going to arrive. There was certainly no one anywhere close by as far as he could see through his scope. He looked at the chateau again stopping every few feet, but he could not even see Erjon moving around. He smiled and felt sorry for the two men who had little chance of survival.

In the courtyard, Patrice told his men to keep alert and handed his Glock to the big man before walking into the chateau.

Inside the main tasting room, Robbie invited Patrice to sit in the middle of the long table. He sat opposite him and was joined by JD and Claude.

"I am a bit lonely over here on my own," Patrice announced in French. "Do we speak in French or English and when do we do the tour? Where is Jack? Will he be here? I like him, he knows what we want from you"

"French is fine, I will get Robbie to help me if necessary, replied JD. He continued in his best Spanish French, Please forgive me, we didn't mean to overwhelm you. We thought coffee and a chat to start before we have a look around. Patrice nodded and suggested they speak English as the American continued, "perhaps Claude you could organise the drinks, then sit at the end. He turned to the Frenchman, "unfortunately Jack will not be here until later he had to meet with Madame Martin this morning.

"Of course, I understand, I will have a coffee, please. What about my men?" he asked

"No worries," replied Robbie. "Lavender and Maria will keep them topped up with coffee, soda drinks and snacks until we are finished here."

"Good, then we're ready," Patrice smiled, relaxed into his seat and waved with one hand to give JD permission to begin. He was thinking about how good it felt to be the victor and listen to these grovelling English or Americans or whatever they were.

"As you know we have agreed on a deal with Astrid Martin and will be handing over a large sum of money for her to look after our interests in France," JD explained in a jaunty manner. "Those interests lie in this chateau and other wine investments in Bordeaux and the Rhone regions." He steeled, "your wine scam will cost us and YOU, our new partners, a lot of money if we don't get rid of investments in those vineyards. Madame Martin told us that you would give us a list of the places you have worked with," he lied.

"How do I know that's true?" asked Patrice not sure which scam he was referring to. "Why tell you when we can keep them for ourselves?" he replied sensing he could make some money when he finally found Frederic. "You tell us where you're invested and we'll tell you if we have them signed up."

"Look why don't you just call her?" he asked Patrice, knowing that the call blocker was switched on. "She will confirm what we are saying I'm sure. Here's your coffee and we have some excellent cake for you," he continued still trying to get agreement.

"Okay I will," he said and failed to get a signal. "Alright, I will text them to you later," he suggested hoping that would end the conversation.

Robbie produced a pen and pad and said, "just give us the name of the vineyard and contact and we can do the rest. Would you like anything else partner, please don't let your coffee get cold?"

Patrice decided to write some of the names so he could get out of there and back to Marseille. This was not what he was expecting and turning into a waste of time. He decided it would be better to go home to make sure Pascal did not take over. After writing twenty names he stopped, keeping the names of his private scam a secret.

"That's it as far as I know," he said and handed over the list. Robbie had a look and decided that he knew about half already from Frederic and Claude. Frederic had said that up to one hundred vineyards were producing fake wines. The Frenchman slouched in his chair and asked whether it was time to do the tour. He had done his duty and now wanted to go home with those nice attendants, especially Lavender. *Perhaps she will have dinner with me. I'm a bit surprised she is working here as well but I know she needs the money*, he thought smiling to himself. The Frenchman looked across the table at JD and Robbie who looked very serious.

"Are you sure this is all, we thought you had two hundred vineyards," suggested Robbie. "Perhaps you need a little help?"

Seconds later The Martin man's smile decayed into a grimace on seeing two gendarmes dragging a handcuffed Frederic into the room and dumping him on a chair. For three seconds he stared at the new arrival before erupting out of his seat and staggering backwards. He looked at JD and Robbie who were looking at a horrified Frederic. The two large officers retrieved Patrice and shoved him back onto his seat and stood behind him.

"I think you know young Freddy here," said Robbie "He's been working with you for some time now, hasn't he? He's a good talker though, he told us a great deal about you and the terrible things you have done to THIS chateau," JD shuffled his seat. "Sorry," he said calming down, "and lots of other vineyards not only in Bordeaux but also in the Rhone provinces. He told us," pointing at Frederic, "there were at least a hundred if not two hundred vineyards affected isn't that right Freddy? Astrid Martin was very upset with you for what you have been doing on your own," he bluffed. She instructed us to make sure you told us everything. Clearly, she wants the deal much more than she wants your raggedy arse."

"I thought we were here to………," Patrice tried to say to Frederic as his worst fears were being realised.

"I'm sorry but I tried to get away and they found me and beat me and…," Freddy blurted out.

JD took over, "but before we talk any more, we need to make sure that your men are not going to do anything stupid. So, you are going to tell that big fellow Cyrano and his two men to give their weapons to these big boys, pointing at the police officers. Then he is going to go out the front of the chateau and collect weapons from your other men and have them sit in their vehicle doing nothing. Is that clear?"

"Why would I do that?" he responded angrily realising that he had been tricked.

"Well because if you don't then we will have to shoot them and then you. One of our men is sitting on the roof with his rifle and enjoys shooting holes in bad people.

"Do it, Patty, these men mean what they say," encouraged Frederic.

"Yea come on Patty, do the right thing," Robbie was getting angry again and jiving Patrice.

"Merde, I will do it to avoid violence. But I know you will not harm us, the French officers will not allow it. They will protect us from you English," he turned to look at the two officers who showed nothing.

"Finish your coffees first why don't you?" JD suggested calming things down. He went off to Claude's office to switch off the phone blocker. He was happy with the way things were going, especially as they managed to avoid telling the Martin leader the true situation. He wondered whether he should pray their luck would hold.

Outside the chateau, Erjon had already pounced on Cormeline and silently dispatched him with a knife, watched by a surprised Chinaman. The assassin preferred to kill that way, it was so much more enjoyable he could feel the body struggling as life left it. For him shooting someone with a long gun was no different than shooting at a post. As he crept up on an unsuspecting Evodie, to enjoy another personal experience, he was again spotted by Chinaman who whispered, "watch out buddy'.

"JD someone is out here killing the gangbangers with a knife. What do you want me to do?" he asked whilst watching Evodie having his throat cut. "That's two of them down now," he continued.

JD asked Chinaman if he knew who it was and received a straight no. He carried on, "don't do anything yet, this is not what we expected, maybe they are after Patrice. Keep watch in case someone tries to attack us here. I will get with the guys and decide what to do and get back to you.."

"Roger that, will let you know if I see the guy head towards the ranch house" replied Chinaman.

Terry congratulated Evodie on a job well done and told him to return to his position. The gangster had already decided to hit Patrice as soon as he departed. He would instruct his men to fire on the courtyard while he took out the watcher on the roof. While he was thinking about his next move, Patrice suddenly appeared in his gun sight with another man he had not seen before.

JD returned to the meeting to find Robbie had escorted Patrice into the courtyard to ask Cyrano to join them. Outside they met Lavender and Maria standing in the warm air entertaining the big man and his fellow members.

Terry gave the order and his men on automatic, opened fire at the courtyard. In seconds practically everyone was hit, especially those who ran out to get behind the cars rather than into the safety of the building. Terry fired and missed Chinaman who had moved in response to the gunfire behind him. The American swivelled to face the direction he thought the shot must have come from, saw a glint and fired back. Then fired two more shots in the direction of Terry before sprinting across the roof to face the courtyard. As he ran a brick splinter hit his leg and then his armour as Terry continued to fire. *Shit, what is going on? I've missed that big bastard twice now,* thought Terry who decided to move closer to the action to make sure they finished Patrice.

Chinaman quickly set up at the front of the roof where he found and shot, the overexcited assassin, Evodie who was kneeling so he could spray his bullets better. JD recovered his rifle quickly and using the walls as cover went outside with the two officers. The three men quickly located the other assassin, Mergime, killing him with their overwhelmed firepower. The shooting suddenly stopped. Chinaman shouted a warning there was still a shooter on the loose and he had lost contact with him.

Terry scanned the courtyard where there a lot of bodies and only little movement. Patrice was alive but slumped between two cars, so the English assassin fired twice to finish his job. That was enough, his mission was over, it was time to make a getaway. One of the police ran forward to see if he could help any of the injured or dying. Terry could not resist the opportunity to shoot a French police officer so reloaded and fired. A mistake, seconds later Chinaman and JD located him, fired six rounds at his position. Two bullets hit his rifle which was wrecked, one cut a shallow trench along his left arm which he ignored while the rest zipped over his head which caused him to curse. *It really is time to go,* he thought and ran for his vehicle using the trees as cover. He knew he had to ditch his armour, rifle and anything else that could incriminate him. *I will just keep this little one* for *the moment* and stuffed a Glock into the rear of his trousers.

In the courtyard the scene was shocking, JD shouted at Chinaman to get the shooter ALIVE. He dashed over to a prone Lavender who was alive but holding her neck. She had been hit many times while saving Maria. Gulping for air her throat filling with blood, JD applied pressure to the wound, but she was also bleeding from her back and stomach. He sat, lifted her onto his thigh and cradled her head thanking her for saving the women and for her service. She tried to speak but all he could hear was her gurgling her brother's name. Robbie, blood on his forehead and face from stone splinters, staggered over and knelt next to them. Both men tried to comfort her, they knew they couldn't save her there was not enough time – it was the end for a much loved former Marine and Stones warrior. She closed her eyes and slipped away leaving both men in tears. They had seen so much death in their lives, but this was by far the worst. Claude brought over a blanket for JD to cover her.

The heroic policemen, shot in the chest, was being attended by his colleague. He would survive but not work again. After a few minutes, Robbie walked over to kneel next to Frederic who had died from multiple gunshots while running into the courtyard to make his escape. Patrice lay dead between the cars along with two of his men, Cyrano was slumped in the driving seat covered in blood, he never got to move.

The police from the roadblock ignored instructions after hearing the gunfire and arrived in the courtyard to take charge of the crime scene. The police allowed the Stones associates to cover the bodies in sheets while they waited for the ambulances.

Terry had covered most of the ground to his vehicle when he was pushed forward and crashed to the ground. For a moment he thought he must have tripped but the pain, the blood, and the broken lower leg told him that he had been brought down by a powerful gunshot. He wanted to crawl but knew he would never make it. All he could do now was wait, tie off his leg and hope that he was not about to receive a kill shot.

Chinaman had seen the carnage in the courtyard, knew Lavender had been hit but had to concentrate on capturing the assassin. He followed a hunch the man would head away from the chateau towards the main road where he would have a vehicle stashed. The Stones associate running with his weapon extended, as he had done many times in combat, saw movement amongst the trees decided it was the gangster and took the shot. He carefully worked his way forward expecting to find his quarry lying in wait, with a long gun pointed ready to fire. Terry lay behind a fallen tree with his sidearm ready in case the chaser made a stupid move and he could bring him down. Chinaman shouted an order to throw out his weapons or be shot. Normally Terry would have told him to bugger off, but now he had no armour, no rifle and so no option but to give up. He tried one last diversionary tactic, stuffed his Glock into the front of his trousers, pulling himself onto the fallen tree and shouted he was dying and had no weapons. Chinaman approached, weapon pointed directly at the top of Terry's head and said, "I've used that trick before so I am just going to shoot you," he fired shots right and left of the assassin who fell back in surprise.

"Fuck you," shouted Terry in pain and threw his Glock towards Chinaman.

"Where's the long gun?" Chinaman asked.

"You yanky bastards shot it up so I tossed it away, it was my favourite," he replied and stuck both arms in the air to prove he could not fire back.

The American approached the prone man with the utmost caution, ready to fire in an instant. Terry lay on his front, hands on top of his head moaning slightly but bleeding heavily from the bullet wound to his leg. Terry was bound with plastic handcuffs, dragged to his hidden vehicle and thrown in the back. "Lucky for me these Frenchie's have the wheel on the right side for us yanks, not like you Brits," Chinaman said." Nothing more was said other than the moans from the back seat as the Stones associate rushed back to the chateau for an update on Lavender and to offload his prisoner.

At the chateau, the medics were fixing the injured and loading the dead into ambulances. The casualty report would state:

- **Wounded**: Robbie (head and side), Claude (arm) Gendarme Officer (chest) Terry Lamb (leg).
- **Dead**
  - BloedStone: – Lavender and Frederic.
  - Martin family: - Patrice, Cyrano, plus four other men to be identified.
  - Unknown: – two men presumed to be associated with a British man identified as Terry Lamb.

The doctors were ordered to repair the British criminal on-site so that Stones could question him on who he worked for and what he was hired to do.

More armed police arrived after sealing off the area even though they too had been ordered to stay away. The policeman, who had witnessed Robbie's behaviour towards Frederic, ordered the arrest of anyone not wearing a uniform, after finding Frederic among the dead. JD and Robbie were in no mood to be arrested and refused to allow it. They were an alarming sight covered in Lavender's blood and preparing for another confrontation. Before the face-off could get started a newly arrived gendarme Superintendent intervened and told them all to stand down and leave it to him. They grumbled but stood down.

Speaking in English to the Stones men he said, "it is lucky I am here it was my good friend Jackson who told me where you would be. I came over to help, I work for the Minister and know General de Vries well. I am sorry this became such a mess for you. It looks like there were three sides. I understand you have lost two of your people, one a lady such a shame. I will arrange for the report to be started this evening and finished in the morning when they have the information on the surviving assassin.

While I am here I must thank you for helping us to arrest the gang members in Marseille. I understand they were trying to get the drugs they thought were hidden from us after the first raid.

Unfortunately, we did not get one of their leaders but I understand that you may also have that in hand. His name is Pascal he is the nastiest of the gang leaders. I will say goodbye now and good luck for the future.

They thanked him for his help and promised to send over the information about the Englishman they had captured.

Fortunately, Terry decided to explain why he was there and who he was reporting to. He avoided mentioning Sylvain and positioned himself as a mere hired gun working alongside his dead colleagues. He finished by repeating, "Pascal is your man, he hired us to shoot Patrice because he wants to be head of the family. He went off to Algiers to kill the Martin boy as far as I know. What are you going to do with me? Can't we do some sort of deal where I work for you guys? In case you are wondering I didn't shoot your lady, I shot Patrice."

"You must joking, you're lucky to be still alive, you were in command when one of our people was killed along with the Martin gangsters. That may cost you when the rest of them find out," said JD looking over at an angry Robbie. "See that big guy over there," pointing at Chinaman, "he was a good friend of the lady you guys killed, he's well pissed with you. Best get off to the hospital and get fixed up. No doubt you will be guarded and charged with murder or whatever they do in France."

"But I told you what you wanted, be fair" Terry pleaded. "Who knows what these Frenchies will get up to if I'm lying alone in some godforsaken hospital. What else can I tell you so you get me back home alive?"

"Terry my man, get yourself fixed up, you need to concentrate on staying alive, I will make sure you are not killed, for now. Later we will decide whether you stay in jail or do something useful." Robbie was thinking about the loss of Lavender and his former lover, Freddy, and whether there might be a job to be done to avenge them. Terry was taken away by the ambulance moaning about not getting any painkillers.

JD called for a sit-down chat with his two remaining associates, told them they needed to make contact with the rest of the team in France to explain what had happened to Lavender. He reminded them their colleagues would only answer if they have completed their part of the plan, so be persistent. He finished by announcing that he would start with a brief call to the General then inform Richard, Robbie was to call Jack leaving Chinaman to contact Shamir and Texas. The three men looked tired and drained of energy, three days ago they were having fun in Vegas and now they had lost Lavender.

After a brief conversation with his CEO, JD called Hockey - It was 5.30 pm.

Chapter 52: Algiers, Friday afternoon

Pascal arrived at the Algerian rental return location just ahead of the BloedStone associates, who watched the criminals walk to the terminal. The Americans left their vehicle in an airport car park for recycling by Stones France, before rushing to the private jet departure lounge. On the way, Chinaman called and told them about Lavender and the suspicion that Pascal was the man behind the assassinations. The loss of Lavender left them feeling angry but sad. Arriving at customs Shamir looked somewhat strange, partly dressed as an Arab woman and partly like a soldier. She was stopped by a muscular but attractive dark-skinned woman, who appeared to be in charge, demanding to carry out a search. Shamir wanted to object but heard Texas shout out NO and let it happen.

Her bags were searched in addition to a "touchy-feely" check of her body. *At least it was better than being molested by a man*, she thought Texas might have enjoyed the sight of her irritation in normal times, but not now.

Once they were through border controls, they joined up with the pilot and were led out to the plane where they had a few minutes to wash and change before the arrival of the Martin men.

Inside the Departure terminal, Pascal was yelling at his Toulon pilot who was trying to explain they could not go anywhere because the oil leak had returned. A spare part was on its way but it could be three hours before it arrived. The pilot offered money or vouchers to pacify him but the Martin member ignored him, he wanted to leave immediately. The pilot continued trying to appease the angry man, playing his part with admirable gusto. Thierry wondered what was going to happen next, he was supposed to be going home not stuck in an airport with Pascal. The airport police ambled over to ask the pilot what the problem was. The sergeant listened before announcing he might be able to help. He knew of a private jet that was leaving for France soon and would check to see whether they could join it. The officer using his shoulder radio was passed through to the pilot, they spoke loudly in English. Pascal went quiet and listened to the exchange. It sounded like an American pilot was flying an archaeological group to France and then back to the US.

After the short exchange, the pilot suggested, "why don't you send them through to the Exec area and I will see what our boss man says when he gets here, there is plenty of room. We are on our way to Boston with a stop in Marseille to pick up the rest of the team." The pilot began to tell an unnecessary story of their finds before continuing, "the chief is a good guy and likes to help out when he can." Pascal thought for a moment, his car was sitting in Toulon but getting back to France tonight would be better than hanging around in Algiers.

"We can pay," offered Thierry hearing the conversation. If he was not going to be saved he might at least get out of Algiers and take his chances in Marseille. The sergeant passed on the comment.

"Not necessary, money is not something the dude needs," the pilot replied. Tell the guys I will see them when you get through customs. The sergeant gave instructions and smiled as the four men ran to get their flight. He made a call and laughed as he rang off still watching the disappearing criminals.

The men were waved through passport and customs to the VIP area. The same officials were on duty, everything was progressing well for the Martin men to board the substitute jet they could see waiting on the apron. The female officer took them into the empty lounge and instructed them to sit down while she opened the exit for departure. As she did six police officers walked into the area with weapons holstered. Three waiting by the door while three stepped forward. One instructed the men to stand up. Pascal managed to say "merde," before he and his men were ordered to show their passports again. He could not restrain himself from insulting the officials, who retaliated by making the men hold out their arms for restraining cuffs. Thierry shouted at Pascal to keep quiet and let the police do their jobs. One of the officers at the door beckoned to the jet while the other two stood guard. The four Martin men looked out into the gloomy light and could just make out two figures coming towards them. A few seconds later a transformed Shamir accompanied by Texas entered the lounge area.

Pascal's mouth dropped open as he saw his Saloni dressed in activewear with a short black Jacket and a French Secret Service badge dangling from her neck. Sitting on her belt was a Glock.45 and various other tools including a new baton. Texas was wearing his flight Captain's uniform with a sidearm tucked into a rear holster, he stopped in the door towering over everyone inside. Thierry breathed a sigh of relief, he was going home. The leader of the police whispered something to the lady custom's officer and her face softened. They called Shamir to them and spoke for a few moments out of hearing for Pascal. The lady officer nodded, touched Shamir on the shoulder and the officers stepped forward to release a relieved Thierry who immediately dashed over to Texas for safety. The customs officer told Driton and Dobri their passports and visas were forged, arrested them and led them away protesting their innocence. Subsequently, they would be charged with using illegal weapons, smuggling and murder. They would try to save themselves by telling the authorities about the Martin members and the UK connections. Unfortunately, there was no witness protection scheme to save them from a violent death the following month.

Pascal shouted, "Saloni what are you doing here? Who are you? You look different," he was desperate and not sure what else to say. The reply came in French with a cold and steely glare.

"Before we leave here, I want you to understand you have caused death and a great deal of destruction, you're going to pay. lève toi grosse merde, if you try to run I will shoot you in both legs and if you do anything I don't like I will shoot you in both knees. If I had my way I would shoot you here and let you die slowly." He was insulted, immediately lost his temper stood up to try and attack her just as the police were leaving.

Texas watched thinking, *big mistake what's he doing?* He shouted to Pascal to sit down before he got hurt.

Pascal never accepted insults from women and therefore paid no attention to the warnings. Shamir sensing what he would do swayed back away from him so he fell onto his knees. She drew her alternate "South African friend" to deal a half-power strike, enough to daze and cause him to fall forward. Texas quickly crossed the room in case she felt inclined to mete out some further punishment. The smiling lady customs officer called for the police to return and help the damaged man onto the jet. Shamir thanked her and returned a big smile as she left.

The Stones associates agreed not to interrogate Pascal during the flight, he was still groggy and Texas wanted to avoid messing up the inside of the leased plane. The rough stuff could wait until they arrived at their overnight stay in Marseille where Jack had arranged a place where Pascal would spend the night answering their questions.

Flight ST 0045 for London Stanstead left Algiers at 8 pm local time with stops at Bordeaux and overnight in Marseille. They would arrive at their first destination around 10.45 pm French time. No one spoke, the flight attendants had little to do, except tidy up the captive's injuries.

Pascal was contemplating what happened, convinced there must be a traitor who brought disaster upon him. He ran through the suspects arriving at Patrice as the most likely. Then he decided, *it doesn't matter, my team in Bordeaux must have been successful, otherwise,*

359

why would they be so angry? It couldn't be about the Marseille warehouse, they only had that stupid American there. Salona was here. He thought about all the events that had taken place that day, *they can't tie me to anything,* there's no evidence I was involved in any crimes in France or I would already be in custody* Then stretching credibility, *maybe I can get out of the Algerian shambles as I was only there to rescue the boy. Then I was mistakenly arrested by the ugly Americans.* He was so convinced of his legal, rather than actual innocence, an ugly grin emerged.

A movement caught his attention, he looked around the seatback, to see Shamir's rear end as she picked up fallen earplugs. He forgot about his innocence and thought about what he wanted to do to her when he was free. He owed her for hitting him when his hands were tied. He decided he would make sure she felt la virilite many times and in many places before he killed her.

Chapter 53: Essex Friday, late afternoon.

It was just after 5 pm when a people carrier, with bright headlights and a diesel rattle, announced Lena Peja's arrival. While the sounds echoed, the Martin members sat watching her park, a short distance from their trucks. No one moved they waited in the gloomy silence. Finally, Lena emerged from the driver's door to open the sliding middle door before walking over to the trucks. She was goth-like wearing black clothes that accentuated her white skin and her sinister snake. When she reached Saville's open door he jumped down to embrace her and kiss both cheeks.

"Hi Sav," she continued to hold him, "It's good to see you again. I hear we lost Henri's truck. Is everything else okay? Do you still have Sylvain's women?" This was no time for pleasantries.

"Good to see you also, luckily the girls were in Ynon's truck over there," he replied. "Can't understand it," he blurted out. "Henri was talking to me, everything was good and then the pigs asked him to open his truck. They were checking another truck that had illegals in it so they wanted to check his too just because he was there. It could have been any of us." Saville was still upset by the loss of his friend. "Do you know what has happened to him?" he asked knowing it was too early to tell. Then he speculated, "maybe it was your present that got him in the end, he had it in the cab."

"We've not heard anything about what will happen, but the English don't like finding people with guns, so it could be bad. Such awful luck being stopped this time," she replied shaking her head. Lena looked up to see the other drivers emerging and waved at Nichol before walking over to see her friend Ynon. "Who's this," she asked Ynon pointing at Jean. "I don't know him do I?"

He's okay, he's the brother of our usual driver and got us out of that trouble in Dover." He decided not to reveal that Jean had a

361

brother-in-law who worked for customs in case it set her off on one of her rants. "He drove us here and speaks good English." Lena lost interest in the new man and returned to discussing the next part of the project - releasing the men while kidnapping the women.

"You need to send the men on their way," she said following Saville to the back of his truck. Nichol pulled up his hoody, before opening up. Nothing happened until Nichol shouted in both English and French that they were in London and it was time to go. He clapped his hands, three men appeared from behind the regular delivery of building materials. Once they reached the doors two of them thanked Nichol and ran off. Lena thought how bad they smelt as they ran past *perhaps the cool air will improve them,* she thought. The third, an older man, climbed down and stood waiting close by, Lena could smell him and backed off a couple of paces, covering her nose.

"GO, what are you waiting for?" Nichol instructed him, he then recollected that one of them came with the girls and a younger male, who was in Henri's truck.

"Where are my son and daughters," he asked in English. Nichol explained that he had been arrested along with their men when their truck was stopped at the services near Dover. Lena and Saville got ready to subdue the man but he just looked distraught at the loss.

In a moment of inspiration, Nichol continued, "I am sorry the police also arrested your daughters when they tried to escape from the truck. They were banging on the doors to get out, I am surprised you didn't hear it. The police opened the truck and took them. They only let us go because they believed that the girls had secretly climbed in. We were lucky to get you and the two other guys out. I believe your daughters are safe with your son, we will go back to Dover in the morning and get them released." The man began to sob and suggested it was a mistake to leave France. Lena and Saville looked at Nichol in awe at his storytelling and joined in to comfort him. Nichol went off to get one of his phone numbers. "Take this and you can call me on Sunday and I will let you know whether we have your family or when we will get them back to you."

The man accepted what he was told, thanked Nichol and left the car park heading towards Ilford town. That night the man would meet his extended family who lived near the Robin Hood Gardens in Poplar. Later in the year in despair over the loss of his family, he would attend a charity event to help families recover trafficked relatives. It would be organised by Elizabeth Manley-James and sponsored by the BloedStones People Recovery Unit – they would help.

With the man gone and Nichol rewarded with a kiss from Lena, Ynon opened his truck. The women were coaxed out by a kindly sympathetic sounding Lena telling them a similar story about their father and brother being captured by the English Border Forces. She even managed to produce some tears for authenticity. The girls were left with little option but to get into the people carrier ready for transportation to one of Sylvain's Kensington properties. After a quick visual inspection, Lena decided that Muna, the older and taller of the three girls, would be fine for her provided when undressed she found nothing unpleasant. The younger sisters, fourteen and sixteen, were perfectly suited to the appetites of Sylvain and his perverted friends. Before leaving, Lena fed them sandwiches, soda and water and sprayed a little of her eau de toilette in the vehicle.

Lena thanked the men, hugging each in turn including the new man. She told them to deliver their loads in the morning and then get back to France. They all smiled and wished her well as she set off for west London. Driving through Ilford town she thought she saw the man from the truck, he was on the roadside looking at her and Muna in the front seat. But when she looked in the rearview mirror he was gone. She dismissed it.

In the lorry park, the four men decided that they would sleep in their cabs. Early in the morning, they would head over to the delivery site to have breakfast before unloading their trucks at a DIY retailer. Then they would rush to Dover to get a ferry back to Calais and do it all again.

However, when they arrived at Dover the next day, three of the men were arrested for smuggling. They were questioned and their trucks confiscated before being sent back to France to be charged with trafficking and jailed.

Jean or John as his friends knew him, would do it all again next week trapping more smugglers and traffickers.

Chapter 54: Kensington, West London, Friday evening

For Lena Peja and the girls, the October traffic was normal - horribly slow. It would take two hours to reach Kensington High Street. Fortunately, the girls would sleep for most of the journey recovering from their ordeal. Lena's earphone rang, it was Sylvain for the third time, checking on her progress. During the last call, she detected a hint of anxiety in his voice giving her the feeling he was holding something back. Most worrying of all, he was being pleasant rather than his usual obnoxious self.

She answered, "I'm very close now, is there a problem?"

"There's been a change of plan," he replied in a whisper. "I think my phone is being tapped so go to that place up north, you know the one where we stayed with Pascal that time, where you complained about it being out in the wilds. Bring the girls with you," he rang off before Lena could protest. She had another twenty miles to drive, this time out of town. She was curious about the change but knew it was best to follow his instructions, especially when carrying his precious cargo.

Sylvain had already taken the difficult decision to abandon ship and run for safety. There were too many indicators that things had gone badly wrong. He could not reach any of the men he sent to France, nor Pascal or Patrice or Madame Martin or M. Labette. He knew about the fire in the Algiers compound and the fiasco at the Maidstone services. He was not blinded by the belief that he was invincible, he had planned for this day. As a long time criminal he took the view he should enjoy what he had when he had it and run to safety when he lost it. He didn't keep his money hidden in a safe, in the walls or a hole in the ground. It had gone offshore to the Isle of Man, Dominica and Switzerland. He had recently established a "warm site," a compound hidden outside Ajaccio in his native Corsica. To make it bearable he would take Lena and the three girls to keep him company. Then he would contribute a little more to the locals and the friendly police who currently looked after the buildings. But before he left for Elstree, he had to close his business in Kensington without arousing suspicions. So far luck had been on his side, starting with him finding a tracker on Lena's vehicle before she left to collect the girls. He did not tell her, he did not want to alarm her but it did confirm he was being watched. That made him believe his phone was tapped and the police were probably waiting for an excuse to apprehend him. It was time to take radical action if he was going to avoid arrest.

He was right to be worried, MI5 and UK customs were operating joint stakeouts of both his restaurant and home, but were in a quandary as to the next move. There was no way of knowing what had spooked the gangster into changing his plans to divert the delivery to an unspecified place north of London known only to Lena. How the mission leader wished he had followed the vehicle rather than relying on a tracking device that had failed to work from the start. They did not even know if the girls would be dumped, kept, traded, killed or let go. The choice now was to wait and follow him when he made his move or carry out raids on his premises. Maybe they would get lucky and they would find drugs and/or illegals of some kind. The listening devices installed a few days earlier suggested nothing more than a regular restaurant with an abusive boss.

Sylvain re-opened the bar and restaurant at the usual time of 6 o'clock following the afternoon break. He told the manager he was not feeling well and would return to his nearby home to take some medicine. Dave Bender drove him for the short trip but had to walk back after leaving the 4X4 in case Sylvain made a miraculous recovery and wanted to return. That left Bendy to join the team waiting outside the restaurant. At 9.30 pm there was an explosion in the building next to Sylvain's house. The watchers decided to leave their post to find the source and help with any casualties.

At that moment Sylvain left his house, head slightly bowed, collar turned up, crossed over the road into his secret house, through it and out of the rear doors to his "emergency car'. He drove away without anyone noticing.

The leader of the security forces standing outside the damaged house abruptly decided it was a deception and raided both of Sylvain's properties ten minutes later. Whilst the authorities were searching for the French criminal and evidence of wrongdoing, Sylvan drove past Lord's cricket ground on his way to the A41. His route took him through Hendon and on to the meeting place at the "emergency" hotel in Elstree. He had his bag of essentials for the flight including, of course, his Rohypnol for the girls. The two gangsters would meet and successfully fly from the nearby airport with their human cargo, to Sylvain's compound in Corsica. They would stay there for the rest of 2019 and some of 2020 before Sylvain went to Zurich to start his next project.

Miss Elizabeth stood in the restaurant watching the search, mortified at their failure to recover the girls from Lena. She obtained some satisfaction in the form of retrieving five women being forced to provide various "services" either in or out of the restaurant.

From this raid, the team would go on to track down several of Sylvain's friends who were involved in the abuse of smuggled or trafficked women. They were arrested and charged with various crimes including offences under the 2015 Modern Slavery Act. Miss Elizabeth wanted to help more, and with financial support from her father and the Stones Company, she would give these and other unfortunate women the chance to start a new life.

Chapter 55: Bordeaux, Friday evening

After making calls to Stones associates, a mournful team assisted the emergency services to collect and label the dead, carefully recording which group they come from. The bodies of the two assassins working for Terry were loaded into separate vehicles from Patrice and his men, before they were all sent to the local hospital for autopsy and identification - none of them carried any ID cards. At Robbie's request, the senior paramedic e-mailed photos of the bodies for Madame Martin and Pascal to identify.

Frederic as a BloedStone associate would eventually be returned to his mother or his missing partner but would be honoured as "lost in action", a parting gift from Robbie.

Lavender would be placed in a transportation coffin ready to go to Marseille to be reunited with her twin for the onward journey to New York.

"That was pretty tough, what did Richard say?" Robbie asked JD. The two men still shaken by events were looking at Lavender lying on a stretcher, ready for emergency services to transport her

"He was on a high having finished the job in Marseille which went well except they didn't find any drugs or money" replied JD. "Of course, when I told him he was devastated, went silent for ages and then started shouting stuff. I wanted to wait until someone was with him but the General told me to get it done in case it leaked. I just hope Jack gets to him before Hockey does something foolish. By the way, can you check with Chinaman he told the guys in Algiers not to kill Pascal? It's not yet proven he arranged it, even though the British shooter said it was the French gangster who paid him. It might end up as one word against the other, and you know these days you can't shoot both just to get the right one." There was no humour it was not a joke.

"Yeah, he did JD, I heard him tell Shamir. I hope she behaves, we still need all the information we can get to arrest that slimeball Frenchie in London," Robbie warned. He knew she could be volatile like him when in desperate or extreme situations, she would need to learn to control such impulses.

"Still a policeman eh Robbie," replied the Commander smirking.

"How do you think Chinaman is?" asked Robbie looking at the associate sitting on the ground at the far side of the courtyard just watching, holding back his emotions. "He looks devastated even though he only met the twins a few days ago, I believe."

"By his desolate look, he might still be thinking it was his fault that Lannie got killed," replied JD. "Earlier he was mumbling something about being quicker. I explained that it was just one of those unfortunate "shit happens" situations. It will take a bit of time for him to grieve but eventually, he will be okay I'm sure. For him, I believe this feels different from the battlefield, more like a relative being killed at a friend's house back home. For us, this is something we are used to whether we like it or not. Remember that shootout last year?" they both nodded and turned to meet an approaching Claude.

The Chateau Manager suggested they all go inside for a glass of something stronger than their wine. JD waved to Chinaman to join them but he refused by indicating he was watching over Lavender now lying in the back of an ambulance.

Once inside, a slightly damaged, happy to be alive and miraculously recovered Maria complete with a smile, served some liquor and biscuits. Robbie started by explaining that although they were not in the best shape mentally they had to finish collating the scam details for a report to the General and French government. So far he had received information from Claude, Frederic and Patrice covering the involvement of more than one hundred businesses. Robbie scanned the list recognising many of the vineyards including some lesser First

Growth Chateaux, with global investors. Though only small in number, in the wrong hands, such news would unsettle all investors in French wine. It would certainly upset the value of Chateau du Carys. Robbie knew there would be more vineyards affected, maybe hundreds or even thousands. He would have to fire up his police brain to devise a strategy to discover the true extent of the problem, then find a solution.

When Claude started to apologise again about his involvement, Robbie reassured him that he would be fine provided he said nothing about the scam or what happened that day.

Claude would become a model employee until he suddenly retired at the end of 2019 to travel on a luxury world cruise. Robbie was surprised they could afford such a treat so he had their finances checked. No abnormalities were found until a smart but bored analyst followed the money and came upon the account of Claude's stepbrother, a café owner in Toulon. It contained transfers amounting to two million euro. The analyst, subsequently employee of the year, carried out a Google maps inspection of the location to reveal an aged and deteriorating property. A visit from two Stones associates led to a confession and the surrender of the money to an Isle of Man account. An unexpected but welcome bonus," Robbie was to tell the General. Unfortunately, Claude and Maria were never able to defend themselves, they disappeared like so many older people on long cruises. Although exactly how, became a subject for discussion at the Stones February 2020 board meeting in Perth, Western Australia.

After a while Chinaman abandoned his guard post, left his heavy weapons by the door and sat at the table with the others. "What time are we due at the airport?" he asked.

"Let me check with Texas," replied JD. Then he announced, "they are on the way back from Algiers and will be landing about half ten. We will leave here around eight, in case they're early."

He turned away to continue the call with Texas. The Stones pilot told him he had spoken with Jack and the team and they were all on the way to Marseille, including Astrid Martin who had returned to her villa to pack. Which raised a snigger from the Commander.

Texas continued, "I've arranged for the hospital at Marseille airport to keep Lannie overnight. I believe that Jack is bringing Richard to see her when we land." He paused, "just so you know, we are currently running ahead of time."

"We've booked rooms for you and Shamir in a hotel near the Martin villa," said JD. Your prisoner is staying in the villa in a VIP room they have there, not sure what it is but Jack was impressed. Perhaps it's one of those spanker places, you know a dominatrix " he chuckled trying to lighten the mood.

"I have no idea what you mean," Texas replied jokingly to help.

"Anyway, we will set off for Bordeaux airport soon with all the information Robbie has collected. See you in the lounge," JD signed off.

Robbie had a final discussion with the senior Crime Scene Investigator to make sure the authorities had everything they needed from Stones. No doubt the French team would be working for many more hours collecting evidence for the enquiry. The material would not be used to tell the story of two rival gangs descended upon a French chateau to attack and kill its owners, guests and ultimately each other. Instead, it would be used to describe how terrorists from Algiers came to France planning to devastate the Bordeaux wine fields but were stopped by the valiant French security forces helped by an unnamed NGO. Of the men who might want to dispute this finding; Pascal was incapacitated and unlikely to have the opportunity, Terry would stay quiet waiting for Robbie to get back to him and Sylvain was in the wind.

The ambulance carrying the body of Lavender followed Robbie's car to the airport. When they arrived at Aéroport de Bordeaux they passed through customs quickly and waited for the arrival of the Gulfstream from Algiers.

Once the plane had landed and stopped the team decamped, embraced their colleagues then all lined up to honour Lavender as she was carried aboard.

During the ceremony, Pascal was left seated to watch and worry as more Americans came aboard to scowl at him. Once everyone was seated he couldn't help thinking how crowded it had become and how happy Thierry looked. Later in the flight, he felt insulted that Saloni spent her time talking with the boy and ignoring him, a real man. He was becoming delusional.

The plane left for Marseille where it would arrive at midnight.

Chapter 56: Cote d'Azur, Friday early evening

Astrid, accompanied by Rosalbe and Yves, left for her Marseille villa with instructions to pack up her possessions and leave by mid-November. To help she enlisted Yasmeen, to hang her art in Le Beaux and Chiara to pack valuable furniture. She would leave the rest to the Stone's Property Manager for incorporation into De Beaux Endroits SARL where it would remain until it was converted or disposed of. As a BloedStone new starter, Astrid would stay at the company's Bandol hotel until she took up her, yet to be defined, new role. Before all of that, she would be chilling some of Matisse's 10-year-old Dom Perignon for Thierry's homecoming.

When they arrived the guards were gone replaced by a green and gold sign announcing the property was protected by BloedStone Security Inc, for those who didn't know, that meant panic rooms, alarms, watching drones and rapid reaction (armed) forces. *What a shame I have to leave this beautiful place,* she thought as they proceeded up the drive. But leave was exactly what she needed, to be free of Matisse's men to start a new life. She was worried but elated at the prospect. To help, her lover had agreed to leave the family business and join Stones. Something she hoped Thierry would also do and make a life as an associate either in Europe or the US. Rosa sitting next to her was wondering whether Thierry would still want to be with her, if not, what would she do?

Once the three were sat admiring the floodlit pool Astrid turned to Rosa and said, "come here my baby, don't worry, I'm sure Thierry loves you. When he finds out what you have been through to get him back, he will love you even more. We will talk about what you are going to do when my boy is back home with us. You must stay with us tonight and as long as you wish," Rosa teared up and accepted the champagne proffered by Yves. They were exhausted, now they waited for word about Thierry.

Jack had been on the phone with Hockey for most of the journey from Bandol to Marseille trying to keep him occupied and help him through the early stages of grief. Jack reckoned as a former soldier he would get to anger very quickly then start thinking about revenge, possibly doing something violent. Jack had so far managed to prevent that from happening and arranged to meet him at the bar where Pascal had taken them on Thursday evening. Once Hockey had calmed down, they would go out to the airport and meet the arriving jet so he could spend some time with Lavender in the quiet of the airport hospital.

At the bar, a tearful Hockey spent hours telling stories about growing up with his sister, fun times, partying and her adventures in the US Marines. Jack listened, happy to keep him talking even managing to avoid the forbidden pastime of talking about company projects in an insecure place. They ate and had a few beers to help pass the time.

When they were on the way to the airport, Jack turned to the events at the warehouse. They discussed how well the plan had gone with the Martin members arrested and soon to be jailed. When it came to the drugs and money, Hockey talked of a mystery. "The crims were convinced it was there but when they got into the cellar there was nothing, I could hear them moaning as I got away. When they came out no one had anything, they complained they had been conned. Someone must have taken it or it was never there. But who could have taken it after the first raid?" He began repeating himself, "it was gone, it can't have been there, they didn't take it out and the police couldn't find it, I know it wasn't stolen when I was there. No, someone, unknown, must have broken in and taken it before we went in. But as far as I could tell afterwards," Hockey rambled on, "no one had broken into the cellar, there was no damage to the door and there was only one way in or out. Perhaps it was never there in the first place and didn't exist. Or maybe someone took it during the original raid but Christ knows how they could have carried it out."

"I suspect this is a mystery we are not going to solve," replied Jack. "Not unless that guy Pascal has it, the rest of the gang have either died or disappeared."

"Is that the bastard who killed Lannie, I know him?" Hockey looked angry.

Jack responded, "Pascal wasn't there, he was getting his arse kicked in Algiers by Shamir, remember. In Bordeaux, there was a battle between two groups from the same gang, we got caught in the middle when we took one of the leaders to our vineyard." They continued to talk.

In Bandol things were more cheerful, the General was spending time with his nephew and Avery. Andre took the opportunity of talking about the business he had created and how well it was doing. He wanted some praise, recognition from his mentor.

"So, you're sure you don't want to join us?" asked the General for the third time. There is a lot of opportunities here in Europe with Jackson and Sir Robbie or over in California with me and Nicky."

"No thanks Unk, I like working for myself. However, you can invest in my business, take an equity stake so I can use the money to scale up around Europe."

"Okay I give up, I will have Jack take a good look, if your business stacks up we can do a deal. Perhaps you can come to the US and open up in our offices," the General suggested. "If you stay here Sir Robbie will be happy to help, provided of course you are a wine drinker. Oh yes," he continued making a face, "that's what started all this in the first place if I remember. You should learn as much as you can from Jack about how to scale up your company. Then from Robbie learn how to control it once it's grown and perhaps more importantly which wines you should drink while doing it," he chuckled.

"Excuse me for a moment I must send a text," said the General heading off to sit at the far end of the room.

General: - When would you like an update; tomorrow (Saturday) or perhaps Sun or Mon?" G.

Minister: I have heard a great deal good and bad. I am sorry for your loss. Let us speak on Sun lunch in Paris at our usual place. I have business on Sat. O.

General: cool G.

Baby Bob was miserable like everyone else, so the General took time to speak with him and agree the young associate was still able to continue with the Iraq mission. He began packing equipment but couldn't shake off the feeling he should be with his teammates when they arrive from Bordeaux. Fortunately, Yasmeen gave him access to a hotel vehicle so he left for the airport. For all his technical ability Baby Bob struggled with the French SatNav but still managed to meet up with Hockey and Jack so they could all wait together. Baby Bob was used to waiting, that was part of the job, wait and see or wait for something to happen.

The Gulfstream landed on schedule and taxied towards Arrivals. The Stones team were quiet, still struggling with losing one of their own. Pascal was in a dark mood still angry about being kidnapped by Americans. He no longer lusted after Saloni nor thought about what was going to happen to him. But others had.

JD and Robbie spent most of the flight deep in conversation with the General. They were telling him what they had discovered about the wine scams and suggesting what could be done to avoid damage to the French wine industry. The three men agreed the General should propose to the Minister that Jack and Robbie carry out the following actions:

1. Assist the authorities in finding further entries for Robbie's spreadsheet of infiltrated vineyards.

2. Stay in France for a while to help develop a process for fixing the vineyards (quietly).
3. Assist a police team to execute the process.
4. Those vineyards invested in by Stones and those on the Frederic and Patrice special list would be removed from the spreadsheet. (Those vineyards would be dealt with by Stones to avoid financial loss or legal liability).
5. Astrid and (the reformed) Yves would be made to help with the work.

Pascal was first to leave the plane and was due to be taken to the Martin villa for interrogation but instead, three gendarme officers arrived to arrest him and take him away to a holding cell. Despite protests from JD and Robbie the officers refused to release Pascal apparently because of Stones failure to recover the Martin drugs and money.

After the short quarrel, the remaining passengers disembarked, to embrace their colleagues who lined up in the cold to wait for their fallen comrade. Lavender appeared in her travel casket to be saluted by the former military associates, while Thierry bowed his head in respect and with thanks. She was transferred to a waiting ambulance and accompanied by Hockey to the hospital mortuary. The rest of the team, along with Thierry, walked to the front car park where they would be driven to Bandol by Jack and Baby Bob.

Before leaving Thierry thanked each of them again, reserving special gratitude for Shamir his "most magnificent badass lady" and Texas, Mr Lonely Ranger. He watched them drive away, shivered, smiled and rushed to the taxi rank only to find his mother and Rosa waiting for him. He stopped for a moment before running to embrace them, the Wineman was no longer missing he had returned home.

Chapter 57: Bandol, Saturday

The General declared Saturday a day of rest with only two events; a team meeting at 5 pm followed by dinner at 8 pm. The weather was typical for autumn, warm with a pale blue sky and a bright but low sun. The three younger US associates surfaced early morning, took a light breakfast and headed off for a relaxing run through the town. They caused a stir amongst the locals who rarely saw a group running through the narrow streets at speeds normally reserved for cyclists. The conversation started with Chinaman describing the events in Bordeaux.

"Man it was shocking to see those shooter dudes firing down into Lannie and the gangbangers," said Chinaman. "Worst of all was the Brit, I'm sure he picked off their leader. He was pretty good, he managed to hit the guy between two cars. He picked him off with a leg shot and when he moved he finished him with a headshot. He almost got away, I just managed to get him before he reached his car. The shit tried to claim he had nothing to do with the shooting and was just passing by. They arrested him, I think they were going to charge him with murder but he dumped the long gun so there was no proof. CSI did a thorough search but no one could find it. Fortunately, he had a Glock so they were able to hold him on possession of an unlicensed weapon. Not much though considering what damage he did."

"It's worse here than at home though," replied Shamir. "How are you feeling?" she continued hoping to help him deal with a death that affected him more than usual. He would need a clear head and emotions in neutral to be safe working in Iraq.

"I'm just pissed at losing Lannie. They staked out the place, we had no chance of stopping it. Poor Lannie, I liked her more than I realised."

"Who do you think is going to replace Lannie" asked Baby Bob changing the subject hoping to lighten the mood, wishing he could have been there to help.

"I don't think Richard is going he will want to bury Lannie, so we will get two new guys," Shamir replied.

"Please don't tell me we are going to have another one of those JD things. Is that dude going to come with us?" he asked. "Although to be fair he was pretty cool for an old guy," Chinaman smiled as he thought about their time in Vegas.

"He's not that old really," Shamir said smiling and thinking about how good he was when she preferred men. The two men looked at her surprised as they slowed for a moment. "I'm just saying he's looked after himself and kept fit like the Lonely Ranger. You know, the pilot, who took me to Algiers. Okay, stop looking at me you two."

"I was just wondering what you are thinking about with a dirty little smile like that," Chinaman replied. "Does that mean you changed....?"

"NO!" and they all laughed and began to feel a little better. It was time to get back and get ready for the mission.

Having passed by the casino and along the seafront to Sanary, they reversed to race along the beach, the lady won – as usual.

"Double-A" lay in bed enjoying the cool breeze from the balcony doors. Andre had already been busy calling Auntie Tess to discover Mills was missing him and meowing for his return, as was the ageing beauty. Avery was thinking about Friday's events and trying to regain his attention. She wanted to know why his uncle had offered him a job and understand why he had turned it down. Andre reminisced about how his uncle had supported the many false starts after his father's death. Now he was successful he believed that the best way to say thanks would be by using Stones money to grow his business into an industry leader before selling up.

"After all, I don't want to be bossed about by you all day and ALL night do I?" he said and promptly received a slap with a pillow.

The three old boys, JD, Jack and Robbie were also discussing the events of the past week. JD was teasing Robbie.

"Now you have been demoted you will have to cook breakfast for Jack every day. I hear that Cass and the girls have already moved into your old gaff with Miss Elizabeth and you're going to live in the flat above the restaurant."

"Listen to you beach boy," replied Robbie. "Last night you were moaning about how tired you were. I thought you said you were servicing all the senioritis in Mexico and yet you fire a few shots at some gangsters and you are so knackered you have to go to bed." They all chuckled but Robbie would not stop, "as for you Jack, you will be working with your new gangster moll Astrid. She sounds like a Swede and just as blonde I hear."

"Haha," replied Jack, "time for us to go and meet with Gendrie and talk about next steps. They jostled each other like young boys on the way to the meeting.

Throughout the day the mood had been improving, they began to look forward to the evening meeting with a mixture of excitement and trepidation. Most of the younger associates had not spent time with their Chairman in such an informal environment. They were encouraged by how the older associates seemed relaxed in his company, almost friend-like – which of course they were. Hockey had returned from the hospital mortuary where Lavender would be for about a week before she could be transported back to New York for burial. The associates took it in turns to welcome him back and give their support. He spent some time with the General plus senior associates debriefing them on the Marseille activities. They agreed on what he would do next.

At just before five the associates entered the private dining room and stood waiting. On the hour the General joined them followed by Robbie. He waved his hands at the seats and everyone took a place but stayed standing. The Stones Chairman turned to Hockey, "Richard we are all deeply sorry for the loss of your sister whom we admired and loved as part of our family. We at Stones and both the French and US governments thank her for her commitment and dedication to us and the Marines. In the Stones tradition, they stood at attention and clapped for nearly two minutes while Hockey and some others teared up. They sat.

The General began, "thank you all for coming I believe most of you know each other except maybe our Sir Robson Manley-James pointing at Robbie. The young associates were surprised as he nodded to them. First, I should announce that he has been reinstated as Chief of BloedStones in Europe. He had briefly stepped down because of **some trouble investing in wine**, which affected our French vineyard amongst others. Everyone nodded even though most never knew.

The General gave the agenda:

1.   Status of the Mission in France.
2.   Outstanding items needing attention.
3.   Where we all go next.

He kept it simple, congratulating the team on a mostly successful outcome to their complicated mission. "Great plans well done, sadly with only one regret, Lavender sacrificing herself to save someone. Always remember, due to your efforts, lives have been saved through the elimination of a vicious crime family. They were involved in drug dealing, people smuggling, trafficking women, and faking French wines. We know the leader and all but one of his key "lieutenants" have been arrested or killed. The wife of the gang leader plus a couple of the former members will be working with us and the French police to clear up any outstanding issues." This explanation avoided unnecessary complications and he failed to mention Stones had acquired certain assets at a knockdown price. *Why complicate things, he thought.* The team felt good and Robbie jokingly asked if anyone would now like to join the Gendarmerie, stay in France and catch more gangsters. That received lots of hoots but no uptakes. Even Hockey managed a smile.

The General moved to outstanding items and started by announcing that Lavender would be returning to New York in about a week. Hockey had decided he would stay in Bandol and travel back with her to a funeral arranged by the Stones US HR dept. Two replacement associates would be joining Shamir in London on Monday. *So much for my integration training,* thought JD.

The General continued, "the French have the remaining gang leader, a guy called Pascal, locked up in Marseille. We believe he is the one who organised the ambush in Bordeaux to eliminate a rival in a leadership battle. Unfortunately, there is no evidence linking him to anything except his activity in Algiers where Shamir and John Huston captured him. No doubt Sir Robbie and Jack will be looking for a way to prove his guilt and have him tried for the murder of Lavender. Currently, the Algerians want him for operating illegally in their country. Which brings me to another gangster, a Brit who was captured by Tyrone," he announced looking at Chinaman. "Mr Lamb is apparently a hitman operating out of London. We think he was hired by Pascal as an assassin but again we have no evidence, his rifle went missing."

"Finally, there is the mysterious case of who took the hidden drugs and cash from the warehouse in Marseille. Two of the gangsters including Pascal swore that the drugs and cash were hidden in the warehouse cellar but when Richard conned them into going to collect it. Guess what? The place was empty. The gangsters got arrested for firearm offences and shooting at the police. Sir Robbie and Jack will try and find out what happened to the hidden loot. The French police are very upset and are suggesting that perhaps we took it," he said looking around the table. "But, don't worry I have assured them that you are already paid too much and don't need more money," which caused laughter around the room. "That brings me to confirm that the standard mission bonus will be paid for what you have done here." This saw the associates nodding and mouthing thanks for a payment of at least $5,000. Not a great deal in comparison to the riches that had been acquired by the Stones owners, even though they didn't have the missing cash or drugs.

JD took over, thanked them all again and officially ended the French mission. The meeting closed, Avery and Andre joined the group everyone began to relax as drinks were served. At dinner, there were lots of toasting and sharing of both happy and sad memories. It was one of the better dinners they would go to.

JD was struggling to explain the travel arrangements for the next morning when the two jets would be leaving. One would go to Paris, London and onto San Francisco while the other would go to London then New York. The team were teasing him about which one they should get until his list was covered in changes. Shamir made sure her team would be with her, travelling to London with JD then RAF Northolt to meet the replacements before the flight to Iraq. JD would take the plane onto New York where he would catch a flight back to Northern Mexico. The Stones UK team would travel to Paris with the General where they would enjoy a late lunch while he had his meeting.

Chapter 58: Paris, Sunday

After breakfast, everyone rushed to the airport in a convoy with all the cars jostling for the front position. The General was praying there would be no accidents preferring to read the e-mails on his phone rather than watch the road race. At the airport, the UK associates helped Shamir's team carry their equipment and push their trollies as they dashed to the VIP lounge ready to get their private jets off on time.

JD took Jack and Robbie aside for a moment, "gentlemen it has been a pleasure to work with you again and despite the sadness, I have enjoyed being here. BUT this really must be the last time I have to come to sort out your mess, I have much catching up to do at home." He laughed as the others hugged him, "See you two in Perth."

"Major, sir, this is most certainly the last time, until the next last time," replied Jack. They laughed out loud as JD muttered something before shouting to Shamir to wait for him and they walked to the plane together waving as they boarded. The New York flight went first, piloted by the Lonely Ranger, with Shamir riding shotgun for part of the London leg.

The Paris flight followed soon after with the lunch party of Jack, Robbie and the Double A's, and with the General on his way to a meeting.

Robbie had already booked Le Fouquet's on the Champs Elysees and they arrived there for lunch at 1 pm. Robbie was warmly greeted by the maitre d" who led the party to one of the best tables. As the meal progressed the conversation turned to the events of the previous week.

"It was you two and Rosa who started all this wasn't it?" suggested Robbie. "How do you think it ended, was it as you expected?" smiling and sipping from his wine glass.

Andre replied, "the whole thing turned out to be much bigger than we could ever have imagined. Initially, we thought it was just an attempt to rip us off for some money."

A thoughtful Avery cut in, "what I am struggling with is how we managed to buy the assets of a criminal gang and no one seems to care. We treated them as if they were a normal company, we have even taken criminals onto the payroll. That seems wrong to me somehow, don't you think?" looking around for support and taking the opportunity to air her concerns. "I'm certain I did not learn about this when doing my audit training," she concluded.

Jack responded first, "yeah it's a bit tricky, there does seem to be a moral conflict taking on assets that might have been grown through the sale of drugs for example."

"I can see why we went to war to deal with the wine scam" said Andre. But Robbie your daughter is working against trafficking isn't she?" They turned to Robbie who looked like he was working on one of his CEO answers.

"I had my doubts about the deal we were proposing and I told the General, as did you Jack. In the end, the decision to proceed was taken by Nicky, our deputy Chairman. He persuaded the boss that it was better for everyone if the assets came to us rather than be absorbed by another gang or some corrupt officials. He argued that he, or we, would make sure the funds went to good causes that had been properly vetted by Stones and not given away by politicians or corrupt appointees to organisations."

"I haven't met Nicky, or should I say the Viscount, but why does he think he knows what's best?" Avery replied getting animated at the arrogance of their deputy Chairman.

"I actually like Nicky," said Robbie. "He's an aristocrat and former Nato Commander who has met some of the most powerful people in the world. He spends most of his time selling our services to politicians, soldiers and the so-called liberal elites based on very clear principles. He doesn't claim to know what's best but he does claim to know what's worst." The table went quiet as the diners thought about the conversation.

Andre intervened, "tell me about who has the drug money that was hidden in the warehouse where we were held, hostage." Avery shivered as she remembered the awful experience which her partner seemed to have discarded. He continued, "having spent all this time finding the Wineman how did we manage to lose the money?" They all smiled at the way he framed the comment. "I bet we have it, don't we? I say we, as you two are going to invest tons of cash into my business," he chuckled as the mood lightened.

"Unfortunately, we don't have it and the General is being harassed for losing it," explained Robbie. "But I'm sure he will be able to plead our innocence with his friend. It would be interesting to be a fly on the wall at that meeting. Anyway someone has it and no doubt we will have to find out who. The criminals and Astrid claim there were millions and millions of euros on pallets waiting to be spent and loads of drugs waiting to be sold. Perhaps we will find the culprits when they start to sell the drugs or spending the money."

Jack intervened, "we might be investing in your company if you can prove that you will make us richer. The first step will be Ms King here, analysing your books", he tittered.

"So watch out and be extra nice to me," she said. "Perhaps you could start by telling us about your new courses. Will there be one on wine investment or have you had enough of that? Perhaps art? What about property? No, no business bridging loans make 12% how cool is that? So much to choose from, do tell us?" Avery was enjoying teasing him.

"I thought about whiskey BUT if you must know we are going to start with Blockchain and the world of Cryptocurrencies. I wonder who amongst us has invested already and bought some Bitcoins?"

At the airport, the General was collected by the Minister's driver and taken to the Frenchman's favourite Michelin star restaurant in central Paris. Once inside he was escorted to a quiet area and asked to wait. His Californian uniform of a blue shirt, with white vest showing at the neck, beige slacks finished off with a suede jacket did not meet with the approval of the smart suited staff and their usual customers. He studied the men wondering whether the ones with bulked shoulders were really security, or just bored with their jobs. His considerations were interrupted by a waitress looking smart in a crisp white shirt, waistcoat and men's black trousers. He asked for a diet soda and as she walked to the bar the General found himself thinking about how sexy a woman looks in men's trousers. He decided it must be to do with the wider hips. His thoughts were once more interrupted as a suited man appeared and asked him to follow. The waitress nodded as he passed by. They arrived in a private dining room where the Minister, in weekend checked suit and cravat at the neck, was talking furiously on his phone. The General sat and sipped his soda while the Frenchman continued speaking and waving his free hand. It was clear to the American that all was not well and he hoped it had nothing to do with him.

"Merde" announced the Minister then walked around the table to unceremoniously shake the hand of a now standing General, before returning to his seat. He continued, "do you remember I told you this is not the wild west but France? Well, some of our friends think that you have gone over the mark and were responsible. Indeed they want me to have your men put into jail for causing so many deaths. They say it does not matter if they are criminal gang members, or bad people, you should not kill them because it is convenient for you to do so. I warned you this would happen." He stopped and looked accusingly at his friend.

"But Olivier we only eliminate REAL assassins in France, it was the gangs who did the rest of the killing, including two of my people," the General offered in defence.

"What about in Algiers where you blew up a whole building," he responded.

"That was down to the trafficking task force, which you supported, asking us to get rid of the gangsters" base whilst we freed a kidnap victim." The General began to worry that he had lost the support of the Minister which could be bad for future business.

"Where have you put the drug gang's money? I am told it was missing when you played your tricks on them, is that true?"

That was enough for the Stones CEO, "Minister we agreed what could happen and it was, worse than we hoped. We did this for you, for France because of your connection with our company. We lost two of our people," he repeated.

The Minister cut in, "your lord Nicky called HIM to explain. I gather it was not a good conversation, HE was angry because both the Police and the Gendarmerie believed that your men behaved like you were dealing with jihadis and not Frenchmen. They say Sir Robbie even used torture on someone, I don't know who. Fortunately, HE agreed with Lordy that our strategy to protect the wine industry was most important for France and decided to forgive you for what you've done provided you give back the money." As the General was about to protest the Minister put up his hand, "Gendrie, I know you did not take the money and I am very sorry for the loss of your person, Lavender isn't it? I believe the other one had been turned by the gang, is that true?"

"Yes she was killed helping to save someone else, we will take care of her family. This business about the missing money is getting out of hand. We DID NOT get any money," an irritated

General raised his voice. "We did, however, take the opportunity to buy some property and retail businesses that were offered to us while we were here. I am sorry if you believe we did too much, it was only because we wanted to help France," said the General appealing to the politician in his friend.

A tap on the door and lunch was brought in, "I took the opportunity to order some chicken as you like it, I believe" Once they commenced eating, the Minister's mood changed. Having completed his official dressing down he was able to return to the beginning and the usual small talk, starting with, "how are you and the family?" Once they arrived at the subject of how Stones could assist French law enforcement to QUIETLY undo the wine scam, the Minister used one hand behind his ear to indicate people were listening. They spent the rest of the meal talking through the suggestions the General had compiled the day before with Robbie and Jack. He explained the recommendations slowly to save the Minister having to repeat them later.

Chapter 59: Paris, Monday

Inside the Hotel de Beauval, once again Hugo tapped on the door before entering the palatial office.

"Mes excuses Minister, I have the Secretary of the Navy on the phone as you asked."

"Mr Secretary," said the Minister. "I hope you are well and enjoyed your weekend."

"Thank you, Minister, I am well it is good to hear from you again so soon. We spoke only a couple of months ago."

"Is it such a short time? you must know that many things have happened here in France."

"Yes, I understand you have been hunting terrorists," said the Secretary hoping he was right.

"Yes we have and I think you have some troubles also to with the Seal who was shooting terrorists in your country," he replied slowly getting around to the point of the call. "I wanted to thank you for the work of some of the people in your US company BloedStone run by General de Vries who you spoke to when we met. They have worked with our law enforcement to break down a gang of drug sellers."

"Yes, I remember he was from the west coast, though originally South African I believe. I will pass your thanks onto the Secretary of Defence, he likes to hear that our contractors are working well with our allies and friends. Is there anything else I can do for you, today Minister?" hoping to get on with his list of calls.

"Unfortunately, one of the team was killed whilst saving a French lady. She will be ready to come home later this week after we honour her if that is alright with you."

"Of course, you go right ahead," the Secretary replied hoping that he could get rid of the Frenchman so he could get on. "Thank you, Minister," he continued "for taking the time to tell me personally," wondering why he bothered to call about a contractor.

"I thought you should know Mr Secretary," the Minister continued, "her name was Lavender Anne Newton and she was a United States Marine." There was a moment of silence.

"Sir, thank you for reminding me, I will personally make sure she is taken care of."

"Thank you, Mr Secretary, now you have a best day'.

Appendix

An assemblage of Associates, Members and Characters

UNITED STATES

BloedStone Missie Corporation - US Associates

General/Unk/Gendrie	Gendrie de Vries	Chairman and Chief Executive Alameda California
Chinaman	Tyrone Jesse Jackson	Associate Chicago Office
Baby Bob	Robert Lee Parker	Associate Atlanta Office.
Black Cat/Saloni	Shamir Ruslana Tehrani	Senior Associate San Francisco Office
Hockey/Lee	Richard Ethan Newton	Associate New York Office
JD	John Wayne Davies	Contractor Mexico
Lannie	Lavender Anne Newton	Associate New York Office
Nicky	Viscount Hadfelt Manor	Deputy Chairman Alameda California
Texas/Lonely Ranger	John William Huston	Associate Texas Office

UNITED KINGDOM

BloedStone Investment Ltd - UK Associates

General/Unk/Gendrie	Gendrie de Vries	Chairman
Ave/Double-A/the King	Avery King	Finance Director St Albans
Jack	Jackson Ritchie	Regional Head and Investment Director St Albans
Miss Elizabeth	Manley-James	Associate for Special Projects St Albans.
Robbie	Sir Robson Manley-James	Chief Executive St Albans
Tinny	Tyndall Jones	Regional Head North of England
Andre/Dev/Double A	Andre Devries	Andre Devries
Bruno		Office Manager/Assistant to Andre
Lydia		Presenter/Trainer St Albans
Roger		Presenter/Trainer St Albans

Criminal gang, South Kensington, West London

Sylvain/Un gros	Sylvain	Gang Leader
Dave/Bendy	Dave Bender	Gang Chauffer and UK Government Agent
Dobo/Dobri	Dobri Ruskof	Member
Jon/Erjon	Erjon Braka	Member
Kot/Mergim	Mergim Kotti	Member
Terry	Terry Lamb	Principal Member/Assassin
Ton/Driton	Driton Osmani	Member

Customs Officers – the UK

Jean	
John	Undercover Officer

English and other and other countries

Anton		Robbie's close friend
Cass	Cassandra Ritchie	Crime Writer/Wife St Albans
Chiara	Chiara Prinzi	Clothes Designer married to the Publisher
Georgie		Ex girlfriend of Andre
Pubs		Publisher and Chiara's Husband
'R'/Traitor		Former Lover of Avery
Mills		Cat of Andre
Nigel		Motivational Speaker
Sahba		Model and Girlfriend of Shamir
Tess/Auntie Tess		Former Glamour Model and Cat Sitter

FRANCE

De Beaux Endroits SARL, owned by BloedStone Investments Ltd

Robbie	Sir Robson Manley-James	Chairman
Claude		Estate Manager, Chateau du Carys
Freddy	Frederic Arsenault	Director
Marie		Estate Worker and Manager's Wife
Yasmeen	Yasmeen Maktoum	Manager le Beaux Hotel

The Martin Crime Family - Headquartered Marseille, France.

Matisse	Matisse Martin	Family Head and Leader
Astrid	Astrid Martin	Deputy Leader, Head of Legal Business and Wife
Armella		Member
Chevy	Chevy Merle	Head of Illicit Drugs
Cormeline		Member
Cyrano		Senior Member, Wine
Evo	Evodie	Member
Revo	Revocat	Member
Hakim		Undocumented Worker
Harbin		Member
Henri	Henri Segal	Head of Smuggling and Trafficking
Lamarr		Member
Lena	Lena Peja	Liaison Officer to Sylvain Gang
Lucian		Senior Member, Wine
M.Labette	M.Labette	Accountant
Mahamid		Undocumented Worker
Nichol		Member
Noell		Member
Pascal/2P's	Pascal Duval	Principle Member and Enforcer
Patrice/2P's	Patrice Barre	Principle Member and Enforcer
Sami		Undocumented Worker
Saville		Senior Member
Sennet		Senior Member
Thierry	Thierry Martin	Deputy Head and Son
Yves/Lucas	Yves Calvin	Head of Wine and Lover
Ynon		Deputy Head and Son

Other French Characters

Wine Woman/Rosa	Rosalba Babineaux	Girl Friend North London
Alexandre		Brothe
Olivier		French Minister
Benoit		Crime Boss and Sylvain's Brother
Emile		Partner of Frederic
Hugo		Private Secretary to a French Minister
Thomas	Thomas Babineaux	Captain in the Gendarmerie and Brother
Wineman/Michel Cannin		Wine Salesman and Boyfriend to Rosalba in North London

Martin Gang outpost in Algiers

| Uranie | Algiers based Member |
| Vedatsie | Algiers based Member |